THE LAST POW WOW

THAT NATIVE THOMAS & STEVEN PAUL JUDD

This is a work of fiction. Names, characters, places, and incidents are either products of both authors' imagination or, if real, are used fictitiously. The true events written in this work are done so by use of common knowledge.

Copyright © 2016 Thomas M. Yeahpau and Steven Paul Judd

All rights reserved. No part of this book may be reproduced, transmitted, or stored in an information retrieval system in any form or by any means, graphic, electronic, digital, or mechanical, including photocopying, taping, and recording, without prior written permission from the publisher.

First edition 2016

Edited by Kimberly Gail Wieser

Cover Art by Ryan Redcorn

Summary: A mysterious pow-wow is set to be held inside a colossal tipi, 200-feet tall and 3-miles wide, which suddenly appears on the outskirts of a town that has never hosted a pow-wow. Advertising fliers blanket the area and all of Indian country, billing itself as "The Pow-Wow of all Pow-Wows." There is a stipulation to the pow-wow though, only full-blooded Native Americans are allowed to dance, drum, or attend the grand event. Mixed-blooded Native Americans and non-Native Americans protest the gathering. Meanwhile, nine journeys are followed to the huge get-together, none of the travelers realize that they are part of something more important, something much bigger than what they all seek from being at the pow-wow. At the story's end, an epic battle between good and evil ensues that will change the world forever.

ISBN: 978-1-5377-6495-5

1. Native American literature - Fiction

Printed in the United States of America

This book is typeset in Cambria

Hosstyle Publishing LLC
509 N. 1st Street., Anadarko, Oklahoma 73005

www.hosstylenation.com

Co-author, That Native Thomas,
dedicates this book to
God, Jesus, and the Holy Ghost.
Also to his son, Jordan Yeahpau,
and his father, Roderick Yeahpau,
who went to the spirit world while
this book was being finished

Co-author, Steven Paul Judd,
dedicates this book to his
family, John, Elaine,
Mike, John-John,
and Caroline

PROLOGUE

The Worst Trick Ever

IN THE BEGINNING, The Great Spirit created the third planet from the sun and named it "Earth." HE knew all of the other planets would eventually take on the names of false Greek and Roman gods and goddesses, but not the planet that was HIS special creation, not Earth. Later, scholars would contend that the third planet's name was derived from various ancient languages. None would ever be able to prove the true origin of the Earth's name though, but it was HE whom named it.

The Great Spirit divided Earth's many lands with giant bodies of water. Then, HE created human beings, whom HE placed on the many lands of Earth. In the beginning, one man and one woman were created for each land, each pair unique from the others. After HE created humans, HE created the animals that would fill the lands of Earth. Finally, HE created protectors, angels for the human beings, who were humanoid, except they had a large pair of white wings protruding out from their backs. HE created animal spirits for all other creatures. Whether it be a butterfly, dog, eagle, raven, or even a coyote, all species had an animal spirit assigned to them. They were the guardian angels over their own kind. Animal Spirits had their place in the home of the The Great Spirit, right next to the angels who protected the human beings of the many lands of Earth. They were considered equal to angels and, except for them having heads like those of the animals they were assigned to protect, even resembled them. They were also humanoid and blessed with a large pair of white wings protruding out from their backs, just like the angels. Everything was balanced, just as HE had intended.

But then there came a great imbalance, right after the angels and animal spirits arrived on Earth to begin their duties. The Great Spirit's greatest angel, known as "Son-of-the-Morning-Star," felt it was beneath him to protect the human beings to whom he was assigned to protect. He felt it was a waste of time to protect such imperfect creatures that would eventually kill themselves off, and he couldn't comprehend why his Creator would create such flawed beings. He began to think that maybe The Great Spirit wasn't as perfect as HE portrayed himself to be. Son-of-the-Morning-Star was the greatest angel ever created, so after suspecting that his Creator might have made a mistake, he saw an opportunity to become even greater by exposing HIS imperfection. He caused an uproar among the angels spread across the lands of Earth. Half of them sided with him, while the other half continued their duties to their Creator.

With half of the angels on his side, Son-of-the-Morning-Star left Earth and flew back to the home of The Great Spirit. Son-of-the-Morning-Star wanted HIS throne for his own and felt that taking it would be an easy victory since HE had sent nearly all of HIS angels to Earth. Since Son-of-the-Morning-Star had half of them following him, what few angels remained in the home of The Great Spirit would not be a threat.

There was a great battle in the home of The Great Spirit between HIS forces and some of those that HE had created. Once HIS remaining angels had done all they could against Son-of-the-Morning-Star and the defiant angels, HE finally intervened, right away putting HIS greatest angel in his place. Though the battle turned quickly into what could have become a massacre, HE didn't kill all who had defied HIM. Instead, The Great Spirit cast them from HIS home back unto Earth. There, the defiant ones would be forced to remain until they submitted to HIM and fulfilled the task for which HE intended for them: watching over the human beings they were assigned to protect.

Son-of-the-Morning-Star and the rest of the defiant angels fell hard from the celestial home of The Great Spirit. Half of them did not survive the fall, leaving the land they fell upon littered with dead angels. Those who survived continued to follow Son-of-the-Morning-Star. They still saw greatness in him. Although their punishment was simple and forgiveness seemed possible, their leader still felt human beings were inferior beings not worthy of protection. So, Son-of-the-Morning-Star decided to show his Creator just how weak of creatures HIS human beings were. And sin was born.

Sin first came about from fruit, but not just regular fruit, Sacred Fruit from Sacred Trees placed on each of the lands by The Great Spirit. Each land had one Sacred Tree with Sacred Fruit, of which the man and woman of that land were forbidden to eat. The Sacred Fruit had special Medicine not yet meant for human beings. After the fall of HIS greatest angel and the other defiant angels, HE ordered all of HIS remaining angels and animal spirits to protect the Sacred Trees of each land. But Son-of-the-Morning-Star was a powerful angel, very persuasive and cunning. One by one, he talked each man and woman of each land into eating the Sacred Fruit from each of the Sacred Trees placed on their lands. By doing so, he showed his Creator just how weak his new creations, the human beings, really were. But there was one land upon which Son-of-the-Morning-Star couldn't prove his point, the land that would come to be known as "America" centuries later after Italian explorer Amerigo Vespucci reached America after Christopher Columbus. America was occupied by the human beings The Great Spirit created to protect and be one with the Earth and protect it. Their bloodline was crucial to the survival of human beings and Earth itself.

The man and woman of America were not at first persuaded by Son-of-the-Morning-Star to eat the Sacred Fruit. His first attempt to tempt them into eating from their Sacred Tree was unsuccessful. They were content and happy with what they already had. The man and woman of America had no interest in taking any more than they needed. So, Son-of-the-Morning-Star had to come up with another plan. He was cunning, but not cunning enough for the human beings of America. And to make things worse, the protectors of America finally arrived, two of them.

One angel and one animal spirit, Coyote, were assigned to protect the Sacred Tree of America. Before they even got settled, there came news from another animal spirit, Hawk, about a great battle in another land that Son-of-the-Morning-Star and the defiant angels were winning. The angel decided to leave to aid his fellow angels in the battle, leaving Coyote to protect America's Sacred Tree by himself. The battle was a diversion and once the angel departed, Son-of-the-Morning-Star returned to America and took the form of a harmless snake. Then, he approached Coyote, who was resting near the Sacred Tree. Coyote paid the serpent no mind, until it spoke to him.

"Coyote," hissed the snake.

"Who goes there?" asked Coyote.

"Jussst a friend, a friend with a proposssition. A proposssition to make you and your kind the mossst powerful beingsss on Earth . . . if you ssseek sssuch a thing," the reptilian answered.

"Oh really?" asked Coyote, who was intrigued by the offer from the belly crawler. He knew the legless lizard was really Son-of-the-Morning-Star, but his offer was one that he had to consider. Coyote did not like the fact that his kind was the lowest of the canine family. The fox was even more highly ranked than him as far as The Great Spirit was concerned.

"Ssso?" the cold-blooded being asked Coyote, who was in deep thought.

"What do I have to do for you to make my kind the most powerful beings on Earth?" Coyote finally asked back, excited by the offer.

"Sssimple, you trick the man and woman placed here into eating a fruit from thisss Sssacred Tree you're protecting, and I'll make sssure your kind are the top dogsss of all beingsss. Deal?" the slithering vertebrae asked Coyote, who only had to think about it for a few seconds.

"Deal," Coyote quickly answered. The serpent disappeared into thin air right in front of Coyote, only moments before the man and woman who were placed on the land of America approached.

"Where did the angel go?" asked the man.

Coyote told him about the battle going on in another land against Son-of-the-Morning-Star, who was out to destroy the men and women of Earth. The man became very concerned about the battle and asked Coyote if there was anything he could do to help. It was then that Coyote realized how he could trick the man and woman of America into eating the Sacred Fruit from the Sacred Tree of their land. Coyote lied for the first time, and it became the birth of lying, for it was the first lie that had ever been told.

Coyote explained to the man and woman of America that the only reason The Great Spirit did not want them to eat the Sacred Fruit from the Sacred Tree was because it would cause them to grow wings, like his, like the angels'. Then, Coyote went on to tell the man of America that if he had wings, he could go join the battle taking place against Son-of-the-Morning-Star and the defiant angels.

The man of America felt a need to do his part in any battle that was taking place against his kind to protect them. That need, the need to be a warrior, was enough to convince him to eat a Sacred Fruit from the Sacred Tree. The woman of America ate the Sacred Fruit with him, wanting to be by his side in the battle with wings of her own, as her primary need was to be of support to him, no matter the cost. So they shared a piece of Sacred Fruit, eating it with no guilt. Then they waited and waited, waiting for their new wings to grow out from their backs, but it never happened. No wings ever appeared. It was Coyote's first trick, the first trick of all tricks forever.

Though Coyote was successful with his first trick, the pleasure he got from it was immediately cut short by the sound of thunder from above him. Lightning crashed down, two lightning bolts to be exact. Both lightning bolts came down on his back, separating both of his wings from his back, leaving him wingless. He knew it was The Great Spirit's doing, but he didn't care because his kind would soon be the most powerful beings of all beings! Coyote accepted his punishment gladly because he felt it would only be temporary. He would soon take his throne as the being of all beings and get his wings back. But suddenly, Coyote heard a thunderous voice, a majestic voice. It was his Creator.

"For your lack of loyalty to me and for being tricked by Son-of-the-Morning-Star, you will no longer be the animal spirit for your kind! From this time on, you will be known as 'The Trickster' since you like playing tricks so much! And you will remain on Earth, to roam it along with Son-of-the-Morning-Star and the defiant angels, not to be allowed back into my home, UNTIL…" The Great Spirit stopped short, not revealing the rest of HIS divine plan to Coyote.

"Until what?" The Trickster yelled. But there came no answer. The Great Spirit apparently wanted him to figure it out for himself. And the word "until" coming from HIM meant it could take a very, very long time, even forever, to figure out. The Trickster didn't want to spend his eternal life on Earth with Son-of-the-Morning-Star and his defiant angels, who had all begun to take gruesome forms, becoming demons. He had to figure out what HE wanted of him. Then, no matter what it was, what it would take, or how long it would take, he had to fulfill that "until." He knew it would be the only way for him to get back home, back to the home of The Great Spirit, where he belonged, right next to the angels, in his seat as the animal spirit of coyotes.

CHAPTER 1

Butterfly Princess

THE BEAUTY OF A BUTTERFLY translated by many Native American tribes was a sign of love. The perfect blend of colors butterflies possessed, which were beautiful together, represented the perfect blend of traits two people in love with each other possessed and the beauty that came when those traits were together. Nature always found a way to balance itself, as did love.

Butterflies were not only a sign of love for one particular young Native American girl named Polacca Nova, they were also a sign of death for her. She was born from both love and death, which together equaled tragedy. The night she came into the world, like a butterfly from its cocoon, her beauty met life alone.

On the night she was born, her dad, a member of the Hopi tribe, was in a fatal car accident while backroading with two of his friends. A coyote crossed the path of her dad's war pony and when he swerved to miss it, the car rolled and rolled. None of them believed in the medicine of a seatbelt, so once the car started to roll, they were all thrown from the vehicle into the air, flying into darkness like butterflies with nowhere to go. But they were drawn to the big sleep like moths drawn to flame, so it was there to which her dad and his friends migrated.

Polacca's parents lived in a small town. It didn't take long for the news of her dad's death to reach her cocoon, her mother's womb. Eight months pregnant with Polacca, her Navajo mother was devastated by the news so much it sent her into premature labor. Her mother was rushed to the hospital although she fought the whole way, screaming and pleading to be taken to her dead husband's body.

The stress, the agony, the sorrow was too much for Polacca's mother to handle while bringing her newborn into the world. Her heartache gave way to a heart attack, a heart attack she did not survive, a heart attack she did not *want* to survive. Polacca's mother could not bear the idea of fulfilling the vow that she had made with the love of her life, until death do they part. So on the night of Polacca's birth, both of her parents left their physical cocoons and became spirits together. Holding hands, they started their migration to the spirit world, leaving Polacca all alone.

But Polacca didn't emerge from her cocoon so

easily. She fought not to come out, as the doctor delivering her later commented. Unbeknownst to the doctor, Polacca tried to follow her mother and father to the spirit world. She cried out to them, extending her hand out to them. They heard her and turned around, but just as her mother took her hand into hers and tried to pull her daughter to her, another force pulled her daughter in the opposite direction. The force pulled Polacca out of her cocoon, out from her mother's lifeless body. It was from that tragic event that Polacca received her gift, just as butterflies received the gift of wings after emerging from their cocoons.

It was a gift witnessed by everyone there in the emergency room where Polacca was born. As infants are conditioned to do once they are born, she cried to assure everyone she was alive. But there was something very peculiar about her cries. They were accompanied by something no one in the emergency room had ever seen in their lives. When Polacca let out her first cry, butterflies flew out from her mouth, dozens of them, each one more beautiful than the previous one, some with colors never seen together. The paired colors ranged from orchid and turquoise, crimson and cream, jade and indigo, to plum and cerise, and on to endless more paired colors. But if that wasn't strange enough, the butterflies weren't real butterflies, they were ghostly, almost like smoke, and disappeared shortly after emerging from Polacca's mouth.

It was the strangest thing, too strange to not investigate its cause. The doctor who delivered Polacca diagnosed her with a fake illness to try to keep her at the hospital so that tests and observations could be done. But Polacca's mother's mother would not have it, nor would she believe that there was something wrong with her granddaughter. She took Polacca away from the hospital, away from the technology and medicine of the blue-eyed tribe. It wasn't the proper place for her diagnosis to be made. From what Polacca's widowed grandma witnessed along with everyone else in that emergency room, her granddaughter had a gift only a medicine man could diagnose and treat.

It wasn't until Polacca was secure in a car seat and her grandma was driving them away from the hospital in Window Rock, Arizona, that Polacca finally stopped crying. She went quiet and stayed that way during the whole early morning trip to see the medicine man to whom her grandma was taking her. It was almost like Polacca knew she had to stop what was happening; even at a few hours old, she knew.

The medicine man they went to still lived in a traditional Navajo hogan, an old and weathered hogan, but a hogan nonetheless. It wasn't along a road like houses were normally located. Instead, it was hidden in a small, desolate canyon about ten miles north of

Window Rock. After parking on a barely-traveled desert backroad, Polacca's grandma carried Polacca to the medicine man's hogan, wrapped in a beautiful Pendleton blanket that perfectly blended the colors Navajo white, salmon, aquamarine, and cardinal. Polacca remained quiet the whole way, comforted by the colors wrapped around her.

Polacca's grandma knew Red-Turtle-Man, a Navajo medicine man, through her mother, which would have been Polacca's great grandma, so the relation was old and would seem almost ancient to one as young as Polacca. Red-Turtle-Man respected their longstanding relationship and invited them inside his hogan once they arrived. There was nothing fancy inside, just jars of medicine, minimal furnishings, cans of food, and a few romance novels, with a fire pit in the middle. He was nothing fancy as well, a skinny, elderly man in a flannel button shirt and blue jeans. His head was adorned with long, gray hair kept in place by a faded red bandana, and he had the brownest of skin, wrinkled to perfection. Red-Turtle-Man and Polacca's grandma each took a seat around the fireless pit. Polacca's grandma held Polacca tight, protecting her, for she was now her new cocoon.

Before anything was said, Red-Turtle-Man lit a bundle of sage and smudged every inch of his hogan with the smoke, chasing out any evil trying to sit in on their conversation. He also prayed in the Navajo language.

Polacca kept quiet the whole time, seeming to know she shouldn't open her mouth and disturb a medicine man at work.

After their visit was blessed, Polacca's grandma filled Red-Turtle-Man in on the details of what had just happened, the two deaths, the birth, and the gift bestowed on the born. It was a lot to take in, even for a medicine man. It was unlike anything he had ever heard of. At first, he didn't have an answer, not even a clue of what the gift meant. He asked Polacca's grandma to see the gift, so she tried to get her granddaughter to cry, but after a few attempts, she was unable to make Polacca cry. She remained quiet, as if she knew better.

Red-Turtle-Man grew impatient and stepped in. He pried open Polacca's mouth using his fingers, and, right before his unbelieving eyes, the ghosts of the most beautiful colored butterflies fluttered out of her mouth. Polacca started to cry again, not liking the unfamiliar feeling of the medicine man's fingers in her mouth. Swarms of butterfly ghosts again emerged from her mouth, a tornado of beautiful colors: burnt orange and black, deep sky blue and emerald, fuchsia and lilac, and so on. The medicine man was beside himself, and it dawned on him what the gift meant. He had heard of a prophecy that mentioned such a gift, but hearing and seeing were two different things. He could not believe the prophecy had come true, that it was happening now.

The prophecy was ancient and known by all medicine men. There would come a time when the Beings of This World and the Beings Not of This World would go to war, good versus evil, and certain gifts would be given to each side. Polacca's gift was a gift prophesied to be given to the Beings of This World, the good side. It was definitely a sign that the war was near. But Red-Turtle-Man did not want to worry Polacca's grandma, so he kept the prophecy from her. It wasn't that Polacca's grandma couldn't take the news, but that knowing what the gift meant would put her in great danger. Beings Not of This World would pick up on the scent of her knowledge, the knowledge of one of the weapons prophesized to be used against them. So no one could know about her gift until the time was right. Polacca was special, a savior, a secret to be kept safe until that time came.

Red-Turtle-Man instructed Polacca's grandma to keep her away from the public. In time, her gift would reveal its purpose. Her grandma agreed to do what he asked, and it was then that he gave her granddaughter her name, Polacca, which in Hopi meant "butterfly," to honor her father's people now that she would be kept safely hidden among her mother's.

For thirteen years, Polacca; who became beautiful, willowy, and winsome, was raised by her grandma. Her grandma was a white-haired, dark skinned

Navajo woman, wearing dresses she had made for herself from fabrics she had owned for a very long time. Her grandma hid Polacca from society the whole first thirteen years of her life; home schooling her, teaching her addition, how to write in cursive, how to cook, and about the ways of the Navajo. Both grandmother and granddaughter alike followed the ceremonial path religiously, saying the Walks-In-Beauty Prayer every morning after they awoke. Polacca, like any thirteen-year-old girl would, grew tired of learning life from books and lessons and yearned to learn from experience. But they lived in the desert in the middle of nowhere, far from people, far from the rest of life. Polacca had no friends. She only read about what it was like to have friends in young adult novels, reading what is was like to share secrets or to talk about someone behind their back, things which most girls her age were all too familiar with. Polacca wanted to experience life so badly that she would have even settled for knowing what being bullied was like.

    Each of Polacca's thirteen birthday parties had consisted of only two people, her grandma and herself. Every birthday wish she ever made after blowing the candles out on her birthday cakes were all the same: to go to town, a town filled with her people, the Navajos and Hopis. The town she dreamt of going to and which was the closest to them was Window Rock, the capital of the

Navajo Nation. But each year, her wish was denied, so she would sit outside of her grandma's house night after night and wonder which canyon Window Rock laid beyond. She hadn't the slightest clue, though.

Although Polacca despised her isolation, she knew it was necessary. She knew it was not normal for a person to talk with ghosts of butterflies shooting out from their mouths as she always did. She kept quiet most of the time. Even her grandma had a hard time getting her to talk. It was rare for Polacca to say a complete sentence. Her grandma still hadn't a clue what her granddaughter's gift meant, but assured Polacca it would reveal itself in due time. Her grandma was a patient woman, but Polacca was becoming less and less patient.

Puberty began to change Polacca in more ways than just one. Other things began to emerge from Polacca's mouth, other kinds of ghosts. It all started when Polacca was given her birthday presents during her thirteenth birthday party. She got her own small television, a DVD player, and some movies on DVD. Her grandma had never owned a television. She was against them, but thought the television might help ease her granddaughter's curiosity about having friends and her yearning to experience life. Polacca's grandma sensed the feelings she was having. Before their annual birthday party was even over, Polacca asked to take her presents to her room to enjoy them. They were the best birthday presents ever as far as she was concerned. She gleamed with happiness, so her grandma could not deny her request. Polacca's grandmother allowed her to cut her birthday party short, even joining her in trying to set up the high tech gadgets.

In about an hour, they had both figured out how to hook up everything and decided to watch the movie, *Star Wars,* which Polacca's grandma had randomly picked out from a shelf of DVDs at a pawn shop. They laid on Polacca's bed together and watched what her grandma still referred to as "talking pictures."

Immediately, they were both mesmerized by the storytelling capability of Polacca's presents. The technology was like nothing either one of them had expected or experienced. They were both enthralled about being taken into space, something neither had previously dreamed possible. The main thing that caught Polacca's attention right away was the way Princess Leia wore her hair, in two twisted buns on each side of her head. It was the traditional style Hopi women, her dad's people, wore their hair. She decided that she would never wear her hair down again, or even braided, instead, she would wear it like the Hopi woman she was becoming, like Princess Leia's hair. All was going good, and they were having the time of their lives, until one particular scene in the movie that they both found so funny it stopped being funny. It was when Princess Leia asked Han Solo, "Will somebody get this big walking carpet out of my way?" She was referring to Chewbacca. Polacca laughed hard, harder than her grandma had ever seen her laugh before, and where the ghosts of butterflies should have emerged, something else did.

Polacca laughed loud and hard until her laughter was joined by other laughter, which came from inside of her mouth at first. Then, before her grandma's eyes, the ghosts of a pack of hyenas emerged from Polacca's mouth, menacing hyenas who bounced around in her bedroom, knocking things over, laughing the whole time. Immediately, Polacca became frightened, as did her grandma. The ghosts of the hyenas lingered longer than the ghosts of butterflies normally did, causing havoc inside her bedroom. One hyena even approached Polacca threateningly, causing her to yell to get it away from her. When she did, her grandma witnessed something even more frightening emerge from her granddaughter's mouth, something she would had never guessed possible, the ghost of a giant grizzly bear. The ghost of the grizzly bear chased the hyena away, then went after all of the other hyenas, chasing them all away, until all of them disappeared into thin air, like smoke. Then, the grizzly bear faded into smoke after them.

The event shocked and terrified both Polacca and her grandma. Polacca closed her mouth and placed her hand over it so nothing else would come out. Her grandma knew right away that the television and DVD player had been a bad idea.

"That's it," her grandma said, "I'm unplugging it all and taking it all back to where I got it!"

"Please, grandma, don't take my birthday gifts away from me!" Polacca pleaded, but as she did, more ghosts emerged from her mouth, this time the ghosts of a pack of wild wolves. The ghosts of the wolves were ferocious and blocked her grandma's path to the television and DVD player. Her grandma stopped in her tracks, unsure if the ghosts of the wolves were able to harm her or not. They lingered even longer than the hyenas and the grizzly bear, growling and snarling, protecting Polacca's television and DVD player. Her grandma gave up on the idea of taking Polacca's birthday presents away from her and left her granddaughter's bedroom, more angry than scared.

For days after Polacca's thirteenth birthday, she and her grandma didn't speak. In fact, Polacca didn't leave her bedroom much at all, so they hardly even saw each other. While Polacca practiced fixing her hair in the traditional style of Hopi women, like Princess Leia's, she watched all of the movies her grandma had given her over and over. One movie made her happy, one made her scared, and one even made her cry. That became her favorite movie of all time, *Titanic.* The emotional rollercoaster the movies sent Polacca on also caused many different ghosts to emerge from her mouth, but she began to learn how to control what came from her mouth and how long each group of ghosts could stay before evaporating. Polacca began to home school herself on using her gift, the gift she had avoided trying to understand for thirteen years. Now, Polacca was embracing it.

It wasn't until almost a week later that Polacca emerged from her newest cocoon, her bedroom, but only because she felt she could now control her gift enough to know she would not harm or frighten her grandma with it. Her grandma was leery at first, unsure if she could trust a word coming from her granddaughter's mouth. But the first words Polacca uttered were two words her grandma was defenseless against, two words any parent was defenseless against.

"I'm sorry," Polacca apologized, as the ghost of a white dove flew from her mouth. It was the universal sign of peace.

Polacca's grandma grabbed her and held her like it was the last time she might hold her granddaughter. They talked about what happened and what it could all mean. Neither one of them had any ideas, but they both knew they had to find some kind of answer because what happened was strange even for someone who spoke ghosts of butterflies. Polacca's grandma decided that she would go back to Red-Turtle-Man and see what he thought.

Polacca's grandma went to Red-Turtle-Man's hogan the next day only to learn from a sheepherder in the area that the medicine man had mysteriously disappeared recently. But the sheepherder gave her the address of a great medicine woman, the last medicine woman alive and keeper of the strongest medicine there ever was, is, and will be, who lived in Oklahoma. It was a long distance away, but Polacca's grandma felt it would be worth the trip, and she had enough money saved up for it. So she returned back home to Polacca and gave her the news. They were going on a road trip. They packed, and, before long, they left their cocoon hidden deep in Navajo country and began their migration to Oklahoma.

It was the first time Polacca had ever been away from home. She was more excited about the trip than she was about finding answers about her gift. They traveled through their home-state of Arizona, which was like a familiar butterfly to them, its colors the most comforting to Polacca; khaki, olive, and sienna. The next state they traveled through was New Mexico, a unique butterfly, its colors very nurturing; gold, spring green, and sarcoline. Then, they traveled through the butterfly known as Texas. It was deep in its shades of forest green, amber, and beige. Finally, they made it to their destination butterfly, Oklahoma, cut with designs of glowing red dirt, mixed with lively pastel greens, and the plush tint of saffron-colored buffalo grass. It was where Polacca hoped her answers might lie.

The medicine woman they sought was Big-Sister, a legendary seer and healer, with powers most medicine men only wished they possessed. They found her in a small Native American town named Anadarko, which meant "home of the bumble-bees." Actually, their destination was a little outside of the town, in the middle of nowhere, just like where Polacca lived with her grandma. Big-Sister's house was modest, plain, nothing that called out a medicine woman might live there. They pulled up to her house and were met by a sixteen-year-old boy, who introduced himself as Little-Red-Man. He let them both know that Big-Sister had been expecting them.

Little-Red-Man led them both inside of Big-Sister's house. Once inside her modest home, they were greeted by their hostess, who was seated at a dining table with two chairs already pulled out for both of them. She was a large, almost ancient Native American woman, a definition of brown, her face sagging with the years. She wore pointy glasses. Her hair was the color of a harsh winter and pulled back into a messy pony tail. She greeted them both with a voice that sounded like it had withstood years and years of sitting in a bingo hall smoking cigarette after cigarette. It wasn't as mystical as either one of them had expected.

"So this thing you have, let me see it," said Big-Sister, right to the point.

Polacca and her grandma looked at each other, neither able to come up with something to say. So Polacca opened her mouth, but nothing came out. She even "awwwed" really hard, but still nothing. So she said the only thing she could think to say.

"Testing, one, two, three. Testing, one, two, three," Polacca said.

And it happened like it always happened; the ghosts of butterflies emerged from Polacca's mouth. It flabbergasted Big-Sister, making it obvious she hadn't ever seen anything like it before. She even swatted at the butterfly ghosts.

"Is this all? This all that can come out?" Big-Sister eagerly asked.

"No, that's why we came to you," Polacca's grandma answered.

Polacca's grandma explained Polacca's life story to Big-Sister, all the way to her thirteenth birthday party and the events that took place. Big-Sister soaked it all in, remaining silent for a long period of time afterward. She even went to her medicine and asked it for an answer, but there was nothing, only silence. Big-Sister even ordered Little-Red-Man to go get her books, and once she received them, she started to read through them. But after a while, it was obvious that they supplied no answers. She wasn't one to care much for prophecies, so she didn't know about the prophecy Red-Turtle-Man and many other medicine men knew about. Big-Sister was baffled. She admitted it was an extraordinary gift, but the question of what it meant could only be answered by one person, one who had seen it all.

Big-Sister explained to Polacca that the best person to ask what her gift meant was Tonto Wayne, who currently held the title as THE TOUGHEST NATIVE ALIVE. He had seen just about every kind of medicine there was that pertained to Native Americans. So it was probable that he had seen her gift before, and he would know what to make of it. She also explained that he was an MC for big pow-wows these days. Big-Sister let them both know that his next gig was being the MC for THE POW-WOW OF ALL POW-WOWS, which was being held in Mankato, Minnesota, in just a few weeks. Big-Sister also let them know that she would be there as well and could introduce them to him. With only that piece of advice, Polacca's grandma and Polacca left Big-Sister's house and started their migration back home.

Polacca's grandma was disappointed in the answer that she had spent all of her savings and driven ten hours to hear, but Polacca saw hope and a new destination. It wasn't until they were safely home that her grandma broke the bad news to her that the journey for answers about her gift was over for the time being.

She explained to her disappointed granddaughter that they should just wait until her gift's purpose was ready to reveal itself to them, as advised by Red-Turtle-Man. Polacca argued with her grandma, begging her to take her to THE POW-WOW OF ALL POW-WOWS. Her grandma refused and explained to her that even if she wanted to take her there, she couldn't because they were broke now. However, Polacca didn't believe her grandma, and anger overcame her. She knew better to not speak another word though, so she went to her room and slammed the door shut.

For a second time, for days on end, Polacca and her grandma didn't speak to each other. For days, Polacca sat in her cocoon of a bedroom and thought and thought. Every thought on THE POW-WOW OF ALL POW-WOWS and its MC, Tonto. Her grandma was just feet away, in the next room, awaiting an apology, but as days passed, it became obvious an apology wouldn't come anytime soon. Finally, one day, it became too much for her grandma to bear, so she went into Polacca's bedroom to apologize to her and make peace. But to her surprise, her granddaughter's bedroom was empty with her window wide open. Polacca was nowhere to be seen. Her grandma knew the place to where she had run away to, but didn't have the money to go after her granddaughter. She really was broke, so all she could do was hope her butterfly would return home, as some butterflies do and some butterflies don't.

The day before, Polacca had emerged from her cocoon through a window with her hair styled in the traditional way of Hopi women. Princess Leia would have been envious of how well Polacca's hair was styled. She felt like a princess too, but her own kind of princess, a Butterfly Princess. Once free from her cocoon, the gift of wings was bestowed upon her. Polacca spread her wings and behold, her colors presented themselves; wisteria, thistle, mauve, and lavender, all bordered by black. The wind smiled and approved of her colors, carrying her up to the awaiting sky above, where she flew. She followed her migration instincts that were taking her to THE POW-WOW OF ALL POW-WOWS, where the answers a Butterfly Princess sought awaited her beauty.

CHAPTER TWO
Chief

Chief awoke at the crack of dawn, as he always did, another day added to his ancient dog life. Describing Chief as a dog was being nice. He was really a mutt. The blood of many breeds of dogs ran in his veins. He was many colors to prove his mixed heritage: white with patches of black and different shades of gray all over his body. He had a strong build for a three-legged dog; lean, muscular, and average-height. Chief awoke to a scent in the air his nose recognized. It was a scent that should not have been so close to the town of Mankato, Minnesota, where he had lived for well over a hundred years, a hundred human years that was. He was old, dirt old in dog years. He should have died long ago, but a curse had been put on him by an evil being he had chased away from Mankato sometime during his mortal life. But there had been many evil beings he had chased away, so he wasn't sure which one put the curse on him. His memory wasn't all that great at his age either. All he knew was that he had seen many generations of his kind come and go, but he always stayed, never joining them in the spirit world. He had a job though, so he couldn't just die and leave. He was the protector of Mankato, the town's fearless guardian, the town's chief. So his name was fitting. His medicine was strong. He had the spirit of Crazy Horse in him, the fearless spirit of the greatest chief in history who had once been his keeper. Chief wasn't just any dog, he was THE GREATEST REZ DOG OF ALL TIME. The word "rez" was a slang term used by Native Americans to describe the reservations they were forced to occupy after the blue-eyed tribe stole their lands through the written lies they called "treaties."

But it was deep in Indian country in a time before reservations were established where Chief's story began. He was born as part of a large litter in a camp of Sioux Indians. Crazy Horse had taken him from his mother once he was too old to nurse from her. From that time on, he carried Crazy Horse's belongings for him, kept evil away from his camps, and even fought side by side him in a few battles. Chief had the scars to prove it too. It was during one of the battles he fought beside Crazy Horse that he became separated from his keeper, never finding him again, but he kept his keeper's spirit within him. He searched high and low for his keeper, but could never pick up on his warrior scent. Crazy Horse was like a ghost when on a warparty. He could even hide his scent trail. So for a long time, Chief wondered the northern plains, looking for his keeper, never finding him. Then one day, he came across a young Sioux brave named Red Otter who took him in as one of his own. Chief became a part of his family, and Red Otter became his new keeper.

It was a bad time for the Sioux. They had surrendered to the blue-eyed tribe, who had defeated them, along with most tribes, by killing off almost all of their food supply, the great herds of buffalo. It was a dirty war tactic. The scent of buffalo on the Great Plains had almost completely vanished. The Sioux camps became pitiful, sad, even to a dog's eyes. He was lucky to even get a bone back then. It was every being for themselves. It was how Chief lost his leg. His family hadn't eaten any meat in weeks, and they were malnourished because of it. So Chief did what family does in times of need, he made a sacrifice. He placed his back left leg on the chopping stump and barked up a storm to his keeper. Red Otter understood him and took Chief's offering, feeding his family the life-saving protein contained in his leg.

Things didn't get better. Instead, they grew worse. The Sioux didn't know how to live without buffalo. It was the only way of life they knew. It was a bad time for all Native American tribes, though, all were starving. And it was starvation, in fact, that drove Red Otter to kill a family of the blue-eyed tribe for just a few eggs, less than a dozen. In that act, he went from a brave to a warrior, but because of that warparty, a war raged between the Sioux and the blue-eyed tribe, a war the Sioux did not win. Once it was over though, Red Otter was taken captive by the blue-eyed tribe. They took him to the town of Mankato, Minnesota. Chief followed, using Red Otter's warrior scent as his guide.

Once in Mankato, Chief sat outside the jail that housed Red Otter the entire time he was incarcerated, each and every second. It was what his original owner, Crazy Horse, would have done. Crazy Horse's spirit was still strong within Chief. Chief wanted to be there when Red Otter was released. He would help guide him back home to his family. But that day never came. A different day arrived instead. Red Otter finally emerged from the jail, but still a captive, still in chains like an animal. Chief was there in the crowd of blue-eyed tribal members who all cheered as Red Otter was hung by his neck. Chief did not understand what had happened or why, all he knew was that he could no longer smell the warrior scent of his second keeper. It faded away as he dangled from a rope, lifeless. It wasn't until the blue-eyed tribe buried Red Otter underneath the ground that Chief understood what had happened. His keeper, the closest friend a dog could have, had gone to the spirit world.

But just as Red Otter's scent had faded away, the scent of Chief's people, the Sioux, was also fading from the land the blue-eyed tribe called Minnesota. Chief decided to stay in Mankato. The blue-eyed tribe were new to the land and knew nothing of the evil that lurked outside the city limits of Mankato. Chief took it upon himself as his duty to protect the townspeople as well as the grave of his keeper from evil. And somewhere between chasing Deer Lady and wolf people away from Mankato, Chief was cursed with immortality. He didn't know why such a curse was bestowed on him, but he lived with it. He was a warrior, he was a chief, and as time passed, he became the oldest dog in the world.

>→ >→ ←< ←<

So on the morning when Chief picked up the scent of something that should not have been so close to Mankato, he went to investigate. But first things first, before he started his investigation, Chief had "ways." There were rituals, routines, and traditions. First, he repositioned the fake warbonnet, which some kids had tied to his head one Halloween night years ago as a joke, on his head. Despite its origin as a prank, Chief was proud of the warbonnet and did everything in his power to keep it secured. The kids had tied it tightly, so it didn't take much effort to keep it there. That warbonnet was how he got his name, Chief. When he was with his Sioux keepers, he was Tasheeka-Watanmee, which meant "Crazy Dog." And before the warbonnet had been tied to his head, the citizens of Mankato had called him "Get" or "Shoo."

But now he was "Chief," warrior dog of Mankato. So on that morning, Chief stood on all three of his legs and wobbled out of his tipi, which was merely a bush in Reconciliation Park. He made his usual stops before leaving city limits to investigate the scent. He drank his morning water from the Minnesota River first. Then, since a few restaurant owners were fond of him and always left leftovers for him in alleyways, he went and had his breakfast. Chief was a stray dog, but he had pride, and he'd be damned if he resulted to dumpster diving. His pride kept him from making friends with his own kind, but he didn't care, far as he was concerned, they were all morons and beggars... cultureless imbeciles.

Once Chief's thirst was quenched and his belly was full, he made his way out of town toward the unwelcomed scent. It was a journey he had made many of times, and all for the same reason. But it was strange to Chief that the stench filled the morning air. Evil beings and evil spirits were nocturnal; sunlight weakened them. But Chief had a duty, a job, and he hadn't kicked evil ass in a long time. He was well overdue for some action. Chief loved it. Maybe it was the Sioux in him, but he loved to fight. He welcomed it whenever he could. The spirit of Crazy Horse was strong in him, always.

The origin of the scent was further outside of Mankato than Chief had thought. What he expected to be a short walk became a five mile journey. But once Chief arrived at the source, he was not surprised by the type of beings from which it emanated. Instead, Chief was flabbergasted to see what they were doing. The scent was coming from Chiye-tankas, known commonly as "Sasquatches." A few dozen of them were gathered just five miles outside of Mankato, all in the middle of a large, open field. Chief watched them as they worked. They were building something. It was the biggest tipi Chief had ever seen. It looked like a circus tent, but the circus stopped coming to Mankato decades ago. The Chiye-tankas were raising the tallest tipi poles Chief had ever seen, two hundred feet high. How the citizens of Mankato could not see what was going on, Chief didn't know. The tipi the Chiye-tankas were erecting was colossal. It had to be at least three miles in circumference.

Then, Chief picked up on another scent, one that was ancient, the most ancient of any scent Chief had ever smelled. It was a scent that came from the beginning of time. It was either an angel or an animal spirit. Neither had he ever encountered before, but he knew they existed. The origin of the ancient scent revealed itself when it ordered the Chiye-tankas to work faster. It was The Trickster in his original form, with the body of a man, but the head of a coyote. He had no wings, though, which Chief found very peculiar because all animal spirits were said to have wings, just like angels. Something was afoot, something big was about to take place, something Chief might have to make war with to protect Mankato.

Chief was fearless, so he approached the Chiye-tankas ready for war, ready for victory. "Get the hell out of here, you stinky, skunk-ape bastards!" Chief barked with all his might. Then, he let out his warcry. The spirit of Crazy Horse was strong in him. Every Chiye-tanka there stopped what they were doing and turned to Chief. There was silence and confusion among them, then they turned to The Trickster, who motioned one of his fingers over his throat, the universal sign for "kill." They all became enraged, grunting and moaning. Then, they began to throw rocks at Chief. Chief had only three legs, but all he needed was three. His having four legs would have put anyone who fought him at a too much of an unfair disadvantage. A true warrior, Chief preferred the odds against him. Chief darted toward the Chiye-tankas, zig-zagging so none of their rocks hit him. Chief was fierce, a force to be reckoned with.

One poor Chiye-tanka felt Chief's fierceness, Chief charged at him and bit him where no male of any species wanted to be bitten. The Chiye-tanka let out a high-pitched shriek. It made all of the other Chiye-tankas grab their private parts and make a painful sound.

"Haha! One down, twenty-three skunk-apes to go! Come on, who's next!" Chief barked. All of the Chiye-tankas retreated, all except one. That Chiye-tanka was bigger and taller than the others. He had to be their chief, Chief could sense it. The enormous, unflinching Chiye-tanka made its way to Chief. Chief growled and showed his teeth, his testicle knives.

"Bring it on, King Kong!" Chief growled.

The Chiye-tanka chief brought it on. He ran toward Chief as Chief charged at him. The joust was on, both in motion, both running at full speed toward each other. The spirit of Crazy Horse was even stronger in Chief than ever. He aimed for testicles, his teeth cocked and loaded. When they were just feet from each other, Chief jumped at his target with his mouth wide open. But then something unexpected happened to Chief. He felt something underneath him, the Chiye-tankas foot. It became very apparent really fast to Chief why they were sometimes called "bigfoot." They had big-ass feet!

And with one really good swift kick from the giant Chiye-tanka, Chief flew for the first time in his dog life. He flew high into the morning sky, passing a few birds on the way. The kick was powerful enough to send Chief the whole five miles back to Mankato, where he landed in a small pond near the fourth hole on Mankato's golf course. Having avoided death hundreds of times before, Chief emerged from the waters of that small pond, with no injuries, but as butt-hurt as could be. Chief did not appreciate being kicked that far at all. It hurt his pride more than anything else. But Chief was smart though, and he didn't want anything to do with whatever The Trickster and the Chiye-tankas were doing outside of town. The citizens of Mankato were on their own. The spirit of Crazy Horse was not strong enough in Chief for him to want to get kicked like that again.

Quietly, however, Chief kept an eye on what The Trickster and the Chiye-tankas were doing. For weeks, he sat daily at the highest point of Mankato and watched them as they set up the colossal tipi. All the while, he barked obscene, vulgar things at them, things he was not proud of barking. But tradition dictated that they had to be warned a warparty awaited them in Mankato. And just after a few weeks, as quick as the Chiye-tankas appeared, they disappeared, leaving THE BIGGEST TIPI EVER BUILT just five miles outside of Mankato, Minnesota. Chief didn't know what to think about it. He never seen nothing like it in all of his years. Something bad was surely amidst.

Strange events followed the arrival of colossal tipi. Chief saw one of the most evil of all beings, the Thunderbird, in the sky one night. The Thunderbird soared over the town, dropping flyers announcing that

THE POW-WOW OF ALL POW-WOWS was going to be held on July 23rd inside THE BIGGEST TIPI EVER BUILT in Mankato, Minnesota. The prize money for all traditional dance and drum contests was ridiculously high, the most ever offered. Chief was a dog, but he could read, especially between the lines. Something about THE POW-WOW OF ALL POW-WOWS didn't seem right to him, especially the fact that only full-blooded Native Americans were going to be allowed into the pow-wow. Chief would have to be on high alert when July 23rd came around if he were to protect the citizens of Mankato.

As July 23rd approached, the town of Mankato was overrun by full-blooded and mixed-blooded Native Americans alike. There were literally hundreds of thousands of them who showed up, if not millions. Weird scents filled the air. It was more than the town of Mankato could handle. Chief became an instant celebrity. All of the Native Americans who came to Mankato posed with him, posting pictures of Chief with his warbonnet on to things he had never heard of, like a book with a face and telegram that was instant. As July 23rd, when grand entry was to take place at THE POW-WOW OF ALL POW-WOWS, approached, a giant city of tents and normal-sized tipis appeared and surrounded THE BIGGEST TIPI EVER BUILT. Chief left Mankato and made his way to the colossal tipi, so that he could represent his people, the Sioux, when grand entry started. The spirit of Crazy

Horse had grown strong in him once again.

The day before THE POW-WOW OF ALL POW-WOWS, there was chaos outside of THE BIGGEST TIPI EVER BUILT. Mixed-blooded Native Americans were protesting the pow-wow, but security around the colossal tent was tight; no mixed-blood was going to be allowed inside, not a single one. They were forced to watch as full-blooded Native Americans entered using their Certificate of Degree of Indian Blood (CDIB) cards as admission tickets to enter and claim their seats for the next day.

Chief laughed at the dilemma the mixed-blooded Native Americans were facing being denied entry into THE BIGGEST TIPI EVER BUILT, but that was until he tried to enter. Security guards denied him entry as well. One security guard even kicked Chief when he tried scramble around them, sending him far over the protesters outside. Chief flew for the second time in his dog life, landing in the bed of an old truck that was driving away from THE POW-WOW OF ALL POW-WOWS to pick up supplies in Mankato. Chief had no choice but to stay in the bed of the truck until it made it into town where he jumped out, butt-hurt even more now. He had to make the five mile journey again. Despite his hurt feelings, Chief did so because he knew in his doggie-heart that something was not right about the pow-wow about to take place.

Chief arrived back at THE BIGGEST TIPI EVER BUILT that evening. The protest was getting heated. Hippies had showed up, busloads of them, all with signs that protested the pow-wow, some signs calling it double discrimination, some signs with pictures of an Indian chief with a tear streaming down his face, and some signs with "Make Love Not War" written on them, left over from a protest long ago. The hippies were kind to Chief and took him in as one of their own. They painted peace symbols all over Chief with warpaint that could only be seen with a black light. Then, they gave him a treat, a cookie laced with LSD. Evening gave way to night, as reality gave way to the mystical.

Before Chief knew it, he was on a vision quest, dancing with the hippies to beats no traditional Native American drummer could keep up with. It was music that was continuous like a heartbeat, never stopping. A black light shined down on them brightly like moonlight from another world. The hippies danced with fire and with sticks that glowed, and they all kissed. Girls kissed guys, guys kissed girls, girls kissed girls, guys kissed guys, and they all kissed Chief. Chief loved the attention, but even more, he loved life more than he ever had at that particular point in time. He could see sounds, hear scents, and feel life itself all around him. It was unlike anything he had ever experienced. The night became a whirlwind of fantastic and wonderful things, diverting

Chief's attention away from his duty, to protect Mankato. Everything was all about love. For all Chief was concerned, love was all that mattered. It was strong in the air, too, because it became apparent very quickly that the hippies were no longer concerned with protesting THE POW-WOW OF ALL POW-WOWS. Instead, they just wanted to dance around the colossal tipi. With a glow stick in his mouth, Chief joined them in their dancing.

Chief had never felt so alive. Vision quests had sure changed since the days of old. They had evolved into something with which Chief was totally unfamiliar with. But he loved it; the dancing, the music, and the touching of energies. Before it was over, Chief began to see things, see ghosts. He saw ghosts of things he didn't know could have ghosts, like butterflies. They were everywhere, their colors lit by the black lights, colors Chief did not know even existed. His dog instincts kicked in, and he began chasing butterfly ghosts, wearing himself out until their beautiful, unrecognizable colors faded into the darkness. Chief ended up falling asleep on top of a hippie couple making love, sending him into a dream of being in a boat all by himself in the middle of an ocean he had never seen. It was absolutely the strangest dream he had ever dreamt.

July 23rd snuck up on Chief. He awoke when the sun was already about to set. Grand entry, which started every pow-wow, was close at hand. Chief had lost focus, but he took care of first things first. He went to find water. His mouth felt like cotton. Drumming suddenly erupted from inside THE BIGGEST TIPI EVER BUILT, and the first song of the pow-wow was underway. A little mixed-blooded Native American girl, maybe ten-years-old, dressed in the regalia of a fancy shawl dancer, gave Chief the water he craved. She poured it into a small Styrofoam bowl for him. Surprisingly, it tasted like Indian corn to him, a taste he hadn't tasted in forever. It was the best water ever, so he drank it like he had never drunk anything before. He wanted a piece of frybread, a Native American traditional bread that was deep-fried to a golden yellowish-orange color and about eight inches in diameter, with it. The Indian corn-flavored water was that good.

The little fancy shawl dancer petted him as he drank from her bowl. It had been forever since he had been petted too. Her parents cautioned her not to do it, but she didn't take their advice. She continued petting him even after he was finished drinking the bowl of water. Chief's warbonnet amused her. She wanted to take Chief home with her, but her mother denied her request, telling her daughter surely a three-legged dog with a warbonnet on had to have a keeper. Traditional Native Americans didn't believe in owning anything, not even animals. They believed they were only their keepers.

Then, the little fancy shawl dancer started to cry and started to tell her mother how sad she already was because she couldn't dance at THE POW-WOW OF ALL POW-WOWS, and now she couldn't keep THE CUTEST DOG EVER. It was then that Chief snapped back into reality. THE POW-WOW OF ALL POW-WOWS was not what it advertised itself to be if it denied such a caring, loving little girl her place in the dance circle. Chief became militant. The spirit of Crazy Horse grew strong in him once again. So he left the little fancy shawl dancer in order to fight for her right to dance at THE POW-WOW OF ALL POW-WOWS.

The protesters around THE BIGGEST TIPI EVER BUILT had more than tripled since Chief had last been there. There were mixed-blooded Native American drum groups drumming traditional songs outside, mixed-blooded Native American chiefs with their highest ranking tribal members with them, and mixed-blooded Native American warriors, all demanding entry into THE POW-WOW OF ALL POW-WOWS. Chief felt their pain because he had been denied entry too, and he was more full-blooded than most full-blooded Native Americans there! His spirit was full-blooded and not corrupted by the blue-eyed tribes' ways in any fashion, except for the fact that he liked pizza. Chief had seen all of the changes from the tipi days to the casino days. So Chief spoke his mind, but with a respectful tongue, since there were women and children present, which his original Sioux keepers had taught him to do.

"This is bullcrap! We came from the same bloodline! You dumb-donkeys!" barked Chief, who was surprised when a crowd of mixed-blooded Native Americans picked him up and lifted him above them all. Chief let out a warcry that was heard all over the world.

Unbeknownst to Chief, a photographer from the *Rolling Rock* magazine was there and took the picture that was set to capture a million hearts. Chief, a dog with a warbonnet on his head, raised high in the air by mixed-blooded Native Americans who were not allowed into THE POW-WOW OF ALL POW-WOWS, was the photograph that would become a symbol. The spirit of Crazy Horse would be seen in him worldwide.

"Being Native American is a way of life, a spirit! It's not a blood-quantum!" barked Chief. The crowd underneath him cheered. "We are all Native American! And if we are not allowed into this pow-wow, then it is not a real pow-wow!!!"

The crowd of mixed-blooded Native Americans cheered. Chief had started a frenzy. He watched mixed-bloods; blonde-haired ones, blue-eyed ones, pale-skinned ones, and even black-skinned ones, became warriors before his eyes. A lot of them gave out warcries for the first time in their lives. But still, the security guards protecting THE BIGGEST TIPI EVER BUILT didn't budge. So Chief protested more.

"And fudge CDIB cards!!!" Chief barked loudly, still being respectful as he was taught to do. The crowd went nuts from that statement. There was a riot, a crazy, out of control riot, more resistance than had been expected from people with only partial warrior blood running through their veins. Mixed-blooded Native Americans bum-rushed THE BIGGEST TIPI EVER BUILT, but they were stopped short when a horde of additional security guards swarmed outside from inside the colossal tent. They were different from the security guards outside though; they had gas masks on. They shot tear gas at the mixed-bloods, released flash bombs, fired guns into the air, and began tasing mixed-bloods left and right. Some mixed-bloods fell, but most backed off, retreating, even dropping Chief back unto the ground, abandoning their spokesdog.

"This will be your only warning! Do not attempt to enter this pow-wow!" one of the security guards warned. But then there was commotion on the ground, and the crowd of mixed-bloods separated like the Red Sea. Chief came running out from the crowd, his eyes on a target, and his teeth cocked and loaded. The spirit of Crazy Horse was the strongest it had ever been in him. Before the Security guard who spoke could figure out what was going on, Chief had his balls in his mouth. There was a shriek, a high-pitched howl that echoed for miles. The riot resumed, as the gas-masked security guards fought dirty, with tasers, rubber bullets, and nightsticks. They stood their ground at the main entrance into THE BIGGEST TIPI EVER BUILT, successful in keeping the mixed-bloods from entering THE POW-WOW OF ALL POW-WOWS.

During all of the commotion of the riot, however, Chief picked up on yet another scent that shouldn't have been anywhere near a camp, and especially near a city of camps. A scent he was familiar with, it belonged to an evil being, one he had chased away from Mankato before. He scurried through the gas-masked security guards and the mixed-bloods, leaving the warparty at hand behind to follow the scent. Something suspicious was definitely going on.

Before Chief knew it, the scent led him to a secret entrance in the back of THE BIGGEST TIPI EVER BUILT. The entrance didn't have any security guards or protesters anywhere near it. He found himself alone with something monstrous, an evil being about to enter THE POW-WOW OF ALL POW-WOWS.

Chief spoke suddenly, stopping the monster short, "Who let the dog out? Who? Who? Who let the dog out?!" he sang from one of his favorite songs. Chief liked to talk shit to evil beings. He knew they feared him, so he toyed with them using a whole repertoire of various punch lines he barked to make his presence known and demonstrate his fearlessness.

The evil being stopped and turned to him. It was Deer Lady, dressed in traditional fancy shawl dancer regalia. Adorned with hot pinks and purples accented with chartreuse, sequins, and rhinestone trim, Deer Lady looked like any other fancy shawl dancer, except for the supernaturally extraordinary nature of her particular beauty and the hoofs Chief could see when her dress lifted up as she walked. Deer Lady was an evil being who hated and mutilated men. She was a shapeshifter permanently shifted, with the upper body of a completely irresistible Native American woman, but lower body with the hindquarters of a deer. Deer Lady was cursed and thus cursed all who came across her. Chief didn't realize he himself was one of the many she had cursed until she spoke.

"I see you're still here. Perfect," Deer Lady snarled at him.

"It was you, bitch!" Chief cursed at her.

"A buffalo dies, an eagle flies, a dog lies, and now a dog dies."

And with that counter-curse, the curse of immortality Deer Lady had put on him long ago was lifted, but not to his advantage. Deer Lady had put the curse on him so that one day, she could have her revenge on Chief and savor his death. She wanted to enjoy being the one that removed Chief from Earth for good.

Chief charged at Deer Lady. He was done with fear. The spirit of Crazy Horse overcame him. With his sharp teeth cocked and loaded, Deer Lady turned her back to him as his mouth made contact. Chief's teeth were not met by the taste of deer legs as he had anticipated. Instead, they were met with the taste of deer hoofs as Deer Lady kicked her legs, throwing Chief backwards, sending him flying high into the air. Chief flew for the third time in his dog life. He flew for miles, landing between THE BIGGEST TIPI EVER BUILT and Mankato. His body landed in a field in the middle of nowhere where no one would ever find him.

As Chief had heard many times, "The third time is a charm."

This time, he could not get up. His heart began beating out of control. He could not catch his breath, as he lay in that desolate piece of land between Mankato and THE BIGGEST TIPI EVER BUILT. He was mortal again. Death could dance a final dance with him, finally.

So Chief did the only thing he could do; he just laid there praying for the pain to stop soon, praying for it to end quickly. After all the years, decades, a century even, he was almost happy about meeting death, but it also made him sad. The people of Mankato would have to protect themselves from now on. Their chief had been denied entry into THE POW-WOW OF ALL POW-WOWS, but had gained entry into the spirit world in the process.

It was something he had always wished for, until now... the irony. He had done his job, though. The Great Spirit and his animal spirit would be proud of him.

As Chief laid there dying, his nose detected two familiar scents from long ago. Then, Chief's dying eyes met the comforting sight of Crazy Horse and Red Otter, both of his keepers, both waving to him from the center of the most beautiful light. He smiled, the first time he had in a century, and his tail began to wag, the first time in a century as well. Then, he got up and went to them like the loyal dog he was.

"Talk about Indian time," Chief joked, as he made his way to his keepers awaiting him in the beautiful light. "Indian time" meaning as it had always meant, better late than never... now.

CHAPTER 3

A Bullet Named Mom

EAGLE VS ROOSTER

ON THE 8TH FLOOR of a beach-side building in Miami, Florida, high above the culture clash and smell of spicy foods on the streets below, a man was in his condo preparing something sacred. Shirtless, the eagle wings tattooed on his back were visible, along with many of the other tattoos that covered his body. Most of his skin was adorned with tribal designs of assorted birds, except for his arms, which were covered with Seminole tribal patchwork. Like a yakuza, his tattoos stopped only at his wrists and neck. He was in a spare bedroom he converted into a bullet-making lab. Most twenty-five-year-old men with a spare room would have made it into their office, their man cave, or their personal gym, but not Eagle. He was a light-skinned Native American man, average in height, and built like a mixed martial art (MMA) fighter, with short, well-styled hair. No, Eagle's spare room was a space where he made his own bullets, so they couldn't be traced back to him. In his profession, ballistics were his enemy.

On that particular day, Eagle was making a special bullet, one which would be his masterpiece. He had melted pure gold for this bullet and even bought the best gun powder money could buy. As always when he did this delicate work, his hands were squeezed into black surgical gloves as to not leave any prints. The long cartridge case of the rifle bullet was securely placed into a vice. Eagle filled the first half of it with the expensive gun powder and the remaining half of it with something that would make it unlike any bullet ever made. The remaining half of the cartridge case Eagle filled with the ashes of his deceased mother, for the bullet had only one purpose: to avenge her death. Once the cartridge case was filled, the golden bullet was put in place and sealed to the powder packed casing that would send it out of his rifle at a killer speed. And since it was a special bullet, it had to be named, so Eagle engraved one word into the bullet's golden point. That one word was, "MOM."

Once Eagle had finished making his masterpiece, he decided to unwind by watching the news. An hour or so later, a large manila envelope was slid under his front door with audible force. Eagle got up from his custom-made black leather couch and went to retrieve the envelope. It was a promise of work. He opened the envelope right away, removing the single piece of paper inside it. The white page had six numbers and the two words, "duck pond," written on it. The job was so top-secret, nothing more could be written; his instructions would only be given orally at the chosen location.

Eagle got ready, dressing in an expensive black suit and white dress-shirt, which were tailored to fit him. His seductive cologne and perfectly styled hair always made the ladies' heads turn. His good looks and taste were his camouflage. Miami was full of rich, sexy people. His light skin, facial structure, and well-mannered behavior made it hard for anyone to make him out as Native American. Most people couldn't pinpoint what race he was. His being ethnically indeterminate was an advantage as he completed contracts all over the world, and it was vital for him to be able to blend in wherever his contracts took him.

On that particular day, he left his condo, bound for the duck pond located in a small park a few miles from where he lived. Walking on their lunch breaks, for exercise, or pleasure, locals gathered there to throw the ducks pieces of bread or crackers into the small pond they called home. The leisurely atmosphere made it the perfect place for Eagle to receive his most sensitive jobs. Something big was going down, but from the appearance of things, no one would know.

At their usual bench, Eagle met Big Bird, an old, obese, Caucasian man in a tailor-made suit that was the most unobtrusive shade of gray. His hair was as gray as his suit and styled to perfection. Big Bird looked like he had been a handsome man at one point in time, but that time had long ago passed. He was coughing when Eagle took a seat on the bench with him.

"You play the lottery any?" Big Bird asked Eagle in between his coughs. The cough sounded bad.

"Yes, usually with the same numbers. 1,2,3,4,5, and 6," Eagle answered in whispers.

"I know it's dumb, but I have to ask every time."

"The numbers are dumb. Who would choose those numbers?"

"That's the point. Nice to see you again, Eagle."

"I would say the same thing, but you don't look or sound so good."

"That's why I named you, 'Eagle,' because of those eagle eyes of yours. I wanted to meet with you in person this time because I'm not sure how much time I have left. It's bad. This may be the last time I see you. And I just wanted to say, 'Bye.' It's been an honor working with you. You're one of the good ones, no, the best one," coughed Big Bird.

"Well, my tribe has no word for 'bye,' only a phrase that means, 'until we cross paths again.' And we believe death is only the start of the big journey," Eagle said quietly, staring at the ducks who were eating crackers a young girl was throwing them about twenty-five yards away.

"What do you Seminoles believe happens after you die?" Big Bird asked.

"You turn into a star, and you slowly make your way to the spirit world by taking the Heaven highway, which is what your people call the Milky Way," explained Eagle.

"Sounds good, I like the idea of turning into a star. But right now, I'm still alive, and I have the target of all targets for you, one I only trust you to take care of," coughed Big Bird.

"Oh yeah? Who?"

"Rooster."

"But he's one of us, one of The Flock," Eagle said, referring to the organization of which he and Big Bird were both part of, which was a small network of killers who carried out high-profile assassinations.

"Was," said Big Bird, "until recently." He coughed for a moment, then continued, "Rooster was sent to New Orleans a few days ago to take care of a mocking bird for a client of ours. It was supposed to go down three days before Fat Tuesday." Big Bird cleared his throat. "To make a long story short, the Big Easy must have gotten the best of Rooster because the mocking bird was allowed to air his tale against our client, which not only makes us look bad, but it cost us a great deal of money," explained Big Bird. He looked exceptionally pale. Trying to talk with his constant coughing was taking a toll on him.

"Rooster's crows are numbered then. I'll take care of it, you have my word," Eagle stated with confidence.

"I knew I could count on you, Eagle. And from our intelligence, he's still in New Orleans celebrating Mardi Gras. It's almost like he has a death wish," Big Bird replied.

"If I know Rooster, and if he's still there, he knows we are coming for him. I'm sure he has a trap for us already put in place, so I just have to avoid taking his bait."

"Well, good luck, not only with this, but with life. I hope you achieve happiness. Most of our kind rarely do," Big Bird wished sincerely. Eagle wasn't accustomed to such a personal wish from anyone, much less while doing business.

"Thanks, but I don't need luck. I just need to find the right hen house, the one where Rooster is waiting for us," explained Eagle, as Big Bird handed him a bulky manila envelope filled with half the cash for the contract. The other half he would receive after completing the job. They shook hands, then Big Bird got up coughing and left walking west. Eagle got up and left in the opposite direction, the ducks behind them both fat and heavy with their secrets.

A few hours later, Eagle was in his '77 black Firebird driving the half day trip from Miami to New Orleans, or as he preferred to call it, "The Big Easy." His car was just like the one in his favorite movie, *Smokey and the Bandit*, with T-tops and all. The job was going to be easy for him, or so he thought. All he had to do was think of where he would go in such a situation. If Rooster had a death wish, Eagle would be the genie to grant it.

During the drive, Eagle tried to make sense of Rooster's failure to complete a contract. It was highly unlike him, something wasn't right. Rooster was dedicated to his work, thorough, precise, never allowing mistakes. He even had a system. It was how he got his name. He always took care of his targets at the crack of dawn, so he had the greatest possible amount of daylight in order to make his getaway. Some targets of his awakened in their beds to a knife sliding across their necks, and some targets were shot in the head as they got up to make their morning coffee. There was something about sunrises that Rooster trusted for his flawlessly delivered murders. Eagle could not make sense of why it was different this time and why was Rooster staying where he had failed to complete a contract. It was insane to do so. It would be the last thing Eagle would do if he ever failed to complete a contract. The first rule after completing a contract, or not completing a contract, was to get the hell out of Dodge.

Eagle knew Rooster well, too. They were somewhat friends, had even worked on several contracts together. Eagle knew his strengths, his weaknesses, and most importantly, what he looked like, which most members of The Flock did not know about each other. He was a tall, skinny, leanly muscled, black man with a shaved bald head. His eyes were beady, and his smile rearranged his face, making it unforgettable. He talked with an accent Eagle could never pinpoint, but he guessed from a country with French influence. Rooster was highly intelligent, cunning, charming, with a good sense of humor. If Eagle ever had a best friend, it was probably Rooster, who always had a joke to make him laugh, even in the dire situations they had been in together. It was almost sad that Eagle had to be the one to take him out, almost. Eagle didn't do emotions, never cared for them, even saw them as weaknesses he wanted nothing to do with, so it was going to be easy in more ways than one in The Big Easy. Irony.

After arriving to New Orleans in the afternoon, Eagle did the usual and checked into a cheap, discretely tucked away motel with no surveillance cameras, using one of his many fake IDs. He didn't unpack, knowing it was probably unnecessary because he planned to kill Rooster before sunrise. He would leave immediately after the contract was complete and check into another motel in some hole-in-the-wall town on his way back to Miami.

It wasn't Eagle's first time partaking in Mardi Gras festivities. He had actually been there on a Fat Tuesday a few years before to complete another contract, so he knew how to blend in with the boisterous crowd celebrating Carnival, the Feast of the Flesh. He drove to a costume shop he had familiarized himself with previously. While debating on whether to be the Mad Hatter, a leprechaun, or Willy Wonka, another costume caught his eye, one Rooster would never suspect Eagle would wear. It was a Jesus costume, complete with a white robe, a fake beard, a brown curly wig, and a crown of thorns. It was perfect. Rooster would be keeping his eye out for something else entirely.

Night arrived as Eagle finished putting his costume on inside his cheap motel room. As Jesus, he screwed his silencer into the barrel of his 9mm Beretta. He didn't need his rifle for this job. This job would take place up close and personal.

First, Eagle had to find the hen house where Rooster would spend his last night alive. It was almost too obvious... Bourbon Street. With so many costumed people there, it was the perfect place for Rooster to hide. Eagle got back into his '77 black Firebird and made his way to the river of drunks flowing all over the heart of the Quarter.

Once Eagle was there walking his way through the chaos of Bourbon Street, he knew he had to find a good place to perch. It cost him a few hundred dollars, but he was able to buy his way to the second story balcony of a bar that overlooked the street below. As Jesus, Eagle scanned through the flood of sinners below him, most in disguise, most with beads to throw to the Jezebels showing their breasts, and most hidden behind masks made of feathers. On Mardi Gras, Bourbon Street became the Babylon of America and its Sodom and Gomorrah.

A few hours passed. As Eagle expected, he saw his prey in disguise. Rooster's face was painted as a skull in black and white paint. He wore a top hat adorned with small skulls around the base. A wig of dreadlocks protruded from underneath it and he was wearing a cheap tuxedo. Rooster was disguised as Baron Semadi, from voodoo folklore.

"How appropriate," Eagle said to himself. Baron Semadi was an evil being found at the crossroads of life and death by voodoo believers. Rooster was with a blonde Caucasian woman dressed as the devil. Her red horns, a pointed tail, and pitchfork set off her sexy dress. She was doing something to him that she shouldn't had been doing, making him happy. He was smiling his unusual big smile and that was how Eagle recognized him.

His smile was bigger than that which Eagle was familiar with from their years working together. It confused him for a second. Rooster seemed the happiest he had ever seen him. It was a time when he shouldn't had been happy at all. Rooster's days were numbered, and he had to know it. So why was he so happy?

Eagle didn't know. Then it dawned on him. Rooster had found love, something usually forbidden to those in their profession. That thought brought Eagle comfort, knowing that his closest thing to a best friend would die happy.

Eagle made his way downstairs and into the river of sinners. He began to follow Rooster incognito, as he was trained to do. Rooster was drunk. He really didn't seem to have a care in the world. It alarmed Eagle. It almost seemed too easy, like a trap of some sort. Maybe Eagle had gotten himself involved in a conspiracy he knew nothing about. Scenarios played out inside his head, as he followed Rooster.

A contract was a contract. He knew what he had to do, so he waited for the perfect moment, staying patient.

After thirty minutes or so, the perfect moment arrived. Rooster's devil-of-a-girlfriend went inside a bar, to use the restroom Eagle assumed. Rooster darted around the side of the bar into an alley. Eagle also assumed he was going to urinate as well. Eagle pulled out his gun from inside his robe, holding it down so it wouldn't be noticed. He snuck up to the corner, took a quick glance around, and then cautiously approached the entrance to the alley where Rooster had disappeared. It was going to be way too easy in The Big Easy.

Eagle walked along the brick wall on his right that led to the alley, his gun out in front of him now in his right hand. Rooster had to be taken by surprise. The brick wall ended at the edge of a dark alley. Eagle turned the corner to the alley fast, still leading with his gun. Before he could get a glimpse of what was around the corner of the brick wall, Rooster grabbed Eagle's stretched out right arm and took his gun out of his hand in a strategic move they both knew well. But as Rooster took the time to turn the gun around and get a grip on it, Eagle shoved him with his left hand, encompassing Rooster's neck and pinning him against the brick wall of the alley. Despite that, Rooster had control of the gun. Choking and lacking oxygen, Rooster maneuvered the gun to the side of Eagle's head, pulling the trigger a half a second later to a dull click.

Rooster pulled the trigger again, but once more, only a click was heard. There were more clicks as Eagle was able to get his right hand around Rooster's neck as well. Eagle knew a lot of things about Rooster, but the most important thing at the moment was that Rooster's reach was significantly shorter than Eagle's. When Rooster dropped Eagle's unloaded gun and began to try to defend himself, it was pointless. Too late.

Rooster scratched, kicked, and even tried to peck, did all he could to release Eagle's talons from his neck, but he was unsuccessful. His arms were just a few inches too short to make any difference. Eagle watched Rooster's eyes become lifeless. His body, no more the weapon it once was, went limp and became heavy by the time Eagle released his grip.

The contract had been completed just as planned. Eagle knew he would recognize Rooster in disguise, just as he knew Rooster would recognize him in disguise. He also knew Rooster would lead him to a dark, discreet place, where he would attempt to disarm him. That was why Eagle had an unloaded gun with him. It was the mistake Eagle needed Rooster to make. He knew he could submit him with a good and unexpected choke if he could divert Rooster for just a few seconds. And only in an alley in The Big Easy would one find Jesus choking a voodoo icon to death.

Voodoo had never stood a chance against Christianity, just like a rooster never stood a chance against an eagle.

EAGLE VS RAVEN

Eagle's real name was ironically John Wayne. Growing up, he swore to himself that he would do whatever he had to do so that no one would ever make fun of him for being a Native American named John Wayne. His profession pretty much guaranteed that.

Already waiting on his next contract, Eagle left his favorite gym in the South Beach, Miami neighborhood in which he lived. It was a blistering, bright sunny day, the streets busy with immigrants and hot shots. The air was thick with the scents of South Beach. As hungry as he was, he ignored the smell of food and got into his Firebird. He had gotten a good workout. He could honestly tell himself that he was in the best shape of his life. His job was his motivation, demanding stamina, accuracy, and strength. Being the only Native American hitman there was at the time, he strived to be the best in honor of his people. He considered himself a warrior who got paid to go on warparties and collect scalps, except his scalps came in the form of completed contracts. Life was good. But John was a quiet warrior, not sociable at all. He liked his solitude, he liked his rules. And he was not a man that lived by the moment. He planned everything he did to a tee. He had a system, a system he never strayed away from, not for anything.

John had not always been a hitman. He had been

a tracker for a few years, working with various agencies like the CIA, which along with the FBI, was hiring Native Americans to do its dirty work. He also worked for some private parties as well. But the work ran out with the invention of cell phones and GPS. People became too easy to locate, so John resorted to working as a bounty hunter for a bail bondsman. It was a decent job, but that's all it was, a job, nothing to make a career out of. John's skills in finding people who did not want to be found was eventually noticed by Big Bird; a man with connections, contracts, and an endless supply of high-paying jobs. Big Bird took John under his wing, away from bail jumpers, and trained him to be the lethal ghost he became. That was how John became a part of The Flock.

It was Big Bird who gave John his assassin name, "Eagle." John loved his assassin name more than his real name. He hated that his father had a sense of humor and had named him "John." He had to know people would associate it with John Wayne, the actor who had killed countless Indians on the silver screen and wasn't too fond of Native Americans in real life, either. But "Eagle" was the only name his clients knew him by. The name Eagle became well known after he completely just a handful of contracts. Eagle's reputation grew and grew and grew until he became the assassin of The Flock that most clients requested. The high demand for his skills meant Eagle worked nonstop, traveling everywhere, experiencing a lifestyle like few Native Americans knew; full of first-class flights, five-star restaurants, and exotic locations. He was on top of the world, at his prime, discreetly assassinating everyone whom he was paid to kill, leaving no trace of his existence. Eagle's existence was that of a ghost.

But "Eagle" was only his killing persona, if he weren't on a job, he was "John," a quiet young man who kept to himself most of the time. He didn't do girlfriends; he preferred escorts. He didn't do friends; he preferred violent video games and forensic science books. He stayed inside his classy condo on South Beach most of the time when he wasn't on a job. His condo was where he was driving to now from his favorite gym. He loved his home. It was decorated with luxuries he could only dream of having while growing up.

↣ ↣ ↢ ↢

John did not have a good upbringing. He was a foster child throughout his teenage years. His mother had died when he was only twelve years old. She was a full-blooded member of the Seminole Tribe of Florida and belonged to their Bird Clan. After her death, various family members took custody of him, since his father was nowhere to be found. John was highly intelligent and a master at every sport from a young age. The blue-eyed tribe took notice of it, so his stay with his family members was cut short after the Department of Human Services intervened and moved him elsewhere, away from his people. From the perspective of the blue-eyed tribe, John could be a threat to their society or an asset. They took him and made him an asset, made him what he became. John learned to fight like a man way before he was a man and became an expert at survival in his teenage years, trained at the various boot camps he was forced to attend. He became antisocial because he was taught to not trust anyone. He became selfish, but only because he had to. It kept him alive in the blue-eyed tribe's world.

When he was sixteen years old, the Department of Human Services found John a good Caucasian family to live with in a suburb of Miami. It was where he learned how to live in disguise, how to pretend to be someone he wasn't, and how to hide his scars. They were good people, never treating John any differently than they did any of the other foster children they took in. It was a comfortable jail, until he turned eighteen-years-old and joined another jail, one he was destined for since the death of his mother, the Marines. The Marines gave John more training, and he became one of the best snipers they had seen in a long time. John did a tour in Iraq and came back with dozens of scalps on his belt, metaphorically. He was a true warrior, but the feeling that he was doing to the people of Iraq what America had done to his own people began to weigh heavily on him. Just a century before, the U.S. Armed Forces attempted the genocide of Native Americans, and now, he was a part of that same armed forces. Something deep inside him felt wrong. He got out of the Marines as soon as he could after that realization.

>→ >→   ←< ←<

Once John arrived to his condo, he parked in the parking garage on the ground floor of the building that overlooked the beautiful Atlantic Ocean. Within minutes, he was in the elevator that took him to the 8th floor. The elevator door opened and John walked down the short hallway lined with the doors to his neighbors' condos until he came to his door. He opened it and entered, noticing a manila envelope on the ground, pushed into his condo from underneath his door. It was a job, a contract, a future paycheck.

His assignments always came in the same kind of 8 1/2" x 11" manila envelope. He picked the envelope up and placed it on his kitchen table, deciding to take a shower before he looked over its contents. Fifteen minutes later, John was seated at his kitchen table, opening up the envelope that contained his next murder. It had been a while since Rooster, a few months.

To his surprise, the envelope wasn't filled with various types of paperwork as it usually was; plane tickets, hotel reservations, falsified passports or driver's licenses, pictures, cash, and the contract. The envelope only contained one very large photograph. John pulled it from the envelope and was shocked to find the photograph was of his father, Tonto Wayne, a famous pow-wow MC/an ex-champion fancy dancer/a warrior/a deadbeat dad. Most Native Americans knew his father as THE TOUGHEST NATIVE ALIVE, which was a title he had won. But John always referred to him as THE WORST NATIVE ALIVE, a title he had also won in his mind. Tonto was the last person he had ever expected to see a picture of inside one of those envelopes. John almost threw it to the ground, in disbelief.

It seemed like a sick joke to John, until he turned the image over and read what was written on the back of the photograph. It was Big Bird's handwriting. He had thought him dead by now. John read the note:

> *"Because of the high level of confidentiality regarding this job, this is all I could send pertaining to the target. The clients feel you are the only one who can get close enough to the target to complete the contract. All I really know is that your cut of the contract is worth two-million dollars if it is completed. I know your feelings toward your father, otherwise, I would not have*

considered offering it to you. It may be a chance to kill two birds with one stone. You could avenge your mother's death and make enough money to retire. If you accept this contract, the specifics of the location and date of the job will be given to you at a meeting with the clients on July 22nd in Washington D.C. at a location to be given to you via text the night before. If you find the terms acceptable, be in D.C. on July 22nd. It's legit. I've checked it out. Hope you decide to take it. Two million dollars!
-Big Bird"

It took a while for John to take it all in. As much as he hated his father, it was still a huge thing to request of someone. But two million dollars was a whole lot of money, enough to fund his early retirement, a dream of his. Killing was John's business, yes, but even though business was good, John was already burnt out on it. He was ready to travel and see what else the world had to offer him. He wanted to do something his mother would have been proud of him for doing. Killing people for money was something she would not have been proud of him for doing. Plus, he wanted to travel on his own terms, go on a vision quest, find himself, find where he belonged, and open up a business there. And two million dollars on top of what he already had saved up would be more than enough money to make his dream come true.

The contract was for his father, Tonto Wayne. John shook his head. He had always told Big Bird that if he had ever ran into his father again, that it wouldn't be good for his father. His hatred for Tonto ran deep, buried in an unmarked grave in his heart. Maybe it was time to give Tonto a marked grave, a real marked grave. If there was anyone who could take out Tonto, it was Eagle, John's alter ego.

Tonto Wayne was well-liked in Indian country all over the U.S. and Canada, though. He was a Native American celebrity, a Native American bad-ass. Tonto held the title as THE TOUGHEST NATIVE ALIVE to prove both, so it would be hard to get close to him without a crowd of on-lookers present. Regardless, it was going to be an easy two million dollars, and it would be the only hit for which John's mother would have been proud of him for. It was a win-win situation.

John had always blamed Tonto for his mother's death. She died only a week after Tonto had left them. A questionable car wreck, coming home late one night from a bar; some believed she drove off the bridge on purpose and some believed she fell asleep at the wheel. Regardless, she was out that night by herself drinking because Tonto had left her, or actually, left them. Tonto's actions poured the alcohol down his mother's throat that night and, ultimately, drove her off that bridge as well.

⇸ ⇸ ⇷ ⇷

They were once a happy family though, Tonto had been a good dad to John for most of his early life. He had been there at his birth, for his first steps, and his first word. He was also a good husband to John's mother during that time. They would all go to pow-wows together during pow-wow season. Tonto was a champion fancy dancer and made his living with prize money from all the pow-wows they traveled to. John had learned most of the ways of his people from his dad. They sweated in sweat lodges together, hunted together, and sang the songs of their ancestors together. Tonto was also very skilled in various martial arts and had taught John how to defend himself and overtake anyone who dared to fight him. John was the warrior he was because of Tonto, not because of all the training he had received from all of the agencies who later controlled him. They made him a killer, but his dad had made him a warrior. John and Tonto were close, too, until that day when John was twelve years old when his dad left and never returned.

John's mother never revealed to him why Tonto had left them; she only drank and cried, then drank more and cried more during that last week of her life. John watched his strong mother succumb to weakness until she became nothing but a tragedy just waiting to happen. And happen it did. Off a bridge she plunged, away from the heartbreak of the world. The job that awaited John was more than just a job; it was a duty, the duty of a warrior to avenge the death of his mother.

↦ ↦ ↤ ↤

John began to pack, only taking a few tailor-made suits and what casual clothing he had. He knew the best place to find Tonto would be at a pow-wow, so he knew he might have to blend in with his fellow Native American men, most of whom didn't dress anything like him. Some dressed like cowboys, some like the hip-hop crowd. Some refused to wear shirts like in the days of old, but most dressed casual and modestly. But John realized he would have to stop somewhere on the way there and shop for cheaper duds that would help him blend in more. Even his casual clothes were all designer brands.

After John figured out his clothing situation, he decided he would drive instead of taking a plane to his destination. For this hit, he wanted to take his favorite high-powered rifle, which he had named "Treaty Enforcer," so flying was out of the question. Treaty Enforcer would be needed if he were to use the special bullet he had made for the occasion at hand. John had never thought in a million years he would actually get the chance to use it. The bullet had mainly stood as a symbol for his hatred of his father and love for his mother, all combined in one object, the bullet he named "Mom" that was created to kill his dad.

It wasn't long before John was packed and inside his '77 black Firebird, stuck in Miami traffic, heading northwest to Washington D.C. July 22nd was a week away, but he didn't see any harm in arriving early. If any obstacles occurred on his trip, John would have enough time to deal with them and still be punctual. He was not very fond of road trips, mainly because of how unpredictable they were; flat tires, overheating of the engine, or storms. But he didn't have anything else to do, and he hadn't seen all of the sights of the nation's capital yet. He decided to make it a little vacation. He had always been fond of Washington D.C. He had done numerous jobs there, but had always been in and out of there like the ghost he was. His job was not there, so he saw no harm in checking things out like the Lincoln Monument or the new National Museum of the American Indian (NMAI) he had read so much about on the internet. Besides, NMAI happened to be home to an exhibit dedicated to his father entitled "The Lone Tonto." It would be rather ironic for him to visit that exhibit before he ended Tonto's so-called bad-ass life.

The drive was long, too long to be driven without a stop at a hotel for sleep, especially since John didn't get out of Miami until the afternoon, but he tried to drive it straight through anyway. He was trained to stay up longer than his body wanted to. And it wasn't a problem for him at all, until night time arrived and he reached the Appalachian Mountains. Something about the monstrous darkness of the mountains caused his eyes to play tricks on him. He began to see animals run across the road that weren't there. His eyelids became heavy. But still, he drove on.

Not stopping for the night quickly became a big mistake, but John did not realize it until it was too late. He fell asleep at the wheel and took an exit he didn't mean to take. John awoke speeding up an off ramp from the interstate, doing a good 70 miles-per-hour straight at a stop sign. The off ramp came to a "T" in the road. It was too late for his brakes to do any good, so he tore right through the aluminum rails that were put in place to stop a vehicle. John remembered rolling and rolling, then he blacked out once his car came to a roaring stop against a tree. He never even heard the crash, he only felt it against his head and when numbness overtook his body. The medicine of his seat belt did little good.

There was darkness. Even when John opened his eyes, the darkness remained. He was not in his car anymore. He was on the ground. He could feel the dirt underneath him, along with some grass. It didn't make sense to him at first. He knew he had been wearing his seat belt. He tried his hardest to regain his sight, feeling out in front of him, but feeling nothing. Then, he heard someone, a deep whisper of some Native American language he didn't understand.

"Who's there?" John asked, but got no answer. Instead, there was a loud flapping noise and more deep whispers that he didn't understand. He rubbed his eyes, feeling a thick layer of mud covering them. After he wiped away the mud, he could see again, but there wasn't much to see. The moonlight barely broke through the trees, revealing his car tangled around a tree nearby. John was relieved to be alive, though, until he saw it, whatever it was, the thing making the loud flapping noise and talking to him in deep whispers of a Native American language he didn't understand.

It was the most unbelievable thing he had ever seen. It was a Native American man, but he had the black wings of a bird protruding from his back, along with the hard, yellow legs of a bird. Black, shiny feathers also stuck out from the top of his head in all directions. He didn't have a beak, but his face was painted black with a stripe of yellow going from ear to ear over his eyes. He was hideous, his feathers blacker than black. John became frightened by his appearance, but then something even more horrifying caught John's attention. He could see himself inside of his car, still secured in his driver's seat by the seat belt he knew he had been wearing. John almost blacked out again, but, instead, a memory hit him from his childhood, from the time when Tonto was still his dad.

>→ >→   ←← ←←

Native Americans used stories, far-fetched stories, to teach children the lessons of life. John had been told many of these kinds of stories by his dad while growing up. One story Tonto had told him when he was only ten-years-old came to his mind, when his dad was trying to teach him how to fancy dance. Fancy dance was the contemporary pow-wow dance into which the war dances of the past had evolved. His dad was a champion fancy dancer, so it was only right that he passed on his moves and skills to his son. But John didn't want to learn how to fancy dance at first and saw it as uncool. But Tonto shared a story with him in order to help motivate his son to learn the traditional dance the men of their family were known for being the best at.

The story involved an evil being called "Raven Man." A Native American version of the Grim Reaper, much like Baron Semadi was to Voodoo, Raven Man was also a gambling death spirit. He was believed to be half human and half raven. It was also believed that he would show up when a Native American died before his or her time, before old age got the best of them, or so his dad said. John's dad explained that Raven Man would challenge the dead person's spirit to a traditional dance contest. Raven Man would even allow the dead to pick the traditional dance for the challenge. It was said that Raven Man could dance like no other, and he was good at every traditional dance there was, so it was a huge gamble. The dead could refuse and face the judgement of The Great Spirit, or the dead could challenge Raven Man, with the prize for winning being life, to be allowed to continue living. The cost for losing to Raven Man was morbid. The dead would become a black feather on one of his wings. Raven Man wanted nothing more than to have enough feathers to fly again and fly back to the home of the Great Spirit, a place from which he had been banished, until he had enough feathers to fly again. He was once the animal spirit of ravens and wanted nothing more than to take his seat again side by side the angels and other animal spirits, as it once was for him.

The story sent a chill down John's spine when his dad had first told him it, like it had done to every Native American kid who had been told the story before. But it motivated them all to learn a traditional dance of their people. John was no exception, so he happily allowed his dad to teach him how to fancy dance. Tonto trained him as his father had trained him when he was a boy. It was brutally hard training, very brutal, but John learned. His dad's moves and skills became his own. Raven Man didn't stand a chance.

But after Tonto abandoned John and his mother,

he vowed to never fancy dance again, ever. It was the only part of his culture he really knew a lot about, but he despised his knowledge of it because it came from the father who had failed him and his mother. And he kept his vow, never fancy dancing, never winning any of the titles Tonto had won at all of the great pow-wows. As far as John was concerned, fancy dancing didn't exist to him.

>→ >→   ←< ←<

John stopped remembering and came back to reality. He could not believe what was happening, as he stared at what he knew to be Raven Man. His father had been right. The story was true, something John never dreamed possible. So he knew why Raven Man was there, and unbeknownst to Raven Man, John was prepared for him. Raven Man's deep whispers in an unknown language soon gave way to English. Finally, John could understand him.

"John Wayne, I have a proposition for you, a bet, if you will. I challenge you to a traditional dance contest, and I'll even let you choose the traditional dance. If you win, you can go back to your body and live on, but if you lose, you will become another feather in one of my wings, forever. Or you can refuse the bet and go to the great tipi in the sky for judgement. The choice is yours," explained Raven Man, although the explanation was not needed.

"I challenge you to a fancy dance contest," John

said, not needing any time to decide. Raven Man smiled, or at least, John thought it was a smile.

"Deal, John Wayne. And to be a good sport, I will go first."

"Deal," was all John could say. It would give him an advantage. He could see the kind of moves he would have to beat.

Suddenly, another being appeared. It was The Trickster, who took his original form of a man with the head of a coyote. He had a small hand drum and drumstick with him.

"Why are you here? Is this some kind of trick?" Raven Man asked The Trickster.

"No, I am here to take Rabbit Boy's place. Thunderbird finally took him from us, so now he is back in the home of The Great Spirit. I'm a better drummer and singer than he was anyway. You will see," The Trickster boasted.

"The deal has already been made, so I guess I have no choice. Hit me!"

The Trickster began to beat the small hand drum and sing a good fancy dance song. Raven Man's hideous bird legs started tearing at the Earth with his claws. He began his fancy dance routine, using his wings and arms to guide his motions. He was a good fancy dancer, stopping when the beat stopped, and performing his special moves when the drumming got louder and harder. It would have been a beautiful sight had it not been for all of his feathers being black as the night above them. Raven Man's fancy dancing became a beautiful blackness.

John had his work cut out for him. But he watched Raven Man's dance routine with a careful eye, seeing how he could do better. It would be hard, but John had faith in what his father had taught him. He did come from a family of champion fancy dancers and that thought brought him confidence. Then, something unexpected happened. The Trickster dropped his drum stick in mid-song. It threw Raven Man off, who didn't stop dancing when the beat stopped, as dictated in a fancy dance routine. The Trickster picked his drum stick up and just ended the song, while Raven Man ended his fancy dance routine with a swift move that twisted a cloud of dust around him in a cyclone. It was pretty impressive.

Once his routine was over, Raven Man laughed a laugh only an evil being could laugh. He was already counting all of his chickens before they hatched. Raven Man wasn't the least bit worried about John winning the challenge. It was going to be hard to beat his moves and skills, but John was still confident, even without having the regalia of a fancy dancer to wear. So he laughed back at Raven Man, stopping Raven Man's laughter, confusing him. Raven Man did not like being laughed at one bit.

"Your turn, John Wayne," interrupted Raven Man,

casting him a 'what up?' glance.

They both fell silent. The Trickster started another fancy dance song. This time, it was John's turn to dance to its difficult rhythm. John started his routine simple, masking his skills, his secret moves. Raven Man was not impressed at all by John's fancy dancing at first. But then, the drumming picked up, and John began to create lightning with his spins, followed by the thunderous sound of his feet stomping on the ground. John had remembered everything his father had taught him; it was like riding a bike. John spun and spun, he dipped to the ground over and over, his legs keeping up with the beat and stopping when the beat stopped. His dad would have been proud of him for remembering the song and the moves that went with it. It was the best John had ever danced. He almost didn't want to stop. It felt that good. But the drumming hit its climax, as did John. He pulled out moves Raven Man had never seen before; flips, twists, kicks, and a finale that involved a high jump into the air and doing the splits just as the drumming stopped. It was the perfect ending to a perfect routine.

And just like that, John got to live again. Raven Man went back to speaking a language John did not understand, but was sure he was only using curse words now. John was not going to have anything to do with Raven Man's flight back to the home of The Great Spirit. He had won.

But just as John watched Raven Man disappear back into shadow, John went back into shadow. Everything went black again, darkness overtook him again.

John woke up moments before he drove up the exit ramp. He awoke in time to avoid taking the exit, taking control of his car, keeping it on the interstate that led to Washington D.C. He wasn't sure if it had been all a dream, but even if wasn't a dream, he believed he had earned a second chance at life. He pulled his car to the shoulder of the interstate, and he did something he hadn't done since his mother's funeral. He cried. He sobbed like a baby. It all hit him at once, everything he buried inside him for so long; the hate, the regret, and something he had never felt before, forgiveness, the emotion he had never allowed himself to feel.

Forgiveness wasn't something with which John was familiar with; he had never forgiven anyone in his life. But after that particular night's events, he felt a strong urge to forgive his father. Without the knowledge his father bestowed on him, John would not be alive. It was a hard pill to swallow. Ultimately, he didn't swallow it. The tears streaming down his face didn't prove anything. John convinced himself they had nothing to do with his feelings toward his father. He only knew tears for his mother. So he decided to press on, to continue to his destination, to avenge his mother's death.

John put his car back into drive and continued his way through the Appalachian Mountains, but using common sense and stopping at the next hotel he came across. And so he soared on, as Eagle, not as John, with hopes to see Tonto again and introduce him to a bullet named "Mom."

CHAPTER 4

Little-Red-Man

ACT I - BIG-SISTER

"Hhheeehhh," Big-Sister breathed out. She was an ancient Native American woman; large and brown as brown could get. Two long braids kept her long, salt and pepper hair from being a nuisance. Her face sagged from her pointy glasses. Her wrinkles cut through her skin like canyons. It was the loudest sound that sixteen-year-old Little-Red-Man, his hearing keen due to blindness, had ever heard. The sound that penetrated his sensitive ear drums, like nothing he had ever heard, was the sound of his mom's last breath. It wasn't her last breath he heard, but her spirit leaving her body. She was old, so old, it was never discussed around Little-Red-Man how exactly old she was, and being blind from birth, it was hard for him to even grasp the concept of what an old person looked like opposed to a young person. All he knew was that she had been on Earth for a very long time and had seen many things, more things than she had time to tell Little-Red-Man about. She was the last medicine woman alive, keeper of the strongest medicine there ever was, is, and will be, until that last breath happened. Now, there were no more medicine women, and the strongest medicine there ever was, is, and will be, was no more. Native Americans would mourn all over Indian Country over her departure to the spirit world.

Little-Red-Man started to cry, only aware of it when he felt tears run down his cheeks from his eyes. He never understood why it happened that way, tears when he cried, but each tear felt more and more soothing to his spirit, almost like a cleansing of some sort. He was the only one next to Big-Sister's bed when she took her last breath. Not that he was her only family, she had one of the biggest families in the area. Little-Red-Man was her youngest son though and the only person that lived with her. Her death came suddenly, so there hadn't been time to notify anyone yet.

Little-Red-Man wasn't her real son. Big-Sister raised him since he was a baby though, since the day she found him on the bank of the Washita River, near an area where she gathered medicine from various plants that grew near the river. It was how he got his Indian name, his only name. He was never given a legal name, so he didn't have a last name, just like Moses from the Bible. It was fitting because just like Moses from the Bible, Little-Red-Man was found on the bank of a river, left in the hands of fate. The Washita River was red in color from the rich Oklahoma soil, and Little-Red-Man was found on the bank of the river covered with red mud from rolling in it. Thus he came to be known as "Little-Red-Man."

Little-Red-Man was not alone in lacking a legal name or a last name. His mother, Big-Sister, only went by her Indian name as well. They were quite well-known all over Indian country as Big-Sister and Little-Red-Man, the medicine woman and her prodigy. Little-Red-Man learned from her, even helped her perform some rituals. He was rich in tradition, knew all the traditional songs and practiced traditional medicine. He had never been to a modern doctor in his life. He knew nothing of shots, pills, or false promises from someone who learned from books. And he was as healthy as could be, except for his blindness.

Big-Sister had always told Little-Red-Man he was blessed to not be able to see the world for what it was. He never understood what she meant. For him, it was a curse, far from a blessing.

Big-Sister's death came at a bad time for Indian country. There was controversy on all tribal reservations, in all Native American populated communities, and amongst all Native Americans. There was an upcoming pow-wow being promoted everywhere as THE POW-WOW OF ALL POW-WOWS, which in normal circumstances wouldn't have been a bad thing. But there was a stipulation with this particular pow-wow; only full-blooded Native Americans could attend and each full-blood had to show their Certificate of Degree of Indian Blood (CDIB) cards as proof to enter the pow-wow. It was also a pow-wow that boasted of having the highest prize money ever given for every traditional dance contest and every drum contest. It even stated there would be per-diems given to all who were in attendance during grand entry.

Full-blooded Native Americans were preparing all over the country to make their way to Mankato, Minnesota, where the pow-wow was to be held. But the mixed-blooded Native Americans were in a frenzy, most protesting racism. Some even tried to take the people responsible for the pow-wow to court, until it was discovered the pow-wow was being funded by the Bureau of Indian Affairs (BIA), the very branch of the U.S. government that oversaw all issues pertaining to Native Americans.

Before she went to the spirit world, Big-Sister could feel there was something not right with THE POW-WOW OF ALL POW-WOWS from the time a friend of hers brought her a flyer that promoted it. Little-Red-Man overheard her discussing it with other elders, chiefs, and medicine men. No one liked the idea of it, but Big-Sister promised every one that she would be there in attendance to make sure all went well. And for months, she prepared for the pow-wow like she never had before. There were things she always did for other pow-wows, since there was always a chance of evil beings and things not of this world infiltrating a pow-wow, but she prepared more than Little-Red-Man had ever known her to prepare for a pow-wow. They went and gathered medicine every day, from the farthest places they had ever gathered medicine. She suspected something very bad might happen at THE POW-WOW OF ALL POW-WOWS. Little-Red-Man wanted to ask her about it, but knew it wasn't his place to do so. Instead, he helped her with everything she needed help with.

Little-Red-Man helped Big-Sister gather medicine day after day, for months, until the day he heard her fall. In the kitchen, Big-Sister's physical being stopped working, failing her, going limp. On the kitchen floor she laid, unable to get up, struggling to breathe. Little-Red-Man carried her to her bedroom and placed her on her bed. It was soon after she was in her bed that she made a dying wish and took her last breath. Little-Red-Man waited by her side, praying she would start breathing again, but it never happened. The wind was no longer in her. He cried and cried until his tear ducts were empty. Then, he just stood there in deep thought. Once he accepted in his mind that she was gone for good, he tucked his mother in properly, kissed her for the last time, and went for help. They lived in the country, miles from town, so it was going to be a journey for Little-Red-Man. He ran into the unseen. For hours he ran, until finally someone saw him. A cab driver named Johnny Butt was coming from dropping off a customer in a neighboring town when he saw Little-Red-Man running through a field near the highway. It was a highly unusual sight, so he honked.

ACT II - JOHNNY BUTT

Little-Red-Man heard the honk. It sounded like a hundred angels singing. He ran toward the honk until he was stopped abruptly by a barbed-wire fence. He bounced backwards and fell to the ground, only to smell a familiar scent in the air, a scent that grew stronger and stronger. It was the smell of butt, stinky butt too. A comforting smile overcame Little-Red-Man's face. He was soon picked up from the ground by a friendly hand, a hand belonging to Johnny Butt, Anadarko, Oklahoma's only cab driver. Johnny was his real first name, but Butt was not his real last name, rather a nickname given to him because he always "smelled like butt" from sitting in a vehicle all day and night. It didn't bother him at all though. There were worse things people could have chosen to call him.

Johnny Butt was a friend. Little-Red-Man had accompanied his mom on many rides to town in Johnny Butt's cab. Johnny Butt was like no cab driver in the world. His rates were in cash, beer, or both. And he always came out even at the end of the day, with a good buzz and enough gas money to cruise around. It was his dream job come true.

Johnny Butt was a long-haired, tough-built, middle-aged Native American man, who was very handsome. He was also an entrepreneur, running his own business, so he was quite the catch. It had always been Johnny Butt's dream to be able to "cruise and booze" and get paid for it. Through his cab business, he achieved his dream. His rates were complicated, but known by every Native American in the area by heart. A one-way trip in town cost five dollars or a 6-pack of cheap beer. A two-way trip in town cost seven dollars or a 6-pack of expensive beer. Out of town trips cost five dollars automatic then two dollars every five miles or a 6-pack automatic and a beer every five miles after. Very reasonable prices for Anadarko, a small Native American town in southwestern Oklahoma. Big-Sister never paid him in either though. She paid him in something more valuable, medicine and blessings.

Little-Red-Man knew he had been saved once he heard Johnny Butt's voice. Not only was his voice a savior, but the sound of his truck instead of his car was another blessing. Johnny Butt owned a black and yellow '84 Ford Taurus and an old, black and yellow '79 Chevy truck. For Little-Red-Man, it was all falling into place, Johnny Butt's truck would be able to transport Big-Sister and take them on the journey that he had promised her he would fulfill for her.

Big-Sister's dying wish to Little-Red-Man was to make sure she made it to THE POW-WOW OF ALL POW-WOWS dead or alive. She proclaimed the importance of her attendance at the pow-wow over and over to Little-Red-Man, no matter what. She even went as far as telling him it was what he was born to do. So when Johnny Butt took his hand, with the sound of his truck blaring in the background, he knew the planets were aligning for the journey bestowed on him.

A promise is a promise, nothing in between mattered. Little-Red-Man filled Johnny Butt in on the details of what happened on the way back to Big-Sister's house. He even told him about her dying wish. He was speechless, only the sound of his drinks of beer were heard until they both were standing there, near Big-Sister's bed, where her lifeless body laid.

"Okay, I'll do it," Johnny Butt finally said, breaking a long silence. Little-Red-Man could hear tears in his voice.

"Thank you so much," Little-Red-Man said, acting

surprised, but knowing it was fate.

"I'll take ya'll, but I can't afford it all by myself."

"I have five hundred dollars she left me, is that enough?"

"Oh, that's more than enough. I don't need all of it though, I'll calculate how much I need and just pay me what I come up with," Johnny Butt answered, his voice cracking from his sadness. He tried to play it off though. "Damn, allergies."

"Whatever it takes to get her there."

"Before anything else, we need to put her body in something, like a coffin of some sort."

"We have some wood in the back," Little-Red-Man answered him.

They both exited Big-Sister's house and went to her backyard, where a pile of lumber laid. Two-by-fours, some plywood, and a few old blankets were enough for what they needed. In a matter of an hour, Johnny Butt made a makeshift coffin for Big-Sister. They put the coffin in the bed of Johnny Butt's truck, then carried Big-Sister's body out of her house, and placed her body inside the coffin as carefully as they could. With no complications and a perfect fit, Big-Sister was put into THE UGLIEST COFFIN EVER MADE.

It didn't take long for Little-Red-Man to pack for the trip and get the five hundred dollars Big-Sister hid in her flour jar for such a time. It was money he had always known she had put there for him for when the time came, when he would be alone without her. One good thing about Johnny Butt was, his honesty, his morals, and his appreciation for Big-Sister. He was actually honored to be a part of granting her dying wish.

But before they left, Johnny Butt did work out what it would cost for the trip, knowing only five hundred dollars was their budget. Mankato, Minnesota was eight hundred miles away, ten hours in highway time. That was equivalent to 40 beers plus 2 full tanks of gas one-way in his truck, which was equal to 30 dollars in beer plus 85 dollars in gas. The trip would be a two-way trip, totaling 230 dollars, but an extra 30 dollars for dollar-menu food since it would take so long. Little-Red-Man was more than happy to pay the 260 hundred dollars Johnny Butt decided to charge. So with finances squared away, their precious cargo secured, and both packed for the journey, they left Anadarko, Oklahoma. Their destination, THE POW-WOW OF ALL POW-WOWS.

It wasn't until fifty miles down the road that they both gathered the courage to talk to each other. Johnny Butt spoke first, he asked a question.

"You see that medicine pouch there?" Johnny Butt asked, pointing at a small medicine pouch hanging from the rear-view mirror.

"No," Little-Red-Man answered jokingly.

"Oh yeah, that's right. But there's some medicine

hanging here from my mirror. You know what a mirror is, right?"

"Not really, but mom used to explain what they were to me. I liked the idea of them, you can see yourself in them right?"

"Yeah, it's like seeing backwards. I have a small one here that I use to see behind me when I'm driving. But back to my point, I have this medicine here, given to me by Big-Sister when I first started my business. She said it was a very special kind of medicine, and only I would own this medicine. She said it would make me invisible, so I could speed or do whatever I wanted and the police wouldn't be able to see me and I wouldn't ever have to worry about getting pulled over. I didn't believe in it at first, until I passed this state trooper on this highway one time. He had his radar gun pointed right at me and I must had been doing twenty miles over the speed limit, but he didn't even flinch at me when I drove by him. I couldn't believe it, it opened up a whole new world to me. Made me who I am. Fuck the police!" Johnny Butt shouted out his window. His buzz was kicking in.

"But what if something happened and you needed their help?" Little-Red-Man asked. The question caught Johnny Butt off guard.

"You know, I never thought of that. I guess I would have to throw it out if it came to that, but then again, I don't think there could ever be anything I needed from the police to make me get rid of my medicine, never."

"Mom always said to never say never."

"Well, you just said it twice," Johnny Butt joked.

Silence fell between them again. But it was far from silent inside the cab of the truck, loud heavy metal music blared from the speakers inside. The more beers Johnny Butt drank, the louder his heavy metal music became. It hurt Little-Red-Man's ears, but he respected Johnny Butt and kept his mouth shut about it. The music was angry, troubled, and reminded him of a bad thunderstorm. The impossible riffs were accompanied with the rhythm of Johnny Butt's instrument of choice, beer cans. The hiss of him popping a can open, the gulping of beer, and exhales after each drink, along with the crushing of empty cans, added percussion to every song.

It wasn't until Johnny Butt had his stereo at maximum volume for a good length of time that he realized he could not go any louder, so it was losing its ability to keep him pumped up, so his momentum began to decrease. Finally, he turned his stereo down all of the way, only the wind hitting his truck could be heard.

"So what kind of music do you prefer, Little-Red-Man?" Johnny Butt asked loudly, even though there was no need to be loud.

Little-Red-Man didn't answer, instead he reached down and opened a gym bag that was near his feet on the floorboard. From the gym bag, he pulled out a small, hand-made traditional drum, along with a traditional drumstick. Without a word said, he began drumming a traditional Kiowa song, then he began singing in the Kiowa language. He was a good singer and knew songs nobody knew anymore, taught to him by his mom, Big-Sister.

"That's what I'm talking about," Johnny Butt tried to say over Little-Red-Man's song, as the sound of a lighter flickering was heard. Soon after, the strong smell of a plant burning filled the cab of the truck. "I got to roll the windows up for this one."

Johnny Butt rolled up the truck windows, all the while, Little-Red-Man drummed and sang his heart out, hoping his mom could hear him from the bed of the truck. She had liked his singing. The aroma of the plant burning was powerful, Johnny Butt breathed it out, as Little-Red-Man breathed it in. Johnny Butt was purposely trying to get his new companion high. It didn't take long for Little-Red-Man to start feeling different, entirely different. He became extremely happy, he could feel himself smiling from ear to ear and his songs never sounded as good as they sounded at that moment. With his drumstick, he was tapping into something significant, he was the heartbeat of their journey, or so he felt. It all began to make sense, everything. Johnny Butt enjoyed the songs of Little-Red-Man, he loved traditional music when he was high, there was nothing like it. It mellowed him out, made him feel at peace with everything, made him feel like... yeah.

Their journey took a detour into the clouds, they floated their way toward the setting sun. They raced a cloud of butterflies but lost, they watched a flying rooster being chased by an eagle, and the sun was wearing a warbonnet. It had become a groovy journey. But it was soon interrupted when Little-Red-Man stopped singing, stopped drumming. The truck fell to the ground, or so it felt.

"Do you hear that?" Little-Red-Man asked in a panic. They both went silent and listened.

"What?" a concerned Johnny Butt asked.

"This, what I am saying right now, do you hear that?"

"I have no idea what you're talking about, man. I don't hear anything but you talking."

"That's exactly what I'm talking about. I sound just like Mickey Mouse, can't you hear it?"

"Mickey Mouse? The Disney dude?"

"Yeah, listen. Howdy boys and girls. M-I-C-K-E-Y M-O-U-S-E."

"You sound more like Donald Duck, man," Johnny Butt barely got out before bursting out in laughter. Little-Red-Man joined him in the laughter. And for miles and miles, the sound of their own laughter became their music, their road trip song. If either one of them had been back in the bed of the truck close to Big-Sister's coffin, they might have heard her laughing with them. But what was so funny, none of them knew.

When the laughter finally halted, countless miles later, they made a pit stop at a convenience store for what they agreed were the necessities for their journey. They bought the most beef jerky and moon pies the cashier working at the convenience store had ever seen anyone buy in one purchase. Once they left the store and were back on the road, they became silent, as Native American warriors do when on a warparty. They had the element of surprise on their side and they surprised their enemy when they tore their wrappers from them and scalped them with their teeth. Their enemies, the moon pie tribe and the beef jerky tribe, didn't stand a chance against them. They were victorious in their warparty and their bellies became full. It was THE BEST WARPARTY EVER as far as they were concerned.

They were almost halfway to their destination, almost through Kansas, when Johnny Butt's beer buzz kicked back in. They were nearing the city of Lawrence, Kansas, where Johnny Butt had spent a semester as a college student at Haskell Indian Nations University, the largest Native American University in the United States. It had been forever since that semester, but he remembered a Native American bar there that was his favorite bar of all time, a bar that was always full of the most beautiful Native American women from tribes across the nation. Johnny Butt was feeling promiscuous, but knew it would take some convincing to get Little-Red-Man aboard to take a pit stop. But Johnny Butt could be convincing when he wanted to. He had to get out of the truck for a little awhile, he needed some fresh air. He turned the radio down again and turned to Little-Red-Man.

"So what do you think about girls? You like girls, right?" Johnny Butt asked.

"I guess I do, haven't really talked to one, well I have talked to some, but not in a way like you're thinking," Little-Red-Man answered.

"So you're a virgin?"

"I guess so. I've had urges, to talk to girls, but I don't really understand anything beyond that."

"Are you shittin' me? So you don't know about the monster with two backs?"

"Monster with two backs?"

"Sex. You do know your lil' thewk-a-loo is meant for more than just peeing with."

"Like what?" Little-Red-Man asked with curiosity.

"When you find a girl you like and a girl who likes you, you will eventually stick your thewk-a-loo inside her. That's why it gets hard."

"What does that have to do with a monster with

two backs?"

"That's just an expression. You see, when a man and woman have sex, the man is usually on top of the woman, and you're facing each other, thus creating a monster with two backs. Never mind, I don't even know why I used that example, you probably can't even visualize that."

"No, I can't, sounds scary. Does the girl like it when you stick your thewk-a-loo in her?"

"Oh yeah, she likes it, but more important, you'll like it even more. Its way better than talking, I tell you that, that urge you have, very little talking is involved. I know I got the urge when I was your age, but I had magazines, pictures to learn from."

"Pictures of what?" Little-Red-Man asked, still curious.

"Naked chicks, they sell magazines full of pictures of naked women," Johnny Butt answered, unsure of how to explain it all to a blind sixteen-year-old boy. There was silence, for miles. Johnny Butt didn't turn the radio back up though. He went into deep thought. "You know, there really isn't a way I can tell you about what I'm talking about, so I want to show you the best way I think I can," Johnny Butt finally said, breaking the silence.

"Show me what?"

"What a naked woman is like. We're coming up on this city I went to college at, I was thinking we could stop at this Native American bar I know of, but now I remember a better place that I could take you. It won't take long, I promise. What do you say?"

"I say, yeah, let's go, if it won't take us long," Little-Red-Man eagerly answered with no hesitation and a big smile on his face.

ACT III - CHRISTMAS

It wasn't long before they exited the Kansas Turnpike and drove into the city of Lawrence, Kansas. Johnny Butt decided to trade off the Native American bar with beautiful Native American college girls for another one of his favorite bars of all time just outside of city limits. It was hidden down a dirt road that separated corn fields, if Little-Red-Man could see how desolate it was, he'd probably think Johnny Butt was going to kill him and leave him somewhere where no one would ever find him. But it led somewhere, to a small building in the middle of nowhere Kansas, known as "The Outhouse," a bring-your-own-beer strip club.

Johnny Butt parked his truck in the makeshift parking lot that was filled with vehicles of all sorts. It was close to midnight, so he knew the best dancers would be taking the stage until closing time.

"But what about mom?" Little-Red-Man finally asked. It was a question long overdue at this point.

"She'll be okay, believe it or not, we are probably not the only ones here with a dead body in the back of our truck," Johnny Butt answered. As much as Little-Red-Man knew it was against his best judgement to leave his mom's body outside of a strip club, the allure of naked women inside diverted his good judgement.

Little-Red-Man got out of Johnny Butt's truck and went to the bed of the truck, where he promised his mom he wouldn't be long. Johnny Butt grabbed a twelve pack, then grabbed Little-Red-Man, leading him toward the entrance of the strip club. Little-Red-Man could hear the bass of a Marilyn Manson song shaking the walls of the small building.

The bass of the song gave way to the full force of the loud song playing inside the strip club, once they entered. They were immediately looked over by a big-ass Native American bouncer, who was tall, built, and stoic, with short hair. The bouncer had to take a double-take at Little-Red-Man, deciding in his mind if he should I.D. him or not. The bouncer decided not to, it was a slow night.

"Sixteen dollars for both of you," the bouncer finally said.

"I thought it was Native American night, no cover charge for Native Americans?" Johnny Butt tried to joke. The bouncer didn't flinch a muscle and was not amused. Johnny Butt handed him sixteen dollars, part of his food money, and just like that, they were in. They were just a lapdance away from showing Little-Red-Man what a naked woman was like. Not to mention, Johnny Butt could have some more beers with naked women in his presence instead of just a blind boy and his dead mother as company.

Johnny Butt led Little-Red-Man to an empty table inside and they both took a seat. There were naked women everywhere, or so it seemed, but in reality, it was an illusion. Every wall was covered completely with mirrors, reflecting the two strippers on two stages everywhere. Little-Red-Man sensed he was in a setting Johnny Butt fit in because he could smell men who had his familiar scent; sweat, beer, and butt. But there was also the scent of different kinds of lotions and perfumes, things sweet in nature. It was quite unique of a place as far as Little-Red-Man was concerned. He liked it so far.

"I'm going to need twenty dollars from your stash," Johnny Butt finally said, yelling over the loud music.

"For what?" Little-Red-man asked.

"I'm going to get you a lapdance."

"What's a lapdance?"

"It's how I'm going to show you what a naked woman is like, believe me, it will be way worth it."

"Okay," Little-Red-Man reluctantly agreed. He pulled his wallet out, opened it, and trusted Johnny Butt to get the amount he needed. Johnny Butt took twenty dollars out. Then, the music stopped, and a DJ spoke on a microphone.

"Give it up for Mercedes, fellows, if you know how to drive stick, well, you know the rest. Next up on the main stage is Christmas, and she only has a list of who was naughty this year," announced the DJ, as he played Mariah Carey's song, "All I Want for Christmas Is You."

If there was one thing The Outhouse could be counted on for, it was having a Native American stripper. There was always at least one Haskell Indian Nation University student that danced there. Christmas was by far the hottest Native American woman Johnny Butt had ever seen take the main stage there. She was dressed in the sexiest Mrs. Santa Claus outfit, complete with ribbons every man in the building wanted to untie, unwrap, and see what was inside. The spirit of Christmas filled the building as she shook what The Great Spirit blessed her with, unwrapping herself on stage. She had the longest brown legs any man could wish for, long black Native American hair, and breasts everyone watching wanted to put under some mistletoe. The mood became cheerful and festive immediately. Some guys even began to clap to the song. By the end of the song, Johnny Butt knew whom he would approach to give Little-Red-Man the lapdance that would teach him what a naked woman was like. There was no need to check his list twice. Little-Red-Man could feel her presence. He wasn't sure what she was doing, but he knew it was something remarkable. He was smiling from ear to ear, rejoicing and he didn't even really know why.

Her set was short because Christmas songs are short, at least the happy ones that she chose were. It took longer than he wished it to, but Johnny Butt managed to make his way to Christmas and ask her for a lapdance. She agreed, as strippers do when a twenty-dollar bill is held up. It confused her though, when Johnny Butt explained it wasn't for him but for his blind friend, who wanted to know what a naked woman was like. She looked Little-Red-Man up and down, knowing he wasn't old enough to be in a strip club. She reluctantly agreed, but only because it was a slow night.

Before Little-Red-Man could even figure out where Johnny Butt went to, he was surprised by a woman, who sat on his lap like she belonged there. It was Christmas, he could tell from her scent; pumpkin spice, pine, and candy cane, plus her bells jingled. Little-Red-Man then heard Johnny Butt take a seat across from them at the table. His scent still strong in the air, butt and alcohol.

"So what tribe are ya'll?" Christmas asked.

"We're Kiowa," answered Johnny Butt. Little-Red-Man couldn't talk, he was speechless, something rare for him. "What about you?" Johnny Butt asked back, eyeing her provocatively.

"Right now, Iapahoe," she joked. They all laughed a little. "No, I'm Kiowa too, from Oklahoma City."

"We're from Oklahoma too, Anadarko, on our way to Mankato, Minnesota," Johnny Butt went to explain.

"Oh, for the pow-wow?" Christmas interrupted.

"Yeah, you heard about it?" asked Johnny Butt.

"It's all I've been hearing about lately, everyone on campus is up in arms about it, since they are only letting full-bloods into the pow-wow. I think it's fucked up."

"Yeah, us, too," Johnny Butt agreed.

"So what's your name, sexy?" she asked Johnny Butt, returning a provocative look. Johnny Butt might have smelled like butt, but he was also a very handsome Native American man. The kind most Native American women liked, fierce-looking, primal.

"They call me Johnny Butt."

"Johnny Butt. Interesting. And you?" she asked, projecting her voice at Little-Red-Man.

"Little-Red-Man," Little-Red-Man answered.

"An Indian name, very interesting too."

"I like your Indian name too, Christmas, because you did make it all Christmassy in here," Little-Red-Man was able to muster out.

"Thanks, but it's not an Indian name, just my stripper name. So you can't see and you want to know what a naked woman is like?"

"I'm trying to show him what men like about women, sexually. You know, the birds and the bees," Johnny Butt interrupted.

"If there's anything I can do, sweetie, it's that. You ready, baby?" Christmas asked Little-Red-Man. He couldn't speak again, so he just nodded his head 'yes' and hoped she saw his answer. The previous song ended and a new one began, Nine Inch Nails song "Closer." The beat was heavy and throbbed throughout the building. Little-Red-Man's mouth became dry as he felt Christmas get off his lap and put her hands on the sides of his head. His pulse quickened.

The song playing hid the sound of Little-Red-Man's heavy breathing. He was excited and scared at the same time. He had never been close to a naked woman, or at least, one he was aware of. Christmas sat back on his lap again, but this time in a way Little-Red-Man never thought possible, backwards. She moved her buttocks in all directions on his lap. He could feel how firm they were, as she grinded on his thewk-a-loo. It began to wake up. He was almost embarrassed but she made it obvious it was the result she wanted. After some intense grinding, she stood up, turned around, and grabbed his head, pulling his face into her breasts. They were the softest thing Little-Red-Man had ever felt, like pillows made of flesh. They smelled good too. Little-Red-Man's thewk-a-loo was definitely awake now. Christmas sat on his lap again, but this time, facing him. Then, she began to thrust. Her pelvic thrusts were almost too much for Little-Red-Man. He never felt anything like it, he didn't even know it was something that could be done. It felt like his birthday, no, it was more like Christmas! He now understood what Johnny Butt meant about sticking his thewk-a-loo inside a girl he liked because he wanted nothing more than to do exactly that to Christmas. Halfway through the song, she stopped thrusting her body unto his, but remained on his lap. It was then that she took his hands into hers, and led his hands to her breasts. They were even softer than they felt against his face. Her nipples were hard, he wasn't sure why he cared so much about it, but he liked that they were. She helped him squeeze her breasts, then she released her hands from his and let him squeeze on his own. He squeezed like he had never squeezed before. He didn't want to stop but had to once she grabbed his hands again. Then, she led his hands down her soft body and behind her, to her buttocks. She released his hands again and he began to squeeze again. Never in a million years would Little-Red-Man guess how awesome it was to squeeze on a woman. It was almost like a naked woman's body was built for just that, to squeeze. Her buttocks were soft and hard, it didn't make sense, but then again, it didn't need to. Little-Red-Man's hands began to wonder on their own, up and down Christmas's body, until the song ended. It was then that she stopped him and climbed off of his lap, taking a seat next to him. Little-Red-Man wasn't into the music of Nine Inch Nails, but the song that just played was now his favorite song of all time.

"So Little-Red-Man, did that help you understand what a naked woman was like?" she asked him.

"Yeah, yeah, yeah," he answered, like a broken record. His pulse was still high, his thewk-a-loo still awake.

"I have to say, I'm jealous, Little-Red-Man. Jealous! That was something else, Christmas," proclaimed Johnny Butt.

"Well if you give me a beer and keep them coming, maybe you'll be next," Christmas said, with a small wink at Johnny Butt.

For the next hour or so, Johnny Butt kept them coming, while Christmas and him became acquainted. They got along good, for strangers, but Kiowas always believed there wasn't such a thing as a stranger. Kiowas believed everyone who met was supposed to meet for a reason, it was so even before it was so. Little-Red-Man tried to join in on the conversations when he could, but he was too embarrassed to talk to Christmas, seeing how she was the only girl to ever feel his thewk-a-loo awake like it was. He didn't know the procedure and wasn't sure if he was supposed to take her to dinner afterwards or what.

Closing time came faster than any one of them wanted it to. But Johnny Butt and Christmas were too into each other to let that stop their conversations. It was decided that Johnny Butt and Little-Red-Man would follow Christmas to her apartment for more drinks and some sleep. She insisted on not letting Johnny Butt continue their journey because of how much he had been drinking. Johnny Butt didn't put up a fight with her about it and it did make sense to Little-Red-Man, they could afford eight hours or so and he was sleepy. He was not a night owl.

So they left the strip club and drove back into the city of Lawrence, Kansas. In just a matter of a beer to Johnny Butt, they were parking in a parking lot outside of an apartment complex in a neighborhood full of apartment complexes. Christmas told them the area she lived in was known as "Frybread Flats" because it was where most Native Americans lived in Lawrence. It was alive with noise and life, even at two in the morning. Little-Red-Man could even hear a pow-wow song playing in a distance that he recognized as a Northern tribal drum song. Little-Red-Man began to softly sing the song, but was soon grabbed by Johnny Butt and led away from his truck. They met Christmas nearby and made their way into her one bedroom apartment.

Once inside, Little-Red-Man smelled all of her smells; lotions, perfumes, incenses. There were so many scents and each one smelled as good as the other. He had never smelled such a place. Girls began to take a whole new meaning to him. He hoped to find a girl so concerned with scents as Christmas someday.

"Okay, first things first, you get a shower," Christmas ordered Johnny Butt.

"A shower? This late at night? What for?" he asked.

"Because I don't mess with dirty boys."

"Okay, okay, where are your towels?"

"In the cabinet above the toilet bowl. While you're showering, I'll make Little-Red-Man here a nice, comfy pallet to sleep on."

Johnny Butt disappeared into the bathroom and soon after, the sound of the shower running was heard. Little-Red-Man listened to Christmas walk back and forth from her bedroom to the living room. He stood where they had left him, near the entrance.

"Okay, you can lay here on my couch, it's pretty comfortable, I even sleep on it sometimes," she finally said.

"Ah-ho, I mean, thank you," Little-Red-Man said, making his way to her voice, running into the couch. He carefully laid down on the couch. She was right, it was comfortable. He then listened to Christmas exit the living room and go into her bedroom, where she opened and closed doors and drawers, until Johnny Butt finished his shower. The bathroom door opened and he listened to Johnny Butt make his way into her bedroom.

"Nice," he heard Christmas say, followed by the sound of her bedroom door being closed shut. Little-Red-Man tried his best to go to sleep, he was tired, but there was a lot of commotion coming from Christmas's bedroom all of the sudden. He could hear her moaning, in a rhythm of some sort, then she began to shriek, louder and louder. He could also hear Johnny Butt grunting, in the same rhythm of her shrieks. Little-Red-Man never heard such noise come from two people at the same time. But then there were words, spoken by both of them.

"Who's your chief? Who's your chief?" Johnny Butt kept asking.

"You are! Oh you!" Christmas kept answering, louder and louder until she proclaimed, "Oh yes, Chief Butt! Oh yes, Chief Butt!"

It became apparent to Little-Red-Man that if he wanted to sleep, it wasn't going to happen in there, so he got up from the couch and carefully exited the apartment, recollecting all the steps they had taken to get there from the truck. Luckily it was on the first floor and he didn't have to worry about stairs. He was good at retracing his steps and made it back to Johnny Butt's truck with no complications. He then climbed into the bed of the truck and laid next to Big-Sister's makeshift coffin. It smelled a little funny but he could still smell her scent. It was comforting and before he knew it, he fell fast asleep, inches away from his mother's arms.

ACT IV - THE TRICKSTER

Little-Red-Man was awakened by wind and speed. He was still lying next to Big-Sister's makeshift coffin, but no longer were they parked in a parking lot in Frybread Flats. Johnny Butt's truck was now speeding down an interstate. Little-Red-Man could feel the warmth of the sun, not the morning sun though, a high noon sun. He had no idea how long he had been asleep or how long they had been traveling or even who was driving. He hoped he was still a customer of Johnny Butt, so to make sure, he climbed his way to the back window of the truck and he knocked on it. The truck slowed down and took a right turn, almost throwing him out of the bed of the truck. Once the truck stopped, he heard the driver exit the truck.

"About time you got up, sleepyhead," said Johnny Butt, who no longer smelled like butt, but still reeked of alcohol.

"Where we at?" Little-Red-Man asked.

"Almost to Des Moines, Iowa. Not too far from the Minnesota border. We're making good time, Big-Sister will definitely be there for grand entry. Come on, get in."

Little-Red-Man climbed out of the bed of Johnny

Butt's truck and got inside the cab. They pulled back unto the interstate they were just on. Soon they were in Des Moines, driving through the city's noise. It was then that Johnny Butt admitted that he hadn't slept yet, but explained why he hadn't. He filled Little-Red-Man in on details he hadn't before, the main one being that he hadn't slept in a few days. It was why he decided not to sleep at Christmas's apartment. He was afraid that if he went to sleep, he probably would not have woken up for a few days, which would have derailed fulfilling Big-Sister's dying wish to attend THE POW-WOW OF ALL POW-WOWS. He knew in his heart she would want to be there for grand entry, the traditional start of every pow-wow, where all of the dancers entered the pow-wow circle, dancing and honoring The Great Spirit. Johnny Butt's admission didn't matter much to Little-Red-Man, he even felt he benefitted from it by getting sleep and they were still making good time. But one thing did bother him, Johnny Butt was slurring his words when he spoke, something he had never heard him do before. He didn't know what it meant.

As they left the Des Moines and made their way back into the countryside, Little-Red-Man rode respectfully, not interrupting Johnny Butt's incoherent, slurred rants, that eventually started to make no sense at all. His voice became loud, his sentences short. His drinks of beer slowed too, far from the pace they had been before. Then, as loud as his mother's last breath was, Little-Red-Man heard another thunderous sound. It was the sound of Johnny Butt snoring. It was a soft snore at first but quickly gave way to a loud, dangerous snore. Little-Red-Man yelled at Johnny Butt, but was only answered with more snores. It was obvious he fell asleep and Little-Red-Man couldn't do anything about it, so he made sure he had the medicine of a seatbelt to protect him. He braced himself and waited.

It didn't take long before it happened. The truck turned sharp and began to roll out of control. Little-Red-Man felt what it was like to be inside a dryer. He tumbled and tumbled, forces throwing him toward Johnny Butt, who wasn't there anymore. He was thrown out of the driver's side window. Luckily for him, he had rolled the window down just moments before to get some air. So he did not crash through glass. He landed hard on soft buffalo grass somewhere along the path of the tornado they had become. With Little-Red-Man still inside, Johnny Butt's truck continued to roll through a field, until it came to a loud crash on its side. Then, there was silence. A bad silence.

The first thing that came to Little-Red-Man's mind was his mom. He unbuckled himself, climbed out of the truck, and ran in what he hoped was the right direction, yelling, "Mom!" all of the way. Being blind didn't stop him from finding her. He tripped over her coffin, falling hard on his face. Her body was still in her makeshift coffin. Immediately, he crawled to her and hugged her coffin, crying tears of happiness. He would've stayed there and never left his mom again had it not been for the sound of Johnny Butt in pain not too far away. Little-Red-Man crawled to him, unsure if it was safe to walk to him. Johnny Butt sounded broken.

"Damn, Little-Red-Man, what happened?" asked Johnny Butt, who was breathing like he didn't know how to breathe anymore. Little-Red-Man took his hand in his.

"You went to sleep," answered Little-Red-Man.

"I know that, but how did I end up here? Where's Christmas? Last thing I remember, I was unwrapping my present," Johnny Butt coughed while blood poured from his mouth at an alarming rate. If Little-Red-Man could see, he would have seen that his chauffeur was badly mutilated and had no business clinging on to life.

"I'll go get help," Little-Red-Man offered, as he tried to get up and go find help.

"No, no, it's too late. I see them."

"See who?" asked Little-Red-Man, who really didn't want Johnny to talk anymore since some kind of liquid was distorting everything he was saying. It was hard to understand him, but he wasn't finishing talking.

"The angels… Hey, listen, I messed up… It's all on me… I didn't factor in how drunk I would get during this trip… my bad… But let me apologize to you now… I have a feeling I'll get the opportunity... to apologize to Big-Sister pretty soon," Johnny Butt spoke in gargles, with pain behind every word. If Little-Red-Man could see, he would've saw how serious the situation was. Johnny Butt had blood coming out of every orifice of his body and his head was swollen to the size of a basketball. He was hideous and should not have been able to talk, but he had to get his last words out.

"What is meant to be will be. The journey is not over," Little-Red-Man tried to comfort him.

"It is for me... I can tell you that... but I do have something for you," gargled Johnny Butt. Then he held up the medicine pouch that hung from his rear-view mirror that Big-Sister had given to him to make him invisible. "It'll protect you... get you to THE POW-WOW OF ALL POW-WOWS... I wish I could be there to see it... I bet it's going to be something else... A buffet of bad-ass Native American chicks..." Johnny Butt tried to joke, but the joke sent him into coughing and gargling on his own blood, until he eventually choked to death on his own blood. Little-Red-Man listened to his last violent breath.

"You will be there and you will see it... Chief Butt," Little-Red-Man responded, taking the medicine pouch from Johnny Butt's hand. Johnny Butt went to the spirit world, but after his last violent breath, came a funny breath. He farted the loudest fart Little-Red-Man had ever heard. It made sense to Little-Red-Man though, it was the only way Johnny Butt's life could have been brought into full circle.

With his mother's "invisible" medicine in hand, Little-Red-Man made his way back to her through the field of buffalo grass. Once he touched upon her makeshift coffin again, he found a place he could use to pull it and he pulled it, making his way back toward the sound of the interstate nearby.

It didn't take long for Little-Red-Man to find his way to the shoulder of the interstate that led to Mankato, Minnesota. It wasn't all that busy, cars and semi-trucks passed him only ever so often, as he pulled his mother's makeshift coffin down the interstate. It started to feel like a lost cause, like he failed his mother. He tired quickly. She was heavy and he was running on only the beef jerky and moon pies he ate the evening before. He finally stopped on the side of the interstate and sat on his mom's makeshift coffin. It was then he prayed to The Great Spirit and to his mom. He began to wonder if it all was a mistake because it seemed everything was against him taking his mom to THE POW-WOW OF ALL POW-WOWS. He remembered how much she stressed the importance of getting her there, but it was starting to feel like it wasn't meant to be. He started to cry and felt tears streaming from his broken eyes.

It wasn't until the moment Little-Red-Man began thinking about how he would get back home to bury his mom properly that it happened. Someone pulled over from the interstate. It was a semi-truck, loud as could be, but a sign of divine intervention. Little-Red-Man dragged his mom's coffin to where his savior awaited. The passenger door of the semi-truck was pushed open just as he arrived there.

The semi-truck was driven by The Trickster, a supernatural being of Native American mythology, who had once been the animal spirit to coyotes. He did not hide who he was and kept his original appearance, the body of a man, but with the head of a coyote. It would have scared anyone else, but not Little-Red-Man, who could not see him for the hideous being he was. Instead, Little-Red-Man could not have been happier that he stopped and was willing to give him a ride. It was divine intervention at its best, or so Little-Red-Man thought.

"So how far are ya'll going?" The Trickster asked with a hillbilly accent.

"Mankato, Minnesota. How far can you take me?" Little-Red-Man asked.

"All the way, I'm headed right through there. What do you have there, luggage?"

"No, my mom. Do you have room for her?"

"Your mom? So you have a dead woman in there?" he asked.

"Yeah, I'm just fulfilling her dying wish," Little-Red-Man answered. There was silence.

"A dying wish is the most sacred of wishes, boy, so I guess we can put her in the trailer. It's full of chickens, but there's room. You will have to put her in there by yourself. It's your mom, not mine."

Little-Red-Man didn't take offense and dragged his mom's makeshift coffin to the back of the trailer. He opened the trailer and clouds of chicken feathers flew down on him. It rained chicken feathers. Somehow, someway, he managed to place his mom's makeshift coffin into the trailer. After securing his mom amongst chickens, he made his way back to the passenger's side of the semi-truck driven by his savior. He climbed in and closed the door. The smell inside of the semi-truck was very peculiar to Little-Red-Man because it was hinted with the scent of a wild animal, along with something not of this world. But the last thing he wanted to do was question the generous man helping him fulfill his mom's dying wish, so he didn't ask anything. There was a lot of silence at first, as they drove on, until the driver finally spoke to his new passenger.

"So you're taking your mom to a family cemetery?" The Trickster asked, breaking the silence. It felt good to him to not have to hide who he really was. From the time he realized Little-Red-Man was blind, The Trickster tried his hardest to come up with a trick to pull on a blind person dragging his dead mom in a coffin. Nothing came to him though, it was a very complicated situation to intervene and have fun with, as he was known for doing.

"No, to a pow-wow. It was her dying wish to be there," Little-Red-Man answered.

"Pow-wow? I didn't know they still had pow-wows. So you're Native American?"

"Yeah."

"Me too, I'm a quarter Cherokee. My grandma was a Cherokee princess. So where are you coming from?" asked The Trickster.

"Anadarko, Oklahoma. A friend brought us this far, but we got into a wreck down the road. Now he's on his journey to the spirit world."

"That mean he's dead?"

"Yeah," Little-Red-Man answered. A single tear ran down one of his cheeks.

"I'm sorry," consoled The Trickster, who saw Little-Red-Man's tear. It was obvious to The Trickster that Little-Red-Man was still mourning, so he spoke no more, instead, he turned his radio on and found a radio station with uplifting music.

The uplifting music wasn't enough to distract Little-Red-Man from all his grief. The single tear multiplied into a countless number of tears. He couldn't stop them, but he tried his hardest, not wanting to make it awkward for his savior. But death was a pill Little-Red-Man had never swallowed and he was now forced to swallow two of them. Big-Sister's last breath echoed in his mind, along with the last gargle of Johnny Butt. And now he was riding with a complete stranger to a strange place, on his own.

The Trickster felt something he hadn't felt in a long time, in centuries, remorse. For all that Little-Red-Man had been through, there was no way The Trickster could play a trick on him. They made their way out of Iowa and into Minnesota. After a while, they started to talk again. It had been forever since The Trickster actually talked to someone without the intention of playing a trick on them. It felt good. They had real conversations, so real, and so serious, that The Trickster almost didn't want their trip together to end. He thought of maybe playing a trick so their trip wouldn't end, but Little-Red-Man was just too good of a kid to pull a trick on.

Once they neared the town of Mankato, Little-Red-Man showed The Trickster a flyer that announced all of the details of THE POW-WOW OF ALL POW-WOWS so he would know where his mom and him needed to be dropped off at. It ended up not being in the town of Mankato at all, but in a field five miles outside of town. The Trickster explained to Little-Red-Man that he was seeing the most cars he had ever seen parked at an event, hundreds of thousands of them parked everywhere, in fields, along roads. He also explained to him that he could see what the flyer described as being THE BIGGEST TIPI EVER BUILT, which would harbor the pow-wow. He described it as more of a circus tent than a tipi, but colossal in size, at least three miles in circumference.

It took a long time of sitting in traffic on a backroad for them to finally make it close to the colossal tent, where there was a lot of commotion. The Trickster explained to Little-Red-Man it was protesters, some carrying signs of racism and things referring to full-bloods and mixed-bloods. Some protesters even threw water bottles at The Trickster's semi-truck, so he didn't stop his semi-truck until he made it a safe distance away from the protesters.

"Okay, this is as close as I can take you, but it's not far from where you need to take your mom. You just have to drag her through a small field and you'll be there. You still have a few hours before it starts," The Trickster explained to Little-Red-Man, who was now crying tears of happiness. He could not believe he had done it. He had fulfilled his mom's dying wish. The Trickster did not get out of his semi-truck to help Little-Red-Man get his mom from his trailer. The protestors nearby were so loud, Little-Red-Man didn't blame him for not helping him. He pulled his mom's makeshift coffin from The Trickster's trailer, then went back to the cab to thank him.

"Thank you, whoever you are," Little-Red-Man said.

"They call me Wild E."

"They call me Little-Red-Man."

"I don't know much about pow-wows but I hope your mom enjoys herself. Thank you, Little-Red-Man, for letting me be a part of this," said The Trickster.

"Before you go, I want to show our appreciation for what you have done by giving you this," Little-Red-Man replied, climbing back up to the cab of the truck, where he handed Johnny Butt's medicine pouch to him.

"What's this?"

"Medicine, it'll make you invisible. Just hang it from your rear-view mirror, whatever that is," Little-Red-Man jokingly said. The Trickster laughed a little.

"Been awhile since I had some medicine. I'm sure I can find a good use for it, but I need it around my neck more than my rear-view mirror. Thanks again."

Little-Red-Man shook The Trickster's hand, then he got out of his truck. The Trickster tried his hardest not to tear up, as he drove away. Moments later, the sound of his semi-truck soon faded and the sound of the protesters nearby was all Little-Red-Man could hear. He found the place on his mom's makeshift coffin he had used to pull her earlier and he pulled his mom through the field The Trickster said he needed to cross to get to THE POW-WOW OF ALL POW-WOWS.

ACT V - THE GOOD, THE BAD, AND THE UGLY

It didn't take Little-Red-Man long to drag his mom across the field to the colossal tent that was going to harbor THE POW-WOW OF ALL POW-WOWS. Once there though, he had a new dilemma to face, he had to find an entrance inside. The tent seemed to be buried in the ground or some kind of medicine was connecting it to the ground because Little-Red-Man could not lift it up anywhere he tried. Since crawling under the tent was out of the question, he dragged his mom's makeshift coffin along the colossal tent. He came upon a back entrance guarded by two security guards from the blue-eyed tribe and one full-blooded Native American security guard from the Tlingit tribe. They were all dressed in black shirts and black cargo pants, all separated by their morals; one had good morals, one had bad morals, and one had ugly morals. They stopped Little-Red-Man in his tracks and questioned him.

"And just where do you think you're going?" asked The Bad in a high-toned voice, standing in Little-Red-Man's way, stopping him. The Bad was a young, skinny man from the blue-eyed tribe with a shaved head and a goatee, his arms decorated with badly done tattoos.

"Yeah, boy," commented The Ugly in a deep voice, who got in Little-Red-Man's face. His size would have intimidated anyone who could see it, but Little-Red-Man could not, so he was not intimidated at all. The Ugly was built like a grizzly bear and just as hairy as one, his long, dirty-blonde hair pulled back in a ponytail and his brown beard down to his chest. He was from the blue-eyed tribe too.

"I am here for the pow-wow," Little-Red-Man answered.

"Is that right?" The Ugly responded.

"This pow-wow is for full-bloods only," butted in The Good, in a regular voice, getting in between The Ugly and Little-Red-Man. The Good was the most civilized-looking of the bunch, average in height but built, his black hair short and styled. He was well-groomed, his face shaved and decorated with a stylish pair of sunglasses. He was full-blooded Tlingit.

"Yes, I know. Could one of you gentlemen please show me inside?" Little-Red-Man asked. No one moved.

"What'cha got in the wooden box?" asked The Bad.

"My mom, Big-Sister, she was the last medicine woman alive, keeper of the strongest medicine there ever was, is, and will be. We came all the way from Oklahoma."

"Medicine woman? Can ya' believe this lil' guy? I gotta admit, that's the best one I've heard yet," The Ugly said, sharing his deep-voiced laughter with The Bad's high-pitched laughter. Their laughter was annoying.

"Is she a full-blood?" asked The Good.

"Yes, one of the only full-blooded Kiowas left. Well, she was," Little-Red-Man answered.

"Was? So you have a dead woman inside there?" asked The Good, concerned.

"Now why would you trying to bring a dead, old hag in here?" asked The Ugly.

"She's not a hag, she's my mom," Little-Red-Man answered, which caused The Ugly and The Bad to laugh out loud again obnoxiously.

"A full-blooded Kiowa, your mom? Now that tops the cake," said The Bad, who could barely speak through his laughter.

"What's your name, kid?" asked The Good.

"Little-Red-Man," he answered, sending The Bad and The Ugly into even more laughter.

"Oh shit, stop it, stop it. This is just too much," added The Ugly, who joined The Bad in even more laughter. It took a while for them to stop laughing. Once they were finished, they had to wipe tears from their eyes.

"What are ya'll doing here, Little-Red-Man, really? What's your angle? This some kind of hidden camera tv show?" asked The Bad, looking around in all directions.

"It was my mom's dying wish that I bring her here."

"Dying wish huh, mind if I take a look at her?" asked The Good, who had just recently lost his grandmother and sympathized with Little-Red-Man.

"Yeah, let's see her," demanded The Bad, looking for another laugh.

Little-Red-Man opened his mom's makeshift coffin to show them the woman who raised him. There was silence. The Good, The Bad, and The Ugly could not believe their eyes, Little-Red-Man was serious.

"Sorry for your loss, Little-Red-Man," The Good finally said, breaking the silence.

"We can see she's legit, but what about you?" asked The Bad, in a menacing tone.

"Yeah, white boy," added The Ugly in his deep voice.

"Stop it, guys," The Good interrupted.

"White boy?" Little-Red-Man asked, confused by The Ugly's comment.

"Did I stutter, boy? What did you do, go and dig up an old Native American woman and come up with this dying wish story so you could get inside the pow-wow? Who do you work for?" asked The Ugly. There was anger in his voice.

"I don't work for anybody, I'm just trying to get my mom inside the pow-wow, like she asked me to."

"This is not your mother, any rat bastard can see that. The Pow-Wow of all Pow-Wows is for full-bloods only, no exceptions," The Bad said, with authority.

"I'm not understanding what the problem is," Little-Red-Man said, still confused.

"The problem is you're fuckin' white, hell, you're whiter than us," answered The Ugly.

"White? No, I'm Native American, full-blooded Native American from the Kiowa Tribe," Little-Red-Man said proudly.

"A freckled, red-headed white boy a full-blooded Kiowa? What do you take us for?" asked The Bad, laughing with The Ugly again.

"Wait a minute, are you really blind?" asked The Good.

"Yes, since I was born. Listen, I don't know what's going on here, but I need to get my mom inside the pow-wow. It's very important that she be inside during the grand entry."

"A blind, honky that thinks he's an injun! This is too much!" exclaimed The Ugly, laughing hard again in his deep voice.

"I told ya'll to stop with that 'Injun' shit!" warned The Good.

"Okay, sorry Kimosabe."

"I'm not white, I'm Kiowa," proclaimed Little-Red-Man

"If you're Kiowa then I'm African," joked The Bad in his high-pitched voice.

"Do you really think you're Kiowa, and a full-blood at that?" asked The Good.

"I don't think, I know I am."

"I hate to be the one to break this to you, kid, but you're as white as they come, a ginger," proclaimed The Bad, trying his best to stop his high-pitched laughter.

"I am Little-Red-Man, Kiowa, from Anadarko, Oklahoma."

"You are no Kiowa, you are a white boy, carrying a dead Kiowa woman around. I gotta say, I like your style," joked The Ugly. The Bad was the only one that found it funny though.

"Listen, I really don't understand what's going on here. I'm full-blooded Kiowa, I can sing the songs to prove it to ya'll. I have the medicine to prove it too, I know the ways. Anyone in there can vouch for me and my mom, if you just let us in."

"So no one has ever told you that you're white?" asked The Good as polite as he could.

"I'm not white," answered Little-Red-Man, who was almost in tears. Then, he thought about it out loud. "Am I?"

"Oh, whiter than white. I've heard of blond-haired Indians, but never of redhead Indians," laughed The Bad.

"You are as honky as honky gets, boy," added The Ugly in his deep voice.

It confused Little-Red-Man and he didn't say

anymore as he went into deep thought. Had his mom misled him, even worse, had everyone he was friends with misled him? He knew in his heart he was Native American, so he could not comprehend what they were seeing. He didn't understand because he had no grasp of colors, more less, the idea that people had different colors of skin that separated them. It made no sense at all to him. He was Native American in mind and spirit and he thought also in body, until that moment, when he heard those words, words he never thought he would ever hear in his life. Those words were "So no one has ever told you that you're white?" And those words confused him. But how could he not be Native American, he wondered? As much as it made no sense at all to him, he had a mission far more important than his inquiries.

"I have to get my mom inside the pow-wow. That's all that matters to me right now," Little-Red-Man finally said.

"That's not going to happen, boy," The Ugly said in his deep voice, who got back in his face. Little-Red-Man could smell the dip in his mouth.

"Yeah, boy, go back to where you came from and tell whoever you are working with that it was a good one, but it didn't work," added The Bad in his high-pitched voice.

"I have to get my mom inside for grand entry," Little-Red-Man repeated.

"They're right, we can't let you in, you have to be a full-blooded Native American to get inside," The Good replied.

"Okay then. I don't care if you let me in, but please, take my mom inside. It was her dying wish that she attend this pow-wow. She was a great medicine woman, I'm telling you, and anyone in there can vouch for her. I just want to fulfill her dying wish, that's all!" Little-Red-Man yelled. He was upset now.

"You are a real piece of work," butted in The Bad.

"Enough is enough, now get the fuck out of here, boy, before we make you sorry you came here," added The Ugly.

"I can't leave, you don't know what I've been through to get here!" Little-Red-Man answered back, only to be met with a shove from The Ugly that sent him the ground. Little-Red-Man immediately curled up into a ball, expecting the worse, which almost came, but The Good stopped The Bad and The Ugly from beating him to a bloody pulp. Little-Red-Man didn't get back up, he didn't even try, and all he could do was cry. He sobbed, unable to control himself. He was about to fail again. But something happened, divine intervention again. The Good became inspired by Little-Red-Man's strength. It was unbelievable that a blind boy could travel from Oklahoma to Minnesota with his mom's dead body. It was a testament that her dying wish should be fulfilled.

He decided to help Little-Red-Man. It was his duty as a full-blood, who traveled all of the way from Alaska to represent his people, but ran out of money and had to take a job as security to protect THE POW-WOW OF ALL POW-WOWS.

"Well, we could use a medicine person inside, since all of the medicine men they invited here haven't showed up yet. Okay, Little-Red-Man, I'll take your mom inside and I'll personally guard her during grand entry. But after grand entry is over, I'll bring her back out here, then will you leave?" asked The Good.

"There's no medicine men in there?" he asked, knowing their absence was not good for a pow-wow of such magnitude. But before an answer came, another question came out of his mouth, "I can't go in with her?"

"No, we were given strict orders to only let full-bloods inside. But you will be granting her dying wish. We have a deal?" The Good asked.

"Okay. But can you make sure she gets a good spot? She likes to be near the drum," Little-Red-Man asked.

"Sure, that's a promise."

Little-Red-Man saw it as better than nothing and let The Good take his mom's makeshift coffin. He listened to him drag her inside the colossal tent, as The Bad and The Ugly murmured insults about The Good. It wasn't how he expected the journey to end, but he fulfilled his mom's dying wish. He was happy, sad, glad, and mad, all at the same time. Once he knew The Good was too far away to help him from The Bad and The Ugly, he took a seat on the grass a good distance away from them and leaned on the colossal tent that harbored THE POW-WOW OF ALL POW-WOWS. He patiently waited for the grand entry to start, singing songs his mom had taught him, songs of his people, tribal songs. He was Native American and there was nothing that could take that away from him, not even the color of his skin or hair. He was Little-Red-Man, son of Big-Sister, the last medicine woman, keeper of the strongest medicine there ever was, is, and will be.

CHAPTER FIVE

Born To Dance

DANCE IS A TRADITION practiced by all cultures. It is medicine and strength. It is sometimes done as part of a beginning, sometimes done as part of an ending. There are dances for celebration and dances for mourning. Various kinds of dance represent not only the people doing the dances, but also their beliefs. Then there is music, the blood that pumps through the veins of dance. All cultures have their own songs to dance to. Dance has been a phenomenon since day one.

Native Americans of days old, were no different from any other culture. They had dance. But the dance Native Americans are the most known for today was not a traditional dance at all. It came about after Native Americans had signed treaties, after the blue-eyed tribe had invaded their territories.

In the 1920s and 1930s, most Native American

dances were still considered religious, having originated from a religion foreign to the foreigners who flocked to America for religious freedom. And since the dances were foreign to the blue-eyed tribe, the Native American religious dances were banned, one by one, until Native Americans couldn't dance the dances that were a significant part of their lives and a big part of their cultures.

And that was how the most popular dance of the Native Americans came about, fancy dancing. Many dances of the Native Americans had to go underground, especially after the blue-eyed tribe began making broken promises with Native American tribes. Most of the broken promises outlawed their traditional dances because it caused Native Americans to gather in big numbers. So tribes began to create new dances that they could get away with doing. The new dances were not traditional dances, so performing them wouldn't violate any treaty they made with the blue-eyed tribe, who forbid them from moving their bodies in certain ways to music. Dancing played no part in the blue-eyed tribe's religion, so there was no way it could play a part in any other religion, as far as they were concerned.

Fancy dancing was loosely based on the traditional war dance. It was invented more for entertainment purposes than for traditional reasons. It attracted visitors, and visitors with money, to various

Native American communities during pow-wows. It was also a highlight in a lot of Wild West shows touring in the 1920s and 1930s.

Crowds flocked to Wild West shows and pow-wows featuring fancy dancers. While the dance itself was an impressive display of athleticism and rapid, complex footwork and acrobatics, the regalia the fancy dancers wore was also a big attraction. Colors on top of colors on top of colors, all moving at a hundred miles-per-hour in various directions it seemed. It was unlike any other kind of dance any person had seen before. It attracted big crowds. New songs were even written to accompany the beauty and fierceness of the new dance.

The fancy dancer's attire was unlike that of any dancer ever seen before. Two U-shaped bustles of large eagle feathers adorned the fancy dancer's back. Moccasins protected his fast feet. White leggings of goat hair ran up to his knees, where he wore a band of bells on each leg, turning his legs into instruments. Both of his arms were decorated with small bustles of feathers and white fluff at the biceps. A porcupine quill roach adorned his head, with two eagle feathers pointing up above them, to help audiences track the movement of his head as he danced. Bead work was also a big part of the fancy dancer's regalia, fit in where ever it could be, on the cuffs, the headband, and the chest piece. But it was the fringes that made the fancy dancer, fringes containing his colors, dictating the colors of his roach, his bead work, and his outfit underneath. The fringes hung off the eagle feathers of his back bustles, from his legs, from his arms, and they blurred his movements into the beautiful display he became once he danced.

Fancy dancing was no easy task either. Only the best dancers could pull off the complicated moves that sent a fancy dancer's body into a frenzy, defying gravity, defying rhythm, and defying the human body in seemingly impossible twists. Fancy dancing songs were the loudest and fastest of those a Native American drum group could drum and sing. The songs were to the traditional music of Native Americans that heavy metal songs were to rock-n-roll music. During all fancy dance songs, the music would come to a complete halt at various points for a measure or two, and the fancy dancer was expected to stop at that same moment, striking a pose. When the dance was first invented, the poses fancy dancers stopped in were simple. But then the greats started to come up with more complex ways of posing at the halts in beat, by doing cart wheels or splits right before the silence. Fancy dancers eventually took the halts in the song even farther with back flips right before the silence. Crowds traveled from far and wide to see what the fancy dancers would come up with next, making it the most well-known dance of Native Americans, even more popular than the "rain dance."

⤻ ⤻   ⤺ ⤺

At seventeen-years-old, Jean White-Raven didn't know much about fancy dancing when she gave birth to her son, Wanbli, nor did she know much about his father. She was raped at sixteen-years-old. It happened one winter night at a friend's house party. She went outside to smoke a cigarette and to get some fresh air when she was overtaken by a man wearing a coyote mask. Her friends didn't even know she was outside when the seed was being planted inside of her. The rape was never reported to the police, only her friends and parents knew of it. They found her outside in the snow, naked and passed out. It changed her, she was never the same cheerful person she once was after that.

Jean was a part of the Sioux tribe and like most Native American girls, her life was based on survival, not traditions. She lived in the poorest Native American community in the nation, Pine Ridge, South Dakota. Although Jean was young, way too young to become a mother, she was going to be there for her son no matter what, even when she heard the doctor curse out loud as he was delivering Wanbli. Whatever was wrong with her newborn son, it didn't matter, she would still be there for him.

The doctor pulled Wanbli out from Jean's womb almost reluctantly, but some would say later, that he danced out of his mother's womb. He was not a normal baby boy when he came into the world, far from it. There was something special about him. The doctor didn't want to give him up at first. He wanted to keep him so that tests and observations could be done because it was a birth unlike anything he had ever seen before. There was something very peculiar about Wanbli, but Jean didn't see it as a big thing, nor would she allow tests or observations on her firstborn. Wanbli was her baby, and she didn't care that he was born with two U-shaped bustles of eagle feathers coming out of his back, bustles like that of a fancy dancer. Being only a baby, Jean thought it was the cutest thing she had ever seen. She grabbed her baby boy from the doctor who delivered him, and she held him, protecting him immediately from the world's ridicule. And in his mother's arms, Wanbli danced for the first time. Even as an infant, his body couldn't resist the songs only he heard. It was the cutest thing ever. It changed her again, she was never the same lost person she had become. She was found. It was her calling in life now, to be a good mother.

Against the advice from the doctor and all of the nurses, even with offers of big money to keep him there, Jean left the hospital with Wanbli only hours after giving birth to him. Jean's mother and father knew it would be best they get him away from the medicine of the blue-eyed tribe and to the medicine of their people. So, they all left the hospital before it became a prison for Wanbli.

Once home, Jean rested for days, as her parents cared for Wanbli. They were amazed by the bustles of eagle feathers growing from his back, not afraid of them at all. They weren't sure what the unusual phenomenon meant, but they were sure it meant something great. Their grandson was a sign of some sort, but what he meant to their people only a medicine man would know. So they waited patiently for their only daughter, Jean, to awaken from her rest. Once she was rested, they would all take Wanbli to the nearest medicine man, who just lived outside of Pine Ridge in the Badlands.

In a few days' time, Jean was ready to take her son to his first visit to a medicine man. So one afternoon, her parents took Wanbli and her to the man they knew as "Blue-Hawk." He still lived in a tipi, still hunted for his food, and still hung hides of various animals to dry around his tipi. Blue-Hawk still lived in the days of old. Once they arrived to his tipi, the gray-haired, small framed, dark brown-skinned, old Sioux man greeted them at their car. The wrinkles on his face were like the rings of the inside of a tree, revealing he was ancient. He had his hair pulled back into a braided ponytail and was wearing a bright yellow and purple jogging suit. Blue-Hawk was gracious and invited them all inside his tipi. They all went inside, where knowledge was passed on, where prayers were answered, and where medicine was strong. As soon as they sat down, they offered him some tobacco and an assortment of gifts, as mandated when visiting a man who was one with medicine.

There was a small fire burning inside the tipi. Blue-Hawk threw some of the tobacco he was given inside the fire. The tipi filled with the aroma of their gift. Before they even had a chance to explain why they were there, Blue-Hawk spoke.

"Let me see him," Blue-Hawk said.

Jean looked at her parents, who both nodded with approval, then she handed Wanbli to Blue-Hawk. He unwrapped him from his baby blankets, and Blue-Hawk was almost as shocked as the doctor who had delivered him was when he saw them. The two bustles of eagle feathers growing from out of his back. Blue-Hawk smiled the biggest smile he had ever smiled in his ancient life. Then, he lifted him up and examined his bustles. Wanbli began kicking his legs in a rhythm to a song only he could hear. Blue-Hawk laughed with excitement, and, for a moment, it seemed he could hear the song as well. He even began to sing softly in an ancient tongue. All the while, Wanbli kicked in the air.

"His name is Wanbli. So what do the bustles mean?" Jean's father asked. Blue-Hawk stopped singing and was barely able to contain his happiness to speak again. He even reluctantly returned Wanbli back to his mother.

"I can't say. All I can tell you is this," Blue-Hawk said, not saying another word, instead, he gave them the universal Native American sign language for 'yes,' curving the index finger on his right hand and whipping his right hand out in front of him and back quickly. It was the strangest thing.

"Tell us what?" Jean's father asked in confusion. But he didn't get an answer, only another hand signal for 'yes' and another big smile from Blue-Hawk.

"I don't get it, dad," Jean interrupted, only to get another hand signal for 'yes' and a smile specifically for her from Blue-Hawk.

"So it's a good thing?" Jean's father asked.

"Yes, a very good thing. To tell you all would put you in great danger. It will reveal its purpose when it is time. Now, I must prepare for my trip to the spirit world. My job here is now done. Take good care of him, protect him with your lives, and never let him stop dancing, ever. You do that, and all of your questions will be answered in the most remarkable way one day. That is all," Blue-Hawk advised.

Jean and her parents left with even more questions than they had arrived with and no answers. None of them could figure out what Blue-Hawk meant by telling them to never let Wanbli stop dancing. It was a strange comment in regard to an infant boy. And they saw no reason to ever stop Wanbli from dancing if that's what he wanted to do.

They took Blue-Hawk's advice once they got home and did exactly what was told of them. They took good care of Wanbli, protected him with their lives, and never let him stop dancing. And the comment made more and more sense with every year he grew because all he liked to do was dance. Wanbli loved to dance. He could dance before he could walk. He was a natural at it. Even if there were no music playing out loud, he danced to the songs inside of his head, which only he could hear, so he was always dancing.

Wanbli didn't dance like normal kids danced. He danced the dances of his people: traditional dances, ceremonial dances, and social dances. He could grass dance, he could eagle dance, he could fancy dance, and he could even hoop dance. No one taught him how to do any of his peoples' dances, they came to him naturally. He rarely walked, rather he danced, shaking his tail-feathers everywhere. The two bustles of eagle feathers growing out from his back grew longer as he grew. They were still a remarkable sight, a sight his mother and grandparents hid from rest of the tribe, though. Wanbli was not allowed to go anywhere and was confined to their home on the outskirts of Pine Ridge.

When Wanbli turned five-years-old, he still hadn't spoken a single word. It concerned his grandparents and his mother. They tried to teach him the importance of speaking, only to have him show them the importance of dance. They weren't sure if he were incapable of talking or that he just didn't want to. It became a feud between them, a feud none of them won. Instead, they decided to meet halfway. Wanbli would speak to them, but not by using words, instead he chose to use dance moves to speak to them.

Wanbli's language became dance. "Yes" became a quick turn to the right. "No" became a quick turn to the left. "I'm happy" became the splits. "I'm upset" became four stomps of his feet. "I'm angry" became a kick followed by a squat. "I'm not sure" became a dance in a circle. And so his own language was born, growing and growing, as he grew. His grandparents and his mother were finally able to communicate with him.

But out of all the traditional dances Wanbli mastered, he lacked the skills to master one, not because he didn't want to, but because he didn't know how. It was the dance he was born to do. He continuously practiced the dance routine to a song only he could hear, never giving up on it, but never mastering it. He could never get it right. His grandparents and mother could never figure out what that dance was, but they encouraged him that practice makes perfect every time he failed to master it.

Wanbli grew up as well as a kid with bustles of eagle feathers growing out from his back could grow up. He didn't know he was poor, he didn't even know what poor was. He loved his life, loved his family, and loved he was always allowed to dance, no matter what. But the older he grew, the more things began to change on his body. Bustles of small eagle feathers, in a complete circle, unlike the two U-shaped bustles on his back, began to grow from the side of his biceps. Fluffy, white hair began to grow from just below his knees to his feet, like leggings. And porcupine hair began to grow from his head in a Mohawk fashion, but in two lines that met at the top of his forehead, like the roach of a fancy dancer. By the time Wanbli was ten-years-old, his body was adorned with the regalia of a fancy dancer, but his regalia was natural, not made, not given as a gift, not won, but grown from his body. It was proof, he was born to dance.

And dance he did, until tragedy struck when Wanbli was only eleven-years-old. His grandmother died of a cancer she didn't know she had. Suddenly, out of nowhere, it had taken her to the spirit world. A few months later, his grandfather died of a heart attack in his sleep. Wanbli was certain it was brought about by the heartache of losing the love of his life. He danced at both of their funerals, a ceremonial death dance that celebrated their lives, rather than mourned them. Their funerals were the first two times his mother allowed him to be around other people, but not the last. The reaction he received from family members was nothing but good, they loved how good he could dance. Some even advised his mother, Jean, to let him dance at pow-wows. They felt Wanbli could win first place at pow-wows easily, which was always accompanied with good prize money. His mother paid the delusions of grandeur no mind though.

As good as a woman as Wanbli's mother was, she was also very spoiled by her parents. It was never even an option that she make her own living and live somewhere other than where she grew up in her parents' home. So once her parents went the spirit world, it left Jean in a bind. She had no income coming in because she didn't have a job. Nor did she know how to run a household. She was thrown into life, unexpectedly, and left vulnerable with Wanbli.

Like all beings left vulnerable, another being picked up on the scent of weakness and preyed upon it. The deaths of her parents left Jean depressed and reaching out to anyone who would give her attention, until she finally found someone. It was a Sioux man, named Nameci, who made her his prey. He was freshly out of prison and in the process of resuming the meth addiction prison had kept him away from. He was a funny guy though, or so Jean thought. He was tall, muscular from countless prison work-outs, with long hair braided roughly. She brought him home one night from a bar in Rapid City where she was spending some of the money her parents had left her. Wanbli was up late, waiting on her, and practicing the dance routine he could never get right. Regardless, he tried and tried. He always tried, dancing to a song only he could hear. His mother's new boyfriend laughed at his dancing, even mocking it, calling him a Native American 'Michael Jackson.' His mother didn't defend him, instead she joined in with his laughter and then told him to 'beat it.'

After their drunken laughter finally stopped, they smoked from a pipe unlike any Wanbli had ever seen. It wasn't a peace pipe. It was made of glass, and the tobacco they smoked gave off an aroma unlike any tobacco he had ever smelled. The tobacco they smoked was white in color, almost yellow, and smelt of chemicals. And before his eyes, his mother changed. Her eyes widened, her movements became fast and unpredictable, and her muscles tightened. Wanbli didn't like what he saw so he went to sleep, leaving his mother with her new boyfriend, Nameci.

Wanbli awoke, eight hours later, and his mother and her new boyfriend were still awake from the night before. His mother's eyes were as wide open as he had ever seen them. She was moving her body erratically, unable to stop herself from grinding her teeth. Although neither she nor Nameci ate any of it, she couldn't stop herself from cooking breakfast for them all. It was weird, but Wanbli went with it. It was the first time he had ever seen his mother with a man. But with his grandparents gone, he knew she needed someone to fill that void left in her. Love was a complicated thing, as far as he was concerned.

So for months, their days blended in with nights, seemingly unending. Their sleep was rare and unpredictable. Wanbli watched his mother become one with the glass pipe Nameci had brought into their home. And right along with Nameci, she smoked that pipe. It became their new air. They breathed in the smoke like they needed it to live. But his mother was happy, and that was all that mattered to Wanbli, Instead of intervening, he danced, like he always had, still trying to perfect the dance routine he could never get right, no matter how much he practiced it. He didn't know what kind of dance it was. All he knew it was important that he learn it.

Then, the money Wanbli's grandparents had left his mother ran out. They were broke. Wanbli went days sometimes without eating, while his mother and Nameci left, sometimes for days. She forgot about him a lot, which never happened before. She was not the same woman she was before his grandparents died. Nameci was obviously the reason for her personality change, but still, he made her happy, and her happiness was all that mattered to Wanbli.

Finally, one day after Wanbli's mother and Nameci awoke from a few days sleep, Nameci came up with an idea to help get them out of their money problems. Food had run out, the electric was in danger of being cut off, and they had run out of their white tobacco. There was a big pow-wow coming up in a reservation nearby with good prize money. Nameci suggested to Jean that they enter Wanbli into the Junior Fancy Dance category. He was a sure win. Jean was against it at first, but it was very appealing to Wanbli because it was a chance for him to get back out in public and amongst his people. He was tired of being cooped up with his mother and Nameci, so he joined Nameci, agreeing it was a good idea. It took a lot of convincing, but after they both assured Wanbli's mother that more good would come out of it than bad, she reluctantly agreed.

So that weekend, they all drove to Rosebud, South Dakota, where the pow-wow was taking place. Wanbli was entered into the Junior Fancy Dance category, which was the only one he was qualified for because he was only twelve-years-old now. The prize money for first place was five hundred dollars.

It was the first time Wanbli had ever been to a real pow-wow. He felt it was where he belonged. He knew he was different and that was why his grandparents and his mother hid him, but the pow-wow was full of dancers wearing regalia, trying to look the way he did naturally. It was where he belonged. There was no doubt about it. But he was nervous. He had never danced in a competition, nor had he ever danced to a real drum and drum singers. His grandpa used to let him listen to some pow-wow music he had on cassette, but this was live. He knew fancy dance songs required the drum group to halt at various points of the songs, and a fancy dancer was expected to stop and pose as the break in the song occurred. The cassettes his grandpa let him listen to he had memorized, so he knew when to stop and pose. But fancy dancing to a live song was different. The drummers might drum songs he never heard before, so for the first time in his life, Wanbli became unsure of his dancing.

But they needed the five hundred dollars, so Wanbli joined the other junior fancy dancers in the pow-wow circle when it came time for their competition to be underway. It was explained to Wanbli by Nameci that the drum group would play three songs. Once the first song was over, the judges would pick half of the fancy dancers to stay out in the circle and continue to dance to the second song. And once the second song was finished, the judges would pick only three fancy dancers to stay out in the circle to battle for third, second, and first place during the last song.

It was a lot for Wanbli to take in, even with how much he loved dancing. Fancy dancing was his favorite kind of dancing too, he had the moves of a champion fancy dancer, or so his grandparents always told him. It was time to see if they were just being loving grandparents or were telling the truth. With his loving mother and Nameci in the audience, Wanbli prepared to dance in the middle of the pow-wow circle with a dozen fancy dancers, who all wore regalia that rivaled his natural adornments.

The drum group started the first song. To Wanbli's advantage, it was a song he recognized, one off of one of his grandpa's cassettes. He just hoped the drummers would stop at the same time of the songs he grew up listening to. He listened carefully, through all of the bells jingling from the junior fancy dancers legs, which he lacked, and through the sounds of whistles, which some of the junior fancy dancers were blowing. He danced to the thunderous beat of the live drum, which he loved the sound of. He couldn't have ever imagined it sounding as good as it did in real life. It took over his legs. His legs started stomping the ground with the beat, overlapping each other. He twisted to the right, which in his language meant 'yes.' He twisted left, a 'no' to all who could speak his language. And then, the beat got harder, the singing got louder, which sent Wanbli in a frenzy. He began to dance out of control. The crowd cheered, the drummers even turned to witness what they had never seen before. Wanbli was doing moves of the days of old, it was less fancy dancing and more war dancing, the way it was meant to be. It had been so long since any Native American had seen war dancing, so it was mind-blowing to all who watched Wanbli bring back the past in dance. Some even wondered if it was still outlawed.

All of the other junior fancy dancers didn't know what to make of it, Wanbli was doing moves they were never taught, moves they thought to be extinct. He had no bells, no whistle, no fringes of color, only his moves, and they were pure medicine. Then, the drum group got to the part of the song that required them to halt for a few measures, so it was time to see if he was for real. They stopped their song all of the sudden, as Wanbli did a backwards flip, landing on the ground in the splits position. He stopped at the very moment they had stopped. The crowd went crazy and cheered so loud that the spirit world heard them. The other junior fancy dancers applauded him too. There was no competition. There was a new champion junior fancy dancer at the pow-wow, and none of the junior fancy dancers wanted to continue against him. Fancy dancing didn't stand a chance against real war dancing.

The drum group didn't continue the song either as they normally would have. Nor did they sing a second song. With what Wanbli showed the pow-wow, there was no need. He was shown instant respect. It was a feeling he couldn't comprehend, to finally be appreciated for doing the thing he knew he was born to do. It felt good. It felt right. His mother was the proudest mother in the world at that moment and that felt better to him than anything else. He just wished his grandparents could have seen it.

They drove away from the pow-wow that night, Wanbli taking first place, second place, and third place trophies home with him. Not to mention the prize money for all three places too, which equaled eight hundred dollars. They celebrated with a stop at McDonalds, which Wanbli had only seen in commercials. It was even better than he imagined. He ate his first Big Mac, and it tasted like the home of The Great Spirit. He would have traded one of his trophies for another one it was so good.

Wanbli's first pow-wow and dance competition was a success. They had food again, the electricity bill was paid in full, and his mother was able to buy more white tobacco to smoke with Nameci. They all saw no reason for it to be the only pow-wow for him to dance at, especially since it was so profitable. Together, they decided to go on what traditional Native Americans called "pow-wow highway," which meant they would drive pow-wow to pow-wow across the country during pow-wow season and live off the prize money won from dance or drum competitions or by selling traditional Native American jewelry or art. It was like a concert tour for traditional Native Americans. During pow-wow season, there were big pow-wows with big prize money and big money crowds every weekend. So they jumped into Wanbli's grandparents' '88 Gold Ford Taurus, which his grandpa named "The Gold Buffalo." It was a rez car, slang for "reservation car," which Native Americans referred to the cars they drove into their graves, most far from being legal to drive. It had one window broken out, one window that didn't roll down, and one door that didn't open. The speedometer didn't work, gas gauge didn't work, but it had a good stereo system, and that was all that mattered. In The Gold Buffalo, they started their journey down pow-wow highway.

For years, they stayed on pow-wow highway. Hotels became their new home, McDonalds their breakfast, lunch, and dinner. Wanbli could not be beaten. After a few years, he was moved up from the Junior Fancy Dance category to the Men's Fancy Dance category, which he still dominated, even though he was way younger than any of his competition. He proved he was the best fancy dancer on the east coast at the Schemitzun (Green Corn Pow-wow) held by the Pequot Tribe in Mashantucket, Connecticut. He beat every fancy dancer who dared compete against him at the Annual Seminole Tribal Festival/Pow-wow in Hollywood, Florida every year. He shut out all who faced him at the great Red Earth Pow-wow in Oklahoma City, Oklahoma; The Haskell Indian Nations University Commencement Pow-wow in Lawrence, Kansas; the Denver March in Denver, Colorado; Crow Fair near Billings, Montana; Morongo Thunder & Lightning Pow-wow in Cabazon, California, and its neighboring pow-wow, the Pechanga Pow-wow in Temecula, California. Those were just some of the great pow-wows on pow-wow highway which Wanbli took first prize in the Men's Fancy Dance category. He even became champion fancy dancer of the greatest pow-wow of all, the Gathering of Nations Pow-wow in Albuquerque, New Mexico.

Life was good for Wanbli. For so long, he had been cooped up at home. Now, he was a celebrity in Indian country. During all of the pow-wows he competed in, he also made friends, which he never had growing up. They all came to know Wanbli's dance language and good times were had by his friends and him. So every pow-wow was a chance for him to hang out with them and get away from his mother, who was not the same person he had known growing up. Nameci had changed her with his white tobacco. Wanbli hadn't paid much mind to it until the winter of his fourteenth year of life. There were no pow-wows during the winter, so every year during that time they went back to their home in Pine Ridge, South Dakota. That winter, he saw that his mother was sick. She began to lose teeth. She lost all of her body weight, to the point to where she was just a walking skeleton. All she seemed to care about was the white tobacco she smoked. Attempts to ask her about her health by using his dance language were only interrupted by Nameci, who told Wanbli that she would be okay as long as he danced and made them the money they needed for the white tobacco. So he continued to dance, but he began to watch Nameci out of the corner of his eye, starting to see what he was doing to his mother with his white tobacco. Nameci kept his glass pipe to his mother's mouth, always keeping her in daze. She had become his zombie. But Wanbli loved his mother and knew how much she liked the white tobacco, so he started down pow-wow highway with her and Nameci the following spring like he had every year since he had started dancing at pow-wows.

Denver March was always their first stop on pow-wow highway. Then, they hit a few smaller pow-wows until they made their way to the greatest pow-wow of them all, the Gathering of Nations. It was there, at the Gathering of Nations, that Wanbli's mother's health began to really deteriorate. After Wanbli won the title as THE WORLD'S GREATEST FANCY DANCER EVER, which he was the first fancy dancer to ever receive the great honor, his mother had to be hospitalized for exhaustion. She had fainted at the Sandia Resort and Casino where they were staying. The hospital recommended sending his mother to rehab, but Nameci wouldn't hear of it, since pow-wow season had just started.

It took seeing his mother in a hospital room hooked up to I.V.'s to realize his dancing was part of the reason his mother was there. He knew Nameci played a big part as well, with his white tobacco, which they could only afford because of the prize money he always won. So, while Nameci was somewhere else smoking his white tobacco, instead of being by Jean's side, Wanbli made a promise to his mother while she was in her long sleep. He vowed to never dance in a competition again, ever, for her sake.

Nameci didn't learn of the promise until they went to their next pow-wow, after taking Wanbli's mother from the hospital sooner than the doctors wanted her to leave. Wanbli refused to dance. Nameci became furious, even becoming physical with Wanbli. His mother had to stop him, only to be forced by Nameci to plead to her son to dance and win the money they needed for the white tobacco. But he denied his mother's request, telling her about the promise he had made to her while she was in the hospital, to never dance in a competition again, ever. His mother understood, but still she pleaded, not for her sake, for Nameci's sake. Wanbli was done though. At fourteen-years-old, he was retiring, ready to pass the crown of THE WORLD'S GREATEST FANCY DANCER EVER to someone else, all for his mother.

And just as quickly as Nameci had appeared in their lives, he disappeared, taking what was left of the money they had made from Wanbli's victories. Wanbli and his mother returned to their home in Pine Ridge with nothing but each other. His mother was still sick, even sicker than when she was in the hospital. She sweated all of the time, her stomach couldn't hold anything, and she screamed to keep the shadow people away from her. His mother suffered for a month. Visits from the reservation doctor and reservation medicine man did her no good. The only thing that could help her was time. The white tobacco attached itself to her body and spirit and would not leave her easily. She could only be released from the grip it had on her through time away from it.

Wanbli understood, and he stayed by his mother's side, even on the nights when she was not his mother, when she begged him to find some white tobacco for her. She slept a lot and when she did, he didn't take advantage of the time alone as he normally would have, by practicing the dance routine he could never perfect. He was really done with it, dancing. And slowly, as days passed, the eagle feathers of his back bustles began to fall off, until there were none. Then, the feathers on his arm bustles fell off as well. He looked like a porcupine, the bustles resembling quills without the eagle feathers that made them usually a beautiful sight. It didn't bother Wanbli, though. He would never need them again anyway.

Then, one bright summer morning, Wanbli's mother awoke, her face glowing with life again. She even wore a smile when she entered the kitchen where Wanbli was cooking them breakfast. It caught him off guard, not her smile or glow, but that she was out of bed, walking around. It was something she hadn't done in a very long time. She hugged Wanbli, the kind of hug that was almost unfamiliar to him. It had been so long since he felt her warmth, her love. Tears ran down his face and for the first time in his life, he spoke.

"Momma," was the only word his lips and tongue could compose before he started crying uncontrollably.

"Wanbli, my precious Wanbli. Where are your feathers?" She asked him, but he was unable to reply through his sobs.

They continued hugging, neither one of them willing to let go of each other. They were all they had, and it was enough to get them through the sickness of the white tobacco. It was a new day, a new start for the retired THE WORLD'S GREATEST FANCY DANCER EVER, who was now fifteen-years-old, and his mother. The hug was long, but they eventually let go of each other and they had breakfast together; powdered eggs from the United States Department of Agriculture (USDA) mixed with real eggs and thick slices of fried USDA luncheon meat. It was their favorite breakfast before McDonalds corrupted their breakfasts.

The first week of Wanbli's mother's reawakening was the best week they had together in many seasons. They spent most of the week getting their home back in order, since they had neglected it for so long. It needed a few repairs, a very thorough cleaning, and the yard needed landscaping really bad, even though it was mostly dirt.

It wasn't until after the first week that reality hit Jean. They had no money, no means to make any money, and no car. They didn't have electricity, the food that Wanbli had gotten from neighbors and family members was running out, and jobs were almost unheard of on the reservation. Most tribal members had to drive off reservation to get work, which was not an option for them because they had no transportation. The bright future Wanbli's mother thought she had awakened to was only an illusion.

All seemed grim for Jean and Wanbli until one day, when she visited the tribal headquarters to fill out paperwork for tribal assistance to help get their electric turned back on. After leaving the office in which she had filled out the paperwork, she passed by a bulletin board with a flyer tacked to it that caught her eye. It was a flyer that promoted THE POW-WOW OF ALL POW-WOWS, which was to take place on July 23rd in Mankato, Minnesota. It also stated that only full-blooded Native Americans would be allowed to enter and partake in all of the dance contests with the biggest prize money that had ever been offered, ever. The flyer then listed the dance categories and the prize money for each category. Wanbli's mother's jaw almost dropped to the floor when she saw that the prize money for 1st place in the Men's Fancy Dance category was one million dollars! It brought tears to her eyes. There was a Great Spirit!!! The grim future that seemed inevitable for them both turned bright again, even brighter than she could have ever imagined it. She took the flyer from the bulletin board to show to Wanbli when she got home.

Jean practically ran home from the tribal headquarters, overly-excited, anxious to tell her son that they had been saved. When she got home, Wanbli was in the front yard digging a hole for a mailbox pole. She went to hug him, as she always did after a trip away from home.

Upon release from their hug, Wanbli could see a bright glow on his mother's face, brighter than usual. She was smiling from ear to ear. He could tell something good had happened or maybe there was good news, maybe their electricity was being turned back on! He gave his mother a chance to tell him whatever it was, ready to share her happiness. But instead of telling him the good news, she handed the flyer to him, which he took and began to read immediately.

As Wanbli read the flyer, his mother anticipated his reaction, waiting for the happiness to hit him as it did her, but it never came. Instead, once he had read it all, he ripped the flyer in half, and wrinkled both halves with his hands and threw them unto the ground. Then, he walked away from his mother without a dance move said and went inside their home. Jean was confused by what had just happened, so she followed him inside. He was getting a drink of water when she spoke to him.

"What's the matter?" Jean asked her son.

"Nothing, as long as you don't ask me to dance at that pow-wow," Wanbli answered in dance.

"But did you see how much the prize money is?"

"Yeah, don't matter though. You know I vowed to never dance again," he danced to her.

"Can't you make an exception, just this once, for me?" she pleaded with her son.

"I made the vow for you. Prize money was what put you in that hospital in New Mexico. What if you died? What would've happened to me? Where would I be? Did you ever think about that when you were smoking that stuff with Nameci? I've had enough with prize money. We might be poor right now, but we are happy and most importantly, you're healthy again," Wanbli argued in dance.

"You're right, son. I was not thinking about you then like I should've been. That stuff clouded my thinking. Nameci clouded my thinking, too. And I'm sorry for putting you through all that. But this prize money should be proof that I'm thinking of you now because if you win it, then I can rest assure that you will be taken care of for the rest of your life, even after I'm gone. I'm not going to be here forever. And I can handle being poor, son, but we are on the verge of being worst off than poor.

I don't even know how we are going to make it through this coming winter with no electricity, no food, nothing for warmth. I think you really need to consider dancing at this pow-wow," Jean pleaded with him, in tears.

"I made a vow," Wanbli danced, almost coldheartedly. It enraged his mother.

"Well, I made a vow as a mother to take care of you, to provide for you. I am your mother, you are my son, and you will do as I tell you! We are going to this pow-wow, and you will win this prize money for us!" Wanbli's mother yelled at him. She almost never yelled. Wanbli was caught off guard.

"But we don't even have a car. We can't even get to the pow-wow," he danced to her.

"You leave that up to me. I'll get us there."

"I don't even have feathers anymore. People will laugh at me," he danced.

"I can get you feathers. We will tie them to your quills, like the other fancy dancers do. You just start practicing your routines. It's only two weeks away. I'm going to start dinner now."

"I'll go, but I won't dance," Wanbli's dancing assured her.

"Then, we will freeze to death this coming winter," she assured him.

It was the longest two weeks ever. Wanbli and his mother gave each other the silent treatment, in tongue and in dance, neither of them ever breaking until the day came that they had to leave. His mother broke the silence that morning.

"Get packed. We leave this afternoon," Jean ordered Wanbli.

"How are we getting there?" he asked in dance.

"By bus. It'll take us a day to get there."

"So, we're going to get there a day early?" he asked in dance.

"Yes, just in case something comes up. We will have a day to spare."

"Where are we going to stay when we get there?" he asked in dance.

"Where Indians in the days of old used to stay at pow-wows, under the stars. So be sure to bring a blanket to lay on and a sheet to cover up with."

"You serious? I told you, I'm not dancing," Wanbli reminded his mother in dance.

"Damn right, I'm serious. This is a chance for us to start over. If you want to make a fool of yourself and not dance, that is up to you, but I'm entering you into the Men's Fancy Dance contest. Everyone around here, all of your people, also believe you should dance and reclaim your title as THE WORLD'S GREATEST FANCY DANCER EVER at this THE POW-WOW OF ALL POW-WOWS. It would make everyone proud to be Sioux. They even donated their most sacred eagle feathers so that I can dress up your bustles. Now, hurry up," his mother ordered him.

Reluctantly, Wanbli gathered some clothes, along with some hygiene products. His clothes weren't what normal boys his age wore. They were made specifically for him to fit around the bustles that grew out from his body and his natural leggings. They were all small articles of clothing, so they all fit into one small backpack. He then packed his blanket, along with a sheet to cover up with, in a small gym bag.

Within a half hour, Jean and Wanbli were walking to the bus stop in Pine Ridge, a few miles away from their home. It was a hot, July day, making the walk more miserable for Wanbli than it already was. He thought himself to be a young man of his word. He vowed to never dance again, so he saw the trip as being pointless. He knew his mother had borrowed money for the bus tickets, which he saw as a debt she was not going to be able to pay back because he was not going to give in to her request. With a million dollars on the line, he was sure Nameci would be there. He would not pass up on such an opportunity, and Wanbli was not sure if his mother could resist him. He had his grip on his mother before, and even though she quit the white tobacco, he didn't think his mother would be strong enough to quit him again. It was going to be a disaster. He could see it and didn't know why his mother couldn't. But then again, he didn't know much about love. From what he saw, it had to be the most powerful medicine there ever was.

By that afternoon, they were on a bus, traveling northeast to Mankato, Minnesota, a place neither one of them had been. As far as they knew, a pow-wow had never occurred there, or at least, not one with contest money. So why THE POW-WOW OF ALL POW-WOWS was taking place there, neither one of them knew. The allure of the biggest pow-wow money ever was taking them there though. While on the bus, Wanbli thought at least he might get to see some of his pow-wow friends he hadn't seen in a while, so the trip would not be a total loss.

The bus was crowded with other Native Americans, all on their way to the same place Wanbli's mother and him were going. There were mostly full-blooded Native Americans on the bus, but there were also some mixed-blooded Native Americans on the bus. They debated with each other, argued some, about blood-quantum, about what makes a Native American a Native American. The mixed-bloods had a good argument, arguing that being Native American was a spirit, something that could not be measured by blood-quantum. The full-bloods didn't have much of an argument, only their Certificate of Degree of Indian Blood (CDIB) cards proving their full-blooded heritage to flaunt in the mixed-bloods' faces. It was their ticket into

THE POW-WOW OF ALL POW-WOWS, which the mixed-bloods CDIB cards could not prove and the reason why they would be denied entry into the epic pow-wow that was sure to make history.

The full-bloods and mixed-bloods all recognized Wanbli. Many had seen him dance and seen him win. He was a celebrity on the bus. It made him feel good to be amongst his people. He didn't see blood-quantum at all, didn't really even understand what it was all about. They were all his people equally to him. He took pictures with the mixed-bloods on the bus, even signed some autographs. They were all honored to be going to THE POW-WOW OF ALL POW-WOWS with THE WORLD'S GREATEST FANCY DANCER EVER. Wanbli didn't want to admit it, but it made him feel good to hear he still had his title, or so the Native Americans on the bus thought, even though he retired. They all felt the same though. He would win the million dollar prize money easily. But he hid the fact that he wasn't going to dance from all the Native Americans on the bus. Only his mother knew of his intentions. She slept most of the way to Mankato.

Within a day's time, the bus arrived to Mankato, Minnesota, a modest little town, almost a city. Jean and Wanbli got off of the bus and immediately, he could feel the energy there. It was offsetting. Positive energy danced with negative energy there. It was like the past was meshing with the present. It was something he had never experienced before, something was overpowering his intentions, like an instinct of some sort.

As Wanbli and his mother walked out of Mankato toward THE BIGGEST TIPI EVER BUILT that would house THE POW-WOW OF ALL POW-WOWS, Wanbli started to do something against his control. He started to dance. He danced down the road, fancy danced at that. His mother smiled, as if she knew something he didn't.

"What's happening?" Wanbli asked her in dance.

"What you were born to do," she answered, trying to hide her happiness.

The closer they got to the colossal tent they could see in the horizon, the more Wanbli danced. It angered him. He didn't want to dance, but every time he tried to turn around to walk back to the town of Mankato, the more he danced toward the colossal tent. He felt like he was walking into some kind of trap. Something was just not right about it all. His mother didn't know what was happening either, but she knew she had to get her son to THE POW-WOW OF ALL POW-WOWS and that was all that mattered to both of them at that moment. She had her reasons for taking him there, and it was becoming apparent he had his reasons for being there, whether he liked it or not. It was going to be like old times, except without Nameci and his white tobacco. The way it should have been from the beginning.

Jean and Wanbli followed a trail of Native

Americans headed to the three-mile wide colossal tent. Cars were parked along the road all of the way from Mankato, and most Native Americans had no choice but to walk the five mile journey from town. The colossal tent was indescribable, with fields of regular-sized tipis, tents, and brush arbors surrounding it. It was a great pow-wow, full of Native Americans from all over Indian country. The energy was strong, and Wanbli wanted it to stop making him dance. But he could not help himself. He danced most of the way there, getting cheers from all of the Native Americans walking to the colossal tent. Most of them recognized him, as the Native Americans on the bus had. He was a celebrity, maybe the biggest celebrity attending THE POW-WOW OF ALL POW-WOWS.

    Wanbli was glad when they finally arrived to THE BIGGEST TIPI EVER BUILT, mainly because the force causing him to dance finally stopped. They walked around the camps that surrounded the colossal tent until they found a good place to camp themselves. They sat their bags down in a small section of grass that was not taken. The urge to dance had left him, but he was still unable to leave, something was keeping him there. So he dealt with it and stayed willingly, just glad he was able to stop dancing. He still wasn't communicating with his mother, so they decided without a word or movement to make pallets for them to sleep on in the very, small open piece of grass that was now the White-Raven camp. It was a very awkward and small piece of grass wedged between four small tents. The day was not over yet, so Wanbli excused himself from their small camp, dancing to his mother that he wanted to look for some of his pow-wow friends. She let him leave with no disapproval, hoping he would find friends who could knock some sense into him and inspire him to win the million dollars.

The camps spread around the colossal tent went as far as the eye could see, so it was not going to be an easy task for Wanbli to find his friends. He knew they would not miss such an epic event, especially with the prize money involved. He was recognized everywhere he went though. Some Native Americans even clapped and cheered when they saw him. He had to admit it, coming to THE POW-WOW OF ALL POW-WOWS was not a bad idea at all. He needed a break from the harsh reality of Pine Ridge. It was not all pow-wows and smiling Native Americans back home. Little by little, camp by camp, he began to see his mother's reason for forcing him to compete in the Men's Fancy Dance category. Walking through the camps, Wanbli wished he lived somewhere where he could see happy Native Americans all of the time. He even wondered if a place existed, but then he realized that it did. It was called pow-wow highway, a road he had vowed to never travel again.

Wanbli walked and walked in his environment, where the oddities growing from his body were not even considered abnormal, even though they were featherless. He blended in with the hundreds of fancy dancers all dancing, rehearsing their fancy dance routines for the next day. There were so many colors everywhere, in every camp, but a certain array of colors caught Wanbli's eyes from afar. Five camps or so away, he saw her, adorned by the most beautiful colors he'd ever seen together, like a butterfly. She looked as if she were lost, not sure where she was going, searching for someone. She was the most beautiful Native American girl Wanbli had ever laid his eyes on. Her hair was styled like Princess Leia, and he wanted to be her Hans Solo. He stared at her until the wind of his stare blew toward her, then she glanced at him. She caught a glimpse of the most handsome Native American brave she had ever laid her eyes on. It was love at first sight, a rare medicine.

Wanbli went to her like a moth to a flame. She stopped in her tracks, playing it cool by acting as if she were tying her shoelaces, even though they were double-knotted already. Wanbli reached her, just as she pretended to be done tying her shoelaces. He smiled at her. She smiled at him.

"Hey," was all Wanbli could come up with to say. He said it in dance though, twirling his arms at her.

"Hey," she said back, the ghost of a rose-colored butterfly fluttered from her mouth. There was an awkward silence. Their eyes roamed up and down on each other.

"I'm Wanbli, what's your name?" Wanbli asked in dance. His dance moves were beautiful to her, and she understood every movement, every word.

"Polacca," Polacca answered, another ghost of a rose-colored butterfly fluttered from her mouth.

"Polacca, that's a unique name," Wanbli danced, knowing he would never get tired of the dance that was now her name.

"Yeah, so is Wanbli. I like it," Polacca said, as more ghosts of rose-colored butterflies fluttered from her mouth.

"It means 'eagle' in Sioux. My mom is Sioux. My dad, well, never met him, so I don't know what tribe he is. My CDIB card says I'm 4/4 Sioux, full-blooded Sioux, so I guess he was Sioux too, so that means they'll let me dance here," joked Wanbli in dance, as he did a funny little dance to make Polacca smile again. He didn't stop the comical dance until she smiled again. She smiled again. In dance, he asked her, "What does Polacca mean?"

"Butterfly," she said, giggling, as the most beautiful butterfly ghost fluttered from her smiling mouth. It was rose-colored, but it shimmered, something she had never seen happen before. Normally, she would have been embarrassed about her gift, but she felt comfortable around Wanbli, enough to not let it bother her because it didn't bother him. It was almost like he didn't even see the ghosts coming from her mouth. "It's a Hopi word, my dad's language. I never met him either, nor my mom. She was Navajo. So my CDIB card says I'm 1/2 Hopi and 1/2 Navajo, a full-blood too, just mixed tribes. So I guess that means they'll let me dance here too."

"You dance?" Wanbli asked by a simple dance move.

"No, I wish. So I take it you fancy dance?" Polacca asked, more ghosts of shimmering rose-colored butterflies seeping through her words. She could feel them coming from directly inside her stomach.

"Yeah," he said with a turn to the right.

"I've never seen a real fancy dancer do the fancy dance before. I've always wanted to. You good at it?" she asked, the air above them, filled with a cloud of shimmering rose-colored butterfly ghosts.

"The best," Wanbli answered with an impressive dance move.

"Get out of here," Polacca joked, pushing on Wanbli's arm, barely missing the small quills that were once a small bustle of feathers protruding from the side of his bicep. His heart dropped at her touch. The ghostly butterflies were now all around them, encasing them in a beautiful shimmering rose-colored hue. It was awesome, Wanbli didn't want it to end, ever.

"No, really. I used to be THE WORLD'S GREATEST

FANCY DANCER EVER," Wanbli danced. It was a complicated dance, but she understood him, somehow.

"Used to be? Well, I hope you get your title back, Wanbli. I'd really like to see some of your moves if you're dancing in the competition. I'll cheer you on. But right now, I have to find somebody," Polacca reluctantly said, not wanting their encounter to end either.

"Who are you looking for?" Wanbli asked in dance.

"Not to be rude, but I have to go. I'll see you tomorrow, okay?" Polacca said, as she started to leave. She turned around though and kissed her palm and blew a kiss at Wanbli. The kiss came from her mouth in the form of a heart-shaped butterfly that fluttered to him and landed softly on his awaiting lips.

"Okay," Wanbli danced, as Polacca continued her journey to find whoever she was looking for. She continued to turn and smile at him until they couldn't see each other anymore. It was like a dream come true to him. He forget all about his original search and returned back to his mother's small camp.

Wanbli reached their small camp just as the sun was setting. His mother was surprised to see him happy, but not only that, he started dancing, rehearsing his fancy dance routines. She got up from her pallet and went to him.

"So you're going to dance?" she asked him.

"Yes, but not for you, for Polacca," Wanbli answered in dance.

Wanbli's mother understood his answer, except for the last part. He danced a dance he made up specifically for her name. His mother had never seen it before so she had to ask.

"For who?" she asked him. Wanbli did the dance again that was now her name. His mother still did not understand, so she asked again. "For who?"

Wanbli didn't do the dance again. He became frustrated that his mother could not understand his new move. So he did something he had only done once before, he spoke again.

"Polacca," Wanbli spoke from mouth. His mother finally understood. Her son had met someone, someone worth real words coming from his mouth rather than his dance moves.

"Polacca, that's a beautiful name. It means 'Butterfly.' Well, continue practicing your dance routines, son, because I know it takes a lot to win the heart of butterfly," Wanbli's mother advised her son, winking at him. She laid back down on her pallet, happy as a mother could be.

And with those words from his mother, Wanbli danced, and he danced the hardest he had ever danced, trying to perfect the dance routine he could never perfect. He danced until his feathers returned to his bustles. They all came back, one by one, reappearing magically, as he practiced his heart out. By midnight, he was full-feathered again and the closest to perfecting the dance routine he had never been able to perfect. But he was going to dance the next day, not for his mother, not for himself, but for Polacca, for LOVE. He prayed to The Great Spirit, giving him thanks for having his gift of dance and natural regalia back. He also prayed to be blessed again with Polacca's presence the next day at THE POW-WOW OF ALL POW-WOWS, where he would prove to her that he was THE WORLD'S GREATEST FANCY DANCER EVER.

CHAPTER SIX

"Across The Red Seas"

THE RED SEA OF DELIAH

THE MORNING OF JULY 23RD started out as most summer mornings did in the town of Mankato, Minnesota; the town's newspaper was delivered promptly to all subscribers, water sprinklers watered the dry lawns of the town, and the sun beamed through every window of every house and business.

It was the bright sun of that morning that awakened ten-year-old Deliah, a young, brown-skinned, long-haired, Native American girl. She was excited about waking up since it was the day THE POW-WOW OF ALL POW-WOWS was to begin just outside of her hometown. Her family was one of the very few Native American families who lived in Mankato, so it was a big deal to them that THE POW-WOW OF ALL POW-WOWS was being held there.

Deliah's parents had promised to take her and her three younger brothers to the grand entry of the pow-wow, which was her favorite part of a pow-wow. The grand entry of a pow-wow was always that, grand, no matter how small the pow-wow or how big. All of the fancy dancers, all of the fancy shawl dancers, all of the grass dancers, and all of the other traditional dancers would all dance their way into the pow-wow circle that they would all compete in. The drum groups, who competed for the drum contest prize money, would sing the songs of their ancestors in unison for the dancers. Deliah could not wait to see the buffet of colors that was her culture. Her mother had even bought her a new summer dress to wear for the occasion. It was the most beautiful summer dress she had ever owned, red with white flowery designs on it and two small straps to go over her bony shoulders to hold it over her small, thin frame.

Deliah didn't awake in her bedroom though. Instead, she awoke in the attic, on the floor, hidden behind some large boxes. It wasn't out of the ordinary for her to awake there. She was known to sleep walk, and her favorite destination when she did sleep walk was the attic. So it was no surprise that her parents didn't wake her, but she was glad the sun creeping through the small attic window had.

Hundreds of thousands of her people, if not millions, were expected to attend THE POW-WOW OF ALL POW-WOWS. It was expected to be the biggest pow-wow ever. If so, it would be the biggest sea of red, the color associated with her people, anyone had ever laid their eyes on since the days of old. Why her hometown, one of the whitest towns in Minnesota, had been chosen to host such an event, Deliah didn't know, but she was glad it was taking place close enough for her to attend it, along with her family. They weren't pow-wow Native Americans usually, but it was a special occasion, so they were going. They were all full-blooded Native American from the Cree tribe. Her father and mother were both Cree, so all of their CDIB cards read 4/4 Cree, so their admittance was guaranteed. Only full-blooded Native Americans were going to be allowed to enter THE POW-WOW OF ALL POW-WOWS.

Deliah went toward the ladder that led out from the attic down to the second story of her family's modest house. It was an old, wooden, cream-colored, two-story house with a small attic under the roof and a big front porch lined with rose bushes. It was built in the middle of a row of houses similar in architecture and color, across the street from another row of the same kind of houses. It was an average American neighborhood, where almost nothing eventful ever happened, just families living and growing up and older together.

Once Deliah made it to the entrance to the attic, it made more sense why she hadn't been awakened. The ladder that led from the attic to the second story of her family's home was pulled up into the ceiling and hidden from anyone downstairs. She pushed it down, and it unfolded as it was designed to do. Carefully and quietly, she climbed down to the second floor. Then, she folded and pushed the ladder back up into the attic, so it was hidden again. Before making her way down to the dining room on the first floor of her family's home where they always ate breakfast, Deliah made a quick pit-stop to the bathroom on the second floor, as she always did in her morning ritual.

After her bathroom trip, Deliah went to her bedroom and changed into her brand new, red dress. Then, she combed her long, dark hair on her own, which her mother usually insisted on doing, but her mother was nowhere around. Once all was done and she was ready for THE POW-WOW OF ALL POW-WOWS, she made her way downstairs, to where she was sure breakfast would be awaiting her.

The morning sun was bright. Deliah's family's house was lit by the natural light, enhancing all colors. But as Deliah entered the kitchen, a color that she normally didn't see in their kitchen was magnified beyond words. It was the color red and it was everywhere; speckles on the ceiling, splashes of it on all the walls, and puddles of it on the floor. It was no longer the yellow kitchen she grew up in. A horrific paint job made it unfamiliar and frightening to her.

The red everywhere was the least of Deliah's concerns. The origin of the red was what concerned her the most. She yelled out for her mother, for her father, and for her brothers, but there was only silence. Carefully, so not to slip on the red all over the floor, she made her way to the living room, only to see more red all over the walls, the ceilings, and in the carpet. Something very, very bad had happened when she was asleep. It was that thought that gave her hope, that maybe it hadn't happened, maybe she was dreaming. She smiled a smile of relief and didn't take the red all over so seriously or with fear. All she had to do was wake up. So, she took a seat on the couch in the living room and waited to wake up.

Minutes passed, possibly hours, as Deliah sat on the couch in her living room, waiting to wake up. It became a very dull nightmare. So out of boredom, she got up and went to the front door, which was open, but the screen door was shut. It had been quiet outside the whole time she had been waiting to wake up, so she didn't expect to see anything outside. But once she stood at the screen door looking outside, that's when she saw them. Her parents were standing in the middle of their front yard, statue-like, not moving at all and staring toward the street.

Terror overcame Deliah, as she noticed things about her parents that could not be, that were impossible. Their backs were turned to her, so she couldn't see their faces, but she didn't need to in order to see something was very wrong. They were both at least three feet taller than usual and a whole lot skinnier than they normal were. From each elbow, they both had two forearms and two hands protruding, and from each knee they both had two shins and two feet protruding. They were grotesque-looking, with what looked to be four arms and four legs, and she would not had believed it were them had it not been for the fact that the clothes they always slept in were dangling from their disfigured bodies, barely covering anything.

Deliah had to put her own hand over her mouth so as not to scream. She could not believe what she was seeing, but what made it even scarier was that neither of them were moving. They were both in what seemed a frozen state. Then she saw more. Across the street, their neighbors were on their porches, in their front yards, and even in the street, all disfigured, in the same grotesque way as her parents, and just like her parents, they were all frozen still. And there was red splattered on every house, with red patches in the grass of some front yards, even some red puddles in the street. It was becoming a very, very bad nightmare. Deliah didn't know what to do.

Then, the most unexpected thing happened. A blue Prius, with a big sign on top of it that read, "Blood Quantum Is Racism!" drove into the neighborhood. It was filled with four mixed-blooded Native American protesters of the hippie-type, two couples to be exact. They were definitely at the wrong place at the wrong time, probably going on a munchie-run. One of Deliah's disfigured neighbors who was frozen on the street suddenly sprang into action and jumped in front of the Prius, landing on its hood. Screams could be heard as the Prius swerved and hit a car parked along the street. It was then that all the disfigured and frozen began to move, including Deliah's parents. They all started making their way to the Prius, but at a slow pace. The occupants of the Prius never got out as the monstrous inhabitants of the neighborhood made their way to the gas saver of a vehicle.

Deliah watched in horror. Deafening screams were heard once the Prius was surrounded. The monsters took turns entering the buffet inside. Red poured from out of the car until there were no more screams, only red dripping from the mouths of the predators of that Prius, including Deliah's parents.

It was then, that Deliah decided to make a run for the only place she knew she would be safe at, awake or asleep, THE POW-WOW OF ALL POW-WOWS. For the sea of red inside the colossal tent would protect her from the sea of red that was now her neighborhood. So she ran to the back door of her house and exited. It was then that she saw Cat Woman Karen, their next door neighbor, an old, seventy-something, widowed Caucasian woman with way too many cats. She was standing in her backyard, completely still, frozen. Her cats were everywhere, keeping their distance from their disfigured owner. Cat Woman Karen was taller, skinnier, and with more limbs than normal, too.

At the sight of Deliah, Cat Woman Karen became unfrozen and started to make her way toward her. Deliah froze in her tracks, not at the sight of her monster of a neighbor, but at the sight of her eyes. They were unlike anything Deliah had ever seen. They were completely black and full of evil, with small tentacles reaching out from them. The tentacles moved too, and were mesmerizing, almost too mesmerizing because she stood there longer than she should have, as Cat Woman Karen just stepped over a fence she normally would have had to climb over.

Deliah snapped out of it and ran, running harder than she had ever run before. In a matter of fractions of a second, she was out of her backyard and down an alley, Cat Woman Karen far behind her because she did not move fast at all. Actually she moved slowly, just as her monstrous neighbors and parents had moved toward the blue Prius. So at least one thing was on Deliah's side, speed.

Deliah cut through red-covered houses, and every red-splattered street she had to cross, was filled with the disfigured and frozen citizens of Mankato. But they all became unfrozen once their completely black and full of evil eyes, with small tentacles reaching out from them, saw Deliah. At a slow pace, the monsters of Mankato gave chase. Speed was her gift in her nightmare, if it were a nightmare. It was hard to tell. The fear felt real. The relief of being able to escape felt real.

And Deliah was making a great escape too, not slowing down for anything, until she turned the corner of a red-covered house and ran right into one of the monsters which became unfrozen immediately. It was like they were playing some kind of sick version of freeze tag. It was then that Deliah found out the monsters had claws. The one she had literally run into swung at her and cut her on the cheek. Red poured down her face, but she did not freeze in fear. Quite the opposite, she went into warp speed, becoming just a blur of red that unfroze every disfigured and frozen citizen of Mankato. They all slowly followed her, their appetite to taste the color red driving them all to her.

Something was terribly wrong with the citizens of Mankato. Deliah's best chance for survival was to get out of Dodge and inside the colossal tipi outside of Mankato that was going to harbor THE POW-WOW OF ALL POW-WOWS. She knew medicine men would be there, along with police and security.

Deliah was not brought up as a traditional Native American. She knew very little of her traditional ways, but she did know some of the stories of her people. One story came to her mind as she made her way out of her red-covered hometown. It was a story that involved a little Cree girl like herself and what that little Cree girl lived through to become the only witness who ever survived the "Wendigos," the original zombies, and their cannibalistic wrath. And as she ran, she was sure of one thing, history was repeating itself. A circle was completing itself.

THE RED SEA OF DANDELION

Deep inside the Boreal Forest, which ran through Ontario, Canada, between the Hudson Bay and Thunder Bay, there was a small portion of the forest known as the "Dead Forest" to the Cree Tribe. They inhibited an area close to the Dead Forest many, many winters ago, in the days of old. It was where Dandelion's story began. It was a forbidden forest, off limits to the tribe, for beings not of the world, dark beings, inhibited the Dead Forest. It got its name because all who dared to enter it ended up dead, mutilated in inconceivable ways. But sometime near

1878, a small nomadic tribe traveling from the north, migrating to the south, settled in the Dead Forest for a summer. The tribe's name was never known, their presence there wasn't even discovered until the day the Dead Forest became known as the "Wendigo Forest."

The fate of that unknown tribe was a story passed down by Cree tribal members, which came from the only survivor of that unknown tribe, a ten-year-old girl named Dandelion. Her recount of the worst massacre in Canada's history sent chills down the spines of every First People who heard it. Native Americans were called "First People" in Canada. It was a massacre of unheard brutality, even in comparison of First Peoples' and Native Americans' experiences with the horrific brutality throughout colonialism and assimilation, after having survived genocide.

Dandelion's people lived in tipis, like most nomadic tribes of Canada at the time. They followed the great buffalo herds that traveled north up to Canada during the summer, then back down to North America during the fall. The Dead Forest seemed like a perfect place for her people to camp for the summer and await the buffalo that they knew would arrive at any time on the large, open plain near the forest. And the land there was bountiful with plants, lakes, and various types of animals to keep them all fed until the buffalo arrived. It was a perfect place for them to camp, or so they thought, until they encountered what Canadian tribes called "Wendigos."

Wendigos were evil, cannibalistic spirits that haunted certain forests and were known to possess humans, giving them an insatiable craving for the taste of human flesh, turning them into a cannibal. Once a Wendigo possessed a human, they would disfigure the human, taking shape close to a Wendigo's true appearance, tall and thin with long sharp teeth and numerous limbs. But the Wendigos never could master how to make the humans they possessed move fast or conserve their energy, so Wendigo-possessed humans were slow and would become paralyzed temporarily after feeding, until their next meal arrived.

Despite their living nearly 150 years and many miles apart, Deliah's story was a cousin of Dandelion's story. She, too, was a browned-skinned, long-haired, bony ten-year-old girl. And just like Deliah was known for doing, Dandelion was also known to sleepwalk. One morning, she awoke hidden in some bushes a short distance outside of her tribe's camp.

It was the bright sun and silence that had awakened her. It was a thick, unnerving silence, highly unusual for her tribe's camp in the morning. Tribal members were normally doing morning chores, which included tending to horses, cooking, and gathering wood, which was one of her chores. She knew her parents would be mad at her for not getting wood for their fire, and they were probably all waiting on her to do so. Her family consisted of her parents, her two little brothers, and her. She rushed up and ran toward her camp, which was only a few hundred yards away, through a thicket of large trees.

But the silence of her camp stopped her from entering once she arrived there. Something wasn't right. She hid behind some bushes to make sure the coast was clear. As suspected, something was wrong, very wrong. The fifty or so tipis that made up her tribes camp were all painted with splatters of red and puddles of red were scattered on the ground. Dandelion had to force her hand over her mouth so as not to scream. She wondered if another tribe had massacred her tribe while she was asleep. But then, she saw them, her tribal members. They weren't themselves, nothing like themselves at all. And seeing them scared her the most. They were disfigured in ways not humanly possible, and all frozen, not moving at all, not even to breath. Dandelion came to the conclusion that she was not awake, that she was in the middle of a nightmare. She laid down near the bush she was hiding behind, closed her eyes, and patiently waited to awaken.

Hours passed and she was still wide awake. She rose back up and peeked out from behind the bush to see what she saw before, each tribal member was disfigured and frozen. They were all taller than normal, skinnier than normal, from each elbow they had two forearms and two hands protruding, and from each knee they had two shins and two feet protruding. They were grotesque-looking, with four arms and four legs. She would not had believed it was her people had it not been for the fact that the tribal garments they always wore, some which she helped make, were dangling from their disfigured bodies, barely covering anything. And their eyes, they were completely black and full of evil, with small tentacles reaching out from them. The tentacles moved, as if seeking the slightest glimmer of life. Then, there was the red that dripped from all of their mouths, fresh red.

Dandelion could not believe what she was seeing, and she couldn't fathom what had happened to them. But she had only one thought in her mind, to make it to her family's tipi and make sure her little brothers were safe. So, she waited patiently for the perfect time, even if it meant waiting until dark consumed the camp.

Dandelion didn't have to wait that long though because a small group of four braves returned to the camp on foot from a scouting expedition for the great herd of buffalo. They were her knights in shining buckskin. She almost ran off from her hiding spot to greet them. She knew them all, teenagers who like to joke around with everyone, never taking anything serious. They were loud with laughter as they entered their camp.

It was the braves' laughter and their movement that unfroze all of the frozen tribal members. The disfigured and unfrozen immediately went toward the four braves, all at once. The four braves didn't know how to react to what they were seeing, so they just began shooting arrows into the monsters that had invaded their camp. Their arrows did no harm to any of them, nor did it stop them. It wasn't until one of the monsters reached one of the braves and subdued him with its four hands so that it could bite into him that the three other braves ran away from the camp in fear. Dandelion watched red spurt and spew from the unlucky brave, as he was consumed by numerous monsters that were once tribal members she respected instead of feared. It was a horrific sight, but also a gleam of light.

The monsters gave chase after the three other braves, leaving the sea of red tipis that were once a camp of white tipis. It gave Dandelion the perfect chance to run to her family's tipi to rescue her little brothers, and hopefully, her parents. She ran from her hiding place faster than she had ever run in her life. Between red tipis and jumping over puddles of red, she ran. It felt almost too easy for her, but the gleam of light was soon darkened when she ran around one red tipi and ran right into a disfigured and frozen tribal member, who wore the buckskin dress of their chief's wife. She immediately became unfrozen. Dandelion was barely able to escape her clutch and ran even harder away from what was becoming a living nightmare. The remaining monsters of her camp gave chase after her, but could not move fast, so Dandelion was safe for the time being.

A few red tipis later, Dandelion was at her family's tipi. It was also a red tipi. She felt her heart drop from her chest to her stomach, as she stopped running and contemplated entering. The hope of a chance that her little brothers may have survived what ever happened gave her the strength to enter her family's tipi. The red was even worse inside, some of it still dripping to the ground from the walls inside. Something bad had happened inside her family's tipi. Dandelion started to cry, sobbing hard, until she heard them. The irregular footsteps of what used to be the chief's wife approaching at a slow pace.

Dandelion darted out of her family's red tipi as fast as she could, her biggest obstacle now being that her family's red tipi was in the center of the fifty or so red tipis that used to house her tribe. She ran through her camp, sickened by what she saw the whole way. Red was everywhere. She kept herself from screaming. As much as she wanted to, she didn't scream. And somehow, someway, she made it out of her camp alive. Then, she ran, again, like she never had in her life, for her life.

After hours of running, Dandelion ran right into a

Swampy Cree camp, full of First People who were all doing their chores of the day. Her urgency caught them off-guard. They almost shot her full of arrows and would have had not an Earth-healing medicine man named Swift-Walker, who was visiting the Swampy Crees, been there to stop them. He was a powerful medicine man who traveled throughout Canada and all of North America, healing animals, plants, trees, waters, and the land. His long hair was white as snow and long as an avalanche. His body covered with the fur of coyotes, the only animal he hunted, along with a coyote-skin hat he was proud of. He often told people that his hat was made from the hide of The Trickster himself. He was old, but his body was that of a middle-aged man, stout and healthy. His appearance was that of someone who had been in the wilderness way too long by himself, so no one could make him out as the important medicine man he was. His medicine was strong though. It could even play a part in the weather. He had the power to heal dying animals, dying trees, dying lakes, dying rivers, dying soil, and even dying mountains. He was said to be able to talk to all of them. He was a medicine man to the Earth, the most sacred kind of medicine man there was, respected by all tribes. He was ancient, with cracks in his brown skin that hid countless stories.

  It was normally a custom for Swampy Crees to kill anyone who came out of the Dead Forest, for fear that they might be possessed by a Wendigo. Since Swift-Walker was there, they made a special exception, but only because he demanded it. All bands of the Cree tribe were very familiar with Wendigos, as was Swift-Walker. From their knowledge, the Wendigos had been known to take physical form only once, ages before the summer of 1878. It had only happened once because the Cree tribe had taken precautions since then so that it would never happen again.

    It had been ages since anyone was naive enough to enter the Dead Forest where the Wendigos dwelled, so it surprised the Swampy Cree camp when Dandelion came running out of it to them. And from what Dandelion had told Swift-Walker and the Swampy Crees, the Wendigos were in the process of trying to take physical form again, for a second time, so they had to be stopped at once.

    It was fate that Swift-Walker had been visiting the Swampy Crees when Dandelion came running out of the Dead Forest with the story of her tribe's bloodbath. Had he not been there, the Swampy Crees would have just moved their camp far away from the Dead Forest and let another band of their tribe deal with the Wendigos. But Swift-Walker was there and his medicine was strong and just what was needed to defeat the Wendigos. Since they were spirit beings of the forest and he was one with the Earth and all its beings, including trees, they were no match against his medicine. But he had to confront them, get close enough to them to use his medicine on them, which meant he would need Dandelion to show him where her tribe's camp was located. He had to ask her to return to the massacre of her people that she had just escaped from. It took some time, but Swift-Walker finally talked the scared ten-year-old girl into being a strong little woman for him. She didn't know why, but she trusted him. He had a confidence about him, just like her father had. After convincing Dandelion to lead the way to the Wendigos, Swift-Walker also had to convince a reluctant band of Swampy Cree warriors to escort them there as well. They all knew, only red awaited them.

And so they went, Swift-Walker, Dandelion, and half a dozen Swampy Cree warriors, into the Dead Forest, a forbidden forest to their tribe, every step more careful than the previous. Every sound taken as a sign, studied before they went any further. It was the longest short journey any of them had ever taken. Dandelion let them know that she did not run far before arriving to their camp, so their camps were not that far apart. The Swampy Crees were also awaiting the summer buffalo herd, as Dandelion's people had been.

Faster than any one of them wanted, they arrived at Dandelion's tribe's camp. It was unlike anything any one of them had ever seen before. There was red everywhere, and like she had described, the disfigured and frozen were there. Swift-Walker, Dandelion, and the Swampy Cree warriors were not detected by the monsters at first because their backs were all turned to them. But then, a Swampy Cree warrior slipped after stepping into a puddle of red and fell to the ground causing a loud commotion. The disfigured and frozen became unfrozen. They all turned around, so that Swift-Walker, Dandelion, and half a dozen Swampy Cree warriors could see their eyes. Their morbid black eyes, with small tentacles reaching out from them. The tentacles moved.

But the disfigured and unfrozen moved at a slow pace toward them. So, Swift-Walker used his medicine to summon what he knew they would be the most afraid of, wolves. It was not the nature of Wendigos to eat anything other than human flesh, and like all beings, it was not their nature to become another being's food supply. Wolves were the only animals that shared their appetite for humans, so Swift-Walker summoned them to help scare the disfigured and unfrozen deeper into the Dead Forest, where he could ask the trees to help capture them. Wendigos could not be killed because they were spirits, but they could be captured and contained.

Just minutes later, hundreds of wolves showed up and surrounded Dandelion's tribe's camp. Swift-Walker started the second part of his plan. He began to talk to the trees of the Dead Forest, and one by one, they began to move, sway, and smash to the ground, in such a way that no one would be able to escape from Dandelion's tribe's camp without being smashed by one of them. The disfigured and unfrozen immediately took notice of the trees behavior, and they all began to slowly congregate together in the middle of the camp, preparing for the battle ahead. It was obvious that the wolves concerned them the most, though. Regardless of their evil, they were still beings, and all beings have the instinct of survival, so even the Wendigo-possessed were afraid to become another being's meal.

The wolves summoned by Swift-Walker charged the camp from all directions except one. It was part of his plan to force the disfigured and unfrozen toward the strongest trees in the area. And so the wolves did, but at a slow pace. They forced the monsters to a part of the forest where the trees were the biggest and the oldest. It was there that Swift-Walker commanded the trees to grab the Wendigo-possessed and consume them, body and spirit both. And so it happened, the trees grabbed and ate all of the monsters, trapping them within their strong bark. They were helpless against the power of the trees. And once again, their evil had been stopped from spreading outside of the Dead Forest.

It was a good victory, but a whole tribe was lost, all except one little girl. So, it became a story passed down by every generation to warn that if it ever happened again, it would be known what to do. But until that time came, the Wendigos were trapped inside of the strong trees of what now would be known as the "Wendigo Forest."

THE RED SEA OF THE QUEEN OF THE WENDIGOS

Unbeknownst to Deliah, as she made her way out of Mankato, and unbeknownst to the Crees of Canada; a mysterious being, one with the head of an animal and body of a man, slyly made its way into the Wendigo Forest just a few weeks prior to July 23rd. It carried a chainsaw, which was forbidden to take anywhere near the Wendigo Forest. The forest was protected by the tribe, ruled as a sacred part of their land that was never to be intruded by anyone. It was heavily guarded by tribal security, cameras, and motion detectors, so how the mysterious being with a chainsaw made it into the forest without detection baffled everyone once it became known. But once it became known, it was too late. The Wendigos were free once again. Their tree prisons destroyed, mutilated by a loud chainsaw no one heard.

Deliah didn't know how, but she made it through the red streets of Mankato and to the edge of town. Only five miles separated her from THE POW-WOW OF ALL POW-WOWS, where she felt she would find safety from the disfigured and unfrozen citizens of Mankato. She could see the colossal tent in the horizon and the fields of cars and camps surrounding it. It was a glimmer of hope and she thought it would be smooth sailing after she got there. Then, she heard a sound behind her, the distorted sound of a march of feet. She turned around to see that all the disfigured and unfrozen citizens of Mankato were following her, hundreds of them. But Deliah had a savior, what would be their demise, and it was called THE POW-WOW OF ALL POW-WOWS, where her people and powerful medicine men would be there to fight them off.

Deliah ran at a safe speed, so not to wear herself out, because the monsters of Mankato were not fast. They moved at the speed of zombies. But what Deliah did not know was that she was leading them to a buffet of their favorite meal, Native Americans, and to what what could become a buffet of the purest red. She had no choice though, it was her only chance for survival. So she ran toward the colossal tent, leading a tribe of hundreds of Wendigo-possessed there. She had no knowledge of the danger she was putting her people in, if she had, she would have known that all she had to do was stop moving, stay completely still, and they would stop following her. But instead, her movements were the very thing leading them to their next feast.

Halfway to THE POW-WOW OF ALL POW-WOWS, Deliah came upon proof that something was not right about what was going on. She almost stepped on a dead dog, whom she knew as "Chief." He was her hometown's stray dog, everyone knew him. Deliah had even fed him more times than she could count. He was a warrior dog, even with just three legs, a kind dog that no one would ever have a reason to harm. She stopped in her tracks and went down to pet him, but that's when she saw the hoof print imprinted on his body and the red that had poured from his mouth. It looked like a deer hoof print to her. Why a deer would want to kick Chief was beyond comprehension to Deliah, he got along with all animals, and he even had a reputation for protecting animals. There was even a story where Chief protected a deer from a deer hunter and was shot full of buckshot in the process, but kept on living. So something was definitely not right.

Deliah petted Chief's lifeless body and realized something, she would not have the wolves she needed to chase the disfigured and unfrozen, the Wendigos, away, like Dandelion had in her story. So, out of respect, she fixed Chief's warbonnet so that it wasn't crooked anymore. Then, she ran on, as the Wendigo-possessed, whom became a dark cloud pouring out from Mankato, followed her.

Since Deliah didn't have the wolves of the story before hers, she prayed there would someone at THE POW-WOW OF ALL POW-WOWS with medicine stronger than Swift-Walker's. But little did she know, all of the medicine men alive had disappeared recently, all of them. There were no medicine men at THE POW-WOW OF ALL POW-WOWS. They were all absent, unaccounted for by their tribes and their families. They were all missing. But also unbeknownst to Deliah, there was a medicine woman there, one with strong enough medicine to ward off the Wendigos. Big-Sister was at THE POW-WOW OF ALL POW-WOWS, but there was only one thing wrong with her presence there, Big-Sister was dead.

So Deliah ran with the greatest of hope, from one red sea to another, not knowing what was in store for her once she reached THE POW-WOW OF ALL POW-WOWS, and not knowing that only disappointment awaited her there. But she ran with hope that her story would end as Dandelion's story had, all the while, leading the Wendigo-possessed to the biggest feast they could ever dream of, a feast of the richest red. Hundreds of thousands of full-blooded Native Americans, if not millions, were in one place at the same time, a rare event. To the Wendigo-possessed following Deliah out of Mankato to THE POW-WOW OF ALL POW-WOWS, she was their savior, their queen, and they had never been rewarded in such a grand way. And so it was, she became the first ever, "Queen of the Wendigos."

CHAPTER 7

The 49ers

A "49" was a Native American social gathering after a pow-wow, mostly attended by young adults and adults, after the kids and elders went to sleep. 49's had their own special traditional songs that were sung to a traditional drum until the sun came up, without the dancing of a pow-wow. They were once peaceful events any Native American could attend. Now, a 49 is still a Native American social gathering after a pow-wow but it has been corrupted by alcohol and violence, so they are mostly held on backroads, fields, or bars allowing their chaos. They are outlawed in most Native American communities and only attended by Native Americans willing to take a chance at it being the last night of their lives. 49's have become a great gamble to attend.

Native Americans have various social gatherings now, depending on the nature of the Native American, whether they are good or bad. The good Native Americans gather at churches, tribal conferences, birthday parties for their kids, sporting events, cookouts, etc. While the bad Native Americans gather at 49's, bars, casinos, house parties, backroads, etc. But both kinds of Native Americans have a neutral meeting ground, pow-wows, where all Native Americans are welcomed; full-blooded/mixed-blooded, drunk/sober, traditional/non-traditional, or good/bad.

⤞ ⤞   ⤝ ⤝

It was the Annual Red Earth Pow-Wow held in Oklahoma City in 1994 that brought four thirty-something-year-old warriors together, who created a great medicine with their unity, a medicine not experienced in a very long time. But they didn't meet at the pow-wow, no, it was at the 49 held afterwards at a Native American bar called, "Crazy Horse." They sat around a drum together and became "The 49ers," who later became known as THE BADDEST DRUM GROUP ALIVE. Their songs blessed their people and brought about feelings their people hadn't felt in a century. At the beat of their drum, men would feel like warriors again and women would feel like war-mothers again. They created a buzz in Indian country, like Nirvana had created in Seattle when they brought "grunge" to the music scene. Every Native American wanted to hear them drum and sing songs of days old, some songs thought to be lost forever. The 49ers consisted of five members; Clyde, Dennis, Leonard, Phylb, and Geronimo.

Clyde, whose Indian name was "Big Mac," which was given to him by his friends and not by an elder, as Indian names were normally given, was the biggest of the group. His Indian name coming from a time when he ate twenty Big Macs in one sitting one day at McDonalds. He ate them all, not because he was hungry, but because a Caucasian friend of his offered to buy as many as he could eat. Native Americans did not turn down free food, it was in their blood not to. He was full-blooded Cherokee and stood at six-feet-eight-inches tall, weighing 275 pounds, mostly muscle. With his hair always in two braided ponytails, he was the definition of a "Wild Indian." He had been a star football player at Sequoyah Indian Boarding School in Tahlequah, Oklahoma, his hometown. It was said that he was offered dozens of scholarships to play football at various universities, but turned down all of them because he didn't like the idea of playing football for the blue-eyed tribe. He was a rowdy Native American that loved to fight and after beating up all the best opponents in his area, he decided to move to Oklahoma City, where he hoped to find a worthy rival. He liked to fight that much.

Dennis, whose Indian name was "Chief X," given to him by The 49ers and not by an elder, was the militant

Native American of the group. He got his Indian name because he had a fire that burned deep in his soul, a fire that hated the blue-eyed tribe and could never forget the injustice Native Americans received from them. The irony of Chief X was that he only dated women from the blue-eyed tribe. He was a stereotype of a Native American; long hair, skinny, average-height, high cheek bones, and his skin a crimson hue. He was full-blooded Chickasaw and grew up in Sulphur, Oklahoma. He attended The University of Oklahoma and was on a path to become a great leader of his people, even founding numerous Native American advocate groups, until he discovered alcohol. In the beginning, it helped fuel the fire that burned deep in his soul, igniting it out of control sometimes. But it quickly started to destroy his credentials, so he went from being a born leader to a born drunk, who could be found in bars on Campus Corner slurring things that no one in bars wanted to hear. He eventually moved to Oklahoma City because there were actually Native Americans there turned on by his militant, incoherent rants.

Leonard, whose Indian name was "Snagging-Eyes," given to him by The 49ers and not by an elder, was the ladies' man of the group. "Snagging" was a term used by Native Americans to describe making out with someone, but the kind of making out hickies and babies came from. And always, when he saw a Native American woman he wanted, he threw them at her, his snagging-eyes. They were his medicine. He had a perfect Mohawk and he was thick in muscle, average in height, with tribal tattoos all over his arms and chest. To most Native Americans, he looked like a poser, but mainly because he was. He was full-blooded Creek and grew up in Muskogee, Oklahoma, but raised by a well-off family. Most Native Americans called his kind "Apples," red on the outside and white on the inside. His family owned ranches and businesses, so he was brought up around the blue-eyed tribe. All of his friends growing up were from the blue-eyed tribe. It wasn't until after he graduated high school that he began to have an urge, an urge to be with a Native American woman, but none were attracted to him. He was advised by a Native American guy he played basketball with one day that he should learn how to drum and sing because Native American women couldn't resist it. And so he did, and so, it worked. But he went through all of the Native American women in his area in no time, so he set his eyes on the prize and moved to Oklahoma City, a mecca of Native American women.

Phylb, whose Indian name was "Santa Hoss," given to him by The 49ers and not by an elder, was the most traditional of the group. "Hoss" was a term used by Native Americans to describe something or someone that was cool or awesome. And since Phylb's physique and personality was jolly, it was where the "Santa" part came from. He was almost bigger than Big Mac, standing at six-feet-five-inches and weighing 350 pounds, but he was all cushion, not muscle. He had long, wild Indian hair, which he never braided, and he was always smiling, far from the definition of a "Wild Indian." He was not very book smart, but he knew the Native American ways, even some that most Native Americans had long forgotten. He was full-blooded Choctaw and grew up in Durant, Oklahoma. His family was a pow-wow family, who spent spring to fall on pow-wow highway. Santa Hoss was the owner of the drum, Geronimo, who had been a gift to his family from Big-Sister, the last medicine woman alive and keeper of the strongest medicine there ever was, is, and will be. But Santa Hoss had witnessed the corruption Geronimo, a drum believed to be owned by the Apache warrior himself, had caused within his family. He took Geronimo and left his family, moving to Oklahoma City, where Geronimo led him. He didn't know anyone there, until that night after The Red Earth Pow-wow at Crazy Horse, where Geronimo introduced Phylb to his new family, The 49ers.

Geronimo, whose Indian name was "Goyathlay," given to him by an elder of his tribe, which meant "the one who yawns." He was the heartbeat of the group. It was believed that he was a drum that once belonged to the Apache warrior himself, but the fact was, it belonged to the small band of Apaches that followed Geronimo to Oklahoma, where he was jailed after his capture. They would use the drum to sing Ghost Dance songs, which were outlawed by the U.S. Government, until the drum was taken away from them by the 7th Cavalry of the U.S. Army, the Indian killers. But when the real Geronimo died, the drum was given back to his people, once it was found not to be a threat. It eventually found its way to Big-Sister, who gave it to the family she thought would protect it best, Santa Hoss's family. Geronimo led Santa Hoss to Oklahoma City to start the completion of a circle he was forged to complete.

After that fateful night at Crazy Horse when The 49ers were formed, they brought back the harmony the 7th Calvary of the U.S. Army, who were formed specifically to kill Indians, had once feared. With their songs, they brought back the spirit of their genocide-surviving ancestors. In no time, The 49ers became celebrities among Native Americans. Pow-wow committees begged them to attend their pow-wows, so they hit pow-wow highway, blessing pow-wows with their medicine. Most of the time, all expenses were paid for their presence, not to mention they always won 1st place prize money in all of the drum contests. They became the Johnny Cash, the Metallica, the Tupac Shakur of pow-wow music, taking it backwards instead of forward, to a place and time most Native Americans had forgotten. They sang songs even the oldest of elders didn't know. The 49ers didn't know how they knew the old songs no other drum group knew, but it made them a force to be reckoned with.

It was a good time for The 49ers, money was of abundance, destinations extravagant, and women plentiful. Big Mac liked the popularity from drumming and singing more than being known as a tough-ass Native American with a good knockout punch. Chief X liked the chance to preach his militant ideas to Native Americans about how the blue-eyed tribe were still doing them wrong and what they could do about it. Snagging-Eyes loved the new abundance of Native American women, from almost every tribe, they all flocked to him. Santa Hoss just liked the drumming and singing he got to do with his new family. Geronimo loved being a part of the circle he was meant to help complete.

But like all good things, it had to come to an end. It was love that finally ended their five year journey down pow-wow highway. And as fate would have it, they all found love at the same time, at a pow-wow in Los Angeles they attended every year. It was at the Annual University of California at Los Angeles (UCLA) Indian Club Pow-Wow that they all met their lifelong snags. "Snags" was a slang term Native Americans used to describe the person they were currently snagging. They discovered The Beach Boys were on to something with their song, "California Girls," because they all fell in love with four women from various California tribes. Big Mac met Laura, from the Pechanga tribe. Chief X met her sister, Sandra. Snagging-Eyes met a beauty from the San Manuel tribe named "Mary." And Santa Hoss met a queen from the Morongo tribe named "Donna." Together, on the night they all met, they had their own little 49 on the sunset strip, like the rock stars they were.

Then, they awoke the next day, on the different reservations of their new snags, captives of their love and beauty. Their snags came from casino tribes that didn't have to struggle as they did before the time of casinos. They all got monthly checks from the profits of their tribes' casinos, so The 49ers left pow-wow highway for easy street. The 49ers made their new homes with their new California dreams come true and began to live even more lavishly than their pow-wow money days had once funded. They retired their warpony, an extended van they named "Mr. Ed," for brand new trucks their new loves bought for them. They gave up eating commodities for expensive organic food from special grocery stores. They went to operas and charity events, and all owned their first tuxedos in order to attend such events. It didn't take long for all of them to make their new loves their wives.

It was a great time for The 49ers, living high on the hog, except for one member of their group. The fifth member of The 49ers only saw darkness of the storage shed Santa Hoss placed him inside. In that small space, he waited, ready to share his medicine with those who needed it, but that time never came again. There was only darkness in California for Geronimo.

The 49ers were treated like kings in California by their new queens, attending high profile parties and sitting by the likes of Michael Jordan, Mike Tyson, and countless other celebrities. And if that weren't enough, they all had hot tubs at their new homes, so they began to have hot tub parties every weekend with each other. Then, one night, they broke out a new drum, which was given to them as a gift from Donna's tribe, and they began drumming on it in the hot tub. They started what they called a "hot tub 49." It became a thing, an almost every weekend thing, hot tub 49's. They started to lose respect for the very thing that was the basis of their livelihood, the traditional drum, which had no place in a hot tub. But their minds were clouded by luxuries and vanity.

Then, The 49ers started to gamble, out of curiosity at first, to see what paid for their new lavish lifestyles and their hot tub 49's. They decided to try the slot machines first, which none of them knew nothing about. At the advice of their queens, they max betted, and after max bet after max bet, The 49ers all had their first jackpot in no time. The jackpots gave them the same feeling they felt when they won a drum contest at a pow-wow. They loved it. The urge they once had to beat on their drum, Geronimo, was replaced with an urge to beat on slot machine buttons. And just like that, The 49ers gave up the pow-wow circles they once blessed for flashing lights, bells, bonuses, and buffets. The pow-wow highway they once traveled became the "casino highway." They got trapped up in a vicious cycle, the gambling cycle, one rivaling the alcohol cycle, both cycles bad for Native Americans. Great pow-wow music was lost to the addiction known as "gambling."

The 49ers, THE BADDEST DRUM GROUP ALIVE, soon faded from familiarity and into legend. Most Native Americans in the pow-wow circuit thought they had all died, rumors went about that there was a plane crash, but the truth was, the casino demons had them. They were captives of Mr. Moneybagz, Red Hot Ruby, Quick Hitz, Kool Kats, Wolves Run, Da Vinci Diamondz, double-downs, and countless other demons.

For a decade, The 49ers stayed legend, until one late 4th of July night, a 42-year-old Santa Hoss was robbed at gunpoint by a man wearing a coyote mask in the parking lot of his wife's tribe's casino. After being robbed, the robber pistol whipped him, knocking him out. He fell to the ground hard and didn't wake up until the next morning inside a hospital. He had to be hospitalized for a concussion and after some tests were ran on him, it was discovered he had an advance stage of

THE LAST POW-WOW • 215

cancer in his stomach that resulted from an untreated tumor. The doctor gave him the diagnosis of only a month to live. He was told the news on July 5th, thirty days away from August 5th, his due date to the spirit world. But to make it worse, the first five days of his last month on Earth would have to be spent in the hospital, doctor's orders.

It was during those five days in the hospital that Santa Hoss got bored of television for the first time in his life. His beautiful wife, Donna, spent most of her time on her laptop. Santa Hoss asked her to show him the internet and how it worked, something he was always curious about, but didn't think he had the intelligence for. It was a lot easier to learn than Santa Hoss had feared and it opened a whole new world to him, a world he didn't even know existed. He could watch pow-wow videos on Youtube, even videos that featured The 49ers at various pow-wows. He could also get in touch with old friends and family on Facebook, and he could google anything that came to his mind, like who held the record for the longest fart, which he thought should have been him because he had farted one time for four minutes straight. The 49ers timed it. But the internet was amazing to him and it upset him that he waited until his last thirty days on Earth to get familiar with it.

Then, one night, as his beautiful wife slept, Santa Hoss hit a jackpot, hit the mother-lode, found a gold mine, while surfing the internet. A website was promoting THE POW-WOW OF ALL POW-WOWS, which was a pow-wow to be held specifically for full-blooded Native Americans only. But that wasn't the only thing unusual about it, the prize money for every category was unusually high, a million dollars for every category. A big smile overcame his face and tears streamed down his cheeks when saw that the pow-wow was to take place on July 23rd, so he would still be alive. He couldn't think of a better way to leave the world than taking 1st place at THE POW-WOW OF ALL POW-WOWS before he left. It would solidify that The 49ers were truly THE BADDEST DRUM GROUP ALIVE, for the time being that he was still alive.

On the day Santa Hoss was discharged from the hospital, he had a dinner at his home that night and invited The 49ers over. It was after dinner that he took them to a shed in the back of his home and he pulled out from that shed someone they hadn't seen in a decade, the fifth member of The 49ers, Geronimo. They all thought Santa Hoss wanted to drum and sing for old times' sake, but he surprised them with the news of THE POW-WOW OF ALL POW-WOWS and his intention of winning 1st place there. The 49ers were skeptical about it at first because drumming and singing traditional songs took a unity of skill, rhythm, pitch, soul, love, tradition, and medicine, all of which they were unsure they still possessed together. But Santa Hoss made it his death wish, the most sacred of wishes.

The 49ers had no choice but to become THE BADDEST DRUM GROUP ALIVE again, so they started a bonfire and sat Geronimo near it, for traditional drums had to be warmed by heat to expand the hide and give it the sound that became its medicine. But the heating took longer than it should have and upon further inspection, Geronimo wasn't doing so well either. It was common for a drum to take the health of its owner, so Santa Hoss's dying wish also became Geronimo's dying wish. They would definitely be buried together.

Once Geronimo was okay to drum on, The 49ers drummed and sang the night away, as their beautiful wives watched and listened. They were their biggest fans, their biggest groupies, so The 49ers all got laid that night. THE POW-WOW OF ALL POW-WOWS was only thirteen days away, so time was not on their side. But it was like riding a bike for them, in no time, The 49ers got their groove back. They would take their last drive down pow-wow highway together, to a town called Mankato in Minnesota, which none of them had ever been to and found it odd for such a great event to be located. It had never been a stop on pow-wow highway ever before.

On July 16th, The 49ers all met at Santa Hoss's house to start their week long journey from Southern California to Mankato, Minnesota. Their beautiful wives had already agreed they would fly to Minnesota and meet them at THE POW-WOW OF ALL POW-WOWS, so their husbands could journey together one last time, like old times. Santa Hoss surprised them again, not with something he had in his shed, but with something he had in the barn behind his home. From inside the barn, Santa Hoss drove out a Winnebago. Big Mac, Chief X, and Snagging-Eyes were all immediately captivated at the most hoss warpony they had every laid their eyes on. The side of the Winnebago even had a painted portrait of The 49ers all sitting around Geronimo, with the words "The 49ers" painted above them. Santa Hoss parked and got out, inviting them inside. Like kids in a candy shop, they all went inside and saw its luxuries; a hot tub, four beds, a state-of-the-art entertainment system, a bar, a hookah pipe, and a little kitchen area. Santa Hoss went on to explain the Winnebago, which he named "Big Sexy," was a project he had been working on for years, with the hope that The 49ers would hit pow-wow highway again someday. Someday had finally arrived.

With goodbye kisses from their beautiful wives, along with ten-thousand dollars from each of them as gifts to help them have fun, The 49ers climbed into Big Sexy. Snagging-Eyes murmured something about his wife taking all of his Viagra pills, which sent the rest of them into laughter. It was like old times again. The 49ers started their journey not as THE BADDEST DRUM

GROUP ALIVE, but as THE HAPPIEST DRUM GROUP ALIVE instead, until they could prove their former title. The 49ers were back!

Hours later, the sun was setting and Big Sexy entered the brightest city in the world, Las Vegas, Nevada. It was the first time any of them had been there without their beautiful wives, so anything could go. They could do whatever they wanted, but they all wanted to do only thing, gamble. It became a two day long vision quest for them, one that took them to places like New York, Paris, Egypt, and places where lions roamed and fountains of water danced.

After two days though, they all awoke inside Big Sexy hungry, but no one wanted to pay for their next meal because it was soon discovered, none of them had any money left. All of them were under the assumption that the others had set aside money for their journey. They were all broke as a joke. They knew they couldn't call their beautiful wives for more money because it would have bad consequences for them because they all knew their beautiful wives were becoming fed up with their gambling ways. So they came up with a plan, to find someone who would buy something from their new warpony. Big Mac, Chief X, and Snagging eyes went to look for potential buyers of some of their luxuries, while Santa Hoss stayed behind to figure out something for lunch. He had a little money left, not much though. It didn't take long for the three to return with a promise from a pawn shop to buy the hot tub inside Big Sexy for a thousand dollars, even though it was clearly worth at least six thousand dollars.

Big Mac drove Big Sexy to the pawn shop, unaware that Santa Hoss had been cooking Ramen noodles in the hot tub for their lunch. Once the pawn broker saw the mess in the hot tub, it took his offer down to eight hundred dollars, but they were allowed to keep the Ramen noodles, which would feed them for at least a day or two. And so, they left Las Vegas with their tails between their legs and two trash bags full of Ramen noodles.

On July 19th, The 49ers were blessed with the beauty of the Rocky Mountains in the horizon. Their beauty was breath-taking, awe-inspiring, and they took it as a sign something great was set to happen, so they took a detour before they got to Denver. They went north to the town of Blackhawk, which was a small town made up entirely of small casinos, a gambler's dream. They were all sick of eating Ramen noodles and couldn't wait to hit a casino buffet and gamble a little, or so their plan was. But after a good meal, the bells, the flashing lights, and the casino demons called them to their sickness. They gambled all of their money away in no time, until they were left with only a hundred dollars, which they decided to put all in one bet on a blackjack table. Santa

Hoss was pretty good at blackjack, so at least they stood a chance of doubling their money. The bet was made and Santa Hoss was dealt a king and queen against a six of hearts card by the dealer. It was an easy win, but then Santa Hoss closed his eyes and began to sing an old traditional song, which led to him banging on the blackjack table like it was a drum. Banging on the blackjack table was also a sign for the blackjack dealer to hit his hand with another card, so the blackjack dealer did just that, dealing a four of spades, taking Santa Hoss's hand way over 21. The 49ers lost their last hundred dollars and because Santa Hoss would not stop banging on the blackjack table like it was a drum and singing loudly, it resulted in them being escorted out of the casino.

They were broke as a joke again, but once they got back to Big Sexy, they discovered a thin, black man of the shady type, looking over their new warpony. He introduced himself as "Frosty, the crackman," the only crackhead that called Blackhawk home. He also went on to explain that since he had no competition from other crackheads, he made a killing selling things he bought or stole. Since he couldn't break into their new warpony, he asked if they had anything to sell him for cheap. They took him inside Big Sexy and showed them their entertainment system, complete with a smart television, a Playstation, Dish Network satellite, dvd/cd player, and big speakers throughout the Winnebago. Frosty offered them five hundred dollars for all of it. Even though it was well worth ten times that amount, they took it. Frosty pulled out a large bundle of hundred dollars bills from his pocket, which looked to be well over ten thousand dollars, and he gave them five Benjamin Franklins. He was the richest crackhead any of them had ever met and quite polite with good manners. And in no time, he unhooked everything, wires and all, and stripped them of their entertainment. One good thing did come from it, no longer would they have to argue about Big Mac wanting to play his Madonna mix CD, or Chief X wanting to play his Public Enemy CD, or Snagging-Eyes wanting to play his Prince and Keith Sweat CDs, or Santa Hoss wanting to play his 'Grease' Soundtrack CD. Now, The 49ers had five hundred dollars, which they weren't sure was enough to get them to Mankato, Minnesota, but they were gamblers and liked the odds against them because the payoff was always better that way.

On July 20th, Big Sexy drove into the city of Omaha, Nebraska, which also happened to be home of several casinos. They used their hunger again to justify going to a casino because a casino buffet was never a gamble, their stomachs would be filled at little cost. But it was the oldest casino trick in the book because their buffets were always located deep inside the casino, so getting out without gambling was a feat of strength, one strength which The 49ers didn't possess. And so, just like before, they left the casino broke as a joke, with only a destroyed hope of flipping their money into more.

They parked Big Sexy in an RV parking lot reserved by the casino for such vehicles. It was there that they all began to knock on the doors of all the recreational vehicles parked there, with the hopes to sell what remained inside their new warpony. A fit, blonde-haired couple from the blue-eyed tribe took interest in their offer and accepted a tour of their new warpony to see what they had to offer. But once The 49ers were inside Big Sexy with them, it took an interesting turn. The only thing that interested the couple inside Big Sexy was The 49ers themselves. They admitted to being swingers and had been seeking to have a Mandingo party for the wife, which meant she sought a group of black men to have sex with her at the same time, but she told them she would settle for a Savage party instead. It caught them off guard and only interested Snagging-Eyes, who had to have sense talked into him by the rest of The 49ers. They denied the couple's offer, but offered anything else. They were disappointed, but decided to buy all of their authentic Native American designed furniture, beds, bar, and a few dreamcatchers and authentic Native American art they had hanging up. By the time the couple left, The 49ers had two-hundred-fifty dollars from their sales. The journey was back on.

But on their way to Mankato, Minnesota, The 49ers had to drive through another casino town, Sioux City, Iowa. They only stopped at a casino to use their clean restrooms, or so they made themselves believe. Just like before, they left the casino broke as a joke. They couldn't resist the allure of the slot machines inside. But luck showed itself to them on their way through the parking lot in the form of a group of "tweekers," meth-addicted folk. They led The 49ers to a salvage yard, where they could make some money from their new warpony. The tweekers stripped Big Sexy of her walls, inside and out, her windows, her cabinets, her toilet bowl, and even her tires, replacing them with donut tires. The tweekers made a deal with the salvage yard owner, took their cut for more meth, and gave The 49ers their cut, a hundred and twenty five dollars. By the time The 49ers drove away from that salvage yard, they owned the very first convertible Winnebago. The wind was too much for them, so they stopped at a dollar movie theater, where Santa Hoss stole four pairs of 3-D glasses, the red and blue kind though, not the new kind. Their eyes were protected now from the wind and bugs flying at them. And outside of Sioux City they stole a porta-potty from a construction site and placed it where their restroom had been.

On the morning of July 22nd, Big Sexy crossed over the border into Minnesota. But just hours away from Mankato, The 49ers luck finally ran out. They ran out of gas near the town of Blue Earth. There was no money left, it had all gone into gas, so it was the end of the road for them all. They tried to hitchhike after that, but no one was willing to fill their cars with four Native Americans, who looked like they had been through hell. Numerous cars filled with Native Americans on their way to THE POW-WOW OF ALL POW-WOWS stopped to aid them, but didn't have enough room for them. Some of them even offered to buy their famous drum, Geronimo, one even a gaming commissioner of a casino, who offered a blank check to them, but Geronimo was the only thing they weren't willing to sell for any price. So, they were left there.

The sun set and getting to Mankato and to THE POW-WOW OF ALL POW-WOWS looked hopeless for The 49ers. Santa Hoss pulled out, yet, another surprise, as they made a camp next to the interstate where their journey had ended. Santa Hoss had brought some Peyote with him, to be taken after they won 1st place and reclaimed their title as THE BADDEST DRUM GROUP ALIVE, but as he saw it, they could have their own THE POW-WOW OF ALL POW-WOWS now. It seemed like a good idea so they made the peyote into a tea and they drank it. Then, they sat Geronimo in the middle of their circle. They began to drum and sing, until a vision came. The Apache warrior himself emerged from the drum and scared them so much that they stopped drumming and singing. The real Geronimo stood in the middle of their circle, complaining at first, about how the drum was just another prison for his soul, but now that he was out, it was time for his last warparty. He told his brothers, The 49ers, to get the fuck up and get back on their warpony because the journey was not over, it had only just begun. With no argument, they grabbed the drum that was apparently one of his prisons and took it with them back unto what was left of Big Sexy. The real Geronimo joined their circle and advised them that they should put their 3-D glasses back on. Then, he started to drum a song none of The 49ers knew, but they joined in anyway. The Native American spirit become strong, so strong, that Big Sexy began to move, without gas, but driven by song instead. The harder they drummed and sang, the faster Big Sexy moved forward. In no time at all, they were back on the interstate and at a speed none of The 49ers could comprehend. It was a good thing that they all had their 3-D glasses on because they reached a speed that was like warp speed in the Star Wars movies. Big Sexy became the famed Millennium Falcon, as Santa Hoss gave out a war-cry that sounded a lot like Chewbacca's war-cry. Then, light just became long streaks to them, as they drummed and sang Geronimo's song with him. And so it happened, Big Sexy became the first vehicle ever to be equipped with a 5-powered Injun!

In milli-moments, The 49ers reached THE BIGGEST TIPI EVER BUILT that was to harbor THE POW-WOW OF ALL POW-WOWS. The odds were finally on their side. Pow-wows had been their first casinos, it was where they always got their jackpots in the form of 1st place drum contest prize money. A lot was on the line this time though, a dying wish, a million dollars, and a chance to solidify The 49ers in the history books as THE BADDEST DRUM GROUP ALIVE, who took 1st place at THE POW-WOW OF ALL POW-WOWS. They were going to have to max bet, double-down, and hope for a bad-beat poker hand to send Santa Hoss to the spirit world properly.

CHAPTER EIGHT

The Toughest Native Alive

IT WAS SAID, that when Tonto Wayne was born, he came out of his mother's womb not crying, but warcrying. He came out a warrior ready to battle the world he entered. It was even said that Tonto's hair was already long and down to his waist, even as a newborn. His father, who was THE TOUGHEST NATIVE ALIVE at the time, adorned his newborn son with warpaint, using his mother's afterbirth to do so. It was a glorious day in Indian Country, another true warrior was born.

Big-Sister, the last medicine woman alive and keeper of the strongest medicine there ever was, is, and will be, was even there at Tonto's birth to bless him. She put an enchantment spell on him to protect him and give him strength like no other Native American, just as she had done for Tonto's father. It was tradition for her to do so because their family had the last of what was left of true warrior blood running through their veins. They fought fights that no other Native Americans would dare fight, so they had to have special protection.

Tonto's father was the one who named him "Tonto," because it was another tradition in his family to name the first born son a name that could be made fun of. It was believed it made the first born son that much tougher, leaving them to fight many fights to defend their name, until it was respected. Tonto's father was a first born son too, and knew the power of having a bad name, seeing how his name was Custer Wayne. Beings of this world and not of this world feared his name though, like innocent Native American women and children of days old feared the name "Custer."

From day one, Tonto was trained by his father to be a warrior. Tonto didn't breast-feed, he ate buffalo meat stew and sucked on deer jerky as an infant. He didn't wear diapers either, only loin cloths. He was wild, untamed, pulling the hair of any other infants that dared come close to him. He wanted scalps right away.

Collecting scalps was the way of Tonto's people, the Crow tribe, it was all the men in their tribe knew. The more scalps a warrior had, the wealthier they were considered. And there were many wealthy Crows in Montana.

Tonto didn't learn how to walk like most kids, he went straight to running and riding the pony his father had given him. As most toddlers his age were learning how to tumble and fall right, Tonto had already killed his first kill, shooting a rabbit with his small bow and arrow. He was a ferocious little kid. The smell and sight of blood quickened his pulse. His father was the proudest father of all fathers.

By the time Tonto was only five-years-old, when most kids his age were going to kindergarten, he was already going on raids. The police of Billings, Montana were already familiar with the little Native American kid that rode into town on a horse wearing only a loin cloth and adorned with warpaint. At first, Tonto would only raid sheds and garages for supplies to take back to his family, but it soon evolved into grocery stores and hardware stores. Every time Tonto raided, the police chased him, but never once did they ever catch him. He was a skillful horseman, as most his people were. He was a ghost to the police. They could never figure out where he came from or where he went to, only learning of his presence after he had struck.

For years, Tonto made his raids without ever being caught. Most believed him to only be a myth, a phantom of some sort. But the Native Americans in the area were strengthened in spirit by the stories of him. He brought hope back to them that maybe the days of old might be returning. Ghost stories were common of the lil' Native boy that came from nowhere to take from the blue-eyed tribe as they had taken from the Crow tribe and all other Native American tribes.

By the time Tonto was ten-years-old, he was legend. But he progressed from just being a nuisance and thief to being dangerous. The transition of his reputation came from an incident that all Native Americans and Non-Native Americans gossiped about. The story always changing. But it involved another ten-year-old Native American boy that was being bullied by a group of teenage boys from the blue-eyed tribe in an alley. Tonto rode up on the travesty and quickly intervened, scaring the teenage boys from the blue-eyed tribe in all directions, except for one, the one he had jumped on top of from his pony. Once on top of the boy from the blue-eyed tribe, Tonto pulled his knife out and sliced a piece of his scalp off from his head before letting him go. Tonto got his first scalp that day, but was labeled a real threat by law enforcement from that point on.

More years passed, and Tonto still had not been caught. He had some close calls, but always escaped from the Billings police officers that dared to try to catch him. But teenage hormones finally got the best of Tonto and became his demise. It was while he was on his way home after one of his raids, when he was thirteen-years-old, that he locked eyes with a teenage Native American girl. She was walking in his direction along a park trail. He felt something he had never felt before, a jolt, a force that ran through his whole body, and became his reason to live. On his pony, he blocked her path, she stopped. She wasn't afraid, instead, intrigued by what she only knew to be a myth, but there he was, right in front of her. She was a pretty teenage Native American girl; dark brown eyes, dark brown skin, and dark brown hair, which was pulled back in a fancy braided ponytail.

Tonto said "Hi." She said "Hi" back. She smiled. He smiled back.

"I'm Tonto," he said.

"I'm Jennifer, but you can call me Jenny," she said.

"I have to get home, but I would like to see you again, Jenny. Would that be okay?" Tonto asked with urgency, since he had just finished a raid and didn't have much time to talk.

Jenny didn't answer him, instead, she wrote something on a small piece of paper and handed it to Tonto. Tonto took her answer and disappeared, like the ghost he was known for being.

Tonto rode home that day, not excited about what he got from his raid, which was usually the case, but this day he had gotten something sacred. It was a piece of paper with an answer from a girl that he hoped said that she wanted to see him again too. He couldn't read though, so he had to wait until he got home to ask his mother or father to read the small piece of paper Jenny had given him. It was the longest ride home ever.

Once Tonto got to his home in the middle of nowhere, he was met by his mother first, who came out of their home ready to help him unload his haul. She was a beautiful Native American woman; her beauty never needed make-up, her hair always welcomed the wind, and her skin brown as the richest soil. Before she could start helping Tonto unload though, he shoved the small piece of paper from Jenny into his mother's hands. She unfolded it and began reading it, as he jumped off of his pony.

"What's it say?" Tonto asked. He was the most excited he had ever been to hear words.

"It says, *'Jennifer Twenty-Elks, 401 East Colorado Street, 406-867-5309.'* Where did you get this?" Tonto's mother asked him.

"What does it mean?" Tonto asked, paying his mother's question no mind

"Apparently it's some girl's address and phone number. Where did you get this?" she asked him again.

"Jenny gave it to me."

"Jenny?" Tonto's mother asked with concern.

"I met her after the raid. So does this mean she wants me to come see her?"

"I guess, or call her. But we don't have a phone so I don't see how you are going to call her."

Tonto's father, Custer, emerged from inside their home to help too. He was a splitting image of what a

Native American middle-aged man was supposed to look like, as far as Hollywood was concerned. He was stoic, built like a warrior, long hair, and handsome as handsome could get. Once he reached his son, he was surprised to see something was going on.

"Something the matter?" Custer asked.

"Your son met a girl today, and she gave him her address and phone number," Tonto's mother answered.

Custer gave out the loudest warcry a warrior could give for his son. It had become time, his son was on the verge of becoming a man.

"Who is she? What does she look like? Who's her family?" Custer asked, just as excited as Tonto was.

"Her name is Jennifer, but she said I could call her Jenny. She's the most beautiful girl I've ever seen, and she's from the Twenty-Elk family," Tonto answered.

"Wee-cha, my heart soars like an eagle for you, son," Custer answered, only to be met with a shove from his wife.

"So what do I do now, dad?" Tonto asked his source of knowledge.

"Now, we must talk," Custer answered his first born son and together they walked off, leaving Tonto's mother to unload his haul all by herself. It was a chore she needed help with but was more than happy to do it by herself knowing her son was about to become a man. It brought an ear-to-ear smile to her face that would not go away. She would have a daughter-in-law soon, she always wanted a daughter.

Tonto and his father returned an hour or so later. His mother could sense the change in her son. He was on the path to become a man. It was decided that he would win the hand of Jenny the traditional way, by the gift of horses to her father. So Tonto and his father rode off together, to find horses to capture for his offering. It didn't take long, only hours, before they were back home with a dozen horses they stole from a nearby rancher.

The next morning, Custer gave his son some last words of wisdom before letting him leave on his own, to Billings, where his future wife awaited him. After a kiss from his mother, Tonto left, with the hopes of not returning alone. It was a glorious day for the Wayne family.

Tonto followed his father's instructions to get to Jenny's home, which to his luck, was on the outskirts of town, so he didn't have to ride through town. In no time, he arrived to his destination, with the dozen horses he had acquired. His new herd had caused enough commotion to get Jenny's father's attention right away. He was the first to emerge from their small, modest house, shocked and confused at what he was seeing. Jenny's father had heard of Tonto, but like all other people in the area, he thought Tonto was just a myth, but there he was, on a horse and in a loin cloth, just like the stories described him.

"I come for Jenny, and I offer you my finest horses for her hand!" Tonto proudly proclaimed.

Jenny's father didn't know what to think, but feared Tonto might kidnap his daughter. So he pretended to go along with it, even inviting Tonto into his home, hoping to distract Tonto enough to buy time to call the police. Tonto took the bait and accepted his invitation into their home.

Tonto entered Jenny's home and met eyes with her again, the girl he would have stolen a hundred horses for. She was beautiful, a real Crow princess. Her father asked Tonto to take a seat, even though her mother was not happy about having a sweaty Native American boy sit on their couch wearing nothing but a loin cloth. He took a seat and looked around their living room and found it very odd that they had a lot of paintings of coyotes hanging up in their living room, along with coyote knick-knacks placed everywhere. It was very strange and it should have alarmed Tonto because he knew coyotes represented The Trickster, which in turn, represented tricks. Jenny's parents were assimilated Native Americans, professional types. They didn't appreciate his traditional style of courting their daughter, but they both knew they had to distract him long enough for the police to get there and handle the situation.

Jenny's parents pretended to be impressed by his offering and they started small talk with Tonto. He was distracted by his yearning for Jenny and didn't sense the danger he was in. The sheriffs, the highway patrol, and the Billings police all surrounded Jenny's house without Tonto realizing it. He was too busy trying to make a good first impression to see what was really going on outside. Jenny didn't know either, for she seemed just as mesmerized by Tonto as he was by her.

Then, it happened. Members of the blue-eyed tribe with badges, guns, and the hope of taking down one of the last true Native American warriors left stormed into Jenny's home. Tonto tried to run, but he was thrown to the ground and handcuffed. When he looked up, he saw something very disturbing. Jenny and her parents had vanished, along with all of their furniture, paintings, and knick-knacks that were just there. He realized that he was in an abandoned house. How that came to be, he had no idea. But somehow, someway, through bad medicine maybe, the law had caught the myth, the phantom, the ghost of the wild Native American boy that had tormented the city of Billings for so many years. He did exist and now they had proof.

Tonto was taken into custody and sent to a juvenile detention center, where he spent the rest of his teenage years. The list of crimes he was found guilty of ran long, his case file took three folders to contain all of his charges. He was a trilogy in the eyes of the state of Montana.

For five years, he was a supervised by the state of Montana. He was forced to wear clothes and speak English. They even cut off his long hair. The state taught him how to read, write, and do math. He didn't stop getting into trouble though, he fought his way to top dog in the detention center, respected by all, even the guards there, some of which experienced his fighting skills. The true warrior in him would not go away, no matter how much they locked him in solitary confinement or beat his ass with night sticks. But it did change him, the true warrior that once only lived in the days of old, now was able to live in two worlds. Tonto became familiar with the blue-eyed tribe's world in that juvenile detention center.

Tonto's mother visited him every chance she got, but he never received one visit from his father. His father's bloodline had a tradition he didn't know about though. It was a tradition, in which, fathers were expected to leave their family once their first born son reached manhood. So Custer left Tonto and his mother, rambling on, as Custer's father had done to him, and his father had done to him, and so on. The news of his departure made no sense to Tonto. All he knew was that it hurt his mother incredibly so and left her with nothing. She began to struggle, sometimes not even having enough money to visit him. Little by little, he began to hate his father, so much, that he finished his last year in the juvenile detention center with good behavior. He wanted out, for two reasons, to take care of his mother and take revenge on his father for leaving them.

But upon Tonto's release, when he turned eighteen-years-old, he was visited by a government recruiter, who laid out a deal for him that he could not refuse. A chance to be a true warrior again and get paid for it. The government recruiter had heard so much about the true warrior that was Tonto, so much that he wanted to offer Tonto an opportunity to undergo special training, from the best of the best, and become a government operative. The thirteen-year-old Tonto that walked handcuffed into the juvenile detention center five years ago would have spit in the government recruiter's face. But the eighteen-year-old Tonto that learned the value of making money and who wanted to provide for his mother, since his father was no longer around, considered the offer. The pay was very good. The government recruiter gave him a few days to spend with his mother, before deciding if he would take the offer.

There wasn't much to think about, Tonto's mother was having a hard time making ends meet, barely able to even put food on the table to celebrate his release. Her health was deteriorating because of how malnourished she had become. Their home was falling apart too. As much as Tonto wanted to fulfill the second thing on his to-do list, which was to take revenge on his father for leaving them, he knew he had to accept the government recruiter's offer first. He didn't know anything about getting a job, nor were there much jobs in Billings, so getting paid for what he knew best, which was kicking ass, was an offer he couldn't refuse.

The government recruiter showed up at his home a few days later, by helicopter, and took Tonto away from his home and his mother's loving arms. Tonto was taken to special training camp after special training camp, where he excelled in all of the training he received. He was a pro at martial arts, stealth training, and he became one of the best snipers the armed forces had ever seen. All the while he trained, the checks the government paid him with went directly to his mother. It made it all worth it, the agonizing drills, sometimes being left in a jungle for days with nothing but a knife. The government was making Tonto the ultimate warrior, one they could send anywhere to complete top secret missions for them.

Training lasted for years, but when it finally ended, Tonto was moved up a few pay grades. His mother always sending him a thank-you letter after every check she received, grateful and now even more grateful that the checks had gotten bigger. She was healthy again, and living comfortably. It was the greatest happiness Tonto could wish for.

His first mission didn't seem like work at all, he would have done it for free. They dropped him into another country, where he made his way into his target's house undetected. He slit his target's neck while he slept. Then, he peeled off his scalp, as his target's wife slept next to him, unaware of the brutal act occurring next to her. It was the first of many scalpings he committed while employed by the U.S. government.

Tonto had many bosses, sometimes the CIA, sometimes the FBI, sometimes the president himself ordered his missions. They were all against him collecting scalps. They even tried to stop him from leaving his calling card, but Tonto never listened, always completing a mission with a scalp or scalps to take back home. His mother proud every time he returned with them, she even had a special shed built at their home, where she stored his collected scalps.

For years, Tonto did the government's work, storming into places no American dared to go. He was sometimes accompanied by Navy Seals, Delta Force, or other government operatives, like himself. Killing was his business and business was good. His father had prided himself as being THE TOUGHEST NATIVE ALIVE, but Tonto aimed higher and prided himself as being THE TOUGHEST MUTHAFUCKER ALIVE. He had the scalps to prove his title too, far more than his father had or even dreamed of having.

But it was during a mission in North Vietnam that everything changed for Tonto. He was dropped inside a North Vietnam city to take out one of their mastermind generals. The Intel on his target painted him as a cold-blooded American-killer with no heart. So Tonto could not wait to collect his scalp. But when Tonto infiltrated his target's home, he was surprised when he didn't see what the file painted his target to be. Instead, the target was a family man, a loving father and husband, with a passion to protect not only his family, but also his people from America's terrorism. His target had just put his children to sleep, while his wife was taking a shower, when Tonto encountered him. Tonto didn't know why, but he didn't kill his target right away. He gave his target enough time to say something. The general's English words caught him off guard, so before killing him, Tonto decided to listen to what he had to say first.

"What's your name?" the target asked, but only received silence from Tonto. "I just want to know the name of the man who takes my life, to honor you in the afterlife."

"Reuben," Tonto answered. It was his favorite fake name to use.

"Reuben, tell me this, is English your people's language?" the target asked.

"No," Tonto answered.

"Then, why do you speak it?"

"Why do you speak it?" Tonto asked, amused by his question.

"I believe for this moment at hand."

"Well choose your words wisely because you only have a few more to speak."

"We are brothers, you and me, both brown in skin and righteous in heart. And we both share the same enemy, those Yankees who call themselves Americans. You are American Indian, like on the John Wayne movies, right?"

"And just how do you know that?" Tonto asked, puzzled.

"I know a brother when I see one."

"I'm no brother to a communist."

"Oh no, you got it all wrong, brother. We are not communist. It is just what your country has labeled us, so they can come into our country and kill more brown people, as America is known for doing. America hates brown people; Vietnamese, Koreans, Middle Eastern Indians, Arabs, Mexicans, Pacific Islanders, and of course, American Indians. You, of all people, should understand that."

"Why should I understand that?" Tonto asked the general.

"America, that isn't even what your people called your land, is it? They named it America, the ancestors of the white people you serve, after an Italian explorer, right? Like it was new found land that no one occupied! They wanted your land for themselves and they did everything they had to do to take it from your people. Now, they are here, but I don't understand why because our land is not valuable to them."

"It's because you kill innocent people."

"As did your people. Didn't your people massacre settlers to send a message, to protect your people from Americans? Their greed is never ending and can never be satisfied until they have it all. They are the black hole of this world and they will be the end of it. They will never stop until they have it all. I do what I do to buy time, to keep them away from my people just a little longer. Eventually, they will win and will take over my people, my land, as they did with your people and your homeland. I know this, but still, I fight. I am a true warrior too, just like you."

At that moment, Tonto was hit with a hard truth. He was so obsessed with outdoing his father and being THE TOUGHEST MUTHAFUCKER ALIVE that he hadn't realized that he had become THE BIGGEST SELL-OUT ALIVE. He had become an "Uncle Tomahawk." His father was right in naming him "Tonto" because he was living up to his name. He was exactly that, a "Tonto," and the American government was his "Lone Ranger." He wasn't the hero he thought himself to be, he was only a sidekick. Tonto really was a "Tonto."

Tonto didn't kill his target, instead he returned from his mission with a story that his target escaped after brief gunfire exchange. It was the only mission he didn't return from with a scalp to show for it, so it became his last mission. He resigned, leaving the Lone Ranger to fight his battles alone.

Tonto didn't return home immediately after resigning, instead, he went on a vision quest to try and find himself. He grew his hair long again and traveled all over America, taking various jobs to see where he fit in. For a year, he lived in San Francisco and became a book cover model, posing for the covers of books about white women giving in to a savage lover. Tonto had the body for it, he was like the Native American Fabio.

Tonto's modeling career took him to Hollywood, where he hoped to become the first Native American movie star, but he was only cast as a long-haired Mexican villain in a few exploitation films. Hollywood was not his cup of tea, so he went east to New York City, where he hoped to hone his talent as a painter. But Native American art was not in fashion in the New York City art scene, so New York City was a bust for Tonto too.

So with his tail between his legs, Tonto returned to his home in Montana during the spring, after a few years on his vision quest. He knew it was going to take time for him to adjust back to his quiet home life, after all he had experienced since leaving his home. But it would make his mother happy and she deserved her happiness. And she was more than happy when he arrived back home, their home not looking nothing like the home he grew up in. His mother had their old home demolished and had a new house built with the checks Tonto had sent her when he worked for the government. It was a good house too, modern, and way bigger than the small box of a house they used to live in.

Tonto's mother was glad to have her son back home and Tonto was glad to finally be home for good. They spent their days and nights together, catching up on old times, not mentioning his father, Custer, in any of their stories. It still sickened Tonto though, the way Custer bailed on his mother, but he pushed it back on his to-do list once again. He knew when the time was right, his revenge would be had. He decided to focus on what was first on his to-do list, his mother's happiness.

Tonto shared his adventures with his mother, the exotic places he had been to, the things he tasted, and the cultures he encountered. They had no use for their television, Tonto supplied all the entertainment they needed. His mother loved his stories and was always all ears, not knowing a lot of her son's stories were classified information that he wasn't supposed to be telling anyone. But Tonto's mother never journeyed out of the Crow reservation, her homeland, so Tonto's stories were her only escape from what she was familiar with.

Then, one late spring morning, Tonto's mother didn't wake up to listen to another one of his stories. She went to sleep for good, but she left the world with a smile on her face. Her dying smile gave Tonto a lot of comfort, enough to mark the first thing off of his to-do list. It wasn't until after his mother's funeral, the cutting of his hair again, and when the mourning ended, that he decided to concentrate on number two of his to-do list. It was time to get revenge on his father for leaving them.

Tonto's father, Custer, wasn't hard to find at all either. Since leaving his mother, Custer had become somewhat of a Native American celebrity, concentrating on his skill as a traditional fancy dancer, winning titles and prize money at every major pow-wow on pow-wow highway, even at his old age. To Tonto, it was just a matter of what pow-wow he wanted to exact his revenge on his father at. There were so many to choose from, so it was a decision Tonto decided to take time to figure out.

It didn't take much time though, Tonto knew the best pow-wow to confront his father at would be their tribal pow-wow, which was known as the Crow Fair, the largest gathering of tipis in the world. It took place during the fall every year, so it gave Tonto plenty of time prepare for the biggest battle of his life. His plan involved him entering the fancy dance contest his father normally won every year, but this year a different champion would emerge. Custer had taught Tonto how to fancy dance when he was a kid, so it came natural to him. But to beat his father in competition was a whole different story, so Tonto knew he would need to spend the whole summer practicing and coming up with a routine to rival his father's routines. So all that summer, Tonto fancy danced, every day, from morning to evening, teaching himself moves that had not been seen before. Once he perfected his routine, he paid an elder of his tribe a good amount of money to make him fancy dancer regalia like no other, a dance outfit that would make him look hoss. And so she did, using colors that had never been used together before, and making a hidden pocket in the outfit, as requested by Tonto.

But Tonto's plan was not going to stop at beating his father at fancy dancing, there was also going to be a fight, a fight only one of them would walk away from. So Tonto also practiced his fighting skills all summer long. He conditioned himself by spending his nights jogging and lifting weights until he was a mean and lean fighting/dancing machine.

When fall came, Tonto was in the best shape and the strongest he had ever been in his life. He almost felt sorry for his father, who had no clue what awaited him. The Crow Fair finally arrived and Tonto entered himself into the fancy dance competition for the first time in his life. His father showed up as expected and entered himself into the fancy dance competition as well. The news went through the pow-wow like wildfire that THE TOUGHEST NATIVE ALIVE would be competing against his first-born son in the fancy dance competition. It was an event that rarely ever happened at pow-wows, a father and son competing for the same title.

Tonto kept his distance from his father during the pow-wow, not giving him a chance to apologize or even wish him good luck. He thought it would make his victory that much sweeter if his father knew he was there to take away his legacy with no respect for him. Surprisingly though, Custer made no attempt to apologize or even talk to Tonto during the pow-wow. He also kept his distance.

Then, the night came, the night all Crow tribal members and pow-wow attendees had anticipated since they heard it was happening. It was time for the fancy dance competition, time to see who was better, father or son. Big-Sister, the last medicine woman alive and keeper of the strongest medicine there ever was, is, and will be, was even in attendance. She was just as curious as everyone else, but especially since she had blessed both of them with the same enchantment spell when they were newborns. Her medicine would be competing against itself.

Thirteen of the best fancy dancers in the nation entered the pow-wow circle for the competition. The drum group started their song, it was an epic song, one not heard in a long time, one to test father and son.

Tonto became one with the beat, his body and regalia doing things some had never seen before. Custer pulled out moves and spins he had been saving for such a battle, some never seen before too. The crowd cheered. The other eleven fancy dancers didn't have anything to compare to the real competition going on between father and son. Colors flew everywhere, colors blurred, until colors became one with song. It was fancy dancing like never seen before; fast, complicated, but yet, graceful. The Great Spirit himself was there to witness their praise to him with their moves.

The first song ended and there was a standing ovation. The crowd went nuts, it was like a Rolling Stones concert at the Crow Fair. Normally, half of the fancy dancers would be eliminated and the remaining half would compete during a second song, but it was obvious only two fancy dancers should remain for the second song. And so, all of the fancy dancers were asked to leave the pow-wow circle, except for Custer and Tonto.

The crowd stood, applauding, cheering for their favorite. It was an epic battle; like it was Muhammed Ali vs Mike Tyson, Michael Jordan vs Kobe Bryant, or Michael Jackson vs Prince. Some were for Custer, but most were for Tonto. Custer was the champion though, he had been in this situation before, he had been against the ropes before, but never against his son. Son or not, he had a reputation to protect, along with a fancy dance title and big prize money. Custer was THE TOUGHEST NATIVE ALIVE and he would be damned if he let his offspring show him up in front of his own people. It was on!

Tonto's plan was working out just as he had planned it and it was only a matter of a song that he could mark number two off of his to-do list. With his father just feet away from him now, Tonto stared at him, a war stare. Custer stared back with his war stare. Then, the drum group started the second song.

Custer and Tonto fought, with dance moves, they fought. Tonto showcased moves never thought of before. Custer showcased moves he was known for being the only one to pull them off. It was medicine against medicine, a fancy dance competition for the ages. When the song came to its sudden halts, they both stopped on a dime with the song, both in very impressive poses when they stopped. But when the song hit its climaxes, Tonto was faster at spinning and pulling off harder moves. Custer began to move his arms and legs in ways never seen before too. It wasn't long before they were both glowing, both their auras shades of their regalia's colors. Tonto's was green, while Custer's was red. Their energy so powerful it showed itself.

Then, when the song was coming to an end, to its final climax, the drum group drummed as loud as they could drum and sang as loud as they could sing. It was legendary. Custer began to squat down and jump up, squat down and jump up, as Tonto went into an F5 tornado spin, becoming what most called an F5 tornado, "the finger of The Great Spirit." He spun and spun his way toward his father, Custer unaware of his approach, until the song came to an abrupt end and Custer's life came to an abrupt end with the final beat of the drum.

Tonto stopped spinning at the very exact moment the song ended, which placed him right in front of his father. Little did anyone know, Tonto had danced the whole second song with a pair of tomahawk numbchucks in one of his hands, but he was moving so fast, they just seemed to be a part of his regalia. So once the song ended and he was in front of his father, no one noticed that Tonto had already struck his father's neck with his new weapon of choice, not even his father was aware since it had happened so fast.

And just like that, the traditional dance known as "fancy dance" went back to its origin as the "war dance." Tonto made war on his father and won. His father's head flew from his body and landed in the middle of the pow-wow circle. The crowd went completely silent, not one person screamed. Tonto went to his father's head and picked it up like a trophy. Then, he took a knife to his father's scalp, peeling it off, in honor of his mother. In front of his people, Tonto won two titles. He was now the best fancy dancer of their pow-wow and also the new

THE TOUGHEST NATIVE ALIVE.

The crowd's silence eventually gave way to cheers, as Tonto held up his father's scalp for all his people to see. They had a new protector of pow-wows, the main job of THE TOUGHEST NATIVE ALIVE, which Tonto knew nothing about.

Tonto thought he was just getting revenge on his father, but little did he know, his father held a lot of responsibility as THE TOUGHEST NATIVE ALIVE. Now, the responsibility was passed on to him. As glorious as the moment was, to avenge his mother, there came a rude awakening. It was Big-Sister, who approached Tonto and filled him in with the details, after all was said and done. A prayer was said for Custer, as his wife gathered his lifeless body and scalpless head. Then, the pow-wow continued, but now with a new protector. The murder that occurred didn't seem to be a big deal at all, it was almost like it had happened before. Unbeknownst to Tonto, it had.

Tonto didn't know it, but he was part of a circle, a family tradition he was unaware of. But Big-Sister was there to explain it to him. She caught him before he tried to disappear from the pow-wow, scared the police would be coming for him soon. She assured him, the police would not be coming after him, so he took the time to hear her out. He knew about the blessing he had received from Big-Sister at his birth from what his mother had told him about it. His mother never filled him in on the details of the blessing though.

Big-Sister explained that what happened was expected because it had happened before, many of times before. The last time it happened was when Custer killed his father at the pow-wow, and the time before that, when Custer's father killed his father at the pow-wow. That was the circle, the first born sons of their family had medicine that made them THE TOUGHEST NATIVE ALIVE until their first born son took their place, but only achieving it by killing their father though. There could only be one protector of pow-wows.

Tonto let Big-Sister know that he knew his father was THE TOUGHEST NATIVE ALIVE, but didn't know anything about being protector of pow-wows. It was then that she explained the true warrior blood running through his veins was sacred. She went on to explain that was why she blessed him when he was born by putting an enchantment spell on him to protect him and give him strength unlike any Native American. She also explained that evil beings and evil spirits were known for trying to infiltrate pow-wows. In the days of old, they were known to massacre pow-wows, so a protector of pow-wows had to be appointed and given special medicine to defeat any evil being or evil spirit that tried to infiltrate a pow-wow, which later that true warrior became known as THE TOUGHEST NATIVE ALIVE. But there was only enough medicine for one protector of pow-wows, so it became a vicious circle that dictated every protector of pow-wows would pass his medicine on to his first born son through death. With his father's scalp in his hand, Tonto only had one thing to say to Big-Sister.

"I don't even like pow-wows," Tonto admitted.

"You should have thought about that before you killed your father, instead of just asking him why he left you and your mother. It is done, like it has been done many times before. If you decide to not attend pow-wows, people will die, a lot of people like your mother. She loved going to pow-wows. She would have been proud of you tonight and proud that you are now the protector of pow-wows," Big-Sister advised.

Tonto thought hard on it, and it all made sense, as crazy as it all sounded. He had been prepped for it all of his life and didn't even know it. His mother would have been proud of him and she would want him to take on the responsibility to protect their people. Tonto had faced many evil beings already and had collected their scalps, so he saw it as working for his people, instead of the government now. The evil beings and evil spirits he would protect pow-wows from couldn't be much worse than the people he protected America from. So he thanked Big-Sister, even guaranteeing her he would make her proud too.

Then, Tonto left his tribe's pow-wow, not scared

that the police might be after him, but on a mission. He drove to the graveyard where his mother was buried. And on her tombstone, he placed his father's scalp. Number two on his to-do list crossed off in her honor.

After that night, it took Tonto awhile to embrace his title as THE TOUGHEST NATIVE ALIVE and protector of pow-wows. He wasn't sure which one sounded the coolest, so just for shit and giggles, he made some business cards with both titles under his name. It started out as a joke at first, since he never came across an evil being or evil spirit at any pow-wow he attended. But after he handed out some of his business cards, he started receiving phone calls and invitations to pow-wows that were being bothered by an evil being or evil spirit.

Tonto's first experience happened at an annual pow-wow held at Haskell Indian Nations University in Lawrence, Kansas. Every year, a number of male students went missing from the all-Native American university after they held their graduation pow-wow. The missing male students went unnoticed for a while, until it became obvious something was happening. Then, one male student came forward and told a story about meeting a sexy Native American girl at the pow-wow. His story went on to explain how she talked him into driving to a backroad where they made out. But while he was making out with her, he went to rub on her booty and felt really course hair, then he ran his hands down her legs, and felt even more hair. It was then that he figured out he was making out with Deer Lady, a powerful shapeshifter known throughout Indian Country to hate men and known to kill them. He barely got away, only escaping because a highway patrol car pulled up on them before she got a chance to stomp him to death. She pranced out of his car and ran off right before the highway patrol car pulled up, jumping into the woods, like a deer in headlights. He got a ticket for indecent exposure, since his pants were still down to his ankles, so his story was never considered credible.

But the pow-wow committee offered Tonto a good amount of money and airfare, so he took on the task to protect their pow-wow from Deer Lady. Tonto had faced many different kinds of danger and never shunned away from anything, but dealing with things not of this world would be a first for him. He didn't have any medicine, only a blessing he had received from Big-Sister when he was born that was supposed to give him the strength to fight and beat whatever crossed his path.

It was a big pow-wow, held at the Haskell Indian Nations University's football stadium every year. Native Americans from all over Indian country were in attendance, most families of students graduating that year. The prize money was modest, so traditional dancers of all sorts were competing in various traditional dances. It had a good vibe. Tonto understood why an evil being would want to infiltrate it, since most of the Native Americans there were visitors from far off lands, a victim could go unaccounted for with a number of reasons for their disappearance. The main reason being that there was a lot of partying going on during the pow-wow, so it was not unusual for someone to not return home with their family right away. The family of the victim would only suspect that the victim might be on a drinking binge with his/her college friends.

    Tonto considered entering the fancy dance competition, but decided to concentrate only on protecting the pow-wow from Deer Lady, who he had no idea what she looked like. All he knew was that she had the torso of a beautiful Native American woman, but her lower body was that of a deer. She didn't have the four legs of a deer though, only the hind legs of a deer, complete with hoofs, hair, and strength. It was said that she liked to stomp a man's private parts with her hoofs, until he died from her brutal stomping.

    The first night of the pow-wow, Tonto didn't encounter anything out of the ordinary. It went smooth. But the second night, he noticed a beautiful Native American woman walking about the crowd adorned in the most beautiful fancy shawl dancing regalia he had ever seen, heavy with the colors pink and turquoise. He met eyes with her and she smiled. Tonto smiled back and it was almost love at first sight. He had forgotten all about Deer Lady and started a new mission, to find out who the beautiful Native American woman was. He had to know, for it had been a long time since Tonto yearned for a woman's attention. She was definitely girlfriend material, the kind of girl he would take home to his mother, if she were still alive. Something about her captured his heart and he wanted nothing more than to make their hearts one.

Tonto followed her around the pow-wow, but she never stayed in one place long enough for him to catch up to her. It was almost like she wanted him to chase her and chase her he did. The allure of finding out who she was overcame him. It made the pow-wow vulnerable, but Tonto didn't care. First things first, and it had been forever since he saw a woman he was that attracted to, since Jenny from his teenage years. And it was the kind of pow-wow where a Native American could leave, never to return again, starting their journey back home, which could be hundreds of miles away. For all he knew, she could be on her way out of the pow-wow and to her hotel room to get some sleep for an early departure from Lawrence to wherever she called home. Time was of the essence. Deer Lady had to wait.

It was at an Indian Taco stand, where she was standing in line, that Tonto finally caught up to her. It was the perfect place too. Tonto got in line right behind her. She smelled good, even better than the frybread scent in the air. Her scent was unlike anything he had ever smelled. He didn't know women could smell that good. There was silence at first, then Tonto finally broke the ice.

"You smell good, what perfume is that?" he asked her.

"Something I put together myself from various roots and berries. I call it Buate by me," she answered and giggled.

"Smells better than anything I've ever smelled."

"Thank you."

"Hey, do you know anything about the frybread here? Been looking for a good Indian taco all weekend, but had no luck yet," Tonto asked the beautiful Native American woman.

"I don't eat frybread, so I don't know. Sorry," she answered.

"What? You are the first Native American girl I met that don't like frybread."

"Oh, I like it, love it, but its pow-wow season, so I lay off of it."

"Frybread could only make you look better, not that you need any help. Oh, excuse me, I'm Tonto," he introduced himself, extending his hand out to her. She took it and shook his hand with a big smile that comforted Tonto, like his mother's smile use to do.

"Tonto? Like the Lone Ranger and Tonto?" she asked, still smiling. She had red warpaint running from the corners of her eyes to her ears, typical for a fancy shawl dancer to be adorned with.

"Yeah," he answered, almost ashamed, but she laughed a comforting laugh, so he joined in with her.

"I like it. So what tribe are you, Tonto?"

"Crow."

"Crow, warrior tribe of the North. Are you a warrior, Tonto?"

"You could say that, among other things. I fancy dance too."

"Really? Then why haven't I seen you around before?" she asked.

"Well, I just started recently."

"You any good?"

"Good as they get."

"Then why aren't you competing here?"

"I have other business here," Tonto answered, as the beautiful Native American woman made it to the front of the line and ordered a Royal Crown soda. She paid for it, but didn't leave right away, instead, she waited for Tonto to order an Indian Taco and pay for it. He was told it would take a few minutes, so he waited nearby with the best company he had in a long time.

"You would like my frybread," the beautiful Native American woman finally said to Tonto, while they waited together. It was the sexiest comment Tonto had ever received from a woman. It could have meant so many things, been a metaphor for so many things, and all of those things were great things. It was almost an invitation into her life, to her lips, and to her heart. Tonto almost lost his cool, but he managed to compose himself.

"I bet," was all he could come up with to say to her. It was enough though. The tension between them was thick. The kind of tension that keeps Native Americans alive and a race that will always survive. It was the reason for pow-wows, so soul mates could meet.

There was an awkward silence between them for a few moments, then, an old Native American woman let Tonto know his Indian taco was ready. He went to get it, as an announcement was given over the loud speakers.

"Okay, snagging break is over, so stop giving that hickey to your wife, your husband, your girlfriend, your boyfriend, your mistress, or your other mistress! Gah! I know I'm bad! But it is now time for the women's fancy shawl dance competition, so ladies, take the circle!" announced the pow-wow MC over loudspeakers.

The beautiful Native American woman Tonto was captivated by started to leave, making her way to the pow-wow circle, but Tonto stopped her with a question.

"What's your name? So I can cheer for you," Tonto asked the beautiful Native American woman.

"Rosemary," she answered with a wink, making

her way to the pow-wow circle.

It was going to be an Indian taco Tonto would never forget because it would be embedded into history. It would become part of the legend of when he met the love of his life. So as the fancy shawl dance competition was about to begin, Tonto bit into the frybread and he tasted it, bliss. It was all going so great, everything. His life had new meaning and he was about to watch his future wife dance for the very first time.

The drum group started their first song. The fancy shawl dance competition was always the favorite of all Native American men because the women danced so gracefully, twisting colors in ways that were mesmerizing and sexy. It was the female version of fancy dancing. It was almost like the fancy shawl dancers never touched the ground at all, since they danced mostly on the tips of their toes, or so it seemed.

Tonto watched his future wife swing her colorful shawl in circles and waves, like a gentle tornado. Her moves were swift, yet more powerful than any move he could pull off as a fancy dancer. Her moves were medicine, a medicine Tonto had to obtain. There was no doubt about it in his mind, he wanted her, needed her, and had to have her. And so far, it was looking like he was going to get what he wanted, needed, and had to have. She met his eyes ever so often during her routine, smiling every time. Tonto felt more like THE LUCKIEST NATIVE

ALIVE than THE TOUGHEST NATIVE ALIVE.

    He was hypnotized by the woman of his dreams, as she danced. But he was not the only one, every man in the crowd also shared his fixation. She was that beautiful, that breath-taking, and her moves, moves that no Native American man's eyes could stop watching. Even some of the Native American women in the crowd were enthralled by her. Something about her put them all in a trance. Her routine was powerful medicine.

    But Tonto had an enchantment spell and blessing that protected him from such medicine, so he was the only one that saw it. It broke his heart into a million pieces when he saw it though. As the beautiful Native American woman spun and spun around with the beat of the drum at one point, her dress twirled up, revealing something only Tonto could only see. The beautiful Native American woman didn't prance on the ground with beautiful moccasins, as her competition did, instead, she danced on hoofs, deer hoofs to be exact. Tonto saw them, her hoofs, along with her deer legs, every time she spun around and her dress lifted up.

    Tonto could not believe his eyes, but realized just how important his position was, because she was there, and there to take more victims, Deer Lady. So he did what he was trained as a government operative to do against an enemy; strike first, strike fast, and ask questions later. He threw his Indian taco unto the ground and ran right out into the pow-wow circle. Deer Lady never saw him coming, so he reached her undetected and he did the unthinkable. He stopped her from dancing by lifting her multi-colored satin dress up from her legs for all to see. The drumming stopped, quickly replaced by horrifying screams from every one at the pow-wow, who went running in all directions. Chaos consumed the pow-wow.

Deer Lady tried to run from Tonto, but she wasn't strong enough to tear away from his grip, which surprised her more than anything else. He had medicine. Tonto grabbed her by the waist and forced her to face him. Their eyes met again. The tension was still there. Another awkward silence fell between them again. They almost kissed. But Tonto had to respect his title as protector of pow-wows and Deer Lady had to be taught a lesson.

"I'm so sorry, Deer Lady," Tonto apologized to her, knowing her real name now. He quickly reached down to her deer legs and got a good grip on them. Once he had a good grip, he began to spin her in circles by her legs, faster and faster, until they were a finger of The Great Spirit together. Then, he let go and watched the woman of his dreams fly into the night sky. She left his hands at such a force that Tonto expected her to land at least twenty miles away. He didn't kill her like he knew he was supposed to do, instead, he made an example of her. Every evil being and evil spirit would now know there was a new sheriff in town and his name was Tonto.

That was the first experience Tonto had as protector of pow-wows and THE TOUGHEST NATIVE ALIVE, but it was far from the last. He learned from it, as he did with every experience. He protected pow-wows from the human-wolves more than once, from the Thunderbird that tormented some of the Pueblos' feasts, and even from the Chiye-tankas that were known to interfere with plains tribes' pow-wows.

There were even special cases where he took on some of the most powerful evil medicine men in Indian Country, along with special cases involving very powerful ghosts, who haunted some pow-wows. Tonto became familiar with the unfamiliar in no time. He even began to love his new job. It all made sense to him, it was what he knew best, kicking ass. So to get paid for doing what he knew best once again, was more than Tonto could ask for and he knew his mother was smiling down on him from the spirit world for doing what he was born to do.

Tonto even began to fancy dance at the pow-wows he attended. At first, he entered the competitions to take titles at every pow-wow he went to, along with the prize money. But he won first place everywhere so many times that it lost its luster fast and he stopped competing as a fancy dancer. It wasn't fair to all of the other fancy dancers, none of them stood a chance against him.

Years passed, even a decade, and before long, Tonto achieved everything he could as protector of pow-wows because no evil being or evil spirit dared to come near a pow-wow. It was a good time for pow-wows. THE TOUGHEST NATIVE ALIVE was not to be reckoned with. But then, Tonto decided to take a break from pow-wow highway and settled down in Florida, on the Seminole reservation, where he had many friends. His travels had taken its toll on him and he wanted a place to call home again, until he was needed again. It was there, on the Seminole reservation that he met a Seminole woman and fell in love with her. Nine months after meeting his new love, she gave birth to their son, whom Tonto named "John," as his family tradition dictated. John Wayne was a name that could be made fun of, especially by Native Americans.

Tonto raised his first-born son, as any proud Native American father raised their son, teaching him the ways of their people, along with the vital skills of a warrior. For twelve years, Tonto taught John everything he needed to know. Then, the evil beings and evil spirits began to infiltrate the pow-wows of Indian Country again, so Tonto had to leave his wife and first-born son, as his father had left him and his mother. It had never made sense to Tonto why his father had left his mother and him, until that moment when he had to do the same thing to his first-born son. And he knew the consequences, John would come for him someday, to take his titles away. Tonto wouldn't always be the protector of pow-wows, nor would he always be THE TOUGHEST NATIVE ALIVE. Someday, John would show up to take both titles away from him. Until then, Tonto could do nothing but what he was born to do, kick evil ass.

For another decade, Tonto kicked evil ass. Once he was no longer in shape enough to compete in fancy dance competitions, he retired his titles and came up with another way to make a little money from the pow-wows he was asked to oversee. Tonto loved to make jokes and make anyone he could laugh. So it became obvious to him that he would make a good pow-wow MC. Tonto started a new chapter in his life. He continued traveling down pow-wow highway, but not only as the protector of pow-wows and THE TOUGHEST NATIVE ALIVE, but now as a pow-wow MC.

The pow-wow crowds loved Tonto as a pow-wow MC. He was good at it, almost as good as he was at being a champion fancy dancer. He still fought evil beings and evil spirits, kicking ass as he was known for doing. He even had another run-in with Deer Lady, who was still bitter toward him for throwing her twenty miles when they last saw each other. She became even more butt hurt when he did the exact same thing to her when he caught her trying to infiltrate a pow-wow on the Alabama-Coushatta reservation in Texas.

Tonto also put the cactus people of New Mexico into their place before they got any ideas. They were new evil beings made of cactus, brought to life by a bad medicine man Tonto had yet to find and kick his ass for doing such dumb shit.

Another decade passed, as Tonto continued kicking evil ass, while making Native Americans laugh as pow-wow MCs do at pow-wows. He was living the good life, a life most Native Americans could only dream of having. Tonto was well-respected and for good reason, for as funny and cool as he was, he was also THE TOUGHEST NATIVE ALIVE, a title he was now proud to have.

So when THE TOUGHEST NATIVE ALIVE was asked to MC at THE POW-WOW OF ALL POW-WOWS, he had to accept, although he found it odd that only full-blooded Native Americans, like himself, would be allowed inside. He also found it odd that the prize money for all categories was outrageous, along with the money he was offered to MC at the pow-wow. But what really caught Tonto's attention the most, was where THE POW-WOW OF ALL POW-WOWS was to take place, in Mankato, Minnesota, where a pow-wow had never taken place before, ever.

Regardless, if THE POW-WOW OF ALL POW-

WOWS was what it boasted it was going to be, the protector of pow-wows had to be there and be on top of his game. So Tonto took a break from pow-wow highway to prep for it, for months he conditioned himself mentally, physically, and spiritually. Tonto made sure that when July 23rd came around, he would prove to any evil being or evil spirit that dared to try to enter THE POW-WOW OF ALL POW-WOWS, that he was still THE TOUGHEST NATIVE ALIVE and the protector of pow-wows.

CHAPTER NINE

The Masterpiece

FEIHT TIRIPS was known as THE BEST NATIVE AMERICAN ARTIST ALIVE, even though he was still a young man, in his mid-thirties. Most great Native American artists didn't achieve greatness until they were usually in their fifties, but not Feiht. The portraits he painted were so real that they caused the hair on the back of people's necks to stand up when they saw them. Some people had even claimed to see some of his paintings blink. He was from the Yakama tribe and grew up in Seattle, Washington. A high-class savage was how he liked to describe himself in interviews. He had long Native American hair, which he never braided, brown Native American skin, high cheek bones, and stoic as could be, always serious-looking. Average in height, he had a thin frame, but was thick chested. He almost never smiled. The thing that set him apart from other Native

American men was how he dressed, with a sophistication that most men of all races wish they had. Tailor-made designer suits decorated his body, a Rolex watch gleamed from his painting wrist, and his demeanor was proper, mannerisms that of royalty. Ladies adored him, not only for his looks, but also because of his talent. Most Native American women dreamt of having their portrait painted by him. Most were even willing to have their portraits painted while they were nude. But Feiht was picky about whom he painted, selectively blessing a few with his immortalizing talent of running colors across a white canvas. He could turn nothing into something like no other.

    His latest subject was Red-Turtle-Man, a Navajo medicine man, who lived in a desolate canyon ten miles north of Window Rock, Arizona. He was a frail, elderly Navajo man, with the whitest of hair held down by a faded red bandana. He had the brownest of skin and his body mainly skin and bones, wrinkled to perfection. Turquoise jewelry adorned his neck, wrists, and fingers, as a red flannel shirt covered his torso, his best jeans covering his lower half. Normally, medicine men didn't allow any type of photography or video of them, fearing a camera was capable of stealing their souls. But since Feiht used his eye instead of a lens, Red-Turtle-Man was willing to let Feiht paint him. It was an honor for Feiht and would become a part of his latest project. He was on a mission to paint all of the medicine men who were still alive so people could remember the dying breed forever. So Red-Turtle-Man, usually a humble man that didn't want any recognition for the good deeds he did for his people, didn't dare pass up the chance to have his portrait painted along with all of the other medicine men of Indian Country. It was quite an honor for him as well.

Red-Turtle-Man sat as still as he could inside his small hogan, as a sharp dressed Feiht painted him. It had been hours since he started imbuing the canvas with what his eyes saw. Red-Turtle-Man hadn't said a word or moved an inch for hours, but it finally got to him. Just like most other men, Red-Turtle-Man was not patient and got bored easily. So he asked a question every subject of Feiht's had also asked him.

"So how does a Native American end up with a German name?" Red-Turtle-Man asked, trying his hardest to barely move his lips.

"I was waiting for that question, you lasted longer than anyone else," Feiht answered with a charming smirk. It brought a small, proud smile to Red-Turtle-Man's face.

"So?"

"My mother, who was full-blooded Yakama, was an orphan, and when she was a little girl, she was adopted by a German family from Seattle. Along with English, they taught her their Native language, German.

So she was probably one of the only Native American girls at the time who could speak three languages, because she could speak Yakama, too. But she loved speaking German the most. Well, once she graduated high school, she met my father, who was also full-blooded Yakama, and became pregnant with me. He went off to fight in the Vietnam War and wasn't around when I was born, so she got to name me. She always liked the German name, Feiht, because it sounded like "Fate" to her. Tirips was her adoptive parents' last name, which she took when they adopted her. My father was killed in action, so she never got the chance to legally marry him and change her last name. And that's how I got a German last name, along with a German first name."

"That is a good story, not what I would have guessed."

"I have a picture of her. Well actually, it's a small painting I did of her," Feiht said, as he stopped painting and reached into a bag he had brought with him. He pulled out a small piece of coyote hide. On the hide, there was a painting of a beautiful Native American woman wearing traditional regalia of days old. He handed Red-Turtle-Man the painting of his mother.

"She's wearing a traditional Yakama dress. The sea shells on it look so real, it's like I can almost hear the ocean sound coming from them. Very beautiful woman."

"Yes, she is," Feiht interrupted, grabbing the small

portrait of his mother from him and placing it behind him so it could be seen. "She likes to watch me paint sometimes."

Red-Turtle-Man was confused by his comment, but he decided not to ask another question and let Feiht finish painting. Feiht was almost finished painting and only lacked a few strokes of black paint to mimic the last of the wrinkles that lined Red-Turtle-Man's face. Feiht took his time on the last stroke of his paint brush to get it just right, perfect. And it was done.

But after the last stroke of Feiht's paint brush, something happened to his subject. Red-Turtle-Man disappeared, entirely, without a trace of his existence. The lawn chair he had been sitting on for so many hours inside his hogan was empty. He was gone. The disappearance of a subject would have alarmed any other artist, but not Feiht. It was what he had expected to happen. So, instead of calling the police or whoever else should have been called, Feiht admired his painting of the Navajo medicine man, Red-Turtle-Man. It was perfect, his eyes and hands were captured in paint better than any camera could have captured them.

Feiht had a gift no other artist possessed. Other artists captured a moment in time, but he captured more than that. He captured his subjects physically and spiritually, until they were no more. Once he slid the last stroke of his paint brush across the canvas, they only existed as one of his paintings. It was a medicine never seen before, but obviously it was bad medicine. He also possessed another gift no other artist possessed, he was not only human, but something else as well. In a way, he was like his paintings, captured, but he was trapped in a place between immortality and mortality. He was of this world and not of this world. Imprisoning people in his paintings was not his only bad medicine, he had more of it. Feiht was a rare being, mothered by a Yakama woman of this world and fathered by something not of this world. His story started over four hundred years ago, when the Indians of days old reigned over the land that became America.

⤳ ⤳   ⤝ ⤝

    Many, many moons ago, as the story went, White-Willow-Woman, who was sixteen-year-old, was in charge of gathering wood for her family. Their village was located in what is now the state of Washington. It was the chore of most girls her age, so leaving the camp alone to gather wood was a part of a young Yakama woman's life.

    But one day, as White-Willow-Woman was finding wood for the cold night ahead of her family, she ran into someone unexpected, a stranger. He was a handsome stranger though, a young Native American man, not much older than her. Although it was close to winter, he was wearing nothing but a loin cloth and his body was that of a great warrior. She could not stop looking at his body, it was mesmerizing, every deep contour and bulge. His hair was long and black, not adorned with a warbonnet or any feathers, instead, she noticed he had two horns sticking out from the top of his head, like a buffalo's horns. Once she was able to peel her eyes from his body, she became alarmed, until she realized that he was alone. War parties always consisted of more than one warrior, so since he was alone, she was not threatened by him. Instead, she suspected he must had been wounded or was lost because warriors did not travel alone, especially close to a camp. She felt an overwhelming yearning to help him.

The handsome warrior didn't say anything at first, he just stared. His stare was unlike any stare White-Willow-Woman had ever gotten from a man before. It wasn't how he stared at her that was different, it was what he stared at her with. The handsome warrior's eyes were unlike any eyes she had ever seen before. His eyes were black, all black, with no white in them. But his stare captivated her and led her to say "Hi" in her language. He said "Hi" back in her language. How he knew her language she didn't know, nor did she really care. He smiled and she smiled back. There was something about him that kept her from running away from him and warning her tribe of his presence like she should have done.

Instead, White-Willow-Woman, who got her name as a little girl because she had a dream of turning into a white willow tree, felt like she needed to know who the handsome warrior was. So she spoke to him again.

"Who are you?" she asked, intrigued as she had ever been intrigued to know a human being's name.

"I am Son-of-the-Morning-Star. Who are you?" he answered and asked.

"White-Willow-Woman."

Then, there was silence. The silence filled with a tension so thick, White-Willow-Woman could not get enough oxygen, so she began to breathe hard. White-Willow-Woman was young and new to womanhood, so the allure of meeting a handsome warrior was a strong desire within her.

He stared at her so long that it felt like forever to White-Willow-Woman, but there was something comforting about his stare that she could not deny. She stared back at him for eternity. Fireworks went off, even though both of them knew nothing of fireworks. Something was happening between them, something magical. His eyes were very peculiar, but not peculiar enough for White-Willow-Woman to be threatened by them. She actually had grown to like them in the short time they had encountered each other.

Unbeknownst to White-Willow-Woman though, black eyes were a bad sign. She hadn't been educated by the stories of her people yet. His black eyes, from the stories told by her tribe, could mean he was a shape shifter, a wendigo, or The Less Spirit himself, who came to be known as "Lucifer," among many other names. But White-Willow-Woman and the handsome warrior shared enough smiles to make it okay for them to finally touch each other. They grabbed each other's hands first. They didn't stop there though, their bodies met in ways a handsome warrior stranger and a young woman's body were not meant to meet right away. They made love in the way Indians of days old made love, a ravaging occurred and a new bloodline was created. The handsome warrior planted his seed deep inside White-Willow-Woman's soil. Their union was an unheard of act. Marriage was The Great Spirit's law before such an act could take place. But it happened. White-Willow-Woman laid with a man before the sacred ritual of marriage had taken place and vows were exchanged before The Great Spirit. And nine months after that unheard act occurred, Feiht was born and became proof it had happened.

White-Willow-Woman never saw Feiht's father again after that day. She was forced to raise him on her own. Her people never believed her story of his conception. She didn't tell them the truth though, how she had succumbed to her urges and gave herself to a stranger. Instead, she claimed that she was raped by a warrior from their enemy tribe, the Snoqualmie tribe. Regardless, rumors went around that her newborn was the child of a cheating Yakama chief, or a cheating Yakama warrior, both forbidden acts a Yakama woman wasn't supposed to be a part of. The truth could never be proven, so White-Willow-Woman and her son were both banished from their tribe.

White-Willow-Woman was strong though, and although she and her son struggled, they survived. She taught him the ways of the land, things that his father should have taught him. And it was discovered soon that Feiht had a talent for painting and drawing. His mother knew the plants they needed for paint and what started as simple cave paintings, soon turned into complex paintings on animal hides.

Growing up, all Feiht wanted to do was to make his mother happy. His paintings always put a smile on her face. Nothing else did at the time. They were poor and exiles, living alone, fighting starvation most of the time. The dire situation they were both forced into ignited a fire inside Feiht, one that burned with hatred for his father for abandoning his mother and him. Not to mention, he also blamed his father for them being banished from their tribe.

Days passed, months passed, and years passed, it was longer than any son could sit around and watch his mother unhappy. From the day he was born, he had rarely seen her smile, until the day he drew his first cave drawing. She loved that first drawing and it pleased him so much to see a smile on her face, so he kept on drawing. Drawing after drawing, meant smile after smile to him. His drawings helped both of them forget about being all alone, without the protection of their tribe. They became their own tribe with a new kind of storytelling to keep them entertained. Their tribe could only tell stories, but they could see stories because of Feiht's talent. He could make buffalos appear where he wanted them to appear, make a lightning bolt strike anywhere he wanted it to, or make a drawing of an event that happened in the past. It was a very powerful medicine. White-Willow-Woman was the proudest a mother could be of her son. He was far from a curse, as her tribe labeled him, no, he was a blessing.

But then, one day, when he was a young man, Feiht came up with a way to make his mother even more proud of him, by honoring her through immortalizing her. It would be his first portrait. He talked her into letting him paint her on a small piece of coyote hide. They were poor, so they didn't eat buffalo or salmon, instead, they ate coyotes, rabbits, and other small game. He explained to his mother that when he went on hunting trips, he could take her with him to bring him good luck with the painting of her. White-Willow-Woman dressed in her best regalia for the portrait, feeling honored her son would want such a thing. She was, indeed, the proudest mother of all mothers.

With the most perfect backdrop behind her, White-Willow-Woman posed for her son. Fieht took his time painting his mother, wanting to get it perfect. Every stroke mattered, until the last stroke. But once the last stroke was completed, something happened, something highly unusual, his mother disappeared. She vanished, like she had never been there. Fieht freaked out at first, not knowing what to think, until he looked at the portrait he had just painted of her and saw her blink. It was then, that he knew he had some of his father's powers. His mother's story was true. She had told him the story of how she met his father, the horned, handsome warrior stranger with black eyes, many of times. She knew he wasn't of this world and expressed to her son that his medicine, whatever it was, might be passed down to him. Finally, his father's medicine had revealed itself and it only added to the fire that was Fieht's hatred for him.

It was the saddest time in his life. He cried and cried, begging his mother to forgive him, holding her portrait close to him for over four hundred years. Always, he kept his mother's portrait with him, along with the hatred for his father.

⤞ ⤞ ⤝ ⤝

Each painting Feiht painted was special to him, and he made sure that nothing happened to them, so he had special cases built to protect his art. After finishing the portrait of the Red-Turtle-Man, he put the portrait of his mother back in her special case in which he kept her in. Then, he carefully stored his newly finished portrait in a special case he had built for his Navajo medicine man painting.

Feiht left the desolate canyon outside of Window Rock, Arizona, where Red-Turtle-Man called home, relieved. It was the last of a little over a hundred paintings he had been commissioned to paint of all the Native American medicine men that were still living. Feiht hated Arizona, so he saved the two medicine men who lived there for last. Red-Turtle-Man was the last one off his long list of medicine men he was paid generously to turn into one of his paintings. It was almost cause for celebration, but Feiht was not the celebrating type, not yet, at least. He would not celebrate until he got to paint the portrait he was promised he would get to a chance to paint. But he had to complete the entire mission he recently accepted first. Only half of the mission was now complete, and although he didn't want to celebrate just yet, he was very ecstatic about his new collection.

It really wasn't a collection of art. It was more of a job from the Bureau of Indian Affairs (BIA) headquarters in Washington D.C., a job that he could not refuse. One, in which, he agreed to paint a portrait of every living Native American medicine man alive, along with the last living Native American medicine woman alive, keeper of the strongest medicine there ever was, is, and will be. But that was only half of his mission, the remaining half would be revealed to him once he finished every portrait. Then, he would be expected to paint one last painting, but not a portrait, that would be hailed as his masterpiece, or so the BIA promised him. But the BIA was known for broken promises, so Feiht didn't keep his hopes up. Even half-blooded immortals didn't trust any agency within the U.S. Government.

There was a stipulation to the deal the BIA made with Feiht though. Once his portraits of all the living medicine people were complete, he would have to wait for the instructions for the last half of his mission, which they claimed would be his masterpiece. So once he finished the last portrait of the last medicine man alive, Feiht returned to his home in Seattle to await the instructions to fulfill the second half of his mission.

Once back in Seattle, Feiht gathered up all of the portraits of his new collection and had them shipped to the BIA headquarters in Washington D.C., as he was obligated to do in his deal with them. He was not attached to any of the portraits, even though he had spent a few years traveling all over America, meeting and getting to know the medicine men he had trapped inside of his paintings. Most were good people, but Feiht could not believe not one of them detected he was half of this world and half not of this world. They were supposed to be medicine men and their medicine should had told them that he was an enemy. He figured his medicine must had been stronger than theirs.

Days passed, then months, all the while Fieht waited for word of the remaining half of his mission, but he didn't receive even a syllable from his new employer. Until one day, he received a letter in the mail announcing that all of his portraits would be part of a new exhibit titled *"The Last of the Medicine Men."* And they would be on display during the summer at the National Museum of the American Indian in Washington D.C.

It was every Native American artist's dream, dead or alive, to have their work displayed at the nation's capitol's museum honoring Native Americans, and Feiht was no exception. He normally didn't like the spotlight, but it was part of the Smithsonian Institution, so it was a big deal.

It took over four hundred years for him to finally feel like he made it as an artist. Feiht Tirips was only one of many personas he had taken since his birth. Every thirty years or so, he would change his name and life story, but he was always a Native American artist, and he had never gotten the recognition he knew he deserved, until now. Feiht was flattered by it, so flattered, that he forgot all about the mission and the remaining half of it, for which he was supposed to be awaiting instructions for.

Instead, Feiht began to make preparations to attend the grand opening of his exhibit at the National Museum of the American Indian in Washington D.C. It was not part of his deal with the BIA to be there for the grand opening, but he wouldn't have missed it for the world. He was almost more excited about it than what the BIA had promised him if he completed the mission for them. The mission had to wait for the exhibit appropriately titled, *"The Last of the Medicine Men."*

The grand opening took place on June 7th and it turned out to be a big event, bigger than Fieht had imagined. He was an instant celebrity. He got to wine and dine with the most sophisticated Native Americans in Indian Country, all who admired his portraits of the medicine men still living, or so they thought. No one suspected a thing, instead, they were enthralled at how real the portraits seemed, some even claiming to see some of the portraits blink or move. Fieht assured them it was just proof of how much he paid attention to detail.

"The Last of the Medicine Men" exhibit at the National Museum of the American Indian was a hit that summer, drawing big crowds every day. The whole allure of being a recognized Native American artist was too much for Feiht to resist, so instead of returning home

after the grand opening, which he had originally planned, he stayed instead. Feiht found a nice townhouse in Washington D.C. to call home.

Every day, Feiht could be found near his exhibit in the background ready to answer any questions an admirer of his work might have. He loved talking about his work and although he wasn't especially proud of his latest collection, because it was part of a very dark mission, it gave him happiness when admirers told him it was the best exhibit they had ever seen. His paintings were respected by all who saw them.

It was a good summer for Feiht Tirips, THE BEST NATIVE AMERICAN ARTIST ALIVE. Then, one day, a stranger came to his exhibit and stood in front of one of his portraits. The stranger was a Native American man dressed in a tailor-made designer suit. It caught Feiht's attention right away because he thought he was the only Native American man who wore tailor-made designer suits. Feiht could also sense that the stranger was dissecting his work, so he approached him. He hoped to make a good impression as an artist who talked to his fans about his work without fear of critique, no ego, or time limits, a fan's dream come true.

"So, what do you think?" Feiht asked the stranger.

"They're all breathtaking, very real-looking," answered John Wayne. It was July 21st and John still had not received the text he had been awaiting to give him instructions on the job he recently accepted. July 23rd was only two days away and it would take a day's drive just to get to THE POW-WOW OF ALL POW-WOWS in Mankato, Minnesota, so time was running out. He knew the text was coming soon to tell him when and where to be to get his last minute instructions in Washington D.C. It wasn't an odd thing, it happened that way sometimes, to protect the financier and himself, leaving him just enough time to do the job and not over-think it. Plus, a set-up could not occur in a short amount of time from either side. A lot of his clients were paranoid, so John wasn't surprised he still hadn't heard anything yet. So he decided to visit the National Museum of the American Indian, like he had always wanted to since it had opened. It was a beautiful museum, adorned with Native American artifacts and collections of Native American art. He was especially impressed with its new exhibit, *"The Last of the Medicine Men."*

"Which one do you like the most?" asked Feiht, drawn to John. There was something about his demeanor that Feiht liked. He wasn't like most Native Americans that walked into his exhibit. No, there was something peculiar about him. Feiht was very intrigued by him.

"They are all impressive pieces of work, but if I had to choose, I'd say the one of the Mescalaro Apache medicine man."

"Yes, that one is of Hangy Bedongah, a very good

piece. He was a fire keeper."

"Wasn't that a young woman's job?"

"No, he wasn't that kind of fire keeper, not a gatherer of wood. He kept fire, the kind of fire with medicine. Sometimes, he'd carry it in a bag and it wouldn't burn the bag, as a matter of fact, it wouldn't burn anything. The strangest fire you could have ever seen. Couldn't paint the fire he kept though, it wouldn't let me, so I just painted him outside of his house. He lived way out in the desert, in the middle of nowhere."

"That's what I liked about it, it had a real desert feel to it. I like the desert. So are you the great Feiht Tirips?" asked John.

"In the flesh. So what tribe are you?" Feiht asked him.

"Seminole."

"From Oklahoma?"

"No, Florida Seminole."

"Ah, the ones that never surrendered. Great people. Did you see my painting of your tribe's medicine man?"

"Yeah, Spade Cypress. It was a good one too. I'm not that familiar with my tribe, though."

"Yeah, me neither. So you visiting?" Feiht asked John, who had to think about his answer before answering.

"I'm here for business actually. I'm John, John

Wayne," John answered, shaking Feiht's hand.

"Wayne? Wait, any relation to Tonto Wayne, THE TOUGHEST NATIVE ALIVE?"

"Yes, he's my dad," John admitted, not proud of it though.

"Really? Wow, I was supposed to paint him for this collection but he refused, said he wasn't a medicine man, but everyone knows he has great medicine. Given to him by Big-Sister herself."

"Where's her portrait?"

"She refused to let me paint her too, and what a shame, because I heard she passed recently."

"Really?" John asked, the news a realization that he might be the last first-born son of his family to have received her blessings and medicine.

"That would make you the last THE TOUGHEST NATIVE ALIVE once your dad goes to the spirit world. With a name like John Wayne, how could you not be his first born? I am honored to meet you, really."

"Likewise, but I have no interest in that title."

"Why not?" Feiht asked, very curious.

"Oh, I wouldn't know where to start. It's a long story."

"Well, the museum is about to close. You care to join me for a drink? I know a good place not too far from here. I would like to hear this long story. Or we could just chat about whatever. Your call."

"Sure," John answered, impressed that THE BEST NATIVE AMERICAN ARTIST ALIVE wanted to have a drink with him. So, together, they left, their egos tucked away in their expensive suits. They became just two Native American men with different medicine about to have drinks and conversations together.

Feiht and John took a cab together to a small bar called "Buffalo Billiards" on 19th Street NW, only a short drive away. It was a small, modest bar, with a Native American ambience. A jukebox blared classic rock songs to filter out the few conversations already taking place inside. They both sat at the bar and ordered beers.

"Hoss suit," complimented Feiht to John.

"Thanks, it's an Armani. That Gucci?" John asked Feiht, who looked a little surprised.

"Yeah, how'd you know?"

"I have one just like it," John answered, and they shared a little laugh together.

"I have to say, you'd make a really cool THE TOUGHEST NATIVE ALIVE. So why not want that title? I'm sure you are just as tough as your dad," Feiht asked, not wasting any time to get to his main question.

"Oh, I'm tougher than him, I'm sure of that. But I'm not much of a pow-wow kind of Native American, you know. And part of having the title of THE TOUGHEST NATIVE ALIVE is that you also have to be the protector of pow-wows. I don't like pow-wows enough to protect them."

"I hear you there, I don't do pow-wows either. I might go to one to get me an Indian taco, but that's it."

"Or a meat pie," added John. They shared another small laugh.

"Damn, I haven't had a meat pie in forever. You're making me hungry for frybread now," laughed Feiht.

"Know of any good Indian taco stands in Washington D.C.? Wouldn't that be something, an Indian taco stand in the nation's capital?" joked John.

"Oh, that would be something else. Can you imagine the President of the United States eating frybread?"

"I bet there hasn't been a president who has ever eaten frybread."

"Very true. They don't know what they're missing," Feiht said, finishing his beer and ordering a shot of Captain Morgan. John finished his beer quickly and ordered a shot of Captain Morgan as well.

While they were waiting on their shots, a text alert came from both of their pockets. For John, it was the sound of a gunshot coming from his cell phone that alerted him. For Feiht, it was the soothing sound of a violin that alerted him. They both pulled out their cell phones and then there was a long silence between them. Neither spoke a word as they read their texts. The serious look on both of their faces gave away just how important the text messages they were reading were. Neither of them even noticed the bartender placing their shots in front of them and neither noticed that they both shot their shots. At the same time, they both finished reading the texts they received. Then, they both picked up where they left off, like everything was normal again.

"Good ole frybread," Feiht finally said.

"Yeah. Can't live with it, can't live without it."

"Ain't that the truth. So you said you were here for business, what kind of business do you do?" Feiht asked John.

"Contract work, grants, with the B.I.A. for various tribes. I'm like the middle man," John answered, not expecting the question.

"Cool," Feiht said, seeing right through John's lie. Feiht knew he needed more alcohol and a better setting to get John to be more honest, so he recommended they go to another bar, a real Native American bar. They both left together, sharing a taxi, to Stan's Restaurant, an old Native American meeting place from the days of the American Indian Movement (AIM). Going old school would get Feiht the answers he sought, plus, Stan's had the best drinks in town. As they settled into a booth with no one close enough to hear their conversation, Feiht asked John, "How long you here?"

"Until tomorrow," answered John, who liked the new scenery and the energy there. He could feel it was a place where great conversations between great Native American warriors had taken place before or maybe he was just that buzzed. Either way, his surroundings felt comfortable. And John was rarely comfortable outside of his home.

"Then you headed back to Florida?"

"Not exactly. This is only one of my stops."

"Humor if you will, but is your next stop Mankato, Minnesota?" Feiht asked, as if he knew something John didn't.

"As a matter of fact, yes, it is. Have you heard about THE POW-WOW OF ALL POW-WOWS?"

"Yeah, and I just received a text telling me that my ride to Mankato is here, and that I will be meeting with him tomorrow at the B. I. A. building at noon," Feiht admitted to his new friend. John could not believe it because his text said almost the same thing. It said he had a meeting at the BIA building at noon, but he knew nothing of giving someone a ride.

"Interesting," was all John could come up with to say.

"Yes, very. It all makes sense now. They don't trust me with your dad, so they brought you in."

"What about my father?"

"I don't know. You tell me. It's obvious we are probably going to Mankato together tomorrow. We might as well catch up on the Intel now. I know your dad is supposed to be the MC at this pow-wow, so that means you're going to be the one who takes him out, not me."

"What makes you think that?" John asked, almost threatened by Feiht, He positioned himself to be ready to pull his gun out. Unbeknownst to him though, Feiht had been drawing a portrait of him on a napkin little by little all night and was one stroke of a gel pen away from capturing John inside of his artwork forever. It became a stand-off and silence fell between them again. It was a loud silence, filled with hard breathing and the careful listening for a small twitch that might provoke survival among them. Finally, it was Feiht who gave in and threw his gel pen down.

"Because they don't think my medicine is strong enough to take your dad out."

"Father."

"Dad, father, same thing."

"No it isn't," John let Feiht know.

"Whatever, point being, my medicine isn't strong enough, but yours apparently is."

"What kind of medicine do you have?"

"Bad medicine, very bad medicine. But I'm trying to use it for good for once, to do the same thing you're trying to do. I want my father off the face of the Earth too. And I am the closest I have ever been to achieving it."

"But I don't have any medicine. I'm just a guy that wants to avenge his mother."

"That's some of the best medicine there is, besides, you have medicine Big-Sister gave you. You were born to kill your father whether you want to accept that or not. Then you will be THE TOUGHEST NATIVE ALIVE whether you want the title or not."

"You're not of this world are you? What are you then?" asked John, positioning himself again for a battle. He felt something very wrong about his new friend all of the sudden.

"See, your medicine works. You know your shit, I'm impressed. I am half of this world though, and half not of this world. My father was an evil being who left my mother in a bad situation. I've never seen him, all I know is that he left me with all these bad gifts I possess, and I hate him for that, among many other reasons," slurred Feiht, as he did the unexpected, he teared up and tried his best not to cry. He was feeling the effects of the alcohol. He wasn't a drinker and normally didn't succumb to the evil spirits hidden in bottles.

"So I take it your talent to paint is somehow part of your bad medicine?" John asked, not threatened by Feiht anymore. His buzz was kicking in and he wanted to be Feiht's listening ear, not his enemy. John wasn't a drinker either.

"Yes, so take a chill pill because if I wanted to, I could have already made you disappear in more ways than one before you drew that thunderstick of yours that wouldn't hurt me anyway. I'm just like you, John, I want my dad gone. I've never wanted to paint anyone more in my life than him, but since he is an evil being, it is always difficult to locate him. The same people who offered you the contract on your dad, offered me one on my dad, but I have to complete two missions for them before, I... yeah. And here we are, we might as well embrace the mission we are obviously both a part of. From the way I see it, it will benefit us... both."

"I normally work alone."

"As do I, but we are both trying to fulfill our obligations at 'The Fucking Pow-wow Of All Fucking Pow-wows,' which I'm sure, they will have protected in every way that they possibly can. What I can't do, I'm sure you can do, and vice-versa, so what do you say? Partners? A fucking warparty?" Feiht asked, with his hand extended out toward John. Buzzingly, John accepted Feiht's hand and gave him a longer than needed handshake. Then, John ordered more shots and they raised their evil spirits in the air.

"Fuck dads," John toasted, clinking his shot glass against Feiht's shot glass.

"Fuck dads," Feiht agreed. They both swallowed their shots of liquor, sealing their deal as partners in crime.

Shot after shot soon followed, until they were both shit-faced. The night spun out of control, even though they both knew they had to be at the BIA building by noon the next day. Once the whirlwind of alcohol stopped between them, they separated as brothers. That night, sleep came easily for them both, but with only a few hours of it available before they both had to awake.

The next day, at 11:45 AM to be exact, Feiht and John crossed paths again, but this time in front of the BIA building, both in expensive sunglasses. They both made it to their meeting with the Acting Director of the BIA at noon. Their second encounter with each other was another friendly one. They shook hands and decided to enter together, sharing small talk the whole way up to the highest floor of the building, both dressed in their finest of suits to impress each other, but both smelling like hell.

Feiht and John arrived at the desk of the secretary, who worked for Andrew Whiteman, the current Acting Director of the BIA His secretary was a blonde Caucasian woman, not what they expected. But it was Washington D.C., so Native American secretaries were probably in short supply. She buzzed them into the office of her boss. They both entered, feeling pretty buzzed still and clueless on the details of their missions.

Once they entered Mr. Whiteman's office, he rose from his desk and went to greet them. He didn't look any more Native American than his secretary. He was a white-haired Caucasian man, average in height and weight, with stern features. He shook both of their hands. His handshake was overly-firm, almost painful to both of them. And he had on an even better suit than either one of them.

"Good to finally meet you both in person. I'm Andrew Whiteman, Acting Director of the Bureau of Indian Affairs," greeted Mr. Whiteman.

"Feiht Tirips," quipped Feiht, massaging his hand.

"Eagle," John said. Feiht was surprised by John's response, but didn't question it.

"Please, take a seat," offered Mr. Whiteman. Feiht and John each sat in one of the Pendleton blanket covered chairs in front of Mr. Whiteman's desk, as he went back behind his luxurious desk and to his black leather swivel chair. Feiht and John were both impressed by the Native American decorations in his office.

"Very nice office," complimented Feiht, who was admiring the five paintings hanging on the wall. All five paintings were of chiefs with whom the BIA had probably broken a treaty or two with.

"Thank you. So, talk about 'Indian Time' huh?" joked Mr. Whiteman, having a laugh at their situation, in which, time was of the essence. "Indian time" was a term used by Native Americans to describe better late than never or now. It was an inside joke among Native Americans.

"Exactly," laughed Feiht. John was playing the

silent game, he didn't like to get too personal with any of his clients and only wanted facts and instructions, no small talk. But something had been bothering him since they talked to the secretary so he had to ask.

"So you are the Acting Director? What happened to the Director before you?" John asked.

"Very good question. It's what brought you two here. I don't see any point in beating around the bush or feeding you bullshit. In the end, you'll know exactly what happened and why it happened. I am the Acting Director because the Director before me lost focus on why he held this position. He was supposed to do just enough to make all tribes believe the B.I.A. was actually doing something for them when it really doesn't. To make a long story short, he started to do more than he should have, so he had to go. The Bureau of Indian Affairs has been a pain in the ass for the U.S. Government since it was formed. Since the day the U.S. Government made that crazy treaty with tribes to take care of their people as long as the grass grows and the rivers flows. Ridiculous treaty if you ask me."

"I concur," agreed Feiht. John didn't respond.

"I know you two have great medicine, as do I, and I know you both have been around things not of this world before, so I don't want to hide my true self from you. If you don't mind, I'd like to take my mask off. Don't be alarmed, but I want to make this deal with you as myself, not as this person I'm pretending to be. Is that okay?" asked Mr. Whiteman.

"Sure," Feiht answered, enjoying how the plot was thickening.

"It's okay with me," John answered, keeping his right hand close to the 9mm Glock he always kept hidden near his crotch.

Without any more being said, Mr. Whiteman began to peel his face off. But he was right, Feiht had many previous run-ins with things not of this world, and John had a few as a child. His father, Tonto, had defeated a few beings not of this world right in front of him, not to mention John's recent run-in with Raven Man. But still, it surprised both of them when Mr. Whiteman finished peeling his face off, along with his hair, to reveal who he really was. Once the mask was removed, it revealed the head of a coyote, the most famous coyote of them all, The Trickster. Feiht and John both looked at each other in disbelief. There wasn't a Native American alive who hadn't heard the stories of The Trickster, who was a legend and part of the oldest legends.

"Thank you, I rarely get a chance to make a deal these days as myself, but it would benefit us all if you knew who you were dealing with. Yes, I'm The Trickster, but what I am about to present to you is no trick to you, just to your targets. It will go down in history as my greatest trick of all, if you two can help me pull it off."

"Now that I see who I am working for, I have more confidence that I will get what I was promised for this, so I definitely will complete my mission," added Feiht, impressed by The Trickster's presence.

"What about you, Eagle?" The Trickster asked, his beady coyote eyes fixed on him.

"Same, as long as I get what I was promised, you have nothing to worry about," answered John, who found it suspicious that he was having a second encounter with The Trickster. He remembered The Trickster being there and drumming during his dance contest against Raven Man.

"Good, real good. So, as you both know, THE POW-WOW OF ALL POW-WOWS starts tomorrow and we have promised to pass out cash vouchers to everyone in attendance of the grand entry as per diem for their travels. So we expect everyone who is going to attend the pow-wow to be at the grand entry. And as you both know, only full-blooded Native Americans can attend it. This was all my idea. The U.S. Government asked me what I could do to help get rid of the Native American bloodline that keeps this department alive, because as you know, America is in a recession, so every little bit helps. So gathering up all of the remaining full-blooded Native Americans in one place for one final massacre was my solution. But it won't be a massacre by armed forces this time, instead, it will be a massacre at the hands of all the evil beings not of this world. A quiet massacre if you will. And once all of the full-bloods are gone, it will fulfill the U.S. Government's main treaty with tribes and they can do away with the B.I.A., tribal governments, and even their casinos. Because if there are only mixed-blooded Native Americans left, it could be argued that all obligations to all tribes have been fulfilled because the race would really be no more. Genius, don't you think?" The Trickster asked, amused by it.

"Genius, indeed," agreed Feiht, who seemed to be a fan of The Trickster.

"So where do we come in on your plan?" John asked, not amused at all.

"Another good question. Which brings me to you, Feiht. You did well, getting rid of all the medicine men for us because it would just take one of them being at THE POW-WOW OF ALL POW-WOWS to mess up my plan. Regardless, there are going to be a whole lot of Native Americans at this event, maybe more than we think the evil beings we have showing up can handle. And we have them all coming; Wendigos, Deer Lady, shapeshifters, wolf people, owl witches, Thunderbird, and so on. So what we thought you could do for us, since your paintings trap people in them, we want to set you up inside the pow-wow arena so that you can paint as much of the crowd as you can and trap them in your painting. I'm sure you could take out a good portion of the crowd, which would be a great help to all of the evil beings I have coming," explained The Trickster.

"I've never painted more than one person, I'm not even sure if that would work," admitted Feiht.

"Oh, it'll work, I've talked it over with some big names that watch over the beings not of this world, and it will work. Your medicine is even more powerful than you know. We've already reserved a good spot for you to paint from," added The Trickster.

"It is an interesting assignment, I must say. If I pull it off, it does have potential to be my masterpiece," admitted Feiht, who was intrigued by the second half of his mission. He had almost forgotten about the other masterpiece he was promised, the portrait of his father.

"Yes, and we've already made preparations for all the lights to be on during the grand entry so that you can see everyone in detail. You just have to paint the fastest you have ever painted."

"So I take it, John's father, I mean, Eagle's father, Tonto, will not be one of my subjects?" Feiht asked, still curious about John's role.

"No, he will not be. That brings me to you, Eagle. As you know, your father has enchantment spells and medicine to protect him from someone like Feiht and his medicine. But it is known to everyone that the only person that can kill THE TOUGHEST NATIVE ALIVE is his first born son. So that's where you come in. Because his main duty is being the protector of pow-wows, we can't chance him being alive once the massacre starts. He could really put a wrench in my plan. You will be the one that takes him out, which I know you want more than anything else, for your mother, so it shouldn't be a problem. His medicine is useless against yours. So not only will you get to achieve one of your goals, you will also get paid well for doing it, and you will win the title of THE TOUGHEST NATIVE ALIVE. It's a win win situation for all of us. I will get what I want, you will get not one masterpiece, but two masterpieces, and you, Eagle, will avenge your mother by killing your father. So do I have a deal, fellows?"

"Deal," Feiht answered right away.

"Deal," John answered, even though it didn't seem right. It wasn't how he always pictured avenging his mother. But it was going to be ironic that his father, THE TOUGHEST NATIVE ALIVE, would fall at THE POW-WOW OF ALL POW-WOWS. It would make it that much sweeter for John. It was an offer he could not refuse. The money was just a bonus. He would have done it for free.

"I may be The Trickster, but I am a being of my word. What was promised to you both will be done. After you complete your missions, come straight back here for your monetary rewards. Oh, and some minor details, Feiht, we have a CDIB card that declares you a full-blood, and you will be riding with John, oh, I mean, Eagle, from this point on. Also, we have reserved a vendor booth at the pow-wow with a good view where Feiht will be pretending to sell art, and Eagle, it will allow you to scope out your best position for the assassination at hand."

"Cool with me," was all Feiht could say.

"Well, what are we waiting for, partner?" John asked Feiht, excited about having a new partner and possibly a new best friend.

The Trickster smiled a smile only a coyote could smile. It was menacing. They all shook hands, then The Trickster poured them all a glass of ancient scotch. They all toasted to THE POW-WOW OF ALL POW-WOWS, which would soon become THE GREATEST MASSACRE EVER, then they finished their glasses of scotch in one drink.

"So, any questions?" The Trickster asked, before they left his office. It was then, that Feiht, who had been to every part of Indian Country and to all the big pow-wows, but realized he had never been to Mankato, Minnesota. So he did have a question, and he decided to ask it.

"Why Mankato, Minnesota?" Feiht asked.

CHAPTER 10

This Is What It Means To Say, "Mankato, Minnesota"

THE STORY OF MANKATO, Minnesota didn't start in the town of Mankato at all. It actually started in the Acton Township of Minnesota on August 17th, 1862. It was a Sunday when four young braves from the Santee Sioux tribe, better known as "Dakota," went on a hunting expedition and came across a hen's nest along a fence line of a white settler's home. The nest was filled with eggs, so one of the braves decided to take the eggs, seeing how they were all starving. Promised food and money from the U.S. Government hadn't reached their people in a long time. But one of them warned the brave taking their next meal that it belonged to a white man and that they should not take the poultry's offspring. The brave taking the eggs teased the other brave, accusing him of being afraid of white people. The teased brave did not like being teased, so to prove his bravery, he declared he would go into the settler's home and kill him to show them how much he was not scared of white people. The determined brave then tested his friends' bravery by asking them to join him in doing so. They all agreed to join him on what had quickly became a warparty. So, they rode into the settler's home and minutes later; three white men, one white woman, and a fifteen-year-old white girl were murdered at the hands of the Dakota braves. Braves became warriors over a nest full of eggs, and it would set off a chain reaction that would be carved into Minnesota's dark history with Indian tribes.

Once what was done was done, the four Dakota braves rode to Chief Shakopee's camp, arriving late at night with their story. Their story created excitement to all who heard it. Eventually, everyone in the camp woke up to hear it and praised what they did. Chief Shakopee took the four Dakota warriors to Chief Little Crow's house, who got up from bed to hear their story. It brought joy to his ears, as it had for every Dakota who had heard it so far. But Chief Little Crow knew that since blood was shed, especially blood belonged to white people, war would be declared. It also meant that the money and food the Dakota were promised, which was supposed to be on its way to them, would definitely be stopped in its tracks. So, they would have to gather food and supplies as soon as possible, through raids and more bloodshed.

A late night meeting was called and the majority of the tribe declared war, chanting "Kill the whites and kill all these cut-hairs who will not join us!" And thus, the Dakota War of 1862, also known as the Sioux Uprising, the Dakota Uprising, the Sioux Outbreak of 1862, the Dakota Conflict, the U.S. Dakota War of 1862, or Little Crow's War, had begun. The first order of business for the Dakota was to attack the Lower Indian Agency near Redwood, Minnesota the following morning. Dakota women made preparations throughout the night, as Dakota warriors cleaned their guns, anticipating the sun rising.

The war had been a long time coming. The four warriors did their people a favor by putting it into action sooner than later. The fuse to the bomb that was August 17th, 1862, was actually lit during 1851 when Dakota chiefs negotiated the 'Treaty of Traverse des Sioux' on July 23rd of that year and the 'Treaty of Mendota' on August 5th of that year. The treaties involved the Dakota giving up over a million acres of land in Minnesota in exchange for food, money, and a reservation 20-miles wide and 150 miles long along the Minnesota River.

As most treaties, the treaties the Dakota made with the U.S. Government were nothing more than tricks in written form. The money promised to the Dakota was stolen by either members of the Bureau of Indian Affairs in Washington D.C., Indian agents in Minnesota, or by white traders who demanded money they claimed was owed to them but was not. The Dakota never saw a dime of the money promised to them. The food promised in the treaties was often sold to settlers for a profit, and the food left over, which was usually spoiled and not fit for a dog to eat, was given to the Dakota.

The situation for the Dakota people only got worse as every day passed. When Minnesota became a state on May 11th, 1858, Chief Little Crow led a small negotiating party of Dakota to Washington D.C. to ask for proper enforcement of the treaties they signed with the U.S. Government. Instead of helping, the U.S. Government did just the opposite and took back the northern half of the reservation they gave to the Dakota, opening the land for settlement. The land was divided into townships, clearing out a lot of forest and prairie land, which interfered with the Dakota's way of life. It was land that they used to hunt, fish, and grow crops.

The treaty violations by the U.S. Government caused increased hunger and hardship among the Dakota. They knew the traders and some corrupt Indian agents were stealing their money, so they demanded that they get the annual payments directly from Indian agent, Thomas J. Galbraith, one of the only Indian agents they trusted. It sent an uproar among the traders in the area. They refused to provide any supplies to the Dakota on credit. It became a bad situation because the Dakota needed supplies but had no money until their payments arrived, which they were promised were on their way.

Two days before the four warriors turned their hunting party into a warparty, two bands of Dakota rode to the Lower Sioux Agency for supplies and were not aware of the situation with the white traders and their payments. They tried to buy supplies on credit but were denied. It resulted in a meeting between Dakota chiefs, Indian agents representing the U.S. Government, and the local traders. The chief representing the Dakota asked Andrew Jackson Myrick, who was representing the local traders, to sell the Dakota food and supplies on credit, knowing their payments were on the way. Andrew Jackson Myrick responded with words he would later eat, literally, "So far as I am concerned, if your people are hungry, let them eat grass or their own dung."

The next day, on August 16th, 1862, $17,000 worth of gold coins reached St. Paul, Minnesota, on its way to Fort Ridgely the next day. It was a small portion of the payment promised to the Dakota for the treaties they signed with the U.S. Government, who hoped it would be enough to cool the situation between the Dakota and the white traders. It was said that the payment did reach Fort Ridgely on August 17th, 1862, but it arrived a few hours late, after the four Dakota warriors had already sealed the fate of their tribe. The payment never reached the Dakota. And hell was to be paid for the delay of that payment.

On August 18th, 1862, Chief Little Crow led a warparty, consisting of numerous bands of Dakota, that attacked the Lower Sioux Agency near Redwood, Minnesota. A massacre occurred, a massacre of white people. The Dakota overtook the Lower Sioux Agency, run by Andrew Jackson Myrick. He was one of the first casualties of the war, found trying to escape through a second floor window of a building at the agency. His mouth was said to be stuffed with grass, as Dakota warriors taunted, "Myrick is eating grass himself."

A lot of Dakota didn't support the war that had been pressured on them until they overtook the Lower Sioux Agency. Then they began to support the war. They got a taste of white people blood and wanted more. Forty-four white soldiers and ten Dakota warriors had been killed during the first battle at the Lower Sioux Agency. During the next few days, two hundred more white people died at the hands of the Dakota, most of them farm families. The Dakota plundered and killed as they pleased, destroying the white towns and settlements that invaded their land, their way of life.

Over two thousand white settlers, mostly women, children, and wounded men, became refugees and fled from the area to Mankato, Minnesota, for protection. Meanwhile, the Dakota continued their massacres, attacking stagecoaches and boats, halting all mail carriers and military personnel as they traveled their routes through the area. There were only a few safe places in the area for white settlers. One was the town of New Ulm, where the surviving citizens had built a barricade to fight off all attacks on the town, even though most of it had been burned to the ground. The next safe place was Fort Ridgely, which had done the same, keeping the Dakota from taking the fort after numerous attempts. A full war was in effect in Minnesota, adding to the stress most politicians in Washington D.C. were already overwhelmed with because of the Civil War. The President of the United States of America, Abraham Lincoln, had a lot on his plate, and the last thing he needed was another war within the country that was already at war.

On September 6th, 1862, almost a month after the Dakota uprising, President Abraham Lincoln formed the Department of the Northwest. He appointed General John Pope, who had just been defeated at Bull Run, to command it with orders to end the violence in Minnesota. General Pope declared, "My purpose will be to exterminate the Dakota, and they will be treated as maniacs and wild beasts." General Pope was assisted in his effort when Minnesota Governor Alexander Ramsey enlisted the help of Colonel Henry Hastings Sibley, Minnesota's previous governor. Together, the general and colonel marched against the Dakota.

Once General Pope reached Minnesota with the U.S. soldiers provided him, he met with the militia Colonel Sibley had gathered. The six week war came to a halt. At the Battle of Wood Lake on September 23, 1862, the Dakota were overwhelmed and defeated by American forces. They surrendered shortly after the battle. It wasn't only American forces that forced the Dakota's surrender, but some of their own tribal members helped the outcome. During the Battle of Wood Lake, Dakotas who were opposed to the war aided in releasing 269 prisoners, a mixture of white people and mixed bloods, to Colonel Sibley. Also, Dakotas at the Upper Sioux Agency threatened to kill any followers of Chief Little Crow who came into their area. So the Dakota warriors involved in the war were trapped. They couldn't go south or north and faced severe food shortages, so they surrendered. The butcher's bill at the end of the war totaled 77 U.S. soldiers killed, around 100 Dakotas, and over 800 white settlers.

On September 28th, 1862, Colonel Henry Sibley appointed a five-member military commission to "try" the Dakota and mixed-blooded Dakota involved in the war for "murder and other outrages" committed against Americans. Although Colonel Sibley didn't have the authority to try anyone, the trials were never disputed, even though a lot of them took less than five minutes to reach a verdict. The Dakota tried were not given any representation by a defense attorney. Most of them weren't even given an explanation of what they were being accused of. The first day of trials, sixteen cases were heard, but by the last day of trials, forty cases were heard, an unheard amount of cases in one day. By the end of it all, 393 Dakota and mixed bloods were tried, but only 323 convicted of "murder and other outrages." 303 of those convicted were sentenced to hang, even though most had surrendered with a promise of safety.

As the 303 Dakota and mixed bloods awaited their fate as prisoners, there were two attempts by vigilante groups to execute them sooner. Both attempts were unsuccessful because U.S. soldiers were protecting the jail where they were incarcerated. The Minnesota governor, Alexander Ramsey, who had made a fortune cheating the Dakota, urged President Lincoln to approve the executions to avoid an uprising of Minnesotans against the Dakota prisoners and vigilante justice. It was an ultimatum from the governor of Minnesota to President Lincoln. The President of the U.S. had to either approve the executions or the citizens of Minnesota would carry the executions out themselves.

General John Pope, with the support of editorial writers, politicians, and the citizens of Minnesota, also urged President Abraham Lincoln to approve a speedy execution of the 303 Dakota. It seemed all agreed with General Pope, except for one man. The Dakota had a friend on their side, Minnesota's Episcopal Bishop, Henry Whipple, who traveled immediately to Washington D.C. to give President Lincoln his own account on the events that took place in Minnesota. President Lincoln was so impressed with Whipple's account of what had happened that President Lincoln decided to review all 303 cases personally, although he was very busy with the Civil War.

President Abraham Lincoln carefully reviewed all of the cases and found lack of evidence in most cases. He found 2 cases involving rape and 37 involving the murder of white settlers. As for the other 265 cases, he decided to commute all of their sentences from death, a highly unpopular political move. But President Lincoln was quoted as saying, "I could not afford to hang men for votes."

Once President Abraham Lincoln had reviewed all cases, he offered a deal to the politicians of Minnesota. If they were willing to agree to shorten the list of Dakota and mixed bloods to be hung down to the 39 he approved of, he in return, would promise to kill or remove every Indian in Minnesota. Also, President Lincoln promised to provide Minnesota with 2 million dollars in federal funds, even though the whole situation had started because the U.S. Government would not pay the Dakota the 1.4 million dollars they owed them for the sale of their land. The politicians of Minnesota happily agreed to

President Lincoln's deal.

On December 6th, 1862, President Abraham Lincoln hand wrote the Order of Execution, which included the complicated names of 39 Dakota and mixed bloods. It notified Colonel Sibley that he should "cause to be executed" 39 of the 303 convicted Dakota Indians. The execution date was set to take place on December 26, 1862, a day after Christmas.

President Abraham Lincoln, well-known for being a human rights activist, ordered the largest mass execution in U.S. history, which was nothing more than murder to obtain Dakota land and please the politicians of Minnesota. Not one white politician, white Indian agent, or white trader was convicted of any crime against the Dakota, even though many had embezzled money, stole supplies, murdered, and committed other crimes against the Dakota.

President Abraham Lincoln was a hero to most Americans, but not to the Indian tribes of the land he was elected President over. They suffered at the hands of most of his policies, including the Homestead Act and the Pacific Railway Act of 1862, which approved the construction of the transcontinental railroad. The new railroad resulted in the loss of land and resources vital to various Indian tribes. There was also the corruption in the Bureau of Indian Affairs, which President Lincoln had acknowledged in two of his Annual Messages to

Congress, but he did nothing about it in his term as President. The stealing of money and supplies that were supposed to go to Indian tribes continued uninterrupted.

Some of President Lincoln's most damaging policies were those that oversaw the placement of Indian tribes on reservations. During the year of 1863, the Lincoln administration was responsible for the removal of the Navajos and Mescalero Apaches from New Mexico to Bosque Redondo, which turned out to be a 450 mile march that 2000 Navajos and Mescalero Apaches did not survive. Numerous massacres also occurred during President Lincoln's term, including the Sand Creek Massacre in Colorado in 1864 that claimed the lives of hundreds of Cheyenne & Arapaho children, women, and elders.

President Abraham Lincoln made revolutionary changes with black/white relations, mainly with the Emancipation Proclamation and the Civil War. But he made no impact on Indian/white relations. If anything, his term made things worse. The Emancipation Proclamation was a big step forward in human rights, but it was written at a time when Indians weren't considered "human" by the United States Government or President Lincoln.

In Mankato, Minnesota, at ten o'clock in the morning on December 26th, 1862, 38 Dakota, one was reprieved before the date of the execution, marched onto a giant square scaffold built to hang thirty-eight people at the same time. It was located in the center of town and was surrounded by an audience of hundreds of white people. Each Dakota took their places assigned to them on the giant scaffold, forming a large square, as the nooses that would take their lives dangled near their heads. Instead of fear or resistance, all Dakota were ready and even seemed anxious to meet the fate bestowed on them. They all sang a Dakota death song together, while caps of white cloth were placed over their heads and the nooses were placed around their necks. The signal to cut the rope that held up the platform was to be three taps of a drum. The first tap silenced the crowd watching, as the Dakota began to make attempts to grasp each other's hands. Then, they all began to shout out their names in their Native language, along with what was interpreted as, "I am here! I am here!" Letting each other know that they were there for their brother. The second tap of the drum set the Dakota off, they began to yell out their warcries and they wardanced atop the gallows, as if the third tap were their enemy. Then, their enemy came, in the form of a short and loud tap of a drum. An axe cut through the rope holding the platform up, and 38 Dakota fell to their deaths together. One rope broke though, leaving a Dakota on the ground thinking he had cheated death, until another noose was placed around his neck and he was lifted up into the air by his neck until he joined his brothers in death. Some said it was the most gruesome sight they had ever seen, 38 Dakota hanging lifeless near the bank of the Minnesota River. The sky was clear and blue that day, even though it was late December, so at least, it was a good day to die.

A telegraph was sent to President Abraham Lincoln on December 27th, 1862 which read, *"I have the honor to inform you that the thirty-eight Indians and half-breeds ordered by you for execution were hung yesterday at Mankato at 10 am. Everything went off quietly and the other prisoners are well secured. Respectfully, H.H. Sibley, Brigadier General."*

The travesty of the 38 Dakota and mixed bloods didn't end with their public execution. Before they were taken to be buried, an unknown person, calling himself "Dr. Sheardown," cut pieces of skin from some of the dead Dakota and mixed bloods, which he placed in small boxes and later sold as souvenirs in Mankato. The bodies of the hung were then buried in a mass grave just outside of town. But later that night, the grave was reopened, and the bodies of the executed were given to a long line of doctors for cadavers for anatomical study, a common practice at the time. One doctor, William Worrall Mayo, received the body of a Dakota named "Cut Nose." Mayo dissected the body of Cut Nose with his medical colleagues. Then, he cleaned and varnished Cut Nose's skeleton, using it to teach lessons in Osteology to his students, including his son. Cut Nose's skeleton remained with the Mayo family until the late 20th century, when the Native American Graves Protection and Repatriation Act forced the Mayo clinic to return Cut Nose's skeleton to the Dakota for proper reburial.

After the mass execution, the remaining 265 Dakota and mixed blooded prisoners were held in a concentration camp through the harsh winter. The following spring, they were all placed unto steamboats and transported to Camp McClellan in Davenport, Iowa, where they remained for three years. By the time they were to be released from Camp McClellan, one-third of the Dakota and mixed blooded prisoners had died in the concentration camps they were held prisoners in. Those who didn't die were eventually pardoned and sent to join their families in Nebraska, since all Indians had been forced out of Minnesota. In April of 1863, the U.S. Congress abolished their reservation in Minnesota and declared all U.S. treaties with the Dakota void. Then, all Indians within the state of Minnesota were forced to leave the state, including the Winnebago tribe, who had nothing to do with the Dakota War of 1862. A bounty of $25 per scalp was offered by the U.S. Government for any Indian found within the borders of the state of Minnesota.

After the Dakota surrendered to the U.S. Army,

Chief Little Crow, the leader of the revolt, was not among the Dakota prisoners. He escaped to Canada with a large warparty of Dakota. They hid out there until the next summer, then decided to return to Minnesota with his teenaged son for a horse-stealing raid. On July 3rd, 1863, the father and son pair decided to stop and gather raspberries near Hutchinson, Minnesota. The raspberries were on the land of a white settler named Nathan Lamson, who saw them on his land. Lamson shot Chief Little Crow, killing him, and took his son prisoner. At first, Lamson thought he just killed a trespasser, but it was soon discovered that he had killed Chief Little Crow, and he received a $500 reward from the state. Chief Little Crow's son was taken into custody, tried, and sentenced to death, but later his sentence was reduced to a prison term. Chief Little Crow's fate became that of the 38 Dakota hung. His skull and scalp were saved and put on display in St. Paul, Minnesota, where they remained until 1971 when they were returned to Chief Little Crow's grandson for proper reburial.

Chief Little Crow and his Dakota followers lost The Dakota War of 1862, but the U.S. Government and Sioux conflict did not end there. It would go on for decades. The conflict finally came to an end on December 29, 1890, when the 7th Cavalry/Indian killers did just what they were created to do. The 7th Cavalry/Indian killers massacred 150 innocent Sioux men, women, and children at Wounded Knee, ending the Sioux resistance for good.

The conflict between the U.S. Government and Sioux resulted in some of the most gruesome massacres committed by the U.S. Army and Indian tribes, along with the largest mass execution in U.S. history. But 38 Dakota hung at the same time was not the only record held by Indian tribes in U.S. execution history. Ninety-six years before the mass execution in Mankato, Minnesota, on December 20th, 1786, the youngest person ever to be hung by the U.S. Government was a mixed-blooded girl named Hannah Ocuish, who was only twelve-years-old at the time of her execution.

Indian tribes and the nooses of the U.S. Government were once familiar with each other, a part of U.S. history hidden by U.S. history books, but what was, happened regardless of what U.S. history books hide.

And this is what it means to say, "Mankato, Minnesota."

CHAPTER ELEVEN

The Most Amazing Grand Entry Ever

"I DON'T KNOW ABOUT YA'LL, but I'm an old school Native, I don't know much about today's technology. Whatever happened to Native Americans communicating through smoke signals? Now we have these things called 'cell phones,' the modern smoke signal. And it wouldn't be bad, but a whole new language emerged from cell phones through texting. Texting! I didn't know about this whole new cell phone language at first, a whole language of acronyms mind you. I use to text a friend of mine to try out some jokes on him, and he would always text me back, 'lol.' He was from the Alabama-Coushatta Tribe down in Texas, so I thought 'lol' was an Alabama-Coushatta word for funny or good. Then, sometimes he would text back, 'lmao,' and I thought that was the Alabama-Coushatta word for really funny. But it wasn't until one time when he texted me, 'hmu,' after I told him I was coming to his tribal pow-wow. I was like, 'hmu?' I pronounced it out loud. I could not for the death of me figure out what it could've meant in Alabama-Coushatta, since I just told him I was going to be at his pow-wow. So I texted him, 'hmu?' And he texted back, 'hit me up.' It was then that I realized 'lol' and 'lmao' meant something in English, not Alabama-Coushatta. Gah!" joked Tonto Wayne, who was the MC at THE POW-WOW OF ALL POW-WOWS in Mankato, Minnesota. Laughter filled the colossal tent. July 23rd had finally arrived, and he stood in the middle of a crowd of 144,000 full-blooded Native Americans inside THE BIGGEST TIPI EVER BUILT that harbored THE POW-WOW OF ALL POW-WOWS. "This is an epic event for us all to be a part of, the biggest pow-wow ever held, with the best of the best in attendance. The 49ers are here! THE BADDEST DRUM GROUP ALIVE! Coming out of retirement! I also heard Wanbli White-Raven is here, THE WORLD'S GREATEST FANCY DANCER EVER! He has come out of retirement too! The best fancy shawl dancer to grace a pow-wow circle, Sue Forty-Bulls, is here as well! And if that isn't enough, I stopped by Feiht Tirips' booth earlier and THE BEST NATIVE AMERICAN ARTIST ALIVE is not only selling some of his hoss work here, but he is doing a live painting of the grand entry!"

The crowd cheered like a pow-wow crowd never cheered before. Tonto stopped talking for a few moments to soak in all of their energy. It was beyond anything he had ever experienced at a pow-wow. The energy that filled THE BIGGEST TIPI EVER BUILT was overwhelming. It almost brought tears to his eyes, but he managed to keep his composure. He continued his introduction that would lead to the grand entry of THE POW-WOW OF ALL POW-WOWS. He had thirty minutes to fill before 7:00 pm when the grand entry was to start.

"And like all pow-wows I oversee, I have to bless it with a dance. And I was given a thousand dollars to give to anyone who guesses what traditional dance I bless THE POW-WOW OF ALL POW-WOWS with. So are you ready? I said, are you ready?!?!" Tonto asked the audience. "Okay, The 49ers, give me a beat!"

The 49ers; Big Mac, Chief X, Snagging-Eyes, Santa Hoss, and their drum, Geronimo, began to drum and sing a 49 song. It was the song, "Indian Girls." The audience cheered even louder than before and began to sing along with The 49ers. The harmonic roar coming from inside of the colossal tent would have scared thunder. Tonto began to do a comical dance, a parody of many traditional dances and modern club dances, ending it with dropping-it-like-it's-hot. He squatted down and moved his booty in ways a Native American man should not move his booty. The crowd laughed and cheered him on. Once The 49ers ended the song, Tonto went to the crowd with his microphone to find someone that could guess what dance he was doing. Tonto went through five audience members, who all guessed wrong. He realized no one would guess it right, so he went back to the table he was seated at to share the answer.

"Okay, that was sad. We don't have all night to find someone who knows what dance I blessed this pow-wow with, so I'm just going to tell you. It was the raindance! The raindance!" he admitted. "And know this, my raindance always works, so expect rain soon!"

The audience laughed, then murmurs were heard, traveling through the audience like a wild fire. All 144,000 full-blooded Native Americans in attendance had heard the same rumor, that travel per-diems were going to be a surprise for the Native Americans attending the grand entry of THE POW-WOW OF ALL POW-WOWS. The rumor was cash would fall from the ceiling of THE BIGGEST TIPI EVER BUILT, like a green rain. Or, at least, that was just what they all heard. So all who planned to attend the pow-wow were not going to miss the grand entry and the chance to get their traveling expenses paid back to them. They were all there, all who would be there for the weekend.

But most of the 144,000 full-blooded Native Americans there would not have missed the grand entry anyway. It was the best part of any pow-wow. During grand entry, every traditional dancer at the pow-wow, both male and female, all danced their way into the pow-wow circle, as all of the drum groups drummed and sang traditional songs. Every color fathomable blended together and brought the the pow-wow circle to life in a way that was awe-inspiring. Words could not do a grand entry justice, nor could pictures. It had to be seen to be believed. And the grand entry to THE POW-WOW OF ALL POW-WOWS would be a one-of-a-kind event. The thousands of colors, the hundreds of dance moves, and the powerful traditional songs, all in unison would be a sight to behold!

>→ >→ ←< ←<

Feiht Tirips was even overwhelmed by the number of subjects he agreed to paint. Intertwined with the audience, there were at least five thousand traditional dancers prepping to dance their way into the pow-wow circle. As much as he was enthralled by the beauty of all the dancers, it wasn't the dancers he was interested in painting. He was there to paint the audience. Their colors were just as in abundance as the dancers though. It took a while for Feiht and his assistant, Eagle, to find the best vantage point for him to paint the audience from. Eagle carried Feiht's bags of paint supplies and his own bag. His bag contained his favorite high-powered rifle, which he named "Treaty Enforcer," that had to be put together, once he found a safe place to do so. But the place Feiht decided to paint from was not ideal for what Eagle was there for. He would not budge though, and insisted that it was where they would do their bad deeds from. Eagle helped him set up his easel, canvas, and paints for his masterpiece to come, but he didn't dare open his own bag and set up his own masterpiece.

Eagle would have to assemble his masterpiece somewhere else. There were too many people around. Feiht really didn't care about Eagle's ordeal because he was too busy trying to complete the second part of his mission. So Eagle left him with no argument, taking his bag with him. He roamed around inside the colossal tent, until he noticed a scaffold at the top of one of the beams holding the tent up. He climbed the beam with his bag and made it to the scaffold undetected. It was dark up there, so he was able to put Treaty Enforcer together discreetly. It was the perfect vantage point for him, enabling a clear shot at the MC's table at the edge of the pow-wow circle far beneath him where Tonto was seated. Once he put Treaty Enforcer together and locked his special bullet named "Mom" into the chamber, he began his wait. The banter of 144,000 Native Americans was loud, thunderous, but he could still hear something unusual, a sound that should not have been in attendance. Sometimes it sounded like glass breaking, sometimes like rocks hitting a drum. It took Eagle awhile to figure it out, but he realized it was coming from outside. People were throwing bottles and rocks at THE BIGGEST TIPI EVER BUILT outside, and they were hitting the colossal tent just outside from where Eagle had stationed himself. Something chaotic was going on outside, but he had more important matters at hand to worry about.

>→ >→   ←< ←<

Outside of the colossal tent that was home of THE POW-WOW OF ALL POW-WOWS, the protest by mixed-blooded Native Americans was reaching a boiling point. Security around the colossal tent was thick though. Security guards were almost elbow-to-elbow to each other, surrounding the colossal tent. No one was entering THE POW-WOW OF ALL POW-WOWS who wasn't allowed inside. And the full-blooded Native Americans who were being allowed inside had formed a long line to get in, which was also protected by a line of security guards on each side. Mixed-bloods were not happy at all by the prejudice being displayed against them. It had gotten to the point that full-bloods had to be protected.

By the time Tonto Wayne's jokes could be heard coming from inside the colossal tent, the line of full-bloods entering THE POW-WOW OF ALL POW-WOWS wasn't that long anymore. It was only a few blocks, compared to the miles it had been earlier. Wanbli White-

Raven and his mother were among the last waiting to get inside the colossal tent. THE WORLD'S GREATEST FANCY DANCER EVER was ready to win his title back and impress a girl he had just met in doing so. While they were in line though, Wanbli noticed Polacca walking nearby, like she was lost. Wanbli left his mother without a movement said and went to Polacca, who was happy to see him.

Wanbli had a notebook and pen with him this time and wrote down what he wanted to say to her, instead of dancing it. The notebook and pen also gave her a chance to write what she wanted to say without speaking ghosts of butterflies in doing so. It was perfect for both of them. Wanbli went first.

'Hello again. Glad to see you. I want to introduce you to my mom,' Wanbli wrote, handing the notebook and pen to Polacca.

'Glad to see you again too. Okay,' Polacca wrote back. Then, Wanbli led her to his mother, who was still in the short line into the pow-wow. Wanbli took the notebook and pen from Polacca and began to write.

'This is Polacca, the girl I told you about,' Wanbli wrote to his mother. His mother, Jean, smiled at Polacca.

"Nice to meet you. So, my son tells me you have a gift and don't speak either. I like that, I understand it more than you know," Jean said to a quiet Polacca.

Polacca grabbed the notebook and pen from

Wanbli anxiously. She began to write.

'Nice to meet you, too. And, yes, I do, and I'm here to find out what my gift means. I was told by Big-Sister to come here and speak with Tonto Wayne,' Polacca wrote as fast as she could.

"Tonto Wayne? The MC? Could be a hard feat to get close to him, but I've always said, nothing's impossible. Where there's a will, there's a way. Wanbli tells me you're here alone. Come on, get in line with us. You can sit by me while Wanbli dances. And we can figure out how you can get close enough to Tonto to ask him what you need to ask him," offered Jean.

Without another word written, Polacca accepted Jean's offer. Wanbli smiled ear from ear. He even danced some to express his happiness. He was definitely going to win his title back. No ifs, ands, or buts about it now.

But as Jean, Wanbli, and Polacca were all waiting in line to get inside THE POW-WOW OF ALL POW-WOWS, they were approached by protestors of the pow-wow, mixed-bloods, two of them. Polacca recognized one of them as Little-Red-Man, whom she met at Big-Sister's house before. The other protestor she did not recognize, but he seemed to only be leading the blind Little-Red-Man around.

"This pow-wow is an abomination! I am Little-Red-Man, son of Big-Sister, the last medicine woman, keeper of the strongest medicine there ever was, is, and will be! If I cannot enter this pow-wow, then no one should be allowed to enter! I am full-blooded Native American in spirit! And in heart! I am Little-Red-Man!" shouted Little-Red-Man.

Polacca left the line to talk to Little-Red-Man. It surprised Wanbli and his mother, who hadn't paid too much mind to the mixed-blooded protestors

"I am Polacca Nova. I came to Big-Sister not too long ago. I don't know if you remember me or not," Polacca started to explain to Little-Red-Man, as ghosts of butterflies fluttered from her mouth.

"Yes, I remember you. Butterfly ghost girl, right?" Little-Red-Man asked. Big-Sister had explained her unusual gift to him.

"Yeah, that's me. Is Big-Sister here?"

"Yes, I brought my mother here, and she is inside with the rest of the full-bloods. But I regret to inform you that she went to the spirit world before we came to be here."

"What do you mean?"

"She died, but her dying wish was for me to bring her body here, and so I did. She's inside, in her coffin, but they wouldn't let me in, that's why I'm out here."

"So she's dead, but her body is inside the pow-wow?" asked Polacca, but before Little-Red-Man could answer, a security guard came between them, shoving Little-Red-Man and his protestor friend away from them.

Little-Red-Man's protestor friend had gotten too close to the main entrance of THE POW-WOW OF ALL POW-WOWS and made it too obvious he was casing it.

Little-Red-Man and his protestor friend left quietly. They went back to their camp, where a bus some hippies had driven to the pow-wow was parked. It was an older school bus, painted blinding-orange with black stripes, one black stripe containing the words, "Shamayim Public Schools" in it. Various protestors were working on the bus, placing a battle ram on its front bumper. Little-Red-Man's friend announced that he had observed the entrance to the colossal tent and that it would be defenseless against the battle ram they were building once the line of full-bloods were all inside. The protestors and hippies cheered, as Little-Red-Man hoped it would be the help he needed to join his mother inside THE POW-WOW OF ALL POW-WOWS.

⤳ ⤳   ⤺ ⤺

The Good sat on Big-Sister's casket, not out of disrespect, but because there was nowhere else to sit. He did manage to pull off placing the casket on the outer edge of the pow-wow circle, near where all of the action would soon take place. THE POW-WOW OF ALL POW-WOWS was close to capacity. Every seat was filled or spoken for. It was past the time grand entry was supposed to start and it didn't look like it was going to start anytime soon either, full-bloods were still entering from outside. The Good wanted nothing more than the grand entry to start and be over with so he could return the casket containing Big-Sister to Little-Red-Man, honoring the promise he had made to the red-headed, blind boy. Unexpected, Mother Nature beckoned, The Good had to piss. He could not hold it through the grand entry, so he stopped another security guard walking by and got him to watch the casket as he went outside to piss.

The Good had to go badly, too, so badly, he would've pissed under the colossal bleachers built for the colossal tent, but every section of bleachers had been boarded up so that no one could go under them. It was quite odd, but The Good didn't have time to think about it. He ran out of the back entrance he had just been guarding, along with The Bad and The Ugly, where there were no protestors, just other security guards and other pow-wow personnel. The Good found the first porta-potty that wasn't occupied and relieved himself.

Once done, The Good emerged from the porta-potty a new man. But he was met with something unexpected. A frightened ten-year-old Native American girl ran up to him. She was sweaty and breathing like she had just ran a marathon. The Good asked her what was wrong, but she was too out of breath to talk, mumbling words that didn't make sense. Then, she pointed toward a field nearby. The Good looked at where she was pointing and could see what looked to be hundreds of people walking through a field nearby. They were coming from the direction of Mankato.

"Okay, guys, we have protestors headed our way!" alerted The Good, who was immediately joined by The Bad and The Ugly. A few other security guards lined up and prepared for the possible riot at hand. They were outnumbered, but they had a job they were getting paid good money to do, so they weren't letting anyone through the back entrance of THE POW-WOW OF ALL POW-WOWS.

"They're... They're not protestors... They're zombies..." Deliah, the little girl who ran up to The Good, finally said after catching her breath.

"Zombies?" questioned The Good.

"Zombies?" The Bad laughed.

"Where do you find these kids?" The Ugly added, along with more laughter.

"There's no such thing as zombies. Are you a full-blood?" The Good asked Deliah.

"Yes, full-blooded Cree," Deliah answered.

"Get inside then. We'll take it from here. This may get messy," The Good ordered Deliah, who rushed into the colossal tent, feeling as if she made it to the safety of the sea of red people inside. Meanwhile, The Good, The Bad, The Ugly, and about ten other security guards lined up and prepared for the hundreds of protestors headed their way. The protestors were in no hurry though, walking slowly toward the back entrance of colossal tent.

↦ ↦ ↤ ↤

    Not even five minutes after Polacca ran into Little-Red-Man, she entered THE BIGGEST TIPI EVER BUILT with Wanbli and his mother. Her breath was taken away at the size of it and the number of full-blooded Native Americans who were there. THE POW-WOW OF ALL POW-WOWS was even more spectacular than Polacca could have imagined it. It was her first pow-wow, and she wondered if they were all so magnificent. But from the expressions on Wanbli and his mother's faces, who were both just as blown away as Polacca was, she figured it was unlike any other pow-wow ever. It was like the Super Bowl, like a NBA play-off basketball game, like Woodstock. The number of people there was inconceivable. It was hard to walk through, but Wanbli led his mother and Polacca to the pow-wow circle. Their seats were located just outside of the pow-wow circle. They had only two reserved seats, but Wanbli was gentleman enough to offer his seat to Polacca, as he took a seat on the ground next to her, awaiting the grand entry. His mother was even more proud of her son. She had raised him right. Even after all the bad things she had put him through, he was still a gentleman. Not too long after they took a seat, Tonto walked to the center of the circle.

"That's him, Tonto Wayne," Jean told Polacca.

"I really need to talk to him. It's important," Polacca said as deep-red butterfly ghosts flew from her mouth. The sight of them amazed Wanbli's mother.

"Wow! That is a very unique gift. I'll help you. I'll act like I need to tell him something about how Wanbli wants to be introduced," offered Jean, which brought an ear-to-ear smile to both Polacca and Wanbli's face. Wanbli was no longer mad at his mother, in fact, he was ready to make both of the women in his life proud.

↣ ↣   ↢ ↢

"I have just received word that everyone is in, all 144,000 of us full-bloods, wee-cha!!!" announced Tonto, as the crowd roared. "Talk about Indian time, though. Man, we can't ever start anything on time or be on time. I had to set my watch an hour ahead this morning, just so I'd only be ten minutes late. Gah!" joked Tonto, as the crowd laughed. "Okay, we're about to get underway here, finally, but before we do, I want to share something with all of you, all my brothers and sisters here tonight. This may be my last gig, yes, sad, I know. But it's for a good reason, you see. I'm going to open up my own business, yes, I'm going corporate. I'm doing this because I've been around Native Americans so long that I know what you all need and I hate to say it, but I'm going to capitalize on it. So ya'll are the first to know that I will be opening up a chain of reservation butt implant surgery centers. You know you all need them," joked Tonto, as the crowd laughed loud like thunder. It was what he liked, but even he had never experienced such deafening laughter from so many Native Americans. It was the highlight of his career as pow-wow MC. "That saying about Native Americans being 'all gut and no butt' will be a thing of the past! I'll even offer a special, buy one butt cheek, and get the second butt cheek half price!" joked Tonto, who was on a roll. The crowd laughed more. "Could you imagine that though? Native Americans with buns, good buns too, 'cause I'll only sell the best. Maybe they'll even start putting Native American girls in those hip-hop music videos, ayyyeee!!! That's if they can find a babysitter though, and grandma won't hear of it, unless they give her some of that booty money for the casino. Gah!!! Nah, but all jokes aside, let's get THE POW-WOW OF ALL POW-WOWS started! And I am honored to announce that The 49ers will start grand entry, after a prayer from Chief Moses Blue-And-Orange-Thunder from the Seneca tribe of New York!" announced Tonto, leaving the pow-wow circle to a table placed on the edge of it.

↣ ↣ ↢ ↢

Chief Moses Blue-And-Orange-Thunder started

his prayer, as The 49ers prepared for their first grand entry song together at a pow-wow in a very long time. And what a pow-wow for them to come out of retirement. They all gazed up and around at the crowd in attendance. It was unlike anything any of them had ever seen. It was THE POW-WOW OF ALL POW-WOWS! It was the perfect pow-wow to be the last pow-wow Santa Hoss and their drum, Geronimo, would be a part of. Big Mac, Chief X, and Snagging-Eyes were even a little jealous because they knew they would never have such a grand departure to the spirit world.

But as The 49ers sat and waited to do what they were all born to do, their beautiful wives watched from nearby. They were their biggest fans, their biggest groupies, who were all reminded of why they put up their gambling husbands. Along with the most beautiful, they were also the most proud wives there. The prayer ended.

"Okay, Geronimo. You've proved you still have your medicine, and we all thank you," thanked Big Mac.

"Still as strong as ever too," added Chief X.

"Helluv stronger," Snagging-Eyes added.

"Of course, he's Geronimo, Apache renegade. Are you ready, old friend?" Santa Hoss asked the fifth member of The 49ers.

"We got this," Chief X assured his drum group.

"Damn right, we do," Snagging-Eyes agreed.

"For Santa Hoss!" declared Big Mac.

"For Santa Hoss!" declared Snagging-Eyes.

"For Philb!" declared Chief X.

"For Geronimo!" declared Santa Hoss.

The 49ers raised their drumsticks high into the air in unison, then they all forced their drumsticks unto Geronimo at the same time and THE POW-WOW OF ALL POW-WOWS started. The first beat of Geronimo was like a gunshot going off to start a race.

The 49ers only drummed and sang a few verses of the song they chose. Then, the other four dozen drum groups in attendance, who were all there for the chance to win second or third place in the traditional drum group category, joined in with them. It was like an atom bomb had went off, but in song. The flag bearers were the first to enter the pow-wow circle, as tradition dictated. Native American veterans from various wars led all grand entries of all pow-wows, holding the American flag, the Armed Forces flags, the P.O.W. flag, the M.I.A. flag, and various tribal flags.

The flag bearers of THE POW-WOW OF ALL POW-WOWS did what had never been done before, they led over five-thousand traditional Native American dancers into the pow-wow circle, the most ever gracing one circle. They all danced their traditional dances, with barely even enough room to dance, but they danced. Every color there ever was poured into the pow-wow circle. The crowd stood, every full-blooded Native American there, and they clapped, warcried, and lulued. It was beyond words, an event everyone knew would make history, and they were all proud to be a part of it. Most of the audience had never felt so Native American in their lives. Some even cried at the sight of the spectacle that was the grand entry. But as beautiful as it was, as breathtaking as it was, every full-blood there glanced at the ceiling of THE BIGGEST TIPI EVER BUILT ever now and then, wondering when their travel per-diems, which most hoped would come in the form of cash, would fall on them like a green rain.

>→ >→   ←< ←<

Polacca, who had never been to a pow-wow, was mesmerized by the grand entry. She didn't know Native Americans danced and danced in a way like no other race or culture. From the DVDs her mother let her see, she knew of dance, but she did not know that her race had specific kinds of dances, with specific kinds of dance regalia. She was beside herself, fighting to keep her mouth close, because her jaw wanted to drop open. It was not a time for ghosts. The pow-wow circle was so big, about one-mile in circumference, that she couldn't see the other side of it from where Wanbli's mother and she sat.

The dancers and colors and songs almost made

Polacca forget why she was there. She saw more fancy dancers than she could count, all more extraordinary than the previous, so if Wanbli was THE WORLD'S GREATEST FANCY DANCER EVER then he had to be remarkable. He was somewhere in the crowd of dancers and Polacca had not seen him since he danced away from his mother and her. There were so many different kinds of other dancers there too. The Native American women who were competing in the fancy shawl dance category captivated her, along with the women competing in the buckskin category, and the jingle dress category. She was almost mad that she had never been taught to dance the dances of her people. She also got to see the different male Native American dancers there. The gourd dancers, grass dancers, Northern traditional dancers, Southern traditional dancers, straight dancers, buffalo dancers, eagle dancers, chicken dancers, and the crowd-pleasing hoop dancers all danced past her. It was by far better than any DVD she had ever seen.

↣ ↣   ↢ ↢

Outside of THE POW-WOW OF ALL POW-WOWS, the protest led by mixed-blooded Native Americans was becoming a time bomb ready to go off at any moment. Little-Red-Man volunteered to be the trigger, not for the cause, but to be at his mother's side for the grand entry now taking place. The drumming and singing inside the colossal tent could be heard for miles and miles away. The battle ram built in front of the bus was finished. The mixed-blooded protestors and hippies all agreed it was a good idea for Little-Red-Man to be the one who drove the bus into the main entrance of THE POW-WOW OF ALL POW-WOWS. Little-Red-Man could use his blindness as a defense if prosecuted for the crime. It was a perfect plan, so as many mixed-bloods that could fit into the bus piled into it, while Little-Red-Man prepared to drive them to justice and equal rights.

Little-Red-Man was so happy that he was about to do what his mother and he planned for months, attend THE POW-WOW OF ALL POW-WOWS together. Little-Red-Man's protestor friend gave him instructions on how to start the bus, put it in drive, and press on the gas. The bus wasn't too far from the main entrance, and it was a straight shot there, so not even a blind boy could miss it.

Little-Red-Man started the bus, put it in drive, and pressed down on the gas slowly, holding the steering wheel steady. Then, he pressed the gas pedal all of the way down and the bus took off faster than any of the protestors thought it could go. The bus reached a good speed, in a matter of seconds, to a point it would not be able to be stopped by anything. The mixed-blooded protestors gave out their warcries and lulus. Victory was at hand.

But then something unexpected happened, just as the bus reached the main entrance into THE POW-WOW OF ALL POW-WOWS. The bus crashed into the opening of the colossal tent that was the main entrance, like it hit a solid brick wall. It was a horrific crash, mangling the bus in ways that made it impossible for anyone inside to have survived the crash. And no one did survive it. Buckets of blood splattered out from the bus in all directions as it hit what seemed to be an invisible wall, painting the main entrance of THE BIGGEST TIPI EVER BUILT red with the blood of mixed-bloods and Little-Red-Man.

The accident was unbelievable to all who saw it because there was nothing at the main entrance that could have stopped the bus like it had been stopped in its tracks. Even the full-blooded Native American security guards, who were just a few feet inside the main entrance when the crash happened, could not believe what had just happened. And it became even stranger when the full-blooded security guards tried to leave the main entrance to assist with the accident, but were thrown back unto the ground when they tried to exit. There was an invisible force field protecting the main entrance now. No one could get in or out of THE POW-WOW OF ALL POW-WOWS. Little-Red-Man got his wish to be with his mother again, but it wasn't going to happen inside THE POW-WOW OF ALL POW-WOWS, like they had planned. Instead, they would cross paths again in the spirit world.

>→ >→   ←< ←<

At the back entrance of THE POW-WOW OF ALL POW-WOWS, the Wendigos had reached the line of security guards awaiting them. The security guards were caught off guard, expecting protestors, but being met with tall, bony, four-armed, four-legged creatures, all with black eyes that had small tentacles protruding from them. Their appetite for human flesh was immediately satisfied when they began to devour the security guards, who were not equipped with guns, just nightsticks and pepper spray. They were defenseless against the Wendigos.

The Good managed to break free from a Wendigo trying to devour him, and he ran to the back entrance, but was stopped in his tracks by an invisible force field. The Good fell backwards to the ground, not understanding what he ran into. It was then that he looked behind him and up, where The Bad and The Ugly stood above him. Their eyes were the blackest of blacks, with tentacle-like things protruding from them. They were not themselves anymore. They began to devour The Good. They were Wendigo and part of the growing cannibalistic tribe. Soon, The Good would become one of them, and they would all make their way into THE POW-

WOW OF ALL POW-WOWS, where a feast of full-blooded Native Americans awaited their appetite.

↣ ↣   ↢ ↢

The most amazing grand entry ever was in full force. The thousands of traditional dancers danced to the thunderous songs drummed and sung by all the drum groups there, who all sang and drummed in unison. The Native American spirit was strong, maybe the strongest it had been in centuries. The crowd cheered, their warcries, their lulus, rivaled the drumming, singing, and sound of the dancers dancing.

Feiht Tirips was seated comfortably in front of his canvas, immortalizing the event. He had finished the background of the painting he was painting and was ready to start painting the audience. From his vantage point, he would be able to paint a little over half of the 144,000 full-blooded Native Americans in attendance. But he knew he wouldn't have time to paint the 75,000 full-blooded Native Americans he could see because his portrait of THE POW-WOW OF ALL POW-WOWS would be cut short when Eagle assassinated his father, Tonto. So, Feiht knew he had to paint as fast as he had ever painted in his immortal life to rid the pow-wow of as many full-bloods as he could. Eagle's bullet named "Mom" was expected to start what would become known as THE GREATEST MASSACRE EVER. But the sound of the bullet being fired would be hidden by a coyote howl, coming from The Trickster himself. How The Trickster would be in attendance in his true appearance to howl baffled Eagle and Feiht, but they didn't care enough to question it. The howl would also act as the signal for someone to release piles and piles of cash from the ceiling of the colossal tent. Green rain would pour on all of the full-bloods in attendance. The shower of cash would provide Eagle and Feiht with cover, so they could both escape undetected, or so they hoped.

 Eagle was no longer sitting patiently. He was in assassination mode. Treaty Enforcer in his arms, pointed down at the grand entry. He stared through the scope of Treaty Enforcer, perfecting his aim at his target, his father, Tonto, who had no idea he was breathing his last breaths. His mission required him to take out his target before the grand entry was over. Normally, Eagle would have taken out his target right away, but he had Feiht to worry about and his mission. He decided to give Feiht enough time to complete the second half of his mission. He pointed his scope at Feiht every now and then, who was hard at work painting at a ridiculous speed.

 Eagle could not have dreamed of a better place to avenge his mother or for his father to fall. The grand entry was unlike anything he'd had ever seen. It did live up to its name. It was THE POW-WOW OF ALL POW-WOWS! He was honored to be there and almost disappointed that he would be the one to turn it into chaos. Then, as he scanned the crowd below him through his scope, he began to see full-blooded Native Americans disappear into thin air. One by one, full-bloods disappeared, until a whole section of the colossal bleachers was empty. No one noticed right away because everyone was fixated on the grand entry. But as every full-blood disappeared into thin air, forced into Feiht's painting of the event, Eagle began to feel something he hadn't felt since his mother was alive, compassion, mercy, and the Native American spirit became strong within him.

The full-blooded Native Americans began to disappear into thin air at a slow rate at first, but then they began to disappear at a faster rate. Right before Eagle's eyes, Feiht's medicine was working as planned. But it didn't sit right with Eagle. Something was coming over him, but he didn't know what it was. He began to feel the need to protect the full-bloods there because he knew he was the only one who could. His father, Tonto, who was supposed to be the protector of pow-wows, was not doing his job and was letting Feiht infiltrate the pow-wow. Eagle came to a realization he was not ready to deal with. He was the only one who could protect THE POW-WOW OF ALL POW-WOWS. Then, it became a choice: to protect the pow-wow or complete his mission. It should not have been a hard choice for him at all, but something inside him didn't like what he was seeing.

Eagle pointed his scope at his father, who was smiling and enjoying what he was seeing, unity. Then, he pointed his scope at Feiht, who was hard in concentration, using bad medicine against his people, who were also his mother's people. He pointed his scope back at his father, but then something unexpected happened. Eagle became John Wayne at that moment and he contemplated on what the bullet in his barrel would have wanted. Revenge or what was right?

Feiht was enjoying painting the full-blooded Native Americans of the pow-wow away and was getting a lot more of the audience done than he had anticipated. But then, he heard the gunshot that was the signal for him to stop painting and get the hell out of there. The sound of the gunshot stopped him in a way unexpected. Right after he heard it, his head exploded like a smashed pumpkin and his blood splattered unto his latest work of art. Through his scope, John watched Feiht fall unto his painting and disappear into the painting. He was no more, disappearing into thin air, like all of his subjects had. Then, the painting fell to the ground, its artist now its prisoner.

⤜⤜   ⤛⤛

The sound of Treaty Enforcer going off accompanied by a thunderous coyote howl signaled that it was time. Cash started to rain down from the ceiling. The full-blooded Native Americans in attendance didn't pay the gunshot or coyote howl any mind once they saw the cash raining down on them. They began to cheer and chaos erupted. John stuck to the plan of using it as cover to escape, but as he prepared to make his way down from the scaffold, he witnessed something he could never have ever expected.

The walls that enclosed every section of bleachers, so that no one could go under the bleachers, all burst open at the same time. And what emerged from under the bleachers was not comprehendible, not even realistic, as far as John thought. It couldn't have been real. And he was the only one seeing it because every full-blooded Native American there was reaching up and gathering money, including all of the dancers and drummers. The drumming and singing stopped, along with the dancing. It was about to become unlike any grand entry ever, but in a different way. Distracted by green rain, none of the full-bloods saw them coming, except for John, who watched it all from above.

Out from under one section of bleachers, wolf people emerged. They resembled what most people knew to be werewolves, but even more hideous, almost too grotesque to look at. The thick hair covering their bodies not a perfect coat at all, patches of bare skin speckled their bodies, as if they had mange. Their teeth sharp and longer than any werewolf in any movie, slobber dripping from them. They began to devour unsuspecting full-bloods right away, ripping them in half with their strength and razor-sharp teeth. Their howls were spine-tingling.

From under another section of bleachers, shapeshifters and skinwalkers emerged. There were many different kinds of shapeshifters there, some half human/half goat, some half human/half frog, some half human/half rattlesnake. It was almost like every animal was represented by a shapeshifter. The skinwalkers took full animal form though, emerging from under the bleachers as giant spiders, giant rats, hairless bears, among other hideous versions of animals. Together, they began to devour full-bloods, as they lived to do. Deer Lady emerged from underneath the bleachers with the shapeshifters as well, stomping the private parts of full-blooded Native American men until they were dead.

Then, from under another section of bleachers, a small covenant of six owl witches emerged. The owl witches were human in form, except their mouths and noses were replaced with owl beaks. They were all adorned with old, black robes and snow-white hair, their eyes yellow, but red in the middle. They were grotesque beings and the ones responsible for the force field around THE BIGGEST TIPI EVER BUILT. Their medicine was strong and evil.

From beneath the rest of the bleachers, other evil beings not of this world emerged, such as the little people, mosquito men, Chiye-tankas, feathered serpents, and even the feared Thunderbird. Most of the full-bloods never even saw their deaths coming, it happened so fast. Cash was still raining down on them when the evil beings not of this world were released on them. The green haze from the shower of cash soon gave way to the dark red tint of blood.

But the full-blooded Native Americans were all part of a warrior culture, and they began to fight back. Evil beings not of this world began to fall, along with full-bloods. It became an all-out war of survival. John watched from above, protected by his location, until the Thunderbird, a pterodactyl-like creature, flew toward him with intentions of devouring him. It was stopped when John became Eagle again and put as many bullets into it as he could. The Thunderbird fell, not standing a chance against Eagle. It was then, that Eagle realized he had to help his people. He stared through his scope and pointed his rifle down toward the battle below him, taking out every evil being not of this world that he could. They dropped like flies at the pull of Treaty Enforcer's trigger.

While Eagle was in assassination-mode again, his scope found his original target, his father. Tonto was proving he was THE TOUGHEST NATIVE ALIVE. He had his tomahawk numb-chucks out, killing evil being after evil being with Bruce Lee precision. The massacre planned became more of a battle than a massacre. The evil beings not of this world did not expect such a resistance. And it started to look good for the full-blooded Native Americans, until the cash stopped dropping from the ceiling and more evil beings not of this world poured into THE BIGGEST TIPI EVER BUILT from outside. The Wendigos arrived, their appetite for human flesh their strength. They began to devour full-bloods, turning some of the full-bloods into more of them. Their tribe grew bigger by the minute, to a monstrous size. It looked hopeless for the full-blooded Native Americans, like it was all over, until something else unexpected happened. The drum known as "Geronimo" began to drum itself. It sounded like a drumstick was banging on Geronimo's tight hide from inside the drum. He began to drum a song not heard in centuries. It was a ghost dance song.

CHAPTER 12

The Ghost Dance

DURING A SOLAR ECLIPSE on January 1st, 1889, a Northern Paiute medicine man, named Wovoka, had a dream, a vision of sorts. In the vision, Wovoka was taken into the spirit world and saw all of his ancestors, who had already taken the journey into the spirit world. He saw that they were all happy and doing the things they loved to do before being taken to the spirit world. While in the spirit world, Wovoka's ancestors gave him the knowledge to take back to all of the Indians of days old to achieve the bliss they had once known. It was a prophecy.

The prophecy, the vision given to Wovoka, foretold of a coming spring, when the grass would be high and the land would be covered with a new soil that would bury all of the blue-eyed tribe and all of the things that they had built to destroy the Earth. The new soil would be bountiful with sweet grass, running water, and trees. The great herds of buffalo that once were would return to it. And all of the Indians of days old who practiced a new ritual given to Wovoka in prophecy would be taken up into the air, like they had wings, and suspended into the air, while the new soil was being laid down upon the Earth. Then, once the new soil was laid down, they would float back down unto the Earth to join their awaiting ancestors. Then, they would enjoy the new soil together as it had been in the past before the blue-eyed tribe had arrived and the buffalo were slaughtered. Earth would become known as "New Earth" after the prophecy was fulfilled.

The vision and prophecy gave birth to a dangerous new ritual. But it brought hope to the Indians of days old, who were struggling with starvation and genocide. They all sought to experience the New Earth foretold by Wovoka, who explained to the Indians of days old that it could not happen unless they danced a special kind of dance and sang special songs. Both song and dance would be the medicine to help fulfill his prophecy. The ritual he spoke of became known as the "Ghost Dance."

Right away, Indians of days old began to practice the Ghost Dance and it spread through every tribe like a wild fire. Every member of every tribe dreamed of such a place like the New Earth Wovoka prophesied about, one without the blue-eyed tribe. Wovoka traveled tribe to tribe sharing his prophecy and the Ghost Dance at an unheard of speed for someone traveling alone at the time. And never once was he ever harmed by the tribe's he approached, something else that was also unheard of at the time. Some tribes were not kind to strangers walking up to them.

By April 1890, it had reached Oklahoma, where the first Ghost Dance in the state occurred near the town of Watonga. Then, by September of that year, the biggest Ghost Dance ever took place near the South Canadian River, where over three-thousand Indians of days old gathered and danced every night for two weeks straight. Members of the Cheyenne, Arapaho, Kiowa, Wichita, Caddo, and Apache tribes participated in the grand event, all praying for the extinction of the blue-eyed tribe and return of their ancestors.

The Ghost Dance eventually found its way to the Sioux tribe. In October of 1890, Sioux chief, Kicking Bear, had visited with Wovoka and returned home. He told Chief Sitting Bull about his meeting with Wovoka, who was being hailed as a "new light" for their people, rivaling the sun and moon. Kicking Bear explained Wovoka's prophecy to Chief Sitting Bull, who decided to adapt Wovoka's prophecy and the Ghost Dance to the Sioux tribe. The Sioux tribe, who needed any glimmer of hope that they could get, began practicing the Ghost

Dance immediately. They, more than any tribe at the time, needed the great herds of buffalo to return, and restore their way of life. The Sioux tribe even added in their own practices with the Ghost Dance, making ghost shirts, which were painted with the visions of the Sioux warrior that wore them. They believed the ghost shirts would protect them from the bullets of the blue-eyed tribe. But it was with the Sioux tribe that the Ghost Dance would end.

On December 15, 1890, Sioux spiritual leader, Chief Sitting Bull, was arrested for leading his people in a Ghost Dance. During the arrest though, one of Chief Sitting Bull's warriors fired at the arresting Lieutenant, shooting him on his right side. The wounded Lieutenant fired back, but at the wrong person, shooting Chief Sitting Bull instead. They both died.

After Chief Sitting Bull's murder, the Ghost Dance became more powerful in its meaning. The Sioux tribe began to practice the Ghost Dance even more, until the U.S. Government feared it would provoke war. To prevent any violence brought on by the Ghost Dance, the 7th Cavalry/Indian killers were sent to disarm the Sioux tribe and stop the Ghost Dance. But on December 29th, 1890, something else happened. The 7th Cavalry/Indian killers reached a Sioux camp and during confusion a gunshot rang out, which triggered the Wounded Knee Massacre. Not knowing who fired the gun shot, The 7th

Cavalry/Indian killers opened fired anyway and killed more than 300 Sioux tribal members, mostly women and children.

The Ghost Dance continued to spread throughout Indian country like a wild fire, practiced by tribes all over. But after the Wounded Knee Massacre, the Ghost Dance became outlawed by the U.S. Government and most tribes stopped practicing the ritual in fear of being massacred. And so, the Ghost Dance became what it was, a ghost.

⤳ ⤳ ⤝ ⤝

Geronimo, the fifth member of The 49ers, continued beating itself loudly. It was so loud that it overpowered all of the screams of full-blooded Native Americans being devoured at THE GREATEST MASSACRE EVER. The 49ers all had their backs toward Geronimo, their beautiful wives behind them, when they heard their fifth member call to them. It was a song they had never drummed before, but they could tell it was the medicine needed for the dire time at hand. They all turned around and sat around Geronimo, their drumsticks in hand, their beautiful wives tucked safely between them all. Then, they began to drum with Geronimo as lead drummer for the first time ever, and they sang a song they had never sung before. The syllables just came to them like a vision quest they had waited their whole lives to receive. It was a Ghost Dance song, ancient and outlawed by the U.S. Government, the very sponsors of THE POW-WOW OF ALL POW-WOWS.

The Ghost Dance song reached Wanbli's legs, who began to dance against his will, especially since he was protecting his mother and Polacca from the massacre taking place. Without warning, he started to dance the dance routine he could never perfect, but this time, with perfection. He was finally doing the dance he was born to do! Then, an unexpected thing happened. He began to glow and every evil being not of this world that tried to come close to him was dissolved into nothing. So his mother and Polacca were safe, as long as he danced the dance he knew he was born to do. Unbeknownst to him though, he was doing the Ghost Dance, a dance outlawed over a century before. No Native American of days new had ever seen it done, but its medicine was so strong, that ever full-blood that witnessed it knew exactly what it was.

Deep in the heart of THE GREATEST MASSACRE EVER, a Ghost Dance was taking place, something that had not occurred for many, many seasons. While The 49ers drummed and sang a Ghost Dance song and Wanbli danced the Ghost Dance, another unexpected thing happened. The combination of Ghost Dance song and Ghost Dance did something to Polacca, who was standing near Wanbli, protected by his medicine. Her mouth opened against her will and ghosts emerged as they normally did, but for the first time, they were ghosts of people, warriors of days old to be exact. Twenty warrior ghosts came out of Polacca's mouth, dressed for battle and all giving out their scariest warcries as they came out of her mouth. The warrior ghosts immediately went to war with the evil beings not of this world, taking scalps as they did so.

But Polacca's mouth did not close after the warrior ghosts emerged from it. Next, came the most ghosts at one time to ever come out of her mouth. A giant herd of 200 buffalo ghosts came stampeding out of her mouth. The ghost herd immediately started stampeding in a circle around the pow-wow circle, preventing any evil being not of this world from entering the pow-wow circle. Every full-blooded Native American still alive and fighting cheered at the sight of all the white buffalo. White buffalo were believed by Native Americans to be a sign of great good. But the fight wasn't over, evil beings were still devouring full-bloods, and full-bloods were still killing evil beings.

The twenty warrior ghosts made a huge difference at first, killing evil beings like they were nothing. Because they were ghosts, the Wendigos could not devour or possess them. But the other evil beings numbers were too much, and they began to overwhelm most of the warrior ghosts. The evil beings not of this world also began to find ways to cause some of the buffalo ghosts to disappear and the herd began to get smaller and smaller. It was only a matter of time before there were no more, and the evil beings would infiltrate the pow-wow circle, which they hadn't been able to do yet.

It began to look grim for the full-blooded Native Americans, who could not escape the colossal tent because of the owl witches' force field. Nor could the mixed-blooded Native Americans outside come into the colossal tent to help the full-bloods. It was going as planned, as far as the evil beings were concerned. The Wendigos grew to a great number quickly, turning full-bloods into flesh-devouring beings with four arms, four legs, and black eyes that had tentacles protruding from them.

Regardless of how the outcome looked for the full-blooded Native Americans there, The 49ers continued to drum and sing, and Wanbli continued to dance. The first Ghost Dance song ended, but there were many more to be drummed and sung. It was at the start of the second Ghost Dance song that, yet, another unexpected thing happened. Polacca's mouth opened against her will again, and one very large ghost emerged from it. Polacca recognized the ghost right away. It was the ghost of Big-Sister, the last medicine woman and keeper of the strongest medicine there ever was, is, and will be. And as soon as Big-Sister's ghost exited Polacca's mouth, she flew to her coffin, which was still placed at the edge of the pow-wow circle. Within moments, the coffin flew open and Big-Sister emerged, alive again and angry at what she was seeing. She gave out the loudest lulu ever heard and went to battle, her medicine flying out from her hands as energy bursts, disintegrating every evil being she threw her medicine at.

>→ >→   ←< ←<

Tonto Wayne, THE TOUGHEST NATIVE ALIVE, was nowhere near the pow-wow circle. He had fought his way in between two sections of bleachers and was now trapped there, unable to make his way back out. A swarm of evil beings not of this world had surrounded him. He was a bad-ass though, and his blessed tomahawk numbchucks were making sure no evil being stood a chance against him. But as tough as he was and blessed as his weapon of choice was, there was something else keeping him alive. Unknown to Tonto, his son, John, was playing a big part in keeping him alive. John was shooting evil being after evil being that tried to make their way to his father.

John's father would have been proud of how good his son was with a thunderstick, which was what most Indians of days old called a "gun." It was looking good for his father, the flood of evil beings trying to get to him soon became only a few, until there were no more. Tonto had a clear path to make his way back into the pow-wow circle. He started to run out of the corner he back himself into, but he was stopped by an unseen force. Something grabbed him and held him still, something invisible. John watched through the scope of Treaty Enforcer, as his father struggled to break free from whatever was holding him. Whatever had him was strong, too strong for John's father to escape its grip. Then suddenly, from the most unexpected place, an evil being got hold of Tonto. It even surprised John, who watched the unfortunate event unfold from above.

From out of the ground, a shapeshifter in the form of a large, hideous half mole/half man being, emerged right underneath Tonto. The mole shapeshifter was large enough to swallow Tonto's legs right away, before he even had a chance to react. Tonto dropped his tomahawk numb-chucks and fought his hardest to keep the mole shapeshifter from devouring the rest of him. John watched his father go from THE TOUGHEST NATIVE ALIVE to a man just trying to stay alive. Defeat was inevitable, but his father didn't give up, nor would he go out quietly, even though he was already almost halfway eaten by a mole shapeshifter.

John knew what he had to do. He had to give his DAD the glorious death he deserved. There was no honor in being eaten by a mole shapeshifter, but there was honor in dying at the hands of the new THE TOUGHEST NATIVE ALIVE, the new protector of pow-wows. It was family tradition. So John took aim, placing a cross on his dad's forehead, and he pulled the trigger. His dad died with honor, and John avenged the death of his mom in the most unusual way, by putting his dad out of his misery. It came at a great cost to John though, because he accepted the crown he never wanted to wear. John was now THE TOUGHEST NATIVE ALIVE and the protector of pow-wows. And his first order of business as THE TOUGHEST NATIVE ALIVE was to kill the mole shapeshifting bastard feeding on his dad. John took aim again, then he shot, but only wounded the mole shapeshifter. Then, John continued to shoot, only adding more wounds, making the mole shapeshifter suffer, and never delivering an instantly fatal wound. Instead, he let it bleed to death, slowly.

↣ ↣ ↤ ↤

With so many innocent bystanders mixed in with all of the evil beings not of this world, it was hard for Big-Sister to use her medicine as a weapon. So carefully, she threw her hands in the direction of her victims, causing them to explode into nothing. But because she had to be careful, she could only take out evil beings one by one, hindering her medicine from its full potential. A few times she did catch a group of evil beings together, which allowed her to take out the whole group in just one throw of her hands.

The slow process gave Big-Sister time to look around at the battle at hand, and she came to a realization that the full-blooded Native Americans, the 20 warrior ghosts, and the dwindling herd of buffalo ghosts were not enough. They were outnumbered, and to make it worse, the number of Wendigos grew with every full-blood they feasted upon and turned into one of them. Big-Sister knew they desperately needed help, but the force field created by the owl witches was so strong that the ghosts of the mixed-blooded warriors who were hung in Mankato could not get through Polacca's mouth to aid the 20 full-blooded warrior ghosts they were hung besides.

Owl witches were a peculiar breed of witch. They always traveled in packs, like wolves. But Big-Sister had faced their kind many of times and was the victor in every encounter. Their medicine was only strong when they united their medicine, so Big-Sister knew what she had to do. She had to kill every owl witch there to break the force field put upon THE BIGGEST TIPI EVER BUILT. But with so much chaos inside the colossal tent, it was not going to be an easy task. She decided to call upon a warrior she had recently met in the spirit world. Big-Sister started a chant that caused Polacca's mouth to open against her will again.

Polacca was not happy at first, that her mouth was being forced open and that she was being used as a portal to the spirit world. But then, she started feeling good about being a part of the battle taking place. She began to embrace her gift finally. Expecting another human ghost to emerge from her mouth, Polacca was surprised when the ghost of a dog wearing a warbonnet jumped from out of her mouth. It was Chief's ghost, and he was magnificent as ever. He was the purest white now, tall, muscular, and had all four of his legs again. His warbonnet was now authentic and grand, a real chief's warbonnet. Chief's ghost immediately went to Big-Sister, who whispered something into one of his ears.

Chief's ghost took in what Big-Sister whispered to him, then he ran out of the protection of the pow-wow circle, fearless, as Big-Sister followed behind him. In just a matter of moments, Chief's ghost sniffed out an owl witch in the chaotic crowd. The owl witch tried to run, but Big-Sister rid the world of the owl witch with very little effort. Her medicine was unrivaled. Then, Chief's ghost found another owl witch, and then another, whom Big-Sister sent them both to the great fire from which they came. It was the fourth owl witch that Chief's ghost had sniffed out that Big-Sister decided to not kill right away. Instead, she tortured the owl witch for information.

The fourth owl witch knew she was no match

against Big-Sister's medicine and gave her the information she sought. She told Big-Sister that there were six owl witches in all that had placed the force field around THE BIGGEST TIPI EVER BUILT, so that no one could get in or out, until THE GREATEST MASSACRE EVER was over. Big-Sister thanked the fourth owl witch and showed her appreciation by giving her a painless death. It was instant. With four down and two to go, Chief's ghost and Big-Sister continued on their warpath for owl witches.

↣ ↣ ↢ ↢

Elsewhere inside THE GREATEST MASSACRE EVER, a painting laid on the ground, filled with thousands of full-blooded Native Americans and Feiht Tirips. It seemed like a harmless object amongst great violence. Son-of-the-Morning-Star, who had taken the shape of a warrior from days old, except his eyes were completely black, didn't suspect anything when he stepped over the painting. He didn't have anything to do with THE GREATEST MASSACRE EVER, but he wasn't going to miss it for world. As he stepped over the painting, on his way to help his evil beings kill more full-bloods, a great unexpected thing happened. A hand reached out from the painting and grabbed one of his legs, pulling his leg into the painting.

The hand belonged to Feiht and he knew who

Son-of-the-Morning-Star was. He was his father. Before his father had a chance to pull his leg out of the painting, Feiht's other hand reached out from the painting and grabbed his other leg, pulling it into the painting as well. Then, Son-of-the-Morning-Star fell into the painting, as Feiht had fallen into it after John had blown his brains all over the canvas. But all was justified in Feiht's mind because he had received his reward after all, and in the way he most desired, revenge by art.

After all was done on July 23rd, the painting would be found a time later, and become the most famous Native American relic ever. The painting's artist unknown, but its title known by every human being: "Native American vs. The Indian." It portrayed a long-haired, well-groomed Native American man in a nice suit choking a long-haired, traditional Indian of days old in warrior regalia with pitch-black eyes, as a crowd of full-blooded Native Americans in the background witnessed the timeless iconic metaphor. Unknown to all who saw it though, it was a father and son portrait. Also not known by its admirers, it was the fate of Son-of-the-Morning-Star, who most knew as "Lucifer." He had once been a great angel of The Great Spirit, but now he was nothing more than just a painting.

⤞ ⤞   ⤝ ⤝

But THE GREATEST MASSACRE EVER was far

from over. Two owl witches had to be found and killed, if the battle were to be won against the evil beings not of this world. The remaining two owl witches were not easy to locate either. They must had caught wind of the danger they were in. Big-Sister followed Chief's ghost throughout the battle at hand. She took out as many evil beings as she could along the way, mostly Wendigos, which were everywhere.

Chief's ghost finally picked up on a scent, wagging his tail, alerting Big-Sister to get prepared. The scent trail led Chief's ghost and Big-Sister under one section of the colossal bleachers built specifically for THE POW-WOW OF ALL POW-WOWS. It was pitch black underneath the bleachers, the only light coming from Chief's ghost aurora. He glowed bright, as most ghosts did. They entered the darkness carefully. After only a few steps into the blackness, Big-Sister chanted something and threw her hands so that they pointed toward the ground and a fire appeared, consuming all of the darkness underneath the bleachers.

The light from the fire revealed the two owl witches, who were both on the underside of the bleachers, right above where Big-Sister stood. It was the last place she looked for them, so the owl witches had time to attack. They combined their bad medicine, holding hands as they put a curse on Big-Sister. Before she could retaliate with a spell, something unexpected happened yet again. Big-Sister's mouth disappeared.

With no mouth, Big-Sister had no way of putting a spell or curse on the owl witches or no way of defending herself against them. Chief's ghost jumped up at them, but both owl witches took full owl form and flew away. In full owl form, both owl witches circled above them, flying faster and faster, until they were just a blur. The blur of them flying in a circle soon gave way to a small tornado. The small tornado touched ground and picked up both Big-Sister and Chief's ghost, spinning them uncontrollably, as the owl witches laughed an evil laugh only they could laugh.

The small tornado twisting Big-Sister in the air didn't affect her as much as the owl witches had wanted. It wasn't the first tornado Big-Sister had been inside. One of Big-Sister's gifts was having the medicine to fight tornadoes, which she had done many of times to protect her people from them. But this particular small tornado had something no other tornado she encountered had, owl claws. The owl witches clawed at her as they flew around her, cutting her more and more as the small tornado kept Chief's ghost and her suspended in the air.

With owl claws added into the equation and a brutal clawing by them, Big-Sister knew she had to do something fast or be clawed to shreds. Her answer spun right next to her though, Chief's ghost. Big-Sister could speak through mediums, but all of the mediums she had used before had been alive and of flesh. So she was uncertain if she even could use a ghost as a medium to speak through, it had never been attempted before. But time was of the essence, and she was desperate. With all of the hope in the world bestowed in her hand, Big-Sister grabbed Chief's ghost. They spun out of control together, united. Then, Big-Sister began to channel her thoughts from her mind to her arm, then to her hand, and into Chief's ghost. A moment later, Chief's ghost spoke, but it wasn't his voice coming from his mouth, it was Big-Sister's voice. It worked! Big-Sister channeled a chant to Chief's ghost's mouth. It was the worst kind of curse that could be put on an enemy. Once the chant was finished, the owl witches were turned inside out. Their insides became their skin and their feathered skin became their insides. They both died the most horrible death there was, and the small tornado gave way to nothing more than a small gust of wind. But it wasn't over, Big-Sister channeled another chant through Chief's ghost, which brought her mouth back to her face. Once she was back to normal, she thanked Chief's ghost before they returned to battle. He wagged his tail in appreciation.

Just as Big-Sister thought it would, the force field was lifted after the death of all the owl witches that created it. But Big-Sister and Chief's ghost were the only ones that knew it was gone now. They both rushed from underneath the bleachers, so that Big-Sister could use the force field being gone to their advantage. Before she even reached the protected pow-wow circle, she began to chant, a chant that opened Polacca's mouth against her will once again. More warrior ghosts emerged from Polacca's mouth, but this time, they were mixed-blooded warrior ghosts, eighteen of them to be exact. The battle took another turn and began to look hopeful for the full-blooded Native Americans who were being slaughtered by the evil beings not of this world.

Before Big-Sister went back to aiding the full-bloods in battle, Chief's ghost gave her his puppy eyes. She read his mind and couldn't refuse his request. He was just so cute. So Big-Sister chanted another chant, and Polacca's mouth opened again. This time, only one warrior ghost emerged. But the warrior ghost was one to be reckoned with. It was Chief's first keeper, Crazy Horse. Chief's ghost went to him, wagging his tail as he followed him into the battle at hand. No longer was the spirit of Crazy Horse in Chief, instead, the spirit of Crazy Horse was beside him. They tore through the evil beings on a warpath unlike any warpath ever traveled. The blood of evil beings colored their trail.

Then, something that should have been expected happened again, Polacca's mouth opened against her will for what would be the last time, letting out the last ghost needed for the battle taking place. Little-Red-Man's ghost emerged from her mouth. It shocked and saddened

Big-Sister, who didn't know he had traveled to the spirit world recently. He had sight and joined his mother. At her side, they wreaked havoc against the evil beings. None stood a chance against them.

The 49ers never stopped drumming and singing Ghost Dance songs, as Wanbli continued to dance to every song. It was the perfect soundtrack for the battle at hand, the slaughter of so many beings of this world and not of this world. Victory and defeat were married at THE POW-WOW OF ALL POW-WOWS.

But with all that Big-Sister had pulled from Polacca's mouth, the evil beings still outnumbered them, the Wendigos had grown to a great number. Big-Sister, Little-Red-Man's ghost, Crazy Horse's ghost, Chief's ghost, John Wayne, the 38 ghosts of the hung Sioux warriors' ghosts, and all of the full-blooded Native Americans that remained were only putting a small dent in the army of evil beings they fought.

↣ ↣   ↢ ↢

Then, a greatest of things happened. The mixed-blooded Native Americans protesting outside had figured out that the force field keeping them out was gone. They charged into THE BIGGEST TIPI EVER BUILT by the hundreds of thousands, expecting to break up a racist pow-wow, but instead, becoming witnesses to a battle unlike any they had ever seen. The Native

American spirit was strong in all of them though, and none retreated. Soon, the evil beings not of this world became the outnumbered. Side by side, full-bloods and mixed-bloods fought together, prevailing over the evil beings not of this world. Their unity became great medicine.

Deer Lady's legs were ripped from her body, and she was beaten to death by them. The wolf people were slaughtered like lambs. The skinwalkers and different kinds of shapeshifters there were killed in the most brutal kinds of ways. The little people were trampled to death. The Chiye-tankas tackled and slaughtered. The feathered serpents were cut into pieces, slithering no more. The mosquito men were splattered of all the blood they had just sucked into their bodies. And the Wendigos, all caught and dirt forced into their mouths until they choked to death, as was custom to kill to a Wendigo. It stopped their appetite for flesh and returned them to the great fire they came from.

The 49ers finally stopped drumming and singing once they saw victory was at hand. Wanbli stopped dancing as well and joined his mother and Polacca in rejoicing. They had all survived. Wovoka had been right. His Ghost Dance was a power unlike anything ever seen before.

And just as the evil beings not of this world had wanted THE POW-WOW OF ALL POW-WOWS to become

THE GREATEST MASSACRE EVER, it did. But it was the evil beings that were massacred at the hands of full-bloods and mixed-bloods alike. It solidified the fact that being Native American was not an issue of blood-quantum, but an issue of spirit. And those who had the Native American spirit in them were true Native Americans, regardless of how much Native American blood pumped through their veins.

The Native spirit was as strong as it had ever been at THE POW-WOW OF ALL POW-WOWS, but it came at a great cost. The casualties of the second attempted genocide of Native American people were great. Dead bodies layered the ground and bleachers inside THE BIGGEST TIPI EVER BUILT.

Once the battle was over, full-blooded and mixed-blooded Native Americans began to gather the dead, but they were stopped by Big-Sister, who took the microphone Tonto had used as MC of the pow-wow. His son, John Wayne, THE TOUGHEST NATIVE ALIVE, the protector of pow-wows, was still in the scaffold above everyone, crying, something he hadn't done since after his battle with Raven Man. His tears were definitely for his dad this time.

Big-Sister didn't give the needed encouraging words to everyone, instead she began a chant into the microphone. She was known as keeper of the strongest medicine there ever was, is, and will be, but no one ever knew what it really meant. The ghosts of Little-Red-Man, Chief, Crazy Horse, and the 38 hung warriors were all circled around her, as she began her chant.

Then, the strongest medicine she was keeper of showed itself to all of the Native Americans present. First, all of the ghosts around Big-Sister became flesh, no longer ghosts. Then, every full-blood and the few mixed-bloods who laid dead rose to their feet, healed and unharmed. The Wendigo-possessed full-bloods became unpossessed and back to normal again. Big-Sister was a necromancer, she could bring the dead back to life. It was the strongest medicine there ever was, is, and will be.

John had stopped shedding tears for his dad, instead, his eyes were fixated on the unbelievable happening below him. The dead rose, the possessed became unpossessed, and ghosts became human again. All were like they were before, except for his dad. Tonto still laid dead, half-eaten with a bullet through his head.

Once Big-Sister finished her chant, she grabbed a microphone and spoke to John Wayne specifically. She explained that only one person would go to the spirit world as the result of the war that was waged and that person was his dad, Tonto. Not because she didn't want him to return, but because the medicine she put on him and John prevented it from happening. What was done was done for a reason, and could not be undone never. It was how the medicine she blessed his family with worked. Then, she asked John to come down to the pow-wow circle and honor his dad by being the new MC for THE POW-WOW OF ALL POW-WOWS, which, as she saw it, had no reason to end, but a greater reason to continue. Now, it could be how it should have been from the beginning, for all Native Americans, both full-blooded and mixed-blooded.

John accepted the job and climbed down from the scaffold, with cheers coming from below him. As much as he didn't like attention, it felt good that he now had a real purpose in life, until the day would come when he would have a son, and his son would take his title and responsibility away from him. Before taking over MC duties, Big-Sister and Little-Red-Man helped John carry the remains of his dad's body to the ugly coffin that Big-Sister occupied during her travel to Mankato. Then, John accepted the microphone, calling on The 49ers to start another song, a victory song.

The 49ers started another Ghost Dance song, one that was meant to be drummed and sung last. All other drum groups joined in to make the song thunder. It was powerful medicine. The pow-wow circle became flooded with full-blooded and mixed-blooded traditional dancers, none were left out. None of them caring about the great money that was once promised to them. It was awe-inspiring. THE POW-WOW OF ALL POW-WOWS was truly THE POW-WOW OF ALL POW-WOWS.

All full-blooded and mixed-blooded Native Americans inside THE BIGGEST TIPI EVER BUILT began to rise into the air. None of them even realized it. They floated right through THE BIGGEST TIPI EVER BUILT as it disappeared. Then, something extraordinary started to happen below them, after the colossal tent disappeared. Great herds of buffalo emerged from out of the ground, millions and millions of them stampeding away in all directions. And the ancestors of all Native Americans also emerged from the ground underneath them, not in ghost form, but in the flesh, alive again. They rose into the air as well in preparation for the new soil that was prophesized to be laid down. And as the great buffalo herds that once were left THE POW-WOW OF ALL POW-WOWS, the ancestors of all Native Americans, both full-blooded and mixed-blooded, joined their kin in the sky. The new soil was laid down as prophesized. It crushed all of the cities and destructive devices built, which ended Earth, so that New Earth could be. And as the rest of Wovoka's prophecy was fulfilled, THE POW-WOW OF ALL POW-WOWS never ended, ever. Once the new soil had been laid down completely, Native Americans and Indians of days old floated back down unto the ground as one. It was then that they all went back to what they were originally created to be all along, human beings and one with Earth. But now the human beings were one with New Earth.

EPILOGUE

The Greatest Trick Ever

"**For your lack** of loyalty to me and for being tricked by Son-of-the-Morning-Star, you will no longer be the animal spirit of your kind! From this time on, you will be known as 'The Trickster' since you like playing tricks so much! And you will remain on Earth, to roam it along with Son-of-the-Morning-Star and the defiant angels, not to be allowed back into my home, UNTIL…" spoke The Great Spirit, not revealing the rest of his request to Coyote.

"Until what?" The Trickster yelled. But there came no answer. The Great Spirit apparently wanted him to figure it out for himself. And the word "until" coming from HIM meant it could take a very, very long time, even forever, to figure out. The Trickster didn't want to spend his eternal life on Earth with Son-of-the-Morning-Star and his defiant angels, who had all begun to take gruesome forms, becoming demons. He had to figure out what HE wanted of him. Then, no matter what it was, what it would take, or how long it would take, he had to fulfill that "until." He knew it would be the only way for him to get back home, back to the home of The Great Spirit, where he belonged, right next to the angels, in his seat as the animal spirit of coyotes.

At first, just for his selfish reasons, The Trickster helped the man and woman of America, hoping The Great Spirit was watching and would see his efforts in protecting the Earth protectors and their bloodline. He had hoped it would fulfill The Great Spirit's "until." He showed them how to survive and showed them the many secrets The Great Spirit hid in various plants he created to fill the land of America. Once the man and woman of America became many, he even showed them how to make a drum, how to make songs with it, how to dance to the drum, how to make outfits to dance in, and how it would all praise their Creator. He was the one that taught them their songs and even their prayers. But The Great Spirit's "until" was not fulfilled, for The Trickster continued to remain on Earth.

For centuries, The Trickster showed the human beings of America, who became known as "Indians," and then "Native Americans," how to live and survive on the land chosen for them. He brought them fire, taught them how to hunt the animals created for them, and even introduced them to medicine. After a while, The Trickster felt he had done more than enough to fulfill The Great Spirit's "until," but still, he remained on Earth.

It weighed heavy on The Trickster and he could only take so much punishment. He grew bored of teaching the human beings of America the Earth's ways. He gave up and decided if he was to spend forever on Earth, then he would make it interesting and entertain himself. That was when The Trickster started doing what he was punished for doing, playing tricks. So, instead of helping the human beings of America, he began tricking them. But not only them, he also decided to start tricking all of the beings of America, even the animals.

At first, The Trickster started out with small tricks; like turning the sacred white raven to black, letting people from underneath the ground up to America, and stopping giant sea turtles in the oceans near America, so that they could create new lands. The Trickster's antics were disrupting The Great Spirit's original plans, so much, that The Great Spirit took all of The Trickster's medicine away from him. But Son-of-the-Morning-Star liked what The Trickster was doing and had his own plans with him. So, he gave The Trickster some bad medicine, so that he could continue his mischief. After that, The Trickster lived up to his name, playing tricks on the human beings and animals of America. It came to the point where he started playing his tricks for the sole purpose of entertainment, not teaching anyone anything with them, which he had done at first. He quickly became a nuisance to the human beings of America, instead of the teacher he once was. Finally, one day, he realized that the entertainment of it all had gone. And that's when he realized he wanted nothing more than to just go home, to his real home, which was the home of The Great Spirit. So, he stopped playing tricks and decided he needed time to think. He had to concentrate and figure out how to fulfill The Great Spirit's "until" bestowed on him.

The Trickster disappeared from the lives of the human beings of America he was assigned to protect. He was gone for so long, that in time, they were conquered by other human beings. America was invaded and taken over. The human beings of America were left helpless against their new enemies, with no medicine from The Trickster to protect them. They were almost wiped off of Earth, as The Trickster was out thinking of how to fulfill The Great Spirit's "until."

After years, decades, even a century and then some, it dawned upon The Trickster just what The Great Spirit meant by using the last word spoken to him, "until." Everything The Great Spirit did was a circle. Earth was filled with countless cycles that were all just countless circles. Everything came into full circle on Earth. So, The Trickster realized that The Great Spirit's "until" meant he was put in charge of bringing the human beings of America into full circle.

The Trickster's revelation and realization of what he must do came a little too late though. The people he had taught how to survive on Earth were now captives and were assimilated into a society they did not belong to. They lost touch with all The Trickster had taught them. They didn't believe in him no more, nor did they rely on what he had taught them anymore. They gave up his medicine, for they had alcohol, drugs, money, and television now. The Trickster returned to them, but it was not noticed by any human being of America because they were too far gone. It became very obvious what had to be done. The Trickster could not interfere with what was happening to them, if he wanted to return home. Their loss and suffering became a vital part of his plan, for he felt it had to happen that way. So, he sat by and watched the human beings of America, as they were assimilated into the blue-eyed human beings' society. Their land was ravaged, their bloodline diluted, and all looked hopeless for them to be the people they were meant to be, protectors of Earth. The Trickster could not have asked for a better opportunity to bring them full circle.

The Great Spirit did not like what was happening to the human beings of America though, as The Trickster stood by and let it happen. So, The Great Spirit sent a prophet to them to teach them the Ghost Dance, which would help bring them full circle. The Trickster's plan of waiting and not doing anything had worked, so now all he had to do was just sit back and wait for them to bring themselves full circle. But then something unexpected happened, the people that conquered America outlawed the Ghost Dance and many massacres occurred to prevent the Ghost Dance from taking place. The human beings of America imprisonment in their own land and assimilation continued. It wasn't the outcome The Trickster had hoped for, so he started working on another plan. If there was one thing he was good at, it was tricks. He had to come up with a trick that would not only fool The Great Spirit and Son-of-the-Morning-Star, but also the people that had conquered the human beings of America. He had to bring them full circle. It would be his greatest trick ever.

    Decades went by, even a century, all the while, The Trickster worked on his greatest trick ever. The Great Spirit provided him with what he needed to bring the protectors of Earth into full circle, the Ghost Dance, but it wasn't going to be an easy task to pull off. Especially since, the human beings of America began to lose touch with their traditions and were becoming like the people that had conquered them. He had many failed attempts. Sometimes The Great Spirit intervened it from happening and sometimes Son-of-the-Morning-Star intervened. He was working against the two greatest beings in the universe, but The Trickster was good at what he was known for doing, playing tricks.

The Trickster knew the Ghost Dance needed only several factors to take place. There had to be a drum and singers to sing the Ghost Dance songs, a dancer to dance the Ghost Dance, a portal for ghosts to enter the world from the spirit world, and a gathering of the human beings of America so great that their unity would bring about the prophecy of the Ghost Dance. So, The Trickster worked effortlessly for decades, making sure everything was put in place. He even divided the people he was assigned to protect through blood quantum. Full-blooded human beings of America and mixed-blooded human beings of America would have to be separated so that when they united, it would be glorious enough for the Ghost Dance prophecy to be fulfilled.

THE POW-WOW OF ALL POW-WOWS was the greatest trick ever. And it worked! The human beings of America were brought into full circle. The Trickster didn't know how it affected the rest of the human beings of Earth, nor did he care. All that he knew was, when the human beings of America were raised into the air together and new soil was laid down underneath them, his "until" had to have been fulfilled. There was no question about it. Then, when the cities of America, along with the residents of each city, all disappeared, it was a good sign. He had brought the people he was assigned to protect into full circle.

After the ghost dance had successfully taken place, The Trickster stood in a field near THE POW-WOW OF ALL POW-WOWS. Suddenly, the "until" revealed itself fulfilled to him. He was given back his wings. Then, he was raised into the air along with the human beings of America, but he never stopped raising, his wings began to flutter on their own. He left New Earth and traveled through space and time at a speed only angels and animal spirits blessed with white wings could travel. Moments later, he saw a familiar glorious light, a comforting glorious light he had missed for so long. As the glorious light overcame him, he smiled, because he was finally home again. The Trickster became "Coyote" again, forgiven of all his sins and tricks, and he took his seat next to all of the angels and animals spirits in the home of The Great Spirit. That is how it was, how it is, and how it will be.

AUTHORS BIO

And The 49ers sang That Native Thomas's song:

> "He is a god-fearing man, he is a father, he is a husband, he is Kiowa and Apache, hey yaw, hey yaw, hey yaw, heyyy... He is a storyteller, he is an author, he is a screenwriter, he is a poet, hey yaw, hey yaw, hey yaw, heyyy... He is a filmmaker, he is a stage actor, he is a music producer, he is an auteur, hey yaw, hey yaw, hey yaw, heyyy... He is a graduate of Riverside Indian Boarding School, he is a graduate of Haskell Indian Nations University, he grew up in Anadarko, Oklahoma, so yeah, he is rugged, hey yaw, hey yaw, hey yaw, heyyy... He is a recipient of the 2006 ABC/Disney Talent Development Writing Fellowship, he is a warrior, he is mah-bane, but damn, he is luscious, hey yaw, hey yaw, hey yaw, heyyy... Wee-cha!"

And The 49ers sang Steven Paul Judd's song:

> "He is a son, he is a brother, he is Kiowa and Choctaw, hey yaw, hey yaw, hey yaw, heyyy... He is a humorist, he is a renaissance man, he is a graphic designer, he is an artist, hey yaw, hey yaw, hey yaw, heyyy... He is a filmmaker, he is an activist, he is a screenwriter, he is a director, hey yaw, hey yaw, hey yaw, heyyy... He is a graduate of Broken Bow High School, he is a graduate of Haskell Indian Nations University, he grew up in Oklahoma, so yeah, he is rugged, hey yaw, hey yaw, hey yaw, heyyy... He is a recipient of the 2009 ABC/Disney Talent Development Writing Fellowship, he is a warrior, he is mah-bane, but damn, he is luscious, hey yaw, hey yaw, hey yaw, heyyy... Wee-cha!"

If you liked this book, we recommend from Candlewick Press:

X-INDIAN CHRONICLES: THE BOOK OF MAUSAPE

by Thomas M. Yeahpau

Also, we recommend from Hosstyle Publishing, The Underwear Boy Warparties:

UNDERWEAR BOY VS THE WITCH - Warparty #1
UNDERWEAR BOY VS THE VAMPIRE - Warparty #2
UNDERWEAR BOY VS THE NO-NAME MONSTER - Warparty #3

The Underwear Boy Warparties is a trilogy of Native American children's stories written specifically to be read by a parent out loud in the traditional way of Native American oral storytelling *(sound effects written appropriately throughout)*. The series follows a 10-year-old Native American boy, who is a self-proclaimed super-hero known as "Underwear Boy." They are great bedtime stories, but only available as e-books that can be downloaded for free using the **ibooks** app on an iphone/ipad, or, other apps that are downloadable for free to any smart phone or tablet, such as **Nook**, **Kindle**, **Kobo**, etc. Some apps won't allow the books to be downloaded for free, but not as choice by the author, some retailers reserve the right to offer free e-book downloads or control their price, depending on the demand of the e-book.

by That Native Thomas

And coming soon from Hosstyle Publishing:

NATIVE LOVE: AN X-INDIAN CHRONICLE

The long awaited sequel to X-INDIAN CHRONICLES: THE BOOK OF MAUSAPE, and a Native American romance novel unlike any other.

by That Native Thomas

Printed in Great Britain
by Amazon